Charlotte Sophia
Myth, Madness and the Moor

Also by Tina Andrews

Books

Sally Hemings An American Scandal:
The Struggle To Tell The Controversial True Story

Screenplays

Why Do Fools Fall in Love
Sally Hemings: An American Scandal
Jacqueline Bouvier Kennedy Onassis
Sistas 'n the City

Plays

Charlotte Sophia
The Mistress of Monticello
Why Do Fools Fall In Love - The Musical

Charlotte Sophia

Myth, Madness and the Moor

a novel

TINA ANDREWS

The Malibu Press
New York   Malibu   London

Dedicated to:

My brother Donald and his family

and
to the memories of:

My mentor, Alex Haley
and
My parents George and Eloyce Andrews

Prologue

✠

THE DIARY

*"...History never embraces more than
a small part of reality..."*

Duke de la Rochefoucauld

10 October, 1818

hy should you be shocked? Why should you disbelieve? It is not as though the origin of my being is unique in the annals of history. Stories of miscegenation, conflict and defilement, or even affection, between master and slave, conqueror and conquered have been with us before the Bible chronicled Abraham, Sarah and Hagar.

That said, the story I must tell you, and the resultant secrets and unpalatable truths which emerge, do not begin with me. Nor, if I have studied history correctly, will the disputation inherent in my being end with my demise—especially once the secret of my amulet and me are revealed to you. I find I must concern myself with legacy—and legacy can be such an abstract and ethereal thing, so open to misrepresentation.

I began this diary to correct the record, for in the end, as Napoleon has said, 'History is but a lie agreed upon.'

You see, we all have our little confidences we conveniently sweep under the rug of acceptability. And oh the price we pay for perception as we stand in the face of judgment and tell the occa-sional, little, white lie.

The problem is, this lie is neither little…

…nor white…

Part One

PRINCESS CHARLOTTE

Mirow Palace
Mecklenburg-Strelitz, Germany
1752 – 1761

*"…Everyone alive is, I am convinced, of mixed
ancestry. But some of us are more White, some of us
more Negro, some of us more Chinese…"*

H.G. Wells

One

I sprang forth into the world as Her Serene Highness Princess Char-lotte Sophia Albertina Frederick on 19 May, in the year of our Lord one thousand seven hundred forty four. Raised in the duchy of Mecklenburg-Strelitz, a small German territory, I was the eighth child and youngest daughter of ten born to Duke Charles Louis Frederick and Duchess Elizabeth Albertina from Saxe-Hildburghausen.

I remember being lanky, precocious, and I have been told that I was a child with too many outspoken opinions for a female of royalty and refine-ment. Yet, my memory of childhood was quite the contrary. Having been born a blue-blood did nothing to elevate my sense of self. I had always been unre-markable, so my mother insisted, and according to her there was nothing out-standing or remotely interesting about me.

My home was known as Mirow Palace, the ducal residence of the Grand Duke and Duchess of Mecklenburg-Strelitz. Though it was consid-ered small by royal standards it was vast enough to allow me to disappear in plain sight. No one ever paid much attention, which suited me just fine. Per-haps it was because I was never thought of as beautiful or charismatic like my sister Christiana before her misfortune, and everyone considered my complex-ion far too dark. I would overhear my mother whispering, 'Pity her broad nose,' or 'Keep her out of the sun, she's already too dusky.' Thus, I was per-ennially kept under thick white chalk.

As far back as I can remember I was always happier when I was alone—especially with a good book, sitting on my swing by Lake Ritouro. Other than my two favorite siblings, Christiana and Adolph, father was the only one I was close to. He was my sacred place. He believed in me and told me everything about life's hills and valleys. He read wonderful books to me and was the one who insisted I rely on my intellect. Thus, I immersed myself in books—and in my father's love. They were definitive.

My first memory of the amulet was perhaps at five or six years old. It dangled so proudly about my father's neck and I was ever drawn to its odd shape. The metal was a strange tarnished looking gold, not bright and shiny as most gold is. The top was flat embossed with a five-pointed star and peculiar writing on it, the rest was thick and tubular. On both the front and back were unusual raised symbols and glyphs, and strange letters from some unknown language. It was a majestic, powerful piece and every time father held me I reached for it without knowing why. I would learn the reason in the summer of my eighth year.

☩

On a cloudless early June morning in 1752, Grand Duke Charles Louis Frederick and his daughter, eight year old Charlotte Sophia were walking along the banks of Lake Ritouro near the palace. They often took long walks together to the swing he had hung for his daughter under an oak tree. It was their ritual and theirs alone. Duke Charles had not been feeling well most of that year and was in very bad condition that particular day. When finally they reached the swing he could not pick Charlotte up to put her on his lap as usual because he needed to rest.

As he sat on the swing gathering strength, he looked at his land. What a beautiful property Mirow was—a vast, glorious expanse filled with sheep, tall billowing grass, and so many trees it felt like a forest. It was a perfect day and the Grand Duke seemed to etch every tree, shrub and blade of grass into his memory for eternity.

Little Charlotte reached up to touch her father's amulet and finally asked the question she wanted to ask for a year: "Father, why am I darker than my sister and brothers? Am I adopted?"

Grand Duke Charles looked down at his favorite child and caressed her cheek. He knew the time had come for an explanation despite her young age. "Charlotte, I must tell you something important about yourself." His voice was coming in sporadic intervals. "You are our child. But your beautiful, sun-kissed color is by divine decree and you should be proud of it. Embrace it. For you are one of the chosen."

The princess frowned in confusion as her father pulled over his collar to reveal a red, raised, birthmark on his left shoulder. The girl gasped.

"I have that same mark," she exclaimed, pulling the bodice of her dress over revealing a similar birthmark on her shoulder.

"I know, daughter," said the Duke. "It's the Merovingian mark. Magragana's mark. "

"Magra... who?"

"Magragana ben Bekar, one of our ancestors," he replied as he caressed the amulet. "This talisman is all we have left of her or our connection to her. Since none of my children received her mark except for you, the amulet must go to you when I die."

"Really?" Charlotte asked, not fully understanding.

"Both sides of your family descend from Magragana and from the Merovingians, but not all of us received the mark. For generations, those of us who did assumed we had received it for a reason, but were unsure as to what the reason was. Perhaps, one day, you will be the one to discover it. But for now, just realize that as a girl with the mark, you are a 'Daughter of David' who will one day wear the amulet. Protect it—and Magragana's story, or it will die with me if left to your mother."

"I don't understand," frowned the princess.

Charlotte's father lowered his voice. "Your mother is not a believer even though she is the 'legitimate' progenitor of your circumstance."

It was all too cryptic and confusing for Charlotte, yet she walked with her father as he slowly strolled to the banks of the water. She could hear the wheezing in his lungs as the Duke stared out as if this was the last time he'd see his beloved lake. "I'm dying, child," he said, gazing at his daughter's face as his own became forlorn. "I want you to read and study. I want you to have the gift of knowledge and independent thought—power too long denied women."

The princess nodded without a suspicion of his meaning as he continued.

"Everything you need to know is written down in the bottom of my carved chest. You know the one?"

"The one with the funny star on top?"

He nodded. "Yes. That is the one. When I die, I've instructed that my amulet, the chest, and all its contents go to you. There is great wealth inside it, a great treasure. But also our family secrets." He looked at the amulet again. "Make sure you receive them."

Charlotte nodded. The Duke then took her hand and shook it a particular way.

"Can you shake my hand like this?"

Charlotte shook her father's hand the exact way he shook hers.

"Remember that handshake. It will help identify a friend when you need one someday."

Suddenly, the Grand Duke clutched his chest and crouched to the ground in pain. Little Charlotte panicked and tears sprang to her eyes.

"Father, what is wrong?"

Duke Charles struggled on the grass gasping for air. He tried his best to get the amulet off of his neck, but it became entwined on his tunic collar. "Take the amulet…quickly," he gasped.

Charlotte refused, "No. If I take the amulet you'll die. I won't help you die."

Duke Charles strained on the grass a few moments. "Take…it!" he ordered then collapsed. Charlotte shook him. "Father, please get up," she cried. "Please!" But the Duke's body lay still. Charlotte screamed and ran back to the palace forgetting the amulet and all else.

✠

On 11 June 1752, Grand Duke Charles Louis Frederick lay in his coffin at the Lutheran parish church. He had suffered a massive seizure and succumbed on the great lawn of Mirow Palace that afternoon six days earlier. Charlotte was inconsolable. At the funeral, her favorite and oldest brother, fourteen year old Adolph, kept his arm around her and never let go. As she looked up at the statue of the crucified Jesus, she wondered if she would be forgiven for her sins, for in her young mind she felt she may have contributed to the death of her father. Trying to give Charlotte the amulet in the throes of his attack could have exacerbated his seizure; Charlotte not accepting it could have made matters worse.

Adolph had to be strong for the rest of the nine member Frederick family, for he was now the new Grand Duke of Mecklenburg—despite his mother serving as regent because of his age. He and Charlotte's next older brothers, eleven year old Charles and ten year old Ernest, held their oldest sister Christiana together. She was so broken up she required a remedy of salted bitters and could not control her fainting spells. Many members of their support staff were also visibly aggrieved, and their wails could be heard all the way back to the palace. Old James wept openly while his sister, Lena, the family maid and cook, was devastated as she held the hand of her 9-year-old son Jon. Everyone was clearly grieving...

...except Charlotte's mother.

Duchess Elizabeth just stood there stoic and aloof, holding her youngest son, 4-year-old George Frederick. She stared down at the casket as the workers tossed dirt onto the remains of her husband and never shed a tear. Not one.

Charlotte was thinking about her father and how much she would miss him when suddenly thoughts about the amulet came flooding back. Where was it? She had not seen it on his body, nor was it visible on any of her siblings. Could it have been placed inside of the breast pocket of his funeral robe and buried with him? She wanted to know, for his last words to her were about it—and his carved chest.

Three days later, Charlotte received her answer. She had just climbed the stairs leading to her room munching spatzen Sister Lena had prepared for lunch. But when she had reached the top of the landing she heard raised voices coming from her mother's chambers.

"Do it, I say, if you value your appointment," her mother was scolding someone.

Seeing the door was ajar Charlotte crept closer. There she saw her mother and her 16-year-old cousin Wilhelm James Albertina opening her father's prized wooden chest. Her mother began sifting through the scrolls and documents inside it, and burned some in the fireplace. Though the princess had been admonished before for eavesdropping, she couldn't move. Her feet seemed paralyzed. Her ears, however, were fully operational and as she peered through the open door she became angry. Her father had instructed the chest and its contents were to be hers upon his death, and here were family members burning those precious items. But when Wilhelm pulled the special gold amulet from the chest, Charlotte gasped.

"Give that to me," her mother insisted. "I will get rid of it myself. I detest its meaning."

"No!" cried Charlotte. "That was father's. He said it was to be mine when he died!"

Duchess Elizabeth and Wilhelm whipped around in surprise. Wilhelm, a violent young man with unruly red hair and a pronounced stutter, marched over to her, snatched her by the arm, and pulled her into the room.

"W-what are you d-doing there? Spying?"

"That's father's amulet!" the girl cried.

Duchess Elizabeth, realizing her daughter had eavesdropped, gestured to Wilhelm that she would handle the matter. She handed him the two scrolls in her hand. "Destroy these as well."

Wilhelm nodded, then gave Charlotte a biting look. He left the room with the scrolls and the amulet as the Duchess closed the lid to the chest. Seeing her daughter's tears, her voice softened.

"Charlotte, I loved your father, but he did not adequately provide for us. He lived his life in a utopian pursuit of fantasies he could never realize—whimsies he had about French kings and religious nonsense. We suffer financially because of it," she remarked quietly, forcing back the tightly coiled tendrils bushing out around Charlotte's face. "Now with the war emptying all our coffers, I refuse to reduce this family's dignity by selling our valuables at auction. I must be practical."

"But I'm supposed to inherit the amulet and the chest. Father said so the day he died."

The Duchess froze. After some thought she changed tactics, smiling at Charlotte which was difficult. "If it means that much, I shall have them delivered to you when you are old enough to appreciate them. But never discuss the chest, its contents or the amulet again."

The princess grudgingly agreed.

"Now go change for lunch, and for God's sake get out of that yellow brocade dress. It gives your complexion a dark, disagreeable pallor, and have Lady Hagedorn re-do your chalk immediately."

The princess ran to her room holding back tears. In her chambers she wondered why her mother always made her feel bad. Why didn't the Duchess love her? She wrestled with feelings of hatred for the woman who bore her and, as she silently prayed for God to help her, unconsciously rubbed the special birthmark on her shoulder.

Two

Eight years passed after my father departed this life leaving a void. Mother never delivered the chest or the amulet and I stopped asking. Perhaps it was God's will that I not have them, and I retreated into the solitude of my private self. In times of distress, I resorted to my books or to the sanctity of my imagination for life was simpler there. It was manageable, acceptable, ordered.

But that all changed in 1760. It was the year I turned sixteen and was no longer a girl-child but a woman. The year everyone became obsessed with my marrying; the year that knowledge of man's insatiable sanction over women awoke within me a mission to evolve beyond the constraints of bias of any ilk.

It was also the year which began a passion for one man from which I have never recovered.

On a Tuesday not unlike any other that summer, Charlotte arose, was dressed, and had breakfast. At eleven o'clock, her music master arrived for her weekly lesson. As all of her brothers were out on a hunt, only the women in Charlotte's family were in the palace.

Duchess Elizabeth found she could not contain her excitement for she had just been informed by Sister Lena that couriers had delivered her order of whalebone, silk, taffeta and chiffon. With it came a note from Monsieur Kyle LeCorbiere, her favorite dressmaker from Vienna, saying he would be delighted to design the gowns for Charlotte, her great aunt Albertina, Christiana, and the Duchess for the most talked-about event of the year—King's Ball at Sanssouci Palace in Potsdam.

Their cousin, King Frederick II, known as Frederick the Great, was having a gathering of 400 guests, and every member of the German aristocracy, head of state or celebrity was invited to the grand gala. It was to be held in six weeks on 26 October 1760—and every servant, valet de chambre or lady in waiting at Mirow palace was busy preparing.

Charlotte's mother was especially jubilant about the ball. She had been ill for some months and desired to make a fashionable entrance to let all know she was fit to return to the invitation lists of her royal society. She was also anxious to show off her son, Adolph, who had assumed his duties as the reigning Grand Duke of Mecklenburg upon turning 18. He was now a handsome and intelligent man who, in her mind, had become an exemplary ruler of the duchy since her husband's death forced the duties on him eight years earlier, and she as Regent.

But more than anything else, Duchess Elizabeth needed money. Because of Grand Duke Charles' financial mismanagement she was forced to operate with far less than the doyenne of Mecklenburg required; thus she was always plotting for funds. Everything she did or thought about was in concert with this, and the king's ball fit the agenda perfectly. Her plan was to marry off Adolph, Christiana, or Charlotte, and she needed a venue where she'd be assured her eligible children would intercept suitable royal or titled prospects.

This arrangement, however, would prove to be a feat more arduous than resurrecting her dead husband. At the age of 17, her eldest daughter Christiana had been in love with and engaged to Lord Michael Ihde, the Duke of Saxe-Idhe. The wedding never took place because Lord Michael drowned in a storm on the North Sea when his ship capsized returning from Paris. Christiana went mad for a time and never fully recovered. She still had intermittent bouts of senselessness, oft times repeating the same phrase over and over:

"When is Michael coming?"

Now at age 25, poor Christiana was far beyond the reasonable age for matrimony, and "quality" prospects from the royal registry were almost out of the question. Left for consideration were bottom-rung elderly widowers, titled but physically deficient royals, or lettered men of questionable sexuality in need of "cloak" wives. The latter category concerned her as Adolph appeared to be a member of this group as he exhibited a penchant for men instead of women.

Then there was Charlotte. Of all her children the Duchess felt her youngest daughter had the least female attributes which drew red-blooded men to women. The girl was too dark in skin tone, her nose was too broad and her mouth too large, giving her a distinctly mulatto appearance. Topping it all, Charlotte's hair was an unruly mass of auburn crinkles. The Duchess hoped that Charlotte would be lucky enough to attract Lord Gregory Muldare, the Margrave of Anhalt-Cothen, who at age 71 was a widower in search of a new bride. Purportedly he had commented favorably on the princess when he visited Mirow the previous February, and he enjoyed a woman who could accompany his violin with her own talent on the harpsichord as his deceased wife had.

Unfortunately, Charlotte's musical proclivities appeared dire. Still, Duchess Elizabeth refused to lose hope. She vowed to place Charlotte in prime view of the aging royal and prayed the girl's youth and figure would compensate for what she felt were Charlotte's considerable shortcomings—failings she made the girl aware of every day. Nonetheless, Charlotte was given every chance for success as she had the better chance of attracting him than her insane sister. Thus, the princess was given the best tutors and dressmakers the little money the Duchess had could buy, and she spared no expense on music lessons.

Charlotte's music master was none other than Carl Phillip Emmanuel Bach. Known as CPE Bach, but called "Emmanuel" by friends, he was the most renowned offspring of Johann Sebastian Bach. Her father had been so impressed with him that he had Herr Bach teach all of his children to play the harpsichord and later the pianoforte. "Music like his comes from God," Charlotte remembered her father saying, "And we must have God in this palace—at least for an hour and a half once a week." So Emmanuel Bach came, and continued so after the Grand Duke's death.

The problem was Charlotte despised him. Emmanuel always seemed angry, summarily putting the princess through repetitive exercises which he knew grated on her. He would play a section of music brilliantly then chastise her when she tried and could not duplicate his skill.

It was no different on the day in question.

"Your Highness, your fingering is sluggish. Feel the music and re-lax your fingers," he intoned for the umpteenth time. "It is precisely why you keep missing the C flat in this section."

The princess played the passage again and inevitably made the same mistake, missing both the C flat and the E sharp in the stanza. This irritated the 45-year-old Bach and again he unleashed his wrath. Char-lotte wondered why she allowed him to berate her so. After all, she was a princess of Mecklenburg. He was neither a royal nor married to royalty.

Yet something inexplicable happened that day, causing her to ig-nore his ranting. For some reason she refused to be pushed over the precipice of emotionalism and determined to forge ahead. She allowed herself to feel the music for the first time and began to play from her soul—each note becoming a heartbeat, each heartbeat becoming perfect music in perfect harmony with her spirit. When she finally finished *The Capriccio*, Herr Bach placed his hand upon Charlotte's shoulder and nod-ded, "That was a nice improvement, Your Highness, and I am as pleased as…well…," he gestured pompously, "…as anyone of my deportment can be."

What arrogance, Charlotte thought, raising her hand for him to kiss. Had he not possessed his own father's genius and Charlotte's father's approval she would have had him dismissed for such insolence.

Herr Bach took her hand and bowed.

"I look forward to your presence at King's Ball in October. My younger brother, Christian, has agreed to join me in a string quintet, and we'll perform *The Capriccio* for the king and his guests. You will be able to hear it in its perfection—the way our father wrote it." As teacher and student walked toward the door he added, "In fact, Christian and I are headed to Berlin. We are to play for the Grand Duke."

But before Emmanuel could put on his hat, Duchess Elizabeth en-tered the room. "Oh Herr Bach, your brother is here now," she ex-claimed. "He arrived a few moments ago." When she moved aside, the most stunning creature Charlotte had ever seen came forward to hug his brother. "Forgive my being early," the younger Bach offered, "but my coachman delivered me sooner than expected. The weather turned out to be so much better coming from Hamburg."

"Quite all right," Emmanuel responded. Turning his brother to-ward Charlotte he added, "Permit me to introduce you to my student,

Princess Charlotte Sophia Frederick. Your Highness, this is my youngest brother, Johann Christian Bach, just recently returned from an engagement in Paris. I believe the last time you saw each other, you were eight."

We looked at each other and I was completely unprepared for my reaction. I canvassed this gorgeous creature who was, to my mind, too beautiful to be real. Christian could not have been more different from his brother. He was tall with strong, angular features, a powerful jaw and the greenest eyes into which I had ever gazed. His full mass of dark hair glistening like India ink was fashioned into a queue without powder. It led the eye to the rich contours of his broad shoulders straining against the fabric of his blue morning jacket. I summoned all of my strength to remain calm and steady my buckling legs.

Apparently the two of us gazed at each other longer than protocol dictated, forcing Emmanuel Bach to clear his throat in order to bring Christian back to the realm of reality.

Christian finally took my hand and kissed it, making no effort to let it go. Equally, I made no effort to retrieve it. I couldn't, for my body stood suspended from my mind.

"Enchante le petit reine," he offered. "Merci, Herr Bach. Enchante aussi," said I. He smiled sheepishly. "The pleasure is mine, Your Highness, but please call me 'Christian.' It so distinguishes me from our father—as if my deficient musicianship does not already accomplish that." I offered a curtsy despite myself. "As you wish… 'Christian.' But do not so unfavorably compare yourself to your father. Your brilliance is almost as renowned, sir." "'Almost'…is why I stay on the road for eight months out of the year," he chided as his liquid-green eyes lit up with a renewed sense of self-regard. Again our eyes said more than either of us dared speak forcing Emmanuel to nudge his younger sibling.

"Your Highness, as I stated earlier, you are improving. So until I see you at King's Ball, I leave you with my insistence that you practice," said the older Bach.

"I shall, Herr Bach," Charlotte replied to her teacher, finally tearing her gaze away from Christian who bowed in kind.

"Your Highness, if we see you at King's Ball, may I be permitted to place my name on your dance card?" the younger Bach queried Charlotte.

"Of course."

"I have recently learned the Betty Blue. It is a new English country dance which has become King Frederick's favorite, and I would be most pleased and honored to dance it with so lovely a display of feminine pulchritude as you." Suddenly becoming conscious of the manner in which he was speaking, Christian remembered his place and became reverential.

"Au revoir, Your Highness."

Charlotte blushed and nodded. The brothers Bach left the palace and when they were out of earshot Duchess Elizabeth smirked loud enough for her daughter to hear: "'Lovely display of feminine pulchritude?' You know, his father was blind." Then she proceeded to her chambers.

Charlotte could've cared less about the remark. She had grown used to her mother's verbal abuses. But the girl's inability to catch her breath or move her feet in response to the presence of such an attractive man, was something she was *not* used to.

"He is quite agreeable, is he not?" Charlotte heard from behind, and turned to find her sister Christiana standing in the doorway of the library.

"Unbelievably so," replied the princess as the two of them went to the window in the foyer to look out. Charlotte watched Christian put his arm around Emmanuel and the two got into their carriage. "What just happened?" she asked aloud. "How is it that the most attractive, talented man on earth wants to dance with *me*? He called *me* lovely, kissed *my* hand, looked into *my* eyes and asked to be placed on *my* dance card."

"Such a shame a man like that isn't titled."

"More a shame such a thing matters."

"Nonetheless, I would certainly add him to *my* dance card," Christiana chortled.

The two sisters chuckled in agreement. Suddenly Charlotte was overcome with dread. "Dance card. Oh my. It means dancing."

"Yes, sister. It means actually moving in unison with a partner."

"A partner who is usually male, Christiana. A man, and dancing in a way such as not to resemble a goose that has just been beheaded—which is exactly how I dance."

Princess Charlotte slumped into the nearest chair. "Did you see me with Christian? I was befuddled and awkward. I do not know how to walk like the grand ladies of the court, according to mother, let alone dance. And Christian Bach—a gorgeous, brilliant, famous man is used to dancing with worldly women, I would be a disaster, the laughing stock of the king's ball."

"Why not ask Lady Schwellenberg?" Christiana suggested. "If she does not know this Betty Blue dance herself, she must know someone who could teach you."

Charlotte hugged her sister. "That is a wonderful idea. Swelly knows everything." Then the two girls giggled and made their way out of the room, passing their cousin Wilhelm and ignoring him as they always did. They had a plan in motion, and were going to achieve their objective.

Three

London, England, August, 1760

Augusta Hanover, the 40-year-old Princess Dowager of Wales, was moaning in ecstasy. The bodice of her dress, which had been so meticulously arranged by her Mistress of the Robes, was now down to her waist, and she was against the wall of her private bed chambers with her bare legs flailing around either side of John Stuart's back. The 47-year-old Earl of Bute grunted deliriously as they made passionate love—his hand over her mouth less she scream in rapture. They carried on until both were completely sated and soaked with sweat.

"Ah, so true what they say about men and their insatiable prowess in the morning," Augusta mused breathlessly.

"Only with a woman who inspires," Bute tittered in his Scottish accent, nibbling on her ear. After taking a moment to freshen themselves and get dressed, Augusta and Bute left her chambers and proceeded down the second-floor hallway. "John, will you talk to George about this Hannah Lightfoot business?" Augusta asked, flipping open her fan as it was sweltering.

"Of course. But I doubt he actually went out and married the girl without any of us knowing about it. He's absolutely transfixed by Sarah Lennox. I cannot imagine him seeing anything or anyone else."

As they turned the corner of the hallway leading to the dining hall stairs, Augusta heard the familiar moans of lovemaking emanating from her son George's chambers. Moments later, a young chamber maid eased out of George's room, carefully adjusting her clothing. Augusta remembered seeing the maid enter George's room after nine o'clock the evening before, and she gave Bute a look of exasperation. He patted her sweetly on her bottom and moved on as Augusta approached the maid.

"Miss Periwinkle," she charged.

The chambermaid jumped slightly, turning in embarrassment, eyes cast down in reverence. "Yes, Your Grace?"

"It would appear you are up and about your work quite early this morning?"

"Yes, Your Grace, everything is so…dusty." The chambermaid stammered, then curtsied quickly and started off.

"Just a moment, dear."

The chambermaid froze on the spot as the princess dowager opened the door to her son's room and entered unannounced.

Inside, young George William Frederick Hanover was naked and scrambling to cover himself as his mother icily walked past him to retrieve a feather duster and apron still lying in a heap at the foot of the bed. Giving George a caustic look she brought the items back to the maid with sardonic cynicism.

"Then here, my dear. It is ever so difficult to dust without your…'tools' of the trade."

The maid grabbed the feather duster, curtsied again having gone blanch from humiliation, and scurried off.

Augusta shook her head, reentered George's room, and scornfully looked at her 22-year-old son. "You're pathetic, George. Miss Periwinkle is the second chambermaid in as many nights," her voice as accusatory as George had ever heard. "Your appetite for fleshly desires appears as insatiable as your grandfather's. I don't see how his mistress, Lady Yarmouth, can take it, with two of his courtesans housed right under her nose at St. James. Is there no end to Hanover men and their penchant for common women?"

Before George could respond she threw his clothes at him, glaring. "No need for an answer, my dear. The question is purely rhetorical. Now get dressed. Bute and I want to discuss this business with Hannah Lightfoot. We'll be at breakfast." She turned to leave, then added, "That is, unless you have plans for more fleshly entertainment in the fifteen minutes or so it will take you."

"I'm sorry, mother, but there is nothing to discuss regarding Miss Lightfoot, and I have plans this morning. I'm going to see Aunt Amelia, who's been ill. Then I have an appointment."

Augusta shook her head in disgust. "Is that what they call it now? 'Appointments?' You're pathetic." She stormed out of the room.

George looked at the closed door a moment and sighed. Why couldn't his mother understand him? Why could she not understand men in general, especially the men of his bloodline? There had never been any one woman in the history of the Plantagenet, Tudor, or Hanover dynasties capable of satisfying their male thirst for carnal knowledge. Surely he was only acting on his inherent genetics as the product of his infamous 13th-generation ancestor Henry VIII, who not only bedded women generously, but married and beheaded them with impunity and frequency. Then, there was his great grandfather, King George I, the first in the Hanover dynasty, who imprisoned his own wife for thirty-two years for having an alleged affair with a Swede whose mutilated body was rumored to be kept beneath the floorboards of their residence. Meanwhile, George I himself carried on with not one but three mistresses. Next, his son, the current King George II, openly carried on with Madame de Walmoden while his wife, Queen Caroline, was still alive. Upon the queen's death he conferred the honor of "Lady" to his lover, who is now "Countess of Yarmouth" and a ubiquitous presence at St. James.

Then there was young George's own father, Frederick Louis, Prince of Wales, who, having predeceased his father George II, never became king. Nonetheless, it didn't preclude him from flagrantly parading his mistress, providing her an apartment in Soho Square and an allowance of £1600 a year for all to comment upon. Young George had already hated his dead father for the cold affections the elder man conferred upon him—the heir to the throne; the blatant display of affection for a woman not his mother most certainly fueled the flames.

Yet none of this addressed his regrettable relationship with his mother. The princess dowager was as cold and indifferent toward him as his father had been. In fact, George had never experienced or seen any affection either from or between the two in his entire young life. Still, George loved his mother, and he had at least witnessed her increasing affection for John Stuart, the very married third Earl of Bute.

Lord Bute had been George's tutor for as long as the young prince could remember. George loved him. Princess Augusta found herself relying heavily on the advice of the handsome, charming Earl. Many times he had witnessed Bute use the back stairs of the residence to visit his mother at all hours, and more than once he'd heard the rumors that Bute was far more to Augusta than a confidant, advisor or friend. "Old boots and Petticoats" was the moniker used by gossips at court and in newspapers. Now his mother was deriding him for inappropriate sexual congress with a woman when she herself was involved in the same way with Bute. The hypocrisy was stunning.

Wives and mistresses, queens and concubines, lovers and courtesans, all part of the luxury of being a royal, and George, with his youthful good looks and guaranteed ascension to the throne, was no different than any other. Little else was on his mind except women—beautiful women, charming women. Women who made his heart leap...

...especially Lady Sarah Lennox of Holland House.

He could not stop thinking about her. Morning, night and all times in between. It was the reason he was with the maid—or *any* lower-caste woman, for he couldn't be with Lady Sarah the way his heart yearned and not dishonor her virtue.

He had met the flirtatious Irish beauty and daughter of Charles II, Duke of Richmond last November when her brother-in-law Sir Henry Fox introduced her to the court of St. James. George was speechless at the sight of her. She was tall and voluptuous with blond ringlets cascading down her back. Her eyes were so large and green George marveled at his own reflection in them, and the smattering of freckles that graced her face made her that much cuter. He was instantly drawn to her intellect and lively wit and she kept him laughing all evening. She told him about life in Ireland as the youngest of the four dashing Lennox sisters. She had been orphaned at age 6 and now, at 15, in fulfillment of her dead father's wishes, had come to England to live with her eldest sister, Lady Caroline Lennox-Fox, at Holland House in Kensington, where Caroline's husband, Sir Henry Fox, had become her surrogate father and patron.

Sir Henry, a Whig, had created a social stir when he eloped with Lady Caroline. The former leader of the House of Commons, Secretary of State and current member of the Cabinet under the Duke of Newcastle was ultimately excluded from the Cabinet, and given the lesser post of Paymaster General in a surreptitious rearrangement of the government.

Now Sir Henry had an agenda. He wanted an unimpeachable position of authority and was very much in favor of a match between young George and Sarah. His desire was to become an Earl, a distinction which could be conferred upon him if Sarah entrenched herself in the life of the Prince of Wales. When George ascended the throne Sarah would become queen, and Sir Henry could be commissioned as "the power behind the throne" with the king's ear.

So when Sir Henry discovered young George was love struck by Sarah he went into action, maneuvering her in the path of the young Prince of Wales at every turn. He made sure she was regularly seen at Court looking as appealing as the gods could conceive, and, knowing that George enjoyed taking a ride every morning past Holland House in the hopes of seeing Sarah, he positioned her to be in the front gardens at precisely 10 o'clock in the morning. Today would be no different and George did not disappoint...even though he was late.

The young prince was just coming back from visiting his ailing aunt that morning and was galloping back through the tall grass and hilly meadows of Holland House estate when he saw her. She was in the front garden picking and arranging roses into bunches which she handed off to her lady in waiting. George stopped to observe her the way he did every other morning. Sometimes he hid, afraid to come forth and declare his emotions; oft times he prayed she'd see him and beckon. Still other times he was bold enough to make his presence known. Today was one of those days, and he was feeling bolder and more assertive. He wondered if Sarah could be the one. A woman of high birth, titled, young and so lovely his heart exploded at the sight of her.

Lady Sarah dipped her kerchief in water and stopped to wipe perspiration from her brow when she looked over and saw him. Upon the realization she stood up, dusted herself off and removed her sunbonnet to afford George a better view. Feigning a warm spell, she dipped her kerchief in the water again and pointedly wiped the perspiration beading on her bosoms for George's benefit.

"Well...?" she called out with a flirtatious grin. "Are you going to stand there again today and spy on me, or will you come over and say hello properly?"

George was caught. His heartbeat accelerated as he dismounted his horse and wandered over to her. Sarah opened the wrought iron gate for him and they looked at each other a moment.

"I...I was hoping to see you," said George awkwardly. "In fact, I came purposely."

"I know," replied Sarah, moving in closer. "I'm glad you did."

He couldn't take his eyes off of her. Giving him full advantage of her beauty, Sarah unloosed the pink ribbon supporting her hair, allowing it to cascade demurely down her back. She then turned to her lady. "Please bring us two lemonades."

Her lady curtsied and hurried off as Sarah turned back to the Prince of Wales and surveyed his face. "You look harried, George. Are you well?"

"I am now. A moment ago I was trembling in fear that I might not see you."

"I have become accustomed to you out there lurking in the fields in the wee hours of the morning. But, as it's now 11:30, I thought perhaps your interest was waning."

"Never. I shall always be intrigued by you, milady."

Suddenly, George was overcome with emotion. It was all he could do to contain the growing beast within his loins, and he offered his hand to Sarah. "Walk with me a bit."

Lady Sarah took George's hand and the two strolled through the north garden of Holland House flanked on one side by a pergola laden with honeysuckle and climbing roses, and bordered on the opposite side by delphiniums. The air was fragrant and George was intoxicated by Sarah's perfume and the way the sun highlighted her hair creating a halo around her. *No one should be so beautiful this early* he thought as they made their way toward the upper terrace connected by worn balustrade steps.

"I should like it if you came to court this Friday—with your family, of course," George stammered.

"I should be happy to attend as I have not seen the king in several weeks."

"Not for the purpose of seeing my grandfather, but to be with me, milady."

Lady Sarah was coy. "I know that, George. I only accept for the opportunity to see you." Looking into his eyes and lowering her voice to a suggestive whisper she added, "To be closer to you."

George's body betrayed him and the constraint he so desperately sought evaporated. He took Sarah into his arms and kissed her passionately—almost savagely—on the lips, drawing her tongue into his mouth. Sarah's body melted into his. Her arms circled his neck and caressed his hair. She loved his hair for it was thick, red and luxurious. George was delirious when they both came up for air.

"Sarah. I know I have been restrained, but I am compelled to tell you now for I have adored you from afar for too long. I love you. I truly love you."

"Why has it taken you so long to tell me so?"

"It matters not now. I am thine own. Completely thine own."

They kissed again.

From a window on the second floor of Holland House, Sir Henry Fox saw them together. Turning to his wife he pointed triumphantly, "Our Sarah has him now, Caroline. Look."

Lady Caroline crept to the window following her husband's gaze. She grinned too—for there at the top of the garden steps were George and Sarah kissing as only lovers do who cannot live without each other.

"Your earldom is a whisper away, Henry," Lady Caroline chuckled. "A whisper."

Four

The below-stairs area of Mirow Palace was a small, self-contained industry unto itself. It consisted of the kitchens, the inside servants' quarters, laundry rooms, wine cellar, and soap-making facilities. Over half of the palace's fifty servants, workers, and employees worked down there. Because of the volume of humanity toiling in such close proximity it was always stiflingly hot, and the pungent smell of spices, meats, scented oils, soaps and body odor always hung thickly in the air. The upstairs royals were rarely in this area of the palace, nor were their chamberlains, lords, wardrobe mistresses, valets or ladies—except as instructed.

It was into this cloistered, congested environment that Charlotte, using the back stairs, found several cooks preparing lunch. Most importantly, Lady Schwellenberg, her lady in waiting, was just placing a flower in a bud vase on top of a tray of sliced fruit and biscuits when she noticed Charlotte's presence.

"My word, Your Highness, what on earth are you doing down here? I was just about to bring a tray to your room to hold you until lunch," said the lady in waiting, who then saw Charlotte's anxious expression. "Goodness, child, what is wrong?"

"Dancing," moaned Charlotte. "It's a hopeless business and I am at wit's end, Swelly."

"Why should dancing concern you all of a sudden, my girl?"

"I am expected to dance at the king's ball. Herr Bach has deemed it thus."

"Why do you care if that old harpy Bach wants to dance with you?

"Because it is not old harpy Bach who wishes it. It's his younger, and I dare say, utterly divine brother Christian who is insisting."

Lady Juliana Louisa Schwellenberg, whom Charlotte affectionately called "Swelly," lifted Charlotte's face with fingers placed gently under her chin. She had attended to Charlotte since the princess was two years old and now the 26-year-old lady in waiting had committed herself unconditionally to her young charge, vowing to protect Charlotte with her own life. Charlotte loved Swelly immensely, sometimes feeling guilty for having greater affection for her than for her own mother.

"I see. A handsome, dashing man wants to dance with you, and you are besotted with panic because you do not know how?"

Charlotte nodded regretfully.

Lady Schwellenberg chuckled. "Well, dancing has more to do with your partner leading and you anticipating his every move. All you need know are the steps."

"Knowing the steps is precisely the problem. I don't know how to follow. I don't know what 'leading' means," Charlotte sighed. "The king has learned a dance called the Betty Blue and everyone will be doing it, including Christian. Oh, Swelly. It's going to be just awful."

"I do not think me familiar with the Betty Blue," Lady Schwellenberg frowned. She turned to the servants preparing lunch. "Do any of you here know a dance called the Betty Blue?"

Several shook their heads, but then Sister Lena came forward. "Your Highness, my son, Jon, know dis dance" answered the brown-skinned Jamaican woman with the beautiful smile and scarred cheek in broken patois. "Him show us after him come back from Hamburg with de horses for de Grand Duke last month. Him seen dem dance this Betty Blue in the village and him show us."

"Where is Jon now?" Charlotte questioned.

"In de stables tendin' de horses."

Charlotte started up the stairs, but Lady Schwellenberg stopped her. "Shall I fetch him for you, my Princess?"

Charlotte shook her head. "No, Swelly. This I can venture on my own."

Charlotte had never been inside the stables in her life, for it was not proper for someone of her stature to be there. A lady of breeding, and a royal, had below-stairs servants for such personal necessities. If she should decide to step out, either her carriage was made ready or horse was saddled and brought up to the palace. Also, Albert Papendiek, her hairdresser, would be furious if he knew she was about to enter the barns, where dust, hay and all manner of debris could potentially ruin the hour-and-a-half worth of work performed on her kinky auburn tresses that morning. An angry Albert was the last thing she wished to experience that day.

Nonetheless curiosity prevailed, and two servants opened the great barn door for her and she stepped inside onto the hay. The first thing she saw was Nugget, her favorite Irish quarter horse with the magnificent tan coat. The next thing she heard was broken German mixed with Jamaican patois.

"Your Highness, 'ave you lost yer way?" Turning, she found herself looking into the powerful hazel eyes of Jon Baptiste—the young, honey-colored Jamaican whose mother had been in service to the Frederick family for a generation. Jon instantly bowed. Suddenly Charlotte became nervous and thought better. "No, Jon. I have changed my mind. Thank you for your time." Then, after taking a moment to pet Nugget, Charlotte left the stables.

Jon was perplexed. The moment the young princess was gone the other horse groomsmen appeared. They were as much at a loss as Jon himself.

The princess ran full speed across the lawn back to the palace. She was upset with herself for not asking a simple question which would have relieved her stress. Why couldn't she do it? Why didn't she just say "Jon, please help me to learn the Betty Blue." She was right there. Jon was right there. What held her back?

As she pondered the reasons for her fear she was unaware that her cousin Wilhelm was watching her from the upper window of the palace. He had seen her enter the stables, and now he saw her running out and was curious. Charlotte was oblivious to this as she ran inside the palace to seek the council of her sister, who always had a kind word or good advice.

When Charlotte reached Christiana's room, her sister was having one of her "spells." Charles and Duchess Elizabeth were trying desperately trying to restrain Christiana, who was frantically raving, *"When is Michael coming…? When is Michael coming…?"* Charlotte was prevailed upon to fetch Dr. Geisel. But upon seeing her sister, Christiana, though shaking and ranting, reached out for her. Somehow Charlotte's presence had a calming effect, and as she rocked her ailing sister in her arms, Christiana retreated into a more subdued, child-like state. Her erratic behavior ceased.

Charlotte decided not to compound her sister's mental concerns with her own regarding Jon or dancing. It would be selfish and inappropriate for it was this very thing—being overcome by feeling for a man—which had condemned Christiana to these bouts of insanity in the first place. So Charlotte said nothing—and did nothing.

Two days later, Charlotte had yet to gather the nerve to approach Jon again. Though she thought about it all day, she realized that, for all her bravado, she simply lacked courage. So once she was sure her sister was feeling better, Charlotte, fed up with the stupidity of her fear, put on her favorite cambric dress, gave her reflection a good talking to in a mirror, and worked up the nerve to speak to Jon again. She repeated to herself "You can do it," then waited patiently until the Jamaican entered the stables that afternoon. With a determined stride went in after him.

Jon was walking his colt into a stall when Charlotte approached. Aware of his station the stable boy waited until she motioned for him to be received, then bowed.

"Yer Highness, to what do I owe de pleasure?"

"Jon, I apologize for my behavior two days ago," Charlotte began cautiously. "I just didn't know how to ask you about something that is important to me."

Jon, though subordinate to the princess, stepped out of protocol and spoke up, risking condemnation. "Your Highness, my mama said she tol' you I know how ta dance da Betty Blue. That what you want learn ta do?" he asked.

Charlotte nodded. "Yes, for King Frederick's birthday ball at Sanssouci," she answered.

"Nothing ta dancing, Yer Highness," Jon replied, sensing her trepidation, "'specially the Betty Blue. It's spirited an' lively an' when you hear the music you just find yourself moving gracefully an' following the rhythms."

"You make it sound so easy and I would *so* like to dance that night. But I do not know about 'following rhythms' and 'moving gracefully.' I have not been to King's Ball in years. Not since...," Charlotte paused a moment, the reminiscence suddenly painful.

"Not since your father died," said Jon, finishing her sentence.

She nodded again. Were he alive, Duke Charles would have taught her to dance himself. He would have danced the first dance with her for all to see, just to make her feel pretty and desirable.

Jon saw the memory filling her with melancholy and countered it with an upbeat voice. "Yer Highness, it'd be a honor ta teach you how ta dance da Betty Blue," he beamed, flashing his alabaster teeth with a sweet disposition, "It's somethin' I know like I know horses."

Charlotte was thrilled at the prospect of her dream coming true. "Oh Jon. I so appreciate it. When can we start? What do we do for music? What do we do first?" Her words were tumbling from her mouth in an excited, jumbled rush.

Jon thought about it a moment. "Well, first you need ta get permission from de grand duke an' duchess fer me so I won't be needed while I'm teachin' you. I don' want no trouble."

"It shall be done, and I will send for you when we can begin."

Jon bowed, and the happy princess returned to the palace knowing her wish would soon be granted. As he glanced back watching her leave, a feeling of pride overtook him—something he had not felt in a long while.

Moments later, as Charlotte left the stables, Wilhelm Albertina stood observing her from his upstairs chamber window. Though he frowned in disapproval of her actions, he continued his surveillance with relish, and soon began touching himself inappropriately. As he watched her breasts bounce ever so slightly against the cambric he began rubbing his crotch—slowly at first, then finally masturbating aggressively. The act disconcerted him, but did not stop his arousal or behavior until it reached its conclusion.

Wilhelm was a slow, lumbering 19-year-old with a stutter, and the look of insanity generated from his cold eyes. He had big ambitions and no regard for whomever or whatever may lie in his path to achieving them. All he knew was his desire to become an Earl of Mirow by divine right of succession, and was waiting for the honor to be bestowed upon him by his cousin, Grand Duke Adolph. Whatever was asked of him he did, for it was important to him to become respected in his family's eyes, and most particularly by Charlotte, who appeared repulsed by him. He cared so much for her, and in return she always treated him with disregard and disdain.

Charlotte's cousin was illegitimate. He was the product of Ernst Friedrich II—Duchess Elizabeth's brother—and his favored mistress, Frieda Heidelberg. He lived with his mother for his first seven years. When Frieda died, young Wilhelm had nowhere to go. Not being accepted by Duke Ernst's wife, Carolina, or any of the legitimate heirs left Wilhelm in a state of flux—until Duchess Elizabeth chose to raise him in the home she shared with her husband and gave him the surname "Albertina." More importantly she gave him affection. Wilhelm loved his Aunt Elizabeth and she loved him in return despite his affliction and somewhat malicious disposition. Wilhelm served the Frederick family well and did their "unpleasant duties" in the hopes of better positioning himself.

But lately his obsession with Charlotte had become dire. He was determined to find a way to impress the princess so she would care for him. He would do anything for her, but what could she want from him to bring her closer? This was the question which pervaded his thoughts for the next few days.

Five

I was apprehensive as Christiana and I entered the dining hall. I had meticulously thought out my request and rehearsed over and over how to approach mother about Jon, and my getting permission for him to teach me the Betty Blue. My palms were sweaty and I squeezed Christiana's hand so tightly she whispered, 'Calm down, stay firm and don't waver or mother will see your anxiety and go for your throat.' I nodded. Then, with a comforting smile, my sister patted me on the shoulder. I remember we had a dinner guest that afternoon—Captain Charles D'Eon, a member of the French Dragoons. He had just been to Russia on business for France and stopped at Mirow to pay his respects to my mother and give her his condolences on the death of my father, with whom he had been friends. I assumed that with company present, mother would be more amiable concerning my desire.

Everyone was gathered and engaged in various discourse. Ernst and Charles skirmished over who would get the big slice of stuffed mutton; Aunt Albertina and Wilhelm were in a debate about the vegetable gardens and how the recent drought would affect them; and mother was engaged in reminiscences about father with Adolph and d'Eon. I sat next to my brother Charles and Christiana sat next to me, then finally, I took in a deep breath…"

"Mother, may I speak with you a moment?"

"What is it, child?"

"I have learned that everyone will be dancing the Betty Blue at King Frederick's ball in October. I would like to learn it so I can dance with Herr Bach as he has offered."

Duchess Elizabeth's face rendered a cold expression and she purposely said nothing. Charlotte stewed in her silence, then somehow managed to continue. "Jon Baptiste knows this dance and has offered to teach me. We could begin tomorrow, but you and Adolph must allow him to be relieved of his duties while we practice."

Elizabeth's eyes narrowed in stunned condemnation. "Learn dancing?" she grimaced, "From our *coloured* servant?" She looked at Adolph with a raised, disapproving eyebrow. Then came the attack. "Absolutely not! It's out of the question!"

"But it would only be a few lessons."

"Learning some new dance from our servant is unacceptable," Elizabeth snipped, "There are dance masters for that. But you know our *situation*." She emphasized 'situation' for emphasis.

"But mother..."

"We all know Negroes are adept at music and dancing," she paused to cough, "but their bodies are too carnal and licentious where ardor is concerned. I simply will not permit you to cavort with one—especially a Negro in our employ. You could arouse a latent sensibility resulting in catastrophe. I absolutely forbid it."

Feeling defeated Charlotte looked at Christiana, her eyes filling with tears. Her mother was as intractable as ever and had once again managed to condemn more than object. Charlotte's hurt feelings were obvious to all—and shared, for Sister Lena felt just as maligned. After all, Elizabeth reproached Lena's son Jon even as Lena served dinner.

Adolph also noticed it and reacted. "Lena, there are two bottles of Rhine in the cellar. Will you get them for us please?"

Sister Lena obediently nodded and hurried away, her eyes glazed. The second she was gone Charlotte's brother turned back to his mother.

"That was unnecessary, mother. Jon and his family have been in your employ for years. He was born here. You know him—and his mother, whom you just embarrassed—someone who did not deserve your censure when she is honorable and harmless." Adolph turned to d'Eon in an effort to change the subject. "Captain d'Eon tell us of your escapades in Russia."

But Duchess Elizabeth would have none of it. "Honorable and harmless? Lena Baptiste? Men have been hanged for less."

"Perhaps we should resolve this matter in a more private setting," Christiana offered after a glance at d'Eon, who was obviously embarrassed by what he saw and heard.

"No. The subject will be resolved now and forever," Elizabeth retorted. "I will not permit Charlotte to dance with a Schwartzer, and I will not have the word 'honorable' associated with Sister Lena. The only reason that immoral, ungrateful scullery maid is still here is…"

"Mother!" Adolph interrupted, firmly cautioning her.

Duchess Elizabeth turned away from a vehement tirade against Jon's mother and focused her wrath on Adolph for Charlotte's benefit. "Lena aside, I will not squander what little revenue we have on a dance master. It would be different if Charlotte were appealing or charismatic, then dancing might help. But she is not. My decision is final."

"It is not *your* decision to make. You are no longer Regent. *I* am Grand Duke…"

"…who does *not* control *my* privy purse."

Adolph fell silent a moment as Charlotte felt tears trickling down her cheeks and a veil of anger coiling within her. She kept squeezing her hands together to control herself.

Captain D'Eon, feeling badly for her, quickly came to her rescue. "I find the princess to be quite appealing. She would make any young gentleman a fine spouse."

Duchess Elizabeth turned to her guest and thought for a moment before proceeding, "My dear Captain d'Eon, have you finally married?"

"Not yet," answered d'Eon, "but I do have my eye on someone in London."

"Pity. With your obvious charm and charisma we might have been able to perhaps betroth Charlotte to you—that is, were you a royal. Instead, you have been forced to witness the very real dilemmas of those of us who *are* members of the aristocracy."

This quieted d'Eon and everyone else who became aware he had been put in his place as Elizabeth continued. "I love my daughter, but I know her shortcomings. All she need do is play enough music to impress the Duke of Anhalt. Marrying him would alleviate any *'situations'*…"

"But I have no affection for him," Charlotte interrupted, unable to contain herself.

Duchess Elizabeth lowered her voice and offered an explanation as though her words could shield her daughter from witnessed abuse. "Lord Gregory has a great fortune and seeks a new wife. With an income of 10,000 talers a year, he does not require your paltry dowry, so we could all benefit greatly from such a match. Neither his age nor your dis-affection are material."

"And, on the supposed chance I say "no" what then, mother?" Charlotte swiped.

"Oh you won't say no, dear. You know what's at stake." The Duch-ess then turned to d'Eon feigning tears for his benefit and sympathy. "My husband, God rest him, mismanaged our privy purse and our future grows bleaker by the day unless one of my children marries well and soon. Obviously it will not be Christiana, as she is 25 and unstable."

Christiana and Charlotte held hands. Charlotte's were shaking from forced composure and Christiana's from embarrassment, as Elizabeth continued. "And Adolph's 'peculiar abnormality' appears to restrict his eligibility…"

"Careful, mother," cautioned the Grand Duke.

"…So Charlotte, is the hope of this family." Elizabeth turned back to Charlotte. "That is why music is the key to the Duke and our future. Not dancing with Christian Bach—nor any Schwartzers in our employ!"

Finally Adolph had enough and slammed his fist on the table. "Then *you* marry the old pig, mother. And stop going on and on about Negroes and calling them 'Schwartzers' as though we Fredericks do not possess the stain of Africa in our own veins."

The room fell mute as though all the air had been sucked from it. An intense feeling of dread enveloped everyone at the table and Charlotte could hear her heart beating so loudly nothing else was audible. Had her brother just uttered what she thought she heard? Had he dared to raise the subject of African blood in the family tree? To the one person her father said did not believe in their Merovingian blood much less this an-cestral imbroglio? And was it true? Were they possessed of black blood?

D'Eon excused himself citing a desperate need to smoke his pipe on the veranda. When he left the room, Charlotte looked at Adolph, then at her mother whose response did not disappoint.

The Duchess dramatically stood to her full five-foot-ten-inch frame and bellowed at the top of her lungs, despite her coughing. "Have you lost your mind?!" she vomited, each word punctuated as though she were stabbing Adolph with a knife. "How *dare* you invoke the idea of 'African blood' aloud, much less at the dinner table in front of guests, where no decent member of polite society would deign to discuss it. Something so repugnant and divisive, something we are forever reminded of every time we look at Charlotte! How *dare* you, Adolph!" She tossed her napkin to the table. "For that little affront of indecency you shall leave this table at once!"

My brother's eyes flashed beet-red outrage. He looked at everyone present, then back at mother with every hair on his body standing at attention. 'I am Grand Duke, mother. I am. If anyone is leaving the table, it shall be you and that poison mind of yours!' he bellowed.

I sunk deeply into my chair, feeling small and insignificant. I thought surely I would disappear. Were it not for my brother, thoughts of taking my own life and ending the embarrassment my yellowness caused, would have consumed me. As it was, I watched in humiliation as Adolph continued summoning every ounce of resolve to control his emotions.

'I respect you as my mother, but I'm glad it's out in the open. All of it!" He finished his port and slammed the glass on the table refusing to leave. I could not have been prouder than I was of my brother that day. Adolph became my champion, always there to fight for me no matter what wrath he incurred. I wiped my eyes and wondered how it was that he did not receive the mark, as his actions were so like father's.

But moments later, mother was overcome by a coughing fit. My brother Charles offered his kerchief and called for mother's lady in waiting. We all knew something was seriously wrong as her coughing flare-ups occurred more frequently than ever. But I couldn't help myself and ran out. I was woefully disheartened and kept asking myself why must it always be this way with mother? Why did she always equate everything to my being plain or having a swarthy complexion? Why did she take things out on every member of the family because of me? I knew there was no logical explanation but I hated her for my feeling that way, and I found myself running below stairs to the kitchen to find Sister Lena...

When Charlotte entered the kitchen Sister Lena was pouring the glasses of the wine Adolph requested. She was trying her best not to sob. Charlotte came over and, upon seeing the princess, the Jamaican turned away slightly.

"I'm so sorry they embarrassed you upstairs. It was so cruel," Charlotte said.

"It isn't de first time, chile." Sister Lena responded placing the wine bottle on the tray with the glasses. She started off, but Charlotte stopped her.

"I do not want any tension between you and me. I am not like her."

Sister Lena looked back at Charlotte. Despite her hurt feelings, she did care for the princess. "No, not in personality. But you are part o' de hypocrisy they forward."

"I don't understand."

Lena thought a moment, wondering if she should go on. Finally choosing not to, she turned to leave. Again Charlotte stopped her.

"Lena, what is it? Tell me."

After a moment, Sister Lena turned back to Charlotte lowering her voice. "What they say upstairs is true—about yer family's Moorish blood. But you the only one who looks like it."

Charlotte's heart began to flutter and warm perspiration formed in tiny beads on her upper lip.

"Neither yer mother or yer father could escape the very thing the Duchess fears most: Magragana's African blood in their veins."

"Magragana ben Bekar?" Charlotte queried, surprised the maid knew the name.

"You know about her?"

"Not in detail. Father only mentioned her name before he died."

Sister Lena set the tray down and went to the small window to look out. She was unsure as to whether she should continue. Yet something within her compelled her. "Magragana was your ancestor from twelve maybe thirteen generations ago. Beyond that I don' know any more about her than you, and you mother will never tell you anyt'ing. She will never speak o' it."

"How is it you know about Magragana at all?" asked the princess.

Sister Lena looked away, myriad thoughts traversing her mind. "I overhear you father arguing wit you mother one day years ago. She was angry he was spending too much money lookin' fer clues to Magragana's descendants."

Charlotte joined the Jamaican at the window and looked at the lawn's labyrinth tended by several dark-skinned servants. Suddenly she was struck by the irony. All power in Mecklenburg was in the hands of the Grand Duke, aristocrats, members of the landed gentry, and the upper classes. The lower classes were poor, uneducated and politically impotent. As Charlotte watched them her fingernails dug into her flesh from guilt.

."If it's true we Frederick's have black blood, only an accident of birth has raised us above our servants," she mumbled, leaning into the frustration of her own embrace.

"Indeed," Sister Lena retorted flatly. "An accident of birth."

At that she took the tray upstairs leaving Charlotte to stew in these new revelations.

☩

After that day, I quietly made it a point to learn everything I could about the Moors—especially since my family was reluctant to accept them as our ancestors. I learned that they were not a religion or race of people, but Arabs, Christians, Berbers, or Muslims who had migrated from Northern Africa to Spain and Portugal and conquered those countries. But by 500 AD, they themselves were conquered.

And yet, instead of retreating at the thought of having African blood, I found I felt a sense of pride in my difference. I was no longer an ordinary, unremarkable girl, but an extraordinary woman with a dark secret. A secret that gave me purpose—even if I had no idea what it was.

"Charlotte, I have a plan…and Adolph is going to help."

It was the day after Duchess Elizabeth's rebuke of Adolph at the dinner table. Christiana had run breathlessly down the hall into Charlotte's room. She was excited.

"I thought about it all night and spoke to Adolph this morning. We've decided you *should* learn to dance for Christian, and you should let Jon teach you."

It took Charlotte a moment to respond. This was all so unexpected coming from her sister. "But mother has forbidden it."

"She will never know."

"How will she *not* know?" Charlotte questioned.

With complete lucidity Christiana put forth her plan. "Adolph will give Jon the time off to work with you. On the chosen days, I'll dress as you, go into the music room at two o'clock, close the door and play the harpsichord for an hour as you do. Trust me, I can play just as poorly. Mother will never know."

It was a brilliant idea. *But would it work?* Charlotte wondered, shaking her head.

"Mother's only interest is in you attracting the old Duke. So you will go to her room and announce you're going to practice for an hour so that you'll impress Lord Gregory when next you see him. Of course mother will notice what you're wearing. Then I'll slip into your dress and you'll go and meet Jon. Remember, the harpsichord faces the mirror so one's back is to the door when playing it. Should mother or anyone pass by or get a glimpse in they won't know it's me playing and not you. Then, when you're done, you'll return to the music room through the opened window, we'll change clothes and that will be that."

The princess hugged her sister. "Thank you for this, Christiana. Can we begin this Thursday at two?"

"As you wish. After all, what are sisters for?"

The following day the plan went into action. Charlotte wore her yellow brocade robe de cour with its grand panier and cotton head cap. She wore it because her mother hated it and she knew she would take note of it. Since the Duchess had taken to her bed for rest, the princess went to her mother's room and announced she was going downstairs to the music room to practice so Lord Gregory would be impressed with her. Given their dinner encounter two evenings earlier the Duchess was thrilled and happily waved Charlotte away.

Next, Christiana and Charlotte exchanged clothes. Putting on her sister's blue linen sacque dress, Charlotte snuck off across the wet grounds of the eastern part of the palace to meet Jon. Perhaps it was not so much that dancing would attract Christian, but that it might give her poise and grace. She might even develop those qualities which alluring women seemed to possess but were not Charlotte's God given gifts. Perhaps her mother might be proud of her.

"Look, Yer Highness, I got us somethin' to help us with the dancin'," Jon announced as he sprinted across the moist, cool grass of the great lawn. "It's a music box the Grand Duke threw away a few years ago. I kep' it cuz I liked the music. It's perfect for Betty Blue dancin'."

Charlotte's eyes bathed Jon in admiration as he pulled a small broken music box from his burlap bag. When he lifted its lid it played several stanzas of a tune in a tinkling, sing-song way that made Charlotte chuckle. Several pegs in the box were broken so on occasion the music would skip. But it did make the girl want to dance as he placed the box on a nearby log.

"Now, let me show you." Jon insisted, pulling Charlotte to him, taking her hand, and putting his own around her waist. Suddenly he remembered Charlotte was royalty and his superior, and he quickly removed his hand. He stepped back deferentially. "I'm sorry, Yer Highness. I forgot myself," he bowed. "I meant to say, 'May I be permitted' to show you."

The princess appreciated the gesture, for she knew Jon meant no disrespect. She curtsied, replying, "Indeed you may," then extended her hand. "In fact, you may take my hand, Sir Jon."

Jon grinned. "Did you say 'Sir Jon'?"

"I did. From now on, when we are together out here, you shall be 'Sir' Jon, and I shall be 'Lady' Charlotte. That way we will be equals and it will help us communicate better. Agreed?"

Jon nodded. Charlotte knew he liked being called "Sir" Jon and he bowed deeply, as if being conferred the fabricated title signaled his rebirth. "Agreed, 'Lady' Charlotte."

"Then show me what to do, Sir Jon."

Jon took Charlotte's hand like an aristocrat. "The gentleman always bows an' the lady curtsies. In all proper dancin', you're 'sposed to do what they call 'pay réverénce' at the beginning an' at the end of the dance," he said with his rudimentary language skills, "An' it's important to look at each other. You maintain eye contact with your partner an' not show the top of your head. Same for the Minuet, the Allemande an' the Contredance."

The princess followed his every advice and move.

"Now," Jon continued, "The lady should be at the Lord's right. That's what is proper. So you should be here." He moved Charlotte to his right side, then wound up the music box again. He held out his hand. Charlotte took it, trying hard to follow. She was clumsy at first, but Jon was blissfully patient.

"You see, it looks real graceful when the lady lets the man lead her through the movements. This means the man has to physically lead an' the lady follows him by anticipatin'.' "

His arm then encircled Charlotte's body. "For instance, when I do this, you move the same—like this." His body indicated a move to the left so she moved to the left with him.

"That's good, Lady Charlotte. You felt that, didn't you?"

"I did," said the princess gleefully. "Just wait until Christian Bach sees me doing this."

Jon nodded. "He will be very impressed."

They continued for a well over an hour. Soon, Charlotte found she didn't care that the tinkling music from the broken old music box relentlessly played the same song over and over because, for the first time since her father's death, she was having fun. No longer was she a princess to be placed on a pedestal and bowed to in formal prostration, but a student who enjoyed the company and instructions of her teacher who respected her and thought her charming, funny and a good sport. Never before had she laughed so hard or so often. Even when she made mistakes—and she made many—Charlotte laughed.

So many times she had heard Jon play the violin when he played for the annual "Feast of the Equinox," where a good spring harvest was prayed for, and a celebration was had along with good food and wine. Charlotte had also heard the merriment and hilarity amongst the Africans in our servants' quarters and marveled at the quality of their singing voices, which rivaled the great opera stars of Europe. Now, for just an hour, she felt personally privy to experience and be part of it—and she wanted more. She wanted to move as they did, dance as they did, laugh and let the world and all its ills fall away. But the reality of my life encroached, and the lesson was over.

"Grand Duke Adolph says I only have a hour. So they'll be needing me."

"Then we shall have another lesson on Thursday?"

"That would be agreeable," he responded, taking a step backward and bowing, "Until Thursday." Jon then sprinted away.

Charlotte watched him go and a wistful smile crept over her face. Something wonderful and exciting had happened. The girl closed her eyes and in her fantasy she saw herself dancing with the dashing musician. She saw what she was wearing, she saw the envy of the crowd, and she saw herself loving the attention. No one could have been happier than Charlotte was that day after her first lesson with Jon Baptiste.

Suddenly Charlotte's eyes flew open in realization. *Good Lord!*, she thought in a panic. *The ruse!* She had to get back to the palace else her sister would be angst-ridden. Charlotte quickly raced across the grounds, through the wet prickly patches of aromatic rosemary and coriander and headed toward the west end of the palace. Completely out of breath and making sure no one noticed her, she climbed through the first-floor window Christiana had left open and fell onto the floor of the music room. Christiana stopped playing the piano-forte and rushed over.

"My God, it took you a fortnight. Are you all right? Well? How was it? Tell me everything. Don't leave anything out," Christiana babbled.

"It was wonderful," Charlotte answered breathlessly. "Jon is an excellent teacher. He brought a music box and taught me wonderful movements. I felt as though I'd be one of the most confident, desirable ladies of court. It was such an exciting experience, so unique." She peeled out of Christiana's dress, helped Christiana unhook hers and they exchanged clothes quickly.

"What is dancing with a Negro like?" Christiana asked hastily hooking Charlotte's dress.

Charlotte blushed at the thought of detailing her time with Jon, which was something she had hoped could remain confidential. Yet she found she had to share it with her sister or burst.

"It was exhilarating. He taught me to do this..."

She took Christiana's hand, hummed a melody and showed her sister a few simple steps of the Betty Blue. Christiana giggled as she followed along and they danced with abandon.

"What have we here?" the sisters soon heard from behind.

Whipping around, they were surprised by the presence of Lady Schwellenberg standing in the doorway of the music room with folded arms. Neither of the girls could speak and their eyes grew as large as saucers. Lady Schwellenberg came over to Christiana and examined her.

"Why is your dress wet at the bottom? And why have you the smell of rosemary?"

Christiana swallowed hard and looked down at her blue dress, the one Charlotte had just worn with Jon. Three inches of hemline was wet and soiled with dirt and grass stains. Christiana looked at Charlotte, not knowing what to do. As she could not come up with a reasonable answer, she said nothing. Swelly then fixed her gaze on Charlotte.

"And why is *your* dress mis-hooked, my girl?"

Sure enough, in Christiana's haste, she had not re-hooked Charlotte's yellow dress correctly. The two girls stood motionless while Lady Schwellenberg's eyes narrowed.

"There is something amiss here. The two of you look like a cornered cat having swallowed the canary. What have you been up to?"

Charlotte began to tremble and her eyes fluttered. Lady Schwellenberg placed a hand on the girl's chin, tilted her head up, lifted an eyebrow perceptively, and just waited. Naturally Charlotte was guilt-ridden and glanced at Christiana, who nodded. Charlotte sighed in acquiescence, then closed the door of the music room and turned to her Lady in Waiting. "I beseech your confidence, Swelly. It's imperative." Charlotte then explained about Jon. She confessed to asking her mother's permission and being denied, the dance lessons, the subterfuge, everything. Then she and Christiana waited for a response which seemed to take an eternity. Lady Schwellenberg went to the pianoforte and sat. She began to play "The Capriccio" exactly the way Charlotte played it—with the same mistakes and flourishes. As she played Charlotte and Christiana wandered over.

"A plot such as yours requires someone other than your sister in order for it to work. Both you and she cannot be missing at the same time. Eventually it will arouse suspicion—especially with the Duchess. So, as we are of similar size, let it be *me* who fills in for you here in the music room," Lady Schwellenberg suggested as she continued to play. "Besides, no one will suspect anything if one's lady in waiting has a dirty, wet hem or is seen running through the meadow, or sneaking through a downstairs window, as I saw you do just now."

Though embarrassed by the revelation Charlotte hugged her Lady.

"Now then. When do you meet Jon next?" asked Charlotte's new partner in crime.

Six

Lake Ritouro was the happiest place in Germany to Charlotte. Three days a week for six weeks she and Jon met there, where she learned the Betty Blue, the Allemande, and the Minuet, and also learned how to waltz. Christiana and Lady Schwellenberg's scheme was working perfectly, and most times no one was aware that Charlotte was not in the palace. Charlotte and her lady exchanged dresses, relieving Christiana of the responsibility, and Swelly practiced on the piano for an hour, locking the music room door behind her. Charlotte made sure her actual lessons with Emmanuel Bach were always on days she did not meet Jon.

Two weeks into her lessons, Jon instructed her on the subtlety of movement. He was concerned about her disjointedness. "You're movin' too stiffly, too tentatively, milady," he said in his soft Jamaican patois. "Part of dancing is in the art of the lady's ability ta be flirtatious, alluring—ta make eye contact with the lord an' keep his attention on her."

"But I do not know how to do that," Charlotte lamented. "I am not considered alluring."

Jon became incredulous. "But you are, Lady Charlotte. Any woman can be. All she need do is be confident." He then positioned Charlotte away from him. "Let's begin again." He bowed. "Now you curtsey. Pretend I'm Herr Christian, an' you are the most beautiful, self-possessed dancer at the ball. Feel it. Know it."

He held out his hand. Charlotte awkwardly curtsied and walked toward him, leading with her left arm and left leg. She felt silly, giggled and asked to begin again.

"Use your eyes an' your attitude," Jon instructed affably. "Be flirtatious. Tell yourself, 'I am beautiful. I am confident, an' Herr Christian is impressed.'"

This ploy succeeded. The princess repeated the phrase over and again until her stride to Jon was more assured. She curtsied, coyly dropping her eyelids then raising them again to the stable boy, who nodded, "Good, good." As they danced, Charlotte imagined what it would feel like to be in Christian's arms—how she would touch his hand, perhaps even his body, yet still dance with elegance, poise and regal bearing.

Jon, though pleased with Charlotte's progress, was unprepared for his own reaction. His initial suggestion that the princess be flirtatious was to ensure her development into a seasoned dancer. But he had not counted on his personal feelings toward her escalating into something else over the next several lessons. Here was a princess dancing with and accepting instruction from him, and he, a servant, was permitted to touch her in a manner otherwise deemed inappropriate. There was even a moment during the Minuet when their eyes locked and, as Charlotte became more confident, Jon experienced feelings he knew were improper for a man of his station.

Charlotte, however, was oblivious. Eventually she and Jon stopped meeting solely for the purpose of dance instruction to enjoy each other's company as friends. Sometimes they would talk for the whole hour, other times they laughed under the blooming dogwood trees. Charlotte liked Jon's spirit, his sense of humor, his zest for life, and his obvious patience. Soon she found herself confessing things to him she never told her own sister. On one occasion while Charlotte waited on the swing to meet with Jon she was reading a book. He sprinted up to her moments later and grinned. "You always readin' when I come."

"Just passing the time until you arrive."

Jon looked at the book, fascinated by the gold lettering. "What was you readin' today?"

"My but we're inquisitive," the princess mused.

"In-what?"

"Inquisitive. You know, probing, inquiring. Curious." But Jon's blank stare caused Charlotte to cross her arms in mock exasperation, "Meddlesome?"

"Oh," Jon shrugged good-naturedly. "Why didn't you say that?"

Charlotte grinned and showed him the book. "'As You Like It,' a comedy play written by William Shakespeare. I try to read at least one book or play every two weeks. Sometimes more."

Jon wound up the broken music box and they began their lesson. This time they did the Countredance and Charlotte was more confident. For a change she didn't need to count off the steps in her head anymore, allowing her to ask questions instead. "Jon, what do you do when you're not tending the horses—or teaching wayward princesses how to dance?"

Jon chuckled. "I do a little blacksmithin', some carpentry, draw a little. In fact, I drew some sketches ta redesign the old barn."

"I'd love to see them sometime. Who knows, perhaps you could become an architect."

"What's a archa... tek?"

"Architect," Charlotte corrected. "It's the creator and designer of buildings."

Jon stopped dancing and stared at her a moment. "I could be somet'ing like that?"

"I imagine you could be anything you wanted, Sir Jon."
Jon thought better. "But I'd need ta know readin' an' numbers."

Suddenly a revelation struck Charlotte like a lightening bolt. Of course. After all, they were already meeting three times a week for dance instruction. Why not reading or math?

"Maybe I could teach you."

Jon was ecstatic. "Oh Princess Charlotte, if you taught me to read an' be smart I'd...I'd..." He paused, overcome with emotion. "I would be so grateful. Imagine me—educated." He stopped again not wanting to exhibit more emotion than was appropriate.

Charlotte understood. "It would be my honor, Sir Jon, if only to repay you for teaching me how to dance, for being my friend, and listening to my plight. So, why don't we continue meeting here as we have been, and I'll bring books and paper and we'll start your tutelage."

"Tuta... what?"

"Your education."

"Oh." The two chuckled.

Charlotte concocted a plan and put it into action. She used books from the library for Jon's lessons. Jon was a willing, even eager student. He loved his sessions with the princess, and Charlotte taught him rudimentary reading, mathematics, and European history. Sometimes on their walks, Charlotte taught Jon the scientific names of her favorite flowers such as hydrangeas, chrysanthemum, delphinium, and her much-loved Maiden's Blush roses. During his chores Jon kept an ear out for new words and asked Charlotte to explain their meaning and was excited to use them in a sentence.

Occasionally, Charlotte managed to sneak out to the stables, where she and Jon would meet in the evening. Candles burned quietly and there amongst horses, hay, parchment and pens, Jon would read to her. Though the words were difficult and he struggled at first, he had dogged determination to do better. Since Charlotte's brothers, the Duchess, Wilhelm, Christiana and her Aunt Albertina always retired early, no one suspected a lesson was being taught to a servant. For that hour in the barn, Jon did not feel like a Jamaican servant in the service of the Grand Duke and Duchess of Mecklenburg, but a member of the social aristocracy—and he liked it. He liked it a lot. So much so that he began to forget himself and his place in the world.

☨

One week before King Frederick's ball Charlotte went through her usual subterfuge with Lady Schwellenberg and snuck out of the music room. She had just run past the grape orchard when she heard screams and commotion. As she circled back toward the north side of the palace in the direction of the sounds, she suddenly found herself cringing from disgust.

There was a small gathering of servants around the palace whipping post. Berthoud Werden, one of the Fredericks' servants, was tied to the post with his shirt stripped to his waist. Wilhelm was mercilessly flogging him with his bullwhip and yelling, "How d-dare you steal from this p-palace! This will teach you!" Poor Berthoud's screams could be heard all the way to the lake, and Charlotte's hands instantly went to her ears to block out the sounds. She couldn't take it, nor could she stop it, for she should not have been there. All she could think about as she ran to her swing was why Wilhelm could not abide by the rules her father had set long ago.

Duke Charles did not allow for corporal punishment like this when he was alive. If you did not live by the rules of the palace, you were dismissed from service. Never did he beat or cause there to be beatings at either palace, Mirow or Neustrelitz. To him it wasn't a Christian ideal, and Charlotte felt the same way. Only Wilhelm and the demons which drove him took such joy in dispensing suffering to another human being.

When Charlotte reached the swing she was completely out of breath and in a blue mood. She needed the sweet smells of wild mimosas and hyacinths around her to lift her spirits and alleviate the ugliness of what she had just witnessed. She wanted everything to be pleasurable again. She needed to pretend "All was right at Mirow." Thank God she had the picturesque view of the lake before her.

"Lady Charlotte," she soon heard from behind her. When she turned Jon was there carrying a larger burlap sack than his usual one. Charlotte smiled at the sight of him.

"Sir Jon. Thank goodness you're here. Did you see it? The beating? It was just terrible."

Jon nodded sadly as he opened the sack. "I know. I see Herr Wilhelm's beatin's all the time. He beat on servants for any reason. But today, Berthoud was caught wit silverware he stole in his room. Wilhelm is makin' a example outta him."

Charlotte looked away. "Let's not dance today. I don't feel up to it anymore, and I do not wish to hear that broken music box."

"As you wish, m'lady. I brought something different for today anyway."

Jon pulled a tablecloth from the burlap bag and arranged the dishes, fruit and other delicacies he brought on it. "I brung my mama's spatzen, some fruit…even some wine cuz I thought a picnic after our dance lesson might be nice. Wasn't expectin' all that with Wilhelm." He helped Charlotte from the swing to the tablecloth.

"I wasn't either," Charlotte commented flatly. "But I am glad you did this. I love Sister Lena's spatzen. I always save extras from dinner for later."

"My mama's spatzen got powerful obeah," Jon said, opening a bottle of wine and pouring a glass for Charlotte. "She learned the recipe from her mama. They say her spatzen is what convinced yer daddy ta bring her here ta Mirow."

"Really? I never knew that was how your family came to be here. Father always liked your mother," Charlotte prattled on. "He used to say she was the smartest and most talented of all the servants he had hired."

Jon stopped pouring wine and stared at Charlotte a moment. *How naive and gullible she is,* he thought. *Doesn't she know? Isn't she aware of the way things really are?*

"Yer Highness, yer father didn't 'hire' my mama," he said with forced composure. "He 'acquired' her, grandma Omena, an' my uncle James in a exchange from ole man Gerhardt's estate in Leipzig. We're slaves. Surely you know that."

There was a long pause as Charlotte's gaze intensified into shock.

Jon realized she was completely unaware of his status as a slave. "You didn't know?" He then mused ironically, "No, why should you? Wasn't like yer father's slaves was important ta him past cookin' an' cleanin'."

Charlotte stood, her reaction changing from shock to insult. "That's not fair, Jon," she stated and started off. But Jon leaped up and grabbed her hand to stop her. He instantly dropped it when her look at him suggested he had overstepped his boundaries.

"I'm sorry, Yer Highness. But none of it's fair, or right," he began, a melancholy frown taking residence across his face and a melancholy tone creeping into his Jamaican brogue. "My granddaddy, Vassa, was captured from Africa an' sold into slavery in Jamaica to harvest sugar cane. Eventually he ran away an' became a Maroon rebel fightin' for the freedom of slaves. Then he met Omena, my grandmother, who was the illegitimate daughter of a Jamaican conjure-woman an' a Portuguese plantation owner. They had a son they named James. Eventually my grandfather was caught, and he, Omena and little James was sold ta a shipping merchant. But Vassa couldn't take another voyage 'cross the water, an' he jus' jumped overboard an' killed hisself. By then, Omena had my mama Lena an' they got sold here ta Germany ta Herr Gerhardt, a canon maker in Leipzig. My grandma taught my mother how ta read the tarot cards an' develop her 'eye,' an' it was mama who predicted that Gerhardt would have a heart attack an' leave a pile o' debt. Some o' them was ta yer daddy, who went ta the Gerhardt estate ta claim somethin' as payment. While they was there my mama cooked for them. Then an' there yer daddy decided he wanted my mama, my uncle an' my grandmother in exchange for the unpaid debts. Two years after they got here ta Mirow, I was born. A year later my grandmother died."

"Where is your father?"

"Don't have a father."

"Everyone has a father, Jon. Don't you know who yours is?"

"Mama says though I was descended from kings, I was Joe Herford's boy."

"The blacksmith? I remember him—the big, barrel-chested man. He made such intricate, delicate ironwork. I remember I liked him before he died."

"After I got old enough, Joe taught me how ta use my hands ta build things. Taught me how ta draw an' blacksmith. But he never lived with me an' mama in the quarters. I know he cared for mama, but she don't talk about it. All she say is most white folks got no use to us."

"Is that what *you* think?"

Jon thought a moment. "I think yer father was always good ta me, mama an' my uncle James. Not too many is that way." Jon looked away a moment. "When I think about those poor slaves an' servants who was on the Gerhardt place, I feel bad. They didn't get it good. Gerhardt's kin separated families from each other. Sold them off piecemeal. Some is in England, or the Colonies, or the Islands working hard an' sufferin' bad as slaves."

"That doesn't seem right."

Jon thought about Joe the blacksmith and how he died from overwork and misuse. He thought about his mother and how she toiled in the kitchen making soap, dusting and doing the laundry when she wasn't cooking. Then he thought about his own life shoveling manure, sweeping the stables, and cleaning chamber pots with only three changes of clothes and the rare bath. Then impulsively, almost impetuously, Jon heard himself blurt out:

"It's *not* right. But *you* won't do nothin' about it, so why care?"

Suddenly everything morphed into a slow blur. The words had tumbled out in a small voice but the sentiment was bold and definitive. How he wished he could take them back and desperately tried to swallow the hard knot in his throat. Why did he say it—especially the way he said it? He had looked Charlotte in her eyes and with undue eloquence forced the princess to examine her values and address his and every other slave, serf or indentured servant in Germany—or in fact the world's—question of "Why?"

Jon Baptiste knew their relationship had changed in that moment, and he had to be prepared to accept the consequences. And all of this was prompted with twelve words:

"But you won't do nothin' about it, so why do you care?"

Charlotte was silent for an unbearable amount of time, and neither she nor Jon could look at the other. The princess knew Jon was correct in his assessment. She wasn't courageous—even with the knowledge that she herself was descended from the same incomprehensible inequity as he. Finally, Jon retreated emotionally, wishing he could transport the two of them back to the moment before his blunder. "I…I should go, Princess Charlotte," he offered, racked with guilt. "I need to finish working on the walking stick I'm whittling for mama's fortieth birthday present. In Maroon ways, this is the 'time o' seasoning' for a woman. Forty is a special birthday."

Charlotte, still blinded by his bluntness, nodded. Jon's heart sank and he backed away, and finally ran off in embarrassment. The princess stood there trying to process it all. She packed up the books, parchment, pens and ink and looked after Jon until he became a spec on the grounds in retreat. How sad it all was, she thought—slavery, serfdom, discrimination and their effects on the human spirit. He was right. It was all so wrong.

I felt I was a part of the evil and could do nothing about it. We owned Jon and his mother like we owned our horses and furniture. I never fully understood that it was morally wrong. But did I not understand because I was taught not to care? Because it was acceptable, therefore right? I never had any regard as to our servants' status because we were instructed by word or deed not to interact with below-stairs help for it was not acceptable in polite society. Now I wondered what else did I not know or understand about the world because of my sheltered, royal life confined to Mirow Palace.

☩

Wilhelm turned from the window. He had witnessed Jon earlier hurrying to the stables, and now the princess was sneaking back into the palace in her usual, well conceived pattern of deception. A wicked smirk curled the corners of his mouth upward as he looked at the young servant girl he'd tied to the foot posts of his bed and dressed in Christiana's blue linen sacque dress, pilfered for the occasion. He stole it because Charlotte occasionally borrowed it from Christiana to sneak off with Jon and it still had old grass and dirt stains which could not be cleaned.

Ignoring her pleas Wilhelm bent down over the frightened girl and traced a lone finger across her cheek, snarling, "Stop w-whimpering and do w-what I say or you'll r-regret it."

The girl swallowed back tears, shivering with fear. Wilhelm then reached into his pocket and took out the prized, gold amulet which Charlotte had craved since her father's death. He placed it around the girl's neck, caressing it gently, then untied one of her hands.

"Now p-pull off that dress, Charlotte."

"I am not Charlotte," the girl cried.

Wilhelm slapped her. "D-did I t-tell you to q-question me? P-pull off that d-dress. And don't tear one thread of it."

The girl tried to take the dress off but couldn't with only one hand. Wilhelm became frustrated and unhooked it himself. After it fell to the floor, and the girl was naked save for the amulet, he grabbed her breasts and savagely mauled them, exciting himself in the process.

"Now, tell me you love me, Charlotte."

The servant cried from humiliation. "Please stop," she begged.

"Tell me you love me, Charlotte!"

"I love you, Wilhelm," the girl sobbed barely above a whisper, praying her crazed attacker would let her go.

Wilhelm turned her around and, quickly dropping his pants, grabbed her hips and thrust himself inside her. Ignoring the girl's cries, he enjoyed himself with her until he finally called out Charlotte's name in the ultimate moment of ecstasy. When he was done he took the amulet from the sobbing servant's neck and untied her. "T-take your clothes and get out," he demanded. "And if you t-tell anyone, I will have you b-beaten and sent to the Bavarian m-mines myself."

The defiled girl gathered her own serving clothes and ran out in her stocking feet.

Wilhelm looked after her a moment then picked up the blue dress. After smelling its fabric laced with Charlotte's perfume, he carefully placed it on the bed and put the amulet on the bodice.

"I love you, Charlotte. One d-day I know you'll be m-mine. As soon as I put this amulet around your b-beautiful neck, you'll show me favor."

✠

Upon exchanging clothes with Lady Schwellenberg after sneaking back into the palace, Charlotte, still overwrought from her misunderstanding with Jon, came out of the music room as though she had just finished practicing the harpsichord. She immediately began looking for Adolph. After asking a page as to his whereabouts she was informed that he was in the library. She headed down the hall immediately, and as she reached the door to the library she could hear her brother and mother arguing. Charlotte started to turn away, not wanting to eavesdrop, but the internal struggle between her rational mind and her curious nature raged—and her curious nature won, keeping her in place.

"...I am telling you, it's high time you married. You are the Grand Duke of this duchy—so you keep insisting so vociferously."

"Yes. I am. And I will kindly ask you to give me my respect as such."

But Charlotte's mother remained belligerent. "Can you not find some properly titled young woman to wed who will not only provide a dowry sufficient to advance us, but forward the continuation of the Frederick dynasty?"

"A woman of my choosing would need to be tolerant of...," Adolph's voice trailed off as he searched for the right words.

"...This morally corrupt thing inside you?" the Duchess jousted, seizing on his pause. "The aberrant behavior that precludes you from even bedding a woman?"

"I tire of your limpid accusations regarding my personal life. If you have something to say speak plainly."

"I have," snipped his mother. "Beautiful, capable women from around the duchy have ruthlessly flirted with you, and you never so much as admire their faces let alone their bosoms. Oh, but let a young, virile boy come galloping by and you become a befuddled mess. And it's this preoccupation with boys that forbids your duties to family."

Adolph's silence was likened to an unspoken admission of guilt for Charlotte, and her head dropped. Finally, she heard:

"Mother, I do not wish to be married. Marriage is a burdensome venture."

"Do you not think it burdensome for we women? Laying on our backs while you beasts have your way with us like pigs in a field? Find a wife, dammit! I shall not continue as the cow providing suckling for you grown leeches. My forbearance and privy purse have limits," Elizabeth ranted. "Now I know for a fact Lady Linda Burnell has had her eye on you for some time. Invite her to the king's ball, be charming, and propose. Once you marry her you can do what you will, with *whomever* you will after that."

As their argument escalated Charlotte found she had more questions than answers. Although her beloved brother stood up for her at dinner in August, for as long as Charlotte could remember he and her mother never argued. Adolph always acquiesced to Elizabeth's wishes, whether he agreed with them or not. Now hearing that her brother was as likely as she to be chastised for whom he did or did not marry was revelation enough; but to learn Adolph was also a man who indeed preferred men to women disconcerted her. Charlotte decided this was obviously not the time to broach a subject as volatile as slavery, and she turned to leave.

But there standing at the top of the landing with a burlap bag was Wilhelm, grinning like a Cheshire cat. He quickly descended the stairs and in one swift gesture grabbed Charlotte's arm as she tried to hurry off. "W-where are you off to in such a h-hurry, cousin?" he stammered, dripping false charm. "D-didn't you have a good practice?"

"I did, thank you," answered Charlotte, trying to move off.

But Wilhelm stood in her way, still grinning fiendishly.

"Let me pass, Wilhelm."

"Oh d-don't be so sardonic, cousin," he quipped, "It d-doesn't become you." He opened the burlap bag and showed her the soiled blue linen dress inside. "It wouldn't do to upset my fragile nerves—especially when I can go t-to my aunt while you're 'practicing' out in the woods with your blackamoor, give her this dress, and tell her to open the d-door of the music room."

Charlotte, shocked by Wilhelm's admission of spying on her, became more fearful for Jon than for herself. Her insane cousin might do anything and she was genuinely nervous. Concealing it, she turned in the opposite direction to run, but Wilhelm grabbed her hair just as Sister Lena came down the hall with linen. She saw Charlotte flee from her cousin to her room, then her eyes traveled back to Wilhelm.

"Don't you have s-something to do?" Wilhelm snapped at Lena.

The Jamaican nodded and hurried on, her eyes cast downward. Then she turned back to make sure Wilhelm was gone and rushed to Charlotte's chamber door where she knocked.

"Yes," Lena heard Charlotte inquire from within.

"It's Sister Lena, chile. I wanna know if you alright."

Moments later, Charlotte came to the door and looked at the Jamaican who took Charlotte's face into her hands. "Did he hurt you?"

"He frightens me."

"I know, chile. But Sister gon' make sure to protect you. I'll keep an eye out."

Charlotte impulsively hugged Sister Lena, feeling a sense of maternal safety washing over her. "What would I do without you?"

Seven

"A king must marry. Matrimony must sooner or later come to pass..."

...King George III

The Prince of Wales, once again anxious to see Lady Sarah, galloped down Gunnersbury Lane a little past nine in the morning. Just as he rode across Kew Bridge, he could see his valet de chambre trotting up to him.

"Your Highness, come quickly. There has been a terrible accident at Kennsington," said the man out of breath. "It's the king!"

Prince George instantly rode back to Kew Palace. No sooner had he entered than a messenger arrived with a note. He read it, then sat grief struck for a long moment. Finally he forced himself to dispatch two notes—one to John Stuart, the Earl of Bute, and the other to Lady Sarah Lennox telling them what had transpired. He also warned the servants at Kew Palace to keep quiet about whatever they heard if they valued their employment.

A wave of tears overtook him. His beloved grandfather, King George II, was dead, and now, at age 22, the Prince of Wales, George William Frederick Hanover, was now King George III of Great Britain and Ireland. He knew he had been primed for this moment all his life, but the new sovereign sat there stunned by the level of responsibility now thrust upon him.

An hour later, George was escorted to Kensington Palace, where his grandfather's body had yet to be removed from his bedchambers. The

palace was in mourning. Black cloth was draped on all mirrors and portraits of the deceased sovereign. People were overcome with grief and
Augusta and the Earl of Bute immediately went to George, where he
learned what had happened. King George II had suffered a massive heart
seizure, fallen from his chamber pot, struck his head on the vanity and
died *in situ*. Plans were now being made for the official preparation of the
body and a state funeral. Bute told George that the Privy Council had to
be called into an emergency session for the official "Passing of the
torch" declaring young George as king.

Forcing calm and feigning the appearance of control, George insisted upon going upstairs to see the body. He came through the door
followed by Bute and his mother and was stunned by the number of
people surrounding his grandfather's body. Present were family members, palace staff, and valued members of Parliament. Crying at his bedside holding the deceased king's hand was his 56-year-old mistress,
Amalie Sophie Marianne von Walmoden, known as Lady Yarmouth.

As George worked his way to the bed everyone bowed, calling him
"Your Majesty." It was disconcerting to absorb the events taking place
and also find time to grieve the loss of his favored grandfather. Yet,
through his tears, he hugged his grandfather's lover.

"I am so sorry for your loss, Lady Yarmouth."

"And yours, Your Majesty," responded the grieving woman. Then,
not sure what to expect, Lady Yarmouth eased away allowing George to
kneel at the bedside. He sadly touched the dead king's cold face, noting
how peaceful the old man looked at life's inevitable end.

Suddenly George felt his emotions breaking again, and leaned in
close to the dead king. "Grandfather, what have you done? I am too
young and inexperienced to be king," he whispered.

Augusta quickly took her son's hand and knelt beside him. She, too,
lowered her voice to a whisper. "You have been primed for this moment
ever since your father died. You are not unprepared for the responsibility
now thrust upon you. George II is dead. *You* are king. Be a king!"

Standing well out of earshot but present out of respect was Sir William Pitt the elder, an MP, who furtively whispered to Lord Newcastle
the Prime Minister.

"Woe to us now. We'll have that damnable Bute to contend with
until the boy reaches political maturity."

"Not if I can help it," Newcastle countered with confidence.

Finally, George stood, drew in a deep breath, and collected himself. He *was* king and he had to act like it. Suddenly everyone in the room heralded him with a chorus of, "Long live the king!"

George, though exhibiting self-assurance, was still internally apprehensive.

Across the Thames at Holland House, Lady Sarah Lennox had received George's note. Her brother-in-law Sir Henry Fox was shamelessly gleeful to the point of indiscretion.

"Sarah, he is dead. Can you not imagine? His Majesty is dead and *your* beloved George is king. You—*you*, my angel, will become Queen of England, and nothing would please me more than to supplant his Lordship Bute from the king's ear as his advisor! Oh heavenly day!"

"Careful, Sir Henry, your ambition is showing." Sarah cautioned.

"And yours is not, my dear?" asked her brother-in-law tactlessly. "You've been giddy ever since you received that note from the king inviting you to be at court on Friday."

Lady Sarah had to agree. She knew George's intentions because she knew his heart. It only made sense. That very Friday night Lady Sarah Marie Margaret Lennox would be proposed to by the newly ensconced King of England and she would become queen. How fabulously appropriate. After all, she and George had been conducting their affair in secret. Now, the prospect of marriage would legitimatize their relationship and engender vindication for Sir Henry. He would have the appointment he coveted, and Lady Sarah would have her dream. King George III and Queen Sarah. She loved the sound of it and what it represented—a marriage of political parties in which her brother-in-law would rule Parliament.

This called for a new dress for the occasion and Sarah put her seamstresses to work around the clock. She had to look stunning, and for the next twelve hours, she soaked herself in warm milk with bay leaves and honey, and scrubbed her face with oats followed by a mud mask. She had to be glowing. George needed to see just what a perfect queen she would make and how vital she could be at his side.

✝

Four days later, as the body of King George II was being prepared to lie in state and Lady Sarah plotted her presumed new role as queen, Lord Bute and George's mother Augusta sought audience with the young king. He agreed to see them while being dressed for his first meeting with the Privy Council.

As the two entered the king's chambers George's thoughts were on the speech he had to give as part of the formal transition of power. He had a horrible headache.

"Your Majesty," began Bute with a respectful bow, "this is a delicate subject that must be addressed as soon as possible. As you are king, we must discuss the issue of you taking a wife, as it is a requirement."

"The requirement will be satisfied by Friday, as I intend to propose to Lady Sarah Lennox. She is the only woman I think about as such."

Augusta gasped. Her fan went fluttering to her face in horror as she glared at Bute demanding he act.

"Your Majesty, you cannot marry Lady Lennox," Bute said frankly.

"I do not see why not. She's a royal. She's Charles II's granddaughter."

"Lady Sarah's bloodline is corrupted," Augusta retorted quickly, unable to keep silent. "Yes, her father was the son of Charles II...but with his mistress. Not his wife, my dear."

"More importantly, your queen cannot come from the House of Fox," Bute insisted. "Sir Henry is a Whig and a member of the Opposition. A royal alliance will secure his most coveted prize—an Earldom from you. He will then be free to exert influence over you toward his own agenda."

"You would do much better to choose a bride from Saxe Gotha," Augusta insisted.

"Yes, a German," Bute interrupted. "We need the continued association."

George became furious. "I will not be dictated to in this manner. I am King!"

"A king with enormous responsibility to his country and his government," Bute insisted.

"And what of a king's responsibilities to his own heart?"

Augusta folded her arms in exasperation; she wanted to strangle him. "George, your romantic life cannot be left to Cupid. You must let Bute and I guide you in your choice of queen. Romps with inappropriate women, like chambermaids or that Lennox woman, are a waste. You're King of England, dammit. It's time you find a wife who will appropriately represent the realm."

George dismissed his dressers, then turned to his mother once they'd gone. "I will not marry a woman I do not love…and I love Sarah."

Augusta scoffed, "Love is not a necessary qualification for your future spouse."

"It is for me!" George snapped, slamming his fist against a table causing a vase to break. "Do I not have any say over my own person? I will not be manipulated in this manner. Not by royal convention or by either of you!"

Bute and Augusta were stunned to silence. Never before had George been this forceful. The king, knowing he had become emotional, moved away to collect himself. With his back to them, in a low, respectful voice he offered reflection. "I never expected to rule without a queen, and my first thought upon ascending the throne was having Sarah as my wife at my side. I've sent for her and arranged the proposal for Friday, praying she will have me."

He turned back to his mother and her lover. "Every man in London wants her, and though I am awkward and clumsy, Sarah is who I want."

Lord Bute understood what was happening, but he had a job to do and turned to the princess dowager. "Your Highness, I wish to speak to His Majesty alone, please."

"But…"

"Augusta!" Bute snapped with an authoritative air of familiarity befitting their personal relationship. "I need to speak to George alone."

Princess Augusta acquiesced, bowing brusquely and emitting an audible sigh of annoyance. She gave George a cursory glance and left quickly as a deafening silence overtook the room. The young king, distraught and put-upon, went to the window and looked out.

However, what needed to be said had to be, and Bute used his longstanding friendship with George to convey his feelings. "George, in the nine years since your father died, I have faithfully advised you."

"Yes. And as my Master of the Robes, I've come to rely on and trust your advice."

"Then trust me now. As king, you will be faced with any number of difficult choices which are better for England than they may be for you personally. You will learn to surrender who you are to who you must be. A king must steel himself to make sacrifices for his country. I've taught you that."

Bute turned the young king around to face him and continued with a softened voice, "Your father, grandfather and his father before that, all did the same thing when faced with this situation—they accepted the inevitable and kept the 'loves of their lives' as mistresses. You're a man, George. Women are there for us to promulgate the royal blood line and ease the tensions of our daily responsibilities. If you can find that *and* royal breeding all in one woman, so be it. If not, do what is expected— for England."

"Is that what *you're* doing—with my mother? 'Promulgating the royal blood line and easing the tension of *your* daily responsibility'?"

"That's not fair, George. I love your mother," Bute retorted with irritation.

"Like you *love* your wife, Sir?" snipped George.

Bute stood in silent admonishment. George, feeling victorious in his reproach, continued. "My point exactly."

However, the painful reality of the king's situation was slowly sinking in. George stared out the window again. "I appear born for the happiness and misery of a great nation," he murmured to no one in particular, "and consequently, I am damned to act contrary to my passion."

He finally looked at his compatriot and advisor accepting the inevitable. "All right, my friend, how do I do what is expected?"

Knowing his young charge was suffering through the pangs of a novice reign, Bute was tender. "It is expected for you to marry someone from Germany. Someone Protestant. To make it easier I have a list for your consideration."

George sighed, signifying his acquiescence. Bute knew this was hard for George. "So far there are eleven appropriate choices. The Royal registry shows that the princesses from Saxe-Hildburghausen, Brandenburg-

Schwedt, Brunswick-Wolfenbuttel, Hesse-Darmstadt, Saxe-Gotha, Mecklenburg-Strelitz, and Anhalt-Dessau are the most suitable."

George acknowledged, looking back out the window. He watched his mother leave the palace still in a huff. "Please send for Baron Von Munchhausen," he said to his advisor. "Tell him I am entrusting him with a mission of the strictest secrecy. I trust between the two of you an appropriate choice will be located." George sighed, buttoning up his new redingote jacket. "I only ask that the Princess of Saxe-Gotha be stricken from the list. She is my mother's niece, and I can promise you there would be no children of that union as I won't go anywhere near her."

Bute chuckled as George's expression became cool and exacting.

"And Bute, hereafter, please do not refer to my grandfather or his choices ever again. He is dead. I am king. His choices are history. Mine will change the future."

"Forgive me, Majesty. It shall not happen again."

"And I shall only mention this once. I know you have deep affection for my mother, but do not side with her again against the wishes of your king. Do you understand?"

"As you wish, Your Majesty." Bute then backed out of the room.

The moment Lord Bute was gone George pulled out his cameo of Lady Sarah and looked at it a long while before placing it back in his pocket. His head fell into his hands. *Only for England*, he thought. *Only for England.*

Eight

Charlotte kept her fan fluttering against the heat. The Fredericks' fourteen-member family and entourage were squeezed into four coaches as they were at last on their way to Potsdam. Duchess Elizabeth, Christiana, Aunt Albertina and Charlotte were in the women's carriage. The trip to Sanssouci Palace would take four days with stops at Inns on the way.

Three days into the journey the cortege stopped at Dartmouth Hall in Berlin to pick up Lady Linda Burnell, the fiery daughter of the Duke of Dartmouth. Lady Linda, an intelligent conversationalist, commanded all eyes, and Charlotte and Christiana felt like leftover mutton in her presence. Yet Duchess Elizabeth fawned over her praying Adolph would propose to the beauty so she could start planning an official engagement party and wedding. Charlotte, knowing Adolph's heart after overhearing his argument with their mother, expected nothing.

As they traveled on a shockingly hot day for October, Charlotte thought about Jon who was steering their carriage. It had been two weeks since that day he insulted yet challenged her, and Jon could not bring himself to return to their spot for dance lessons or tutoring. When she saw him in the halls or on the grounds he would avoid her. She so wanted to tell him it was all right—that she had been thinking about what he'd said and was searching for a way to apply it.

But for the moment anything untoward Charlotte felt had to be set aside. She was on her way to King Frederick's ball, at which she would see the object of her desire, Christian Bach. Nothing else mattered. Jon had done his job teaching her the Betty Blue. The rest was up to her.

Princess Charlotte was dressed and coiffed to perfection. Her gown fit perfectly, and the yards and yards of pink chiffon and taffeta covered with hundreds of tiny pearls made her feel beautiful. It flowed with every step she took, and her German-made shoes, dyed to match her gown, fit impeccably. She was ready to dance with the lightness of a cobweb.

Sir Albert had straightened Charlotte's unruly hair as smooth as possible, and her only concern was the heat. In hot summer months or whenever she swam, her tightly coiled tresses became a tangled mass taking hours to unravel. But Sir Albert created an ingenious pomade of bees wax, shea butter and olive oil obtained from Sister Lena who, along with Mirow's servants of African descent, used it on their own unruly hair. He applied it heavily on Charlotte so her natural hair would not indiscriminately peek out from beneath her fashionably formal wig.

In the window of her coach Charlotte saw her own reflection. She was heavily painted by Swelly, who had been instructed by Duchess Elizabeth to thickly apply the chalk milk powder make-up to Charlotte's face, shoulders, arms and hands to make her "a desirable aristocratic white." It was on occasions such as this—when she had to be prepared so specifically for acceptance within her own society, that Charlotte missed her father most. Duke Charles had complimented her, saying that her "beautiful, sun-kissed" color was by divine decree, and she should be proud of it. Yet today, when her mother saw Charlotte after being coiffed and dressed, she exclaimed, "Charlotte looks almost presentable. And what a feat, as she will never be known for her feminine wiles no matter what you do." The Duchess then found a necklace and told Swelly, "Put this on her. It pulls the eye to her bosoms where, thankfully, she was blessed."

Hurt by the comment, Charlotte kept her emotions meticulously veiled. Nothing was going to ruin the ball for her—not even her mother's ravings. She had but one chance to be Cinderella, and she would not have it spoiled.

By four o'clock on 27 October, the Frederick family coaches finally made their way down the cobbled streets of Potsdam. As the late afternoon sun descended behind the western clouds, disquiet enveloped Charlotte. Around them were disgruntled commoners whose rage was evident, and the princess could not believe what she was witnessing. Faces hid behind blackened windows of buildings along the way, cursing their procession of gilded coaches passing by. Each carriage seemed to provoke the ire of the people standing in alleys or on the streets. Some hurled stones.

Prussian citizens were upset by the war King Frederick was waging against Austria, France and Russia. Dissidents blocked the streets, screaming as one angry spokesman incited the crowd.

"Are we to allow King Frederick to bankrupt the very souls of the people?"

"No!" The crowd shouted back.

"We have no food, no work and no say in government! Junkers crush us with high taxes earmarked entirely for the military to support the king's war. The Bourgeoisie are puppets for government officials," the man cried out. "Do we continue to let our children beg in the streets and die of starvation while our debauched king wages war in the name of expansion? I say no!"

Again, the crowd screamed in agreement. Charlotte and Christiana grabbed hands as Charlotte looked around. She witnessed men begging and women with crying, starving babies at their breasts as her carriage rode by. The stench of urine was as putrid as her mother's perfume intoxicated, and the princess turned away.

"Mother, shouldn't we do something? They're starving."

Duchess Elizabeth saw that her daughter was deeply affected by the dismal sights and sounds and drew the curtains to prevent Charlotte's viewing of it. "Such calamities of society must not be allowed to fester within you, daughter," she warned. "You have a job to do—seducing the Duke of Anhalt-Cothen into marriage. As the only eligible female able to help pull us from the specter of our *own* poverty, I do not want your mind distracted by the genuine poverty residing outside that window."

Charlotte said nothing, keeping her focus forward as her mother and Aunt Albertina continued their conversation. Christiana saw that her sister was melancholy and placed her hand over Charlotte's in a show of solidarity, which Charlotte appreciated. Lady Linda and the princess exchanged a quick look, but Linda turned away. Though she was of the same mind as Charlotte, she would do nothing to provoke censure from the Duchess or disturb the status quo, for she, too, was on a mission—marriage to Grand Duke Adolph.

Half an hour later, they could just make out the glittering Palace of Sanssouci through a tiny opening in the curtains. It was the smallest but most impressive of all King Frederick's residences, and Charlotte's heart began racing until it was in synch with the galloping horses. Her mother drew back the curtains all the way and the princess stuck her head from the window. Though there were more angry people gathered at the palace gates, Jon carefully guided their carriage through the melee and, finally, they entered the most ornate of formal gardens.

Sanssouci was magnificent. The palace boasted a breathtaking center-piece garden designed to be viewed by his majesty and his courtiers from their apartments within the court. There were grand open spaces where the gentry could enjoy promenading and socializing in a vista without obstruc-tions. One vast courtyard showcased marble statues of Greek gods inter-spersed with fountains. Forty-six thousand Chinese lanterns were lit around the grounds so that jugglers and acrobatics could perform, and there was even a carousel.

The Fredericks' carriages came to a halt. Footmen instantly appeared to open the doors. Duchess Elizabeth stepped out, offering her hand for assistance, and was led through the walkway up the marble stairs to the reception line. Aunt Albertina and Christiana were assisted next.

As Charlotte was helped from the coach, Jon climbed down and re-spectfully approached her. He bowed then looked at her—his copper eyes apologetic and tender.

"Your Highness, may I please speak with you?"

Charlotte nodded and Jon took a moment to gather his thoughts. "I don't know how or where to begin apologizing for my conduct two weeks ago…," he began in his much improved Jamaican lilted German, "…and before you go inside I…"

"Jon, it is done," Charlotte interrupted, knowing how difficult this was for him and anxious to enter the palace. "You had every right to speak your mind. I was serious when I told you that when we are together, you are to be truthful and uninhibited."

"Thank you, Your Highness. Your friendship means so much to me and I…I…am so sorry. I wish you well tonight. Remember, let your part-ner lead and feel the rhythm of the music as you follow."

"I'll remember, Jon." Charlotte reassured.

Jon's innocent smile emerged. Charlotte reciprocated in kind, then proceeded with a footman to the top of the stairs to join the others who were already in the formal receiving line. For her, Jon's apology as much appeased her own guilt as his, and she, too, was grateful they could move forward with their friendship. Now feeling a sense of relief, Charlotte could enjoy King Frederick's party, as best she could with the commotion attending the king's gates. More importantly, she could concentrate on the real reason she was there...

...Christian Bach.

Nine

Charlotte drew in a deep breath, allowing herself a moment to look around and feel everything. She had anxiously waited for this special evening for three months. The plump palace crier—in his too-tight formal attire and powdered wig—announced the royal family, stamping the polished marble floor with his brass staff: "Presenting Grand Duke Adolphus Louis Frederick, Duchess Elizabeth Albertina Frederick, Dukes Charles, Ernest and George Frederick, Princesses Albertina, Charlotte and Christiana Frederick; and Sir Wilhelm Albertina of Mecklenburg-Strelitz."

When announced the princess felt like an actor on stage with the curtain raised on her new life. The moment they entered the palace and came through the grand doors, heads turned. Then, as the Frederick's promenaded down the grand staircase, Charlotte held her breath at the sight of it.

King Frederick's ball was pure spectacle. The cream of Prussian and European aristocracy was in attendance, and the palace was awash with powdered wigs, satin waistcoats, and merriment. The palace was remarkable. The interior of the main salon boasted high ceilings with a skylight, arched windows showcasing the Chinese lanterns outside, and gold gilded wallpaper. Floors were polished marble and vases filled with fresh calla lilies were positioned on every buffet table, all of which offered pheasant stuffed truffles, goose pate, canapés, and choices of sugared cakes. Wine, champagne and cherry nectar punch flowed served by attendants in black velvet service jackets who came through every two or three minutes carrying a variety of morsels.

When they reached the bottom of the stairs and entered the grand ballroom, seated in the middle of a semi-circle was the elegantly dressed host of the event—King Frederick of Prussia. At 48, the king appeared ancient and worn from his many battle campaigns of the last three months. His deep-set eyes were tired and puffy, and his once trim figure bulged at the belly. As his guests were announced the king was somewhat indifferent—greeting each with a judge-like graveness not generally displayed to those he cared about.

Charlotte observed another curious oddity. An attractive, effeminate man was seated to King Frederick's right—a man who blatantly caressed Frederick's hand. Though there was noticeable gossiping among his guests, the king received his visitors, daring anyone to refer to the man.

Duchess Elizabeth grandly swept up to His Majesty with her train in tow and bowed. "Your Majesty, the Frederick family is pleased to bid thee a hearty thank-you for our invitation to this most fabulous event. We also extend our congratulations on your victory at Tortuga."

The king smiled and kissed her hand, tilting his head to the side to peruse her. "My dear cousin Elizabeth, you look much recovered. I was concerned when I heard about your recent illness. It is good to have you back at court."

The Duchess curtsied, "Thank you, Your Majesty." Raising her fan to her mouth to suppress the cough threatening to expose her continuing illness, she quickly glided away, insisting Christiana and Charlotte follow. As they approached one of seven buffet tables, the sisters were daunted by the variety of magnificent cuisine, and chatted in German about where to begin.

Not far from them was a young African girl about Charlotte's age, perhaps older, with large, almond-shaped eyes and ebony skin who struck her as interesting. Her head was wrapped in a brightly colored gele, and her thickly roped hair hung just past her shoulders. She was obviously in service to one of the guests, but she caught Charlotte's eye and smiled as did Charlotte in return. Just then the princess overheard a woman and a man chatting behind them.

"Who is the young gentleman seated to the right of the king?" the woman asked the man. "The one blatantly holding his hand."

"I have no idea," the man responded, "but he looks to be quite the fancyman."

Christiana chuckled. "The answer is so obvious." She lowered her voice to a sotto voce whisper to Charlotte. "He is the king's latest dandy. Everyone knows King Frederick is a sodomite."

Charlotte's hand flew to her mouth, and her sister chuckled again. "Charlotte, don't be so naive. I've explained such behavior to you before. It's simply the way of the world. Some people are more comfortable in the 'private company' of their own gender. They can't help themselves."

"But our cousin? The king?"

"Why should it be different for him? Is it different for Adolph?"

Charlotte paused in realization. "Then it's true about our brother? Because he doesn't act like it."

"And do you love him any less for it? Remember, not all men *like that* favor plumes."

Suddenly, they heard a loud stamp of the staff followed by the resounding voice of King Frederick's Lord Chamberlain. "May I have your attention, please? His Majesty King Frederick wishes to address his guests."

The room grew quiet as His Majesty regally moved to the center of the room, adjusting his black velvet waistcoat and clearing his throat. "Thank you all for attending this evening. It is my hope that each of you has a remarkable time here at Sanssouci. After the campaign last winter I went to Dresden to allow myself to indulge in my more pacific pursuits and interests. At the opera I heard La Pilaja sing, but she was in such bad voice she sounded like a tooth-carpenter."

The guests chuckled as he continued. "The next evening, however, I was thoroughly entertained by the soprano and the musicians you are about to hear, for tonight we are in celebration. Last year we suffered a crushing defeat in the battle at Kunersdorf. This year we are victorious again with our move into Poland, due to our valiant soldiers and my regiments of hussars to whom we owe the honor." His glass went into the air in a toast. "To the German army. May they forever rule the land and sea for the greater good of Prussia!"

"Here, here," cried the crowd as they held up their glasses to the invited members of the army, acknowledging them in appreciation.

Frederick continued, "Now it is my great honor to present for your entertainment one of Italian opera's most magnificent sopranos: Mademoiselle Maria Monticellini. She will be accompanied by five of the finest music masters in the world: Johann Joachim Quantz, Carl Friedrich Abel, Frantisek Benda and Carl Phillip Emmanuel Bach, performing 'Arteserse,' an aria written by Herr Bach's brother, Johann Christian

Bach, from his latest opera—with the composer himself accompanying Miss Monticellini on the clavier."

Charlotte pushed her way to the front of the gathering and watched as Maria Monticellini, a beautiful, 20-year-old opera star, took center stage. Five musicians appeared from the inner salon and took their places behind their instruments: Emmanuel Bach to his harpsichord, Abel to his viola, Quantz to his flute, Benda to his violin…and Christian to his clavier.

The moment Charlotte saw him, it happened again. Everything else at Sanssouci stood still, as though struck by Thor's lightning rod. Their eyes instantly locked and Christian's expression of recognition warmed her body. A flirtation of the most subtle degree transpired between them as he accompanied Mademoiselle Monticellini, and the princess felt her cheeks flush as she imagined her body as the harpsichord upon which he played. Charlotte found she could not let go of his face.

Duchess Elizabeth became concerned. Charlotte's reintroduction to the dashing Bach could thwart all her efforts for a potential relationship with Lord Gregory and ruin her mission to ensure the family's financial success. So once Mademoiselle Monticellini had her audience enthralled with her vocal dexterity, the Duchess slyly looked around using her fan for stealth. When she found her target she grabbed Charlotte's hand and pulled her toward him—Lord Gregory Muldare, Duke of Anhalt-Cothen. Naturally Charlotte was furious, thus tactless in her behavior.

Lord Gregory, overly powdered and painted even for this event, was listening to the aria with his daughter Princess Helena, who at age 27 was an unattractive, paunchy spinster; and Lieutenant Colonel Charles Cornwallis, a handsome young member of the king's army. The moment Lord Gregory saw Charlotte and the Duchess, he held out his arms dramatically to embrace her.

"Ah, Your Grace, I was hoping to see you and your family this evening." His voice dropped subtly, "You know, to finalize our little agreement, hmmm?"

"As were we, Lord Gregory," the Duchess replied turning to his daughter. "Are you and your father enjoying yourselves, Princess Helena?"

"Very much so, Your Grace," answered the frumpy princess.

"Indeed she is," echoed Lord Gregory. "She was hoping to spend some time with your nephew Wilhelm. She always asks after him."

Charlotte and Princess Helena exchanged a look that, although lasting a second, conveyed that she harbored as much discomfort at being manipulated into a relationship as did Charlotte. Lord Gregory introduced them to Cornwallis, who, after experiencing the same uneasy pause they all did, excused himself. Lord Gregory looked at Charlotte. There had been enough trivial repartee and he needed to forward his agenda. "So, how is our dear Charlotte this evening, hmmm?" he said, taking the girl's hand to kiss it. "I hope we can spend a bit of time together. Perhaps a dance, hmmm?"

Offended by the arrogance of this gesture, Charlotte nonetheless curtsied. "I shall endeavor to set aside some time for you on my dance card later, Lord Gregory."

"Of course, there is nothing like the present, my dear."

"But I am currently listening to the music. Please take no offense. Let us spend some time later perhaps."

The Duke was miffed. He glanced in disappointment to Charlotte's mother then moved off. The princess turned to make her way back to the front of the gathering to resume listening to Christian, but was abruptly whirled around by Duchess Elizabeth who was incensed. "How dare you offend the Duke by not dancing with him? Have you no shame? It was only a dance, Charlotte. Such a small request for you to honor," she hissed in a harsh whisper.

"Mother, I am listening to Herr Bach. Please do not embarrass me by creating a commotion in front of everyone here."

But her mother was livid. She pulled Charlotte away angrily, leading her out of the salon and into the gallery nearby. The princess found herself flush with humiliation as her mother squeezed her forearm so tightly Charlotte thought it would leave a bruise.

"Young lady, I have had about as much of your insolence as I intend to experience. You go out there, you find Lord Gregory, and you tell him you would be most happy to dance with him, talk to him, or hop on one leg should he ask. You are in no position to deny the Duke whatever he requests. And as far as Herr Bach is concerned, it's all quite lovely that you are suddenly besotted by him, but he is nonetheless a commoner. A mere musician. A poor player hired to entertain the masses, not marriage material for a Princess of Mecklenburg. Am I understood?"

"But..."

"...AM I UNDERSTOOD?"

"Yes, mother," Charlotte answered finally.

"Now find Lord Gregory and stay mindful of who you are," the Duchess snapped, then left the gallery in a huff. Charlotte glared after her as she made her exit. Barely an hour had passed and already there was dissention between them. So what if Lord Gregory happened to admire that which Charlotte had prepared to attract the attentions of Christian—a man her mother referred to as a *"mere musician."* Why did she have to jump through hoops for him? Was she just a suckling pig on a spit to be had for a dance? A jester obligated to "hop on one leg"?

Charlotte was so upset she had to fold her arms across her waist to keep herself from falling down. She began to rock back and forth while gazing at King Frederick's art collection, unable to quell the knot in her stomach.

As I absently gazed at King Frederick's artwork I was still upset by my mother's behavior. Very soon after voices interrupted my thoughts and I quickly gathered my composure. When I turned I saw the exquisitely detailed black velvet waistcoat of King Frederick as he entered the room, along with another gentleman. I curtsied to the king respectfully whereupon he asked why I was in there and not enjoying the music. "I...I just wanted a chance to gaze upon some of your magnificent art," I lied. "Well, upon that point is reason for our venturing in here," the king mused as he turned to his companion. "Permit me to introduce Francois Antoine Gaston, the Duke of Levis-Mirepoix. This is Princess Charlotte Sophia Frederick, my cousin from Mecklenburg-Strelitz. Her late father was a frequent guest here. Don't you remember?"

A look of respect and admiration brightened the Duke's face. "So you are Duke Charles Louis Frederick's daughter Charlotte. It is indeed a pleasure. Your father and I spent many an evening discoursing on religion, fraternity and, on occasion, you." I was surprised. "I am most pleased to meet one of my father's friends." Duke Francois moved in closer to me. I could smell his tobacco tinged breath as he spoke softly. "By any chance did your father leave you with instructions for me? I have wondered now for many years." "No, Your Grace," I responded with confusion. "Should he have?" The Duke smiled and patted my head. "Well, should you ever need me I can always be found in Mirepoix, France where I await your word."

King Frederick then led the Duke over to a painting at which they both marveled. Several moments later they moved on to the next room equally devoted to the king's art while I stood there frowning in bewilderment by the Duke Francois' cryptic words. What did he mean by 'Did your father leave you with instructions for me?', and 'I await your word'? It was all so odd.

Then suddenly, as if God had answered a prayer, I felt a tug at the back of my gown. Upon turning, I found myself gazing into his luminous green eyes, and his beautiful long fingers reached out to kiss my hand, whereupon the breath left my body...

"I didn't mean to startle you," he said. "I saw you down in front when I began the aria, but when I finished you had vanished, so I went searching."

It was Christian Bach.

Though grateful for his insistence to find her, Charlotte forced herself to turn away from her preoccupation with his face for fear of revealing the depth of her desire. Yet there was an attraction building—an undeniable magnetism thick enough to slice through.

"You played magnificently," she said. "And to think you wrote that piece for so impressive a voice as Mme. Monticellini."

"Maria does possess the voice of a goddess. But she was not the inspiration for the aria. That distinction belongs to a lovely princess I was reintroduced to last August in Mecklenburg."

A warm fluttering arose at the back of Charlotte's neck. "Christian, you are such a flirt."

"Only when I have reason to be, Highness."

Silenced by the compliment and the need to hide the rush of pink staining her cheeks, Charlotte turned to a painting before stealing another glance at Christian's appearance. He was dressed in a blue velvet waistcoat with crisp white lace at the sleeves, and his hair was powdered instead of covered by a wig. "How does your music come to you?" I asked."

"I'll show you." Christian took Charlotte's hand, leading her from the gallery into the smaller drawing room. In this room, King Frederick had a pianoforte at which Christian sat. He thought a moment until bits of a melody came to him which he played.

"I am thinking about a princess with red hair, a beautifully crooked smile, and the sunniest of dispositions, " Christian mused as he played. "So I shall call this piece 'Ode to a Princess.'"

When he finished Charlotte was so moved her hands flew to her face and she became teary-eyed. "That was a most wonderful gift. Thank you."

Christian took her face into his hands and their closeness overwhelmed the princess like a drug lulling her into euphoria. She wanted him to kiss her but protocol precluded it. Then they heard: "Do forgive me. I was told you were in one of these rooms, Your Highness."

Turning in surprise they saw Lord Gregory. Charlotte thought she had rid herself of this ancient twerp of a man. Christian stood and bowed respectfully as the Duke continued, "Sorry to interrupt, but Duchess Elizabeth said you wanted to speak with me, hmmm."

Caught off guard, Charlotte nodded. "Yes, Lord Gregory. I...I felt I was perhaps rude earlier...and wanted to...apologize. By the way, do you know Herr Johann Christian Bach?"

"Only by talent," the Duke replied, coolly shaking Christian's hand. He looked back at the princess, waiting for her next move. This was her cue to be decorous. She accommodated.

"Lord Gregory, I was wondering if you wanted to dance...with me?" she lied.

The aging Duke's face lit up. "I would indeed."

Christian was heartbroken that their special moment had to end, but he understood. After all, Lord Gregory was nobility. Thus Charlotte and the Duke left the room while Christian boiled in his social pedigree.

Lord Gregory promenaded Charlotte into the ballroom where everyone danced an English Contredance—including the king. As they bowed to pay reverence to each other before starting, Charlotte observed her brother Adolph and Lady Linda along with Christiana and Emmanuel Bach on the dance floor. Wilhelm was dancing with Lord Gregory's daughter.

Dancing with Lord Gregory went on forever, and Charlotte tired of his conversation. Adding indignity to affront, his breath was so foul it could melt gold from gilded walls. He insisted upon his invectives on the virtues of the obedient woman and the princess wondered if God had condemned her. "Charlotte, I know I am not a first or unremitting choice of companion for you," the Duke started, "But you must know by now that I have the deepest, most enduring affection for you. I also know there are a few years separating our longevity together." commented the Duke as they danced.

"Only a few? I am but 17."

"But surely you know I can ensure the dreams your father had for Mecklenburg grow to fruition. I can also ensure that your family's well-being continues unabated with a marital association."

Now Charlotte was livid. "Lord Gregory, surely you are not suggesting my happiness or that of my family can be purchased by marriage?"

"I am indeed," stated the Duke frankly which quieted and broke Charlotte's spirit. From the corner of her eye, she saw Christian dancing with Maria Monticellini, who was completely enchanted by him. As they passed each other, Charlotte and Christian exchanged a regretful glance.

Christiana, noticing her sister's mood, encouraged Emmanuel to promenade her to Adolph, dancing with Lady Linda Brummell. Christiana whispered to Adolph, who kissed Lady Linda's hand and gave her over to Emmanuel. Adolph then took Christiana's hand and with a twinkle promenaded her over to Charlotte. He bowed gallantly, and cut in. "Lord Gregory, my sister has practiced the Contredance so diligently. Would you mind if I danced with her?"

Lord Gregory was reticent, but finally acquiesced. Christiana sacrificed herself for her sister and curtsied before the aging Duke. They danced away, leaving Charlotte relieved.

"Thank you for the rescue, Adolph. You are my hero."

"Not yet, dear girl. Just watch as royalty trumps a commoner," Adolph mused, then corrected himself, "Not that Christian is common." He winked, then grandly waltzed Charlotte around the Italian inspired columns, past the mirrored wall, over to Christian and Maria Monticellini. He bowed to the beautiful opera singer and held out his hand to cut in.

"Mademoiselle Monticellini, I am Adolphus Louis Frederick, Grand Duke of Mecklenburg. May I have the pleasure?"

The soprano was impressed. After all, Grand Duke Adolph *was* major royalty—practically *king* of Mecklenburg. Maria curtsied, took Adolph's hand, and off they went. Charlotte mouthed "thank you" to her older brother, who mouthed in return, "You owe me."

Charlotte and Christian looked at each other and almost on cue the music stopped and the musicians began the Betty Blue. Couples who knew the country dance took to the floor, which instantly became a kaleidoscope of swirling gowns. Christian held out his arms, and Charlotte moved into them remembering what Jon had instructed. Though her heart hammered against her ribs, being in Christian's arms felt like the most natural thing in the world. She closed her eyes and let go, reveling in the moment as the handsome, dashing Bach danced with her while all the other eligible women who were so much more alluring stood by. "Charlotte, I believe you to be the most beautiful woman here," he whispered, "and me, the luckiest man."

"No. Tis I who is luckiest."

No more words were spoken between them. Christian held Charlotte as close as propriety dictated. She could feel his fingers probing—the urgency of his touch piercing through her, and she never wanted the feeling to end. As we exchanged partners, which the dance required, her heart always skipped when her fingers were once again entwined with Christian's.

Finally, the music came to a conclusion and Charlotte was brought back from the cloud she had danced upon. Carl Abel came over and lightly tapped on Christian's shoulder. After a nod to Charlotte he cautioned, "Christian, we perform 'The Cappriccio' next."

Christian acknowledged and turned back to Charlotte. "I'm afraid duty calls."

Charlotte understood. "Will you come to call again at Mirow soon?"

A look of regret enveloped Christian's face. "I would love to come, but I leave for Milan tomorrow, and I do not know when my benefactor will allow my return."

The princess sighed fading into disappointment which Christian saw. "Until I see you again, please know that tonight will always be special to me," he reassured, then, in a gracious gesture, kissed her hand.

Charlotte curtsied to Christian, who moved to the orchestra area while the princess hurried to a food table.

"You danced beautifully, my girl," said Lady Schwellenberg, who was standing across the table having wine. "Well worth the chance taken with Jon."

"Thank you, Swelly."

"But there is something you should know," the Lady continued. "Your Christian apparently has quite the penchant for opera singers. Sopranos in particular." She pointed to the African girl Charlotte had seen earlier. "Do you see Lady Bethany's girl? She told me so."

"Fetch her," Charlotte insisted.

Lady Schwellenberg nodded, and approached the African girl then pointed to Charlotte. The two approached and the girl curtsied to the princess.

"This is Lady Bethany's maid," said Lady Schwellenberg. "It is she who told me about Herr Bach,"

"What is your name?" Charlotte asked the girl, who was so frightened she visibly shook.

"Anne Josef," she answered with her head bowed, never making eye contact. "I am in service to Lady Bethany of Liverpool, England."

It was obvious that her station in life dictated her actions and Charlotte lifted the girl's head. "Do not be afraid. I just want to know how you know such things about these people?"

"Bitte möchte ich nicht in Mühe kommen," Anne said in German, eyes cast downward.

"You won't be in trouble," Charlotte assured, shocked by Anne's perfect German.

The girl sighed. "Aristocracy tends to ignore its help, milady. We're rendered invisible. So when they talk, I listen—and retain everything. It's how I know about the people here."

"And what do you know of Christian Bach?"

Anne finally looked up at the princess. She knew her answer to Charlotte's question was of genuine significance to her. "As I told your lady, other than the bothersome comparisons to his father, Herr Bach is the most talented and ambitious of the Bach siblings—far more so than his older brother Emmanuel. Then there is Count Litta, Herr Bach's benefactor in Milan, who pays for his lifestyle. The Count keeps Herr

Bach on quite the short leash. Yet somehow," Anne looked down again, her voice dropping to a whisper. "Herr Bach has managed to bed half the sopranos in Europe."

This stung, and Charlotte looked across the room at Christian performing *The Cappriccio* along with Carl Abel and the king. Emmanuel Bach had been right. Christian played the sonata brilliantly leaving no doubt as to his genius, and Charlotte indeed heard the music played *properly*. She could also see the effect he had on his audience—especially Maria Monticellini, who couldn't take her eyes off of him and she wondered if Maria was his lover.

"Your German is impeccable," said Charlotte to Anne, trying to conceal disappointment.

"Thank you," the girl demurred. "I am fluent in a few languages."

Charlotte was impressed. Here was an African girl in service who spoke several languages other than her native tongue and carried herself with the comportment of an aristocrat.

"My name is Charlotte Sophia. I am from Mecklenburg-Strelitz. Where are you from?"

"Originally Ethiopia."

It was then Charlotte saw it—an amulet dangling from Anne's neck into her décolletage and she was stunned she had not seen it sooner. Before she could stop herself Charlotte reached out and lifted it from the Ethiopian's neck so she could hold it in her hands. Other than it being stained brown and on a ribbon to match her dress, Anne's talisman was shockingly similar to Charlotte's father's. The glyphs and symbols were almost exact. *How can this be?* Charlotte thought. It was too coincidental. "This is beautiful. So unique."

"It is an heirloom," Anne affirmed proudly, "handed down from my forefathers."

"What are the markings?" Charlotte asked, lowering her own voice upon seeing her cousin Wilhelm was nearby, eavesdropping.

"Some of the symbols are Coptic—an ancient Egyptian language— similar to Greek."

"Can you speak it?"

"I can only interpret some," Anne offered.

Unbelievable, Charlotte thought. There in front of her was someone who may have been able to decipher her father's amulet, which she had not seen since she was eight, and desperately wished she had now. But suddenly Lady Bethany appeared from God knew where in exasperation. She yanked the girl away and snapped, "You are absolutely worthless, Anne. Why can I not find you when I need you!" she yelled, "Pay attention to your job!"

Anne quickly bent down and lifted the train of her lady's tulle gown, then glanced at Charlotte in embarrassment. Her look said all—it was back to work. The princess watched them a moment and the thought of Anne's amulet made her want the one promised her by her father. Now, a new blanket of disillusion swept over her heart. She looked over at Christian, who was still performing, and realized that the exchange between them and her feelings for him would have to remain in perspective. She had to put Christian out of her mind. Thus, she chose to take solace in the fact that she at least accomplished her goal. She did dance with Christian Bach. They had that glorious moment together, and she would always have Sanssouci.

Soon hushed arguing could be heard not far from her. Charlotte turned and saw her mother in a heated discussion with Lord Gregory— who left the palace with Princess Helena in anger. The Duchess marched over to Charlotte and pulled her and her family from the palace. When they reached the bottom of the stairs outside the main entrance the Duchess could not contain herself.

"If your escapades with Herr Bach have cost this family its security, I shall banish you to a convent so help me God!" she threatened with eyes red-hot in vexation. "You had better pray Lord Gregory calms down from his fury over your behavior."

But Charlotte was so upset by news of Christian's predilection for sopranos that she lashed out as well. "I pray Lord Gregory jumps from a bridge!"

Duchess Elizabeth reared back in agitation and slapped Charlotte so hard she thought her teeth had loosened. The princess held her cheek in mortification. The poor girl had planned for the King's Ball to be the most memorable time she would have in the autumn of her youth. Now it would be—but for the wrong reason.

Ten

Young King George had just delivered his maiden speech at Westminster before an uninspired Parliament and he was just as unimpressed with himself as was his audience. Perhaps he should have rehearsed it more, he thought, recognizing that his public speaking voice and demeanor needed improvement. During the delivery, when he would look up from his prepared text, he saw Prime Minister Newcastle, Lord Pitt, Sir Henry Fox, Sir Horace Walpole, and Sir Charles Bunbury sitting with arms folded in boredom. Sir John Wilkes, a noted member of Parliament, had actually fallen asleep, the result of which was his resounding snore. It had all gone very badly.

Now George was back at St. James, rubbing his temples as Newcastle and Pitt harangued him regarding the address, and the only one there in support was the ubiquitous Lord Bute.

Thomas Pelham-Holes—Duke of Newcastle and the current Prime Minister—took the first shot. "Your Majesty, before the text of your address is published we suggest certain passages be altered. The last sentence should say 'in concert with our allies,' and the phrase, 'bloody war' should be changed to 'an expensive, but just and necessary war.'"

George bristled. "Minister Newcastle, it *has* been a bloody war. A bloody and I dare say protracted war. Your suggestions cause *my* address to appear a justification for what was clearly *your* war policy, Sir."

"Nonetheless, the passages must be changed," said Newcastle. Bute, however, was dubious, and moved from the corner to the center of the group. "Minister Newcastle, why did you not suggest these changes when the speech was read to you earlier today?"

Newcastle narrowed his eyes at Bute. "I would like to know why your Lordship was even present at the meeting or why you deign to interject now? You are *not* a member of Parliament, the Privy Council, nor the Cabinet."

George became incensed. How dare these sons of bitches speak their minds so imprudently with no regard for his new eminence, he thought. Bute was the only one he trusted; the only person who would tell him the truth no matter how it offended his sensibilities. One who comforted him when he questioned his own worth and readiness as a king. Such feats went beyond the abilities of his own mother—whose idea of support was the verbal insistence he "Be a king" at the deathbed of his grandfather. How dare Newcastle affront him by challenging Bute's position.

"Sir, the Earl of Bute is my trusted advisor and you will treat him as such," George snapped at Newcastle.

"This is not a question of personal preference, or comfort, Your Majesty," William Pitt interjected, attempting to cushion the effect of the insult just aimed at the Prime Minister. "It is a matter of policy. There should be no one here or any ideas entertained by persons who are not members of the Privy Council."

A knock was followed by the entrance of Sir William Cavendish, the king's Lord Chamberlain. Cavendish respectfully moved to George and whispered to him. George motioned to Bute, who turned to Pitt and Newcastle.

"My Lords, I will recommend the king allow the changes to his speech for publication purposes. And Mr. Pitt...?" Bute pulled Pitt away from the others for privacy. "I propose we bury what is past and work together for the good of king and country. Please offer the same to Minister Newcastle."

Sir William Pitt, however, was too old to be changed by an upstart sovereign or his philandering Tory advisor. "Your management of this country's affairs will never be for the good of His Majesty, but *you*, sir. Do not presume to fool me—or the Prime Minister."

Pitt and Newcastle left as George motioned to Cavendish. "Send Munchhausen in, lest I explode from those horses arses."

Cavendish nodded and seconds later brought in a 40-ish looking man with a neatly trimmed mustache and dark, studious eyes. "Your Majesty, permit me to present Baron Philip Adolphus Von Munchhausen."

Munchhausen bowed deeply. "Your Majesty. I am at your service."

George liked Munchhausen instantly. There was something about his manner and simplicity of dress that was appealing, and after a few moments of idle chat George came to the point of the Baron's summons. "Lord Munchhausen. I have accepted my obligations. A king must marry sooner or later, and I have been informed that for me...it shall be sooner. I want you to make discreet inquiries about each of the prospective German princesses and to be ready to conduct personal interviews with the candidates by March of next year."

"As you wish. Do you have any criteria for your choice, Majesty?"

The king thought about this a moment. "My bride need not necessarily be pretty—for no one will ever be more lovely than my Sarah—although a good face would be preferable. What is most important is that she have a pleasant disposition, a good understanding, the ability to bear children and she should have no political ambition. I shall have no petticoat ruler in my reign. So see that my bride-to-be has no interest in government. Is that understood?

"Indeed."

"Be ready to sail to Germany next month to meet with as many of the princesses as you can before the harshness of winter forbids," George stopped to rub his temples again. Bute became concerned. This was the fourth time in as many days that George was overcome by a headache. "Once you conclude three or four interviews, send your reports directly to Bute until all candidates are accounted for," George finally continued. "Do not discuss them with anyone. Not an MP, the Council or the Cabinet."

"You have my solemn oath," Munchhausen promised.

"Good. My privy secretary will see to your financial needs, and Colonel Von Schulenburg, my emissary in Germany, will weed through a preliminary list for you. Find me a decent queen."

Munchhausen bowed to George, then to Bute, and left. But Bute became concerned with George's health. "Your headaches are appearing more frequently, Your Majesty."

"Much is on my mind, old friend. But in light of what happened earlier I have made a decision. I'm appointing you to the Privy Council."

Bute was surprised. This was not something he expected, nor particularly wanted. He had never had much ambition beyond serving at the pleasure of the prince-turned-king, and wasn't sure a responsibility such as a cabinet post was in keeping with his personality.

"Majesty, I am honored by your faith in me, but you must know how very much I am disliked in Parliament. I am Scottish, I am a Tory, I have your ear and I care for your mother—which is obviously not the best kept secret in London. Between Newcastle, Pitt, Wilkes and Fox, such a post will create an unholy alliance in the Lords. I don't think you're aware how much so."

But George merely smiled through his throbbing head. "Oh, but I am. Now will you accept? Shake things up with that motley group of Whig rabble-rousers?"

Bute was tactful. "I shall you my answer at the next salon."

George smiled through his headache and walked his friend to the door. "Yes. Discuss it with your wife… and my mother. Between those two women, Bute, I have no doubt you'll want an escape to the council."

Lord Bute grinned, bowed and left. George resumed massaging his temples, and for just a moment he thought perhaps something might be more seriously wrong with him.

Eleven

This was it. This was the night. Lady Sarah Lennox, dressed in the finest gown she could have designed, emerged from an elegant burgundy carriage along with Sir Henry Fox, his wife Caroline and his sister Susan Fox-Strangeways, and made her way into St. James palace.

Lady Sarah was excited because this was the first salon given at St. James since George II died and King George III succeeded him to the throne. She knew this would be the night young George would ask her *the* question, and her plan was to be at the ready. Over and over she rehearsed it in her mind. He would ask the question, she would be coy and wonder aloud why it took him so long. She would promise to give him her reply in a few days, gently kiss him, then take his hand and place it on her breast, allowing a sampling of what he'd receive nightly with her as queen, then demurely whisper of her deep, abiding love—and leave. Yes, she had it all planned perfectly—down to her choice of perfume.

Inside St. James, aristocrats, MPs and noblemen, along with their wives and consorts, were enjoying themselves. As the Fox family was announced, Sarah looked around for the king and found him playing cards. George instantly excused himself, and as he made his approach to her, Sir Henry pulled the rest of his family to a gaming table, winking at Sarah as they went.

"Lady Sarah, thank you for coming," George smiled, knowing all eyes were on him.

"Thank you for the invitation, Your Majesty. I would not have missed it."

George motioned to a butler who brought two glasses of port. After a few sips he leaned in close to his beloved. "Why don't we go to the library? It's quieter there and it's important I speak with you."

Lady Sarah nodded in acceptance. This was the moment she was waiting for. She glanced at Sir Henry in triumph as George took her hand and they snuck away up the stairs.

Across the room Lord Bute, standing with his wife Baroness Mary Stuart, witnessed the entire exchange. His concern intensified. He had just informed the king he would accept a position as member of the Privy Council. Now he had witnessed George sneaking into the library with the one person from whom he had warned the king to disengage. This obsession with Lady Sarah had to end so George could travel the road upon which his destiny resided. Yet Bute also knew no one could govern the dictates of one's heart. More than anyone he knew what it felt like to have a wife yet love another, and all he could do was pray the king didn't overrule the politics of his reign with the currency of his passion.

Once in the library, George helped Sarah remove her coat. She looked like an angel and smelled of all things breathtaking. She gazed around the impressive library at the shelves of books, paintings and mementos.

"I have never been in this room—or this part of the palace," she exclaimed in wonder.

"This library contains some of the most beautiful works of art and literature in the world," said George, "but none compare to you." George kissed her—and despite Lady Sarah's meticulous plan she kissed him back. Soon, his hands became as inquisitive as hers, and as fate would have it they lost themselves in the throes of passion in front of the fireplace.

Meanwhile, six different card games were going on in the drawing room. Sir Henry Fox, Sir John Wilkes, Sir Horace Walpole and Sir Charles Bunbury were playing a fierce game of Ruff and Honors, while Bute, Lord Mansfield, Lord Diehl and Sir Robert Mackpeace found enjoyment in a game of Toure.

Dowager Princess Augusta, who had been chatting with a party of Ladies, looked around, excused herself, and found Bute, who slyly felt her derriere as she rounded a table. Checking first to see where his wife

Baroness Mary was, Augusta leaned into him and mused, "You're incorrigible, John. Now where is George? I have not seen him in awhile."

Bute would not answer. He knew exactly where the king had retreated. He had seen him. But revealing it to Augusta would only elicit the response he had all too often encountered when George had hankerings for Sarah—and his hankerings were, of late, more and more intense. For all he knew George was in the library having his way with Sarah with no regard for his guests, his surroundings or his obligations elsewhere.

If only Bute knew how correct he was in his assessment, for inside the library George and Lady Sarah were holding each other, basking in afterglow. Lady Sarah was disheveled, yet incandescent. Finally she sat up on the chaise valiantly trying to arrange herself in a more presentable fashion. As he stood watching her, George's eyes began to tear up. Sarah deserved the truth, he thought. She deserved a man who could give her the love and position she warranted, and he knew he could not honor such a pledge. It was time to tell her.

"Sarah, I have never loved anyone as much as I love you."

"And I, you, my love."

"You are the only one I wish to marry. You must believe that."

Sarah grinned with excitement. He has finally asked. Her plan worked. Now was the time to be demure and coquettish.

"But I am pledged to marry a German Protestant," George continued.

Had she heard correctly? Was she mistaken? *German Protestant? Pledged to marry?* Her world crumbled in a matter of seconds. Had she just given herself to a man who declared himself pledged to another? Was he mad? Was she? These thoughts assaulted her at the speed of light and she did not notice her fingers unconsciously balling up. Before she knew it, she lurched back and without an ability to control herself swung with the force of Goliath making contact with George's face knocking him off of his feet.

"You son-of-a-bitch!" she screamed coming unglued as she gathered her clothing, "You knew this when you brought me in here. You purposely seduced me into thinking you'd propose, you horrible, despicable blackguard!"

Princess Augusta and the Earl of Bute, still in the Grand Hall, looked up moments later to see Lady Sarah fly out of the library incensed, in tears, and adjusting her clothing. Rushing down the stairs she ran out of the palace while haphazardly buttoning her coat. George emerged from the library calling after her to no avail. Everyone now knew the king had delivered the bad news, and when he returned to the Grand Hall, the room was silent.

Bute, seeing the king's discomfort, quickly called out to the musicians. "Music! Where is the music?"

The musicians obliged and palace merriment began again. George sat down to a card game knowing he had lost Sarah forever and there was no turning back. As far as he was concerned, his life was over.

And if he could just place his hands on some arsenic, it would be.

Twelve

December, 1760

"Mother, I have decided to marry Lord Gregory. We have set our wedding date for next July in Neustrelitz, but would like to have an engagement party here at Mirow in April."

With those words Princess Charlotte Sophia made Duchess Elizabeth the happiest mother on earth. She acquiesced to that which her mother required of her when they argued at Sanssouci, and the announcement came on the evening of 28 November. Plans for the engagement party immediately went into effect, and the Duchess, in anticipation of the money to come as a result of her daughter's marriage, began spending precious family funds on it.

But as the promise of fall gracefully morphed into the gray-ochre of winter, Charlotte felt her life was over. As she sat in her room looking out at the snow covering the palace grounds, she thought about the events which led her here.

Lord Gregory had come to Mirow in early November at the suppliant behest of the dowager Duchess. He brought gifts, a bottle of fine brandy and, more importantly, two notes totaling 5,000 talers for the Duchess to use any way she chose as long as Charlotte agreed to an engagement. A half-hour later, after Duchess Elizabeth cleared the family from the parlor to allow Charlotte and the Duke privacy, Lord Gregory was on his knee, diamond ring raised in expectation, asking for Charlotte's hand in marriage. The princess had to think before answering. This was it, the moment, and she told the Duke she would think about it and give him an answer in a fortnight.

As every discussion of marriage to the Duke resulted in discord between Charlotte and her mother, Elizabeth assigned Adolph the task of
influencing Charlotte's decision. He knocked on her door one afternoon
knowing she was melancholy over Christian's departure, her mother's
public censure at Sanssouci, and the Duke's proposal. Charlotte was
reading a book as she sat in her pillowed window seat framed by the
freshly cleaned gold tasseled burgundy velvet drapes. A warm expression
washed over her as Adolph entered. She knew why he was there. As
usual, she had eavesdropped on another in a long line of arguments he'd
had with the Duchess over Charlotte's need to marry Lord Gregory.

"Sister, you must accept the Duke's proposal."

"You know I do not love him, and I will not give myself to a man I
do not love."

"Love is not an option in which a woman of royalty but no means
can afford to engage."

"But he's disagreeable and old. What sane young woman would want
him?"

"A woman with a large title and a small dowry." Adolph reminded,
then took his sister's hand. "My darling, I hate to say this, but Christian is
not an option. Marry the Duke. Who knows, perhaps he'll die within a
year and you'll be the widow Muldare, Duchess of Anhalt with no problems or cares. Or, while you are married to the old prune, you can always
take a lover."

Charlotte absently looked back out of the window and thought. It
was true. She could take a lover. After all why was it acceptable for men
to have mistresses, yet women had to be chaste and pure?

"Besides, you will not be the only member of this family not to be
with the one you love. I suffer the same condition," Adolph admitted.

This caused Charlotte to stare into her brother's eyes and see his
pain for the first time. She touched his face. "My God, what you must go
through."

"No one understands," Adolph said in a small voice filled with frustration, "I am Grand Duke, but have no power as long as our domineer-
ing mother lives. I am a man who struggles with feelings for those of my
same gender, yet I do not act on it. I am forced into decisions which
make others uncomfortable to ease the financial burden of my family.
But I do not do my part to ease that burden…"

"…Then I will," offered Charlotte kissing her beloved brother's forehead having made a decision. "I will shoulder some of that burden. I will marry Lord Gregory."

And with that, Charlotte sealed her marital fate.

Two weeks later, when Lord Gregory returned to Mirow Palace, the princess asked him to take a turn with her about the grounds. He agreed. Knowing all eyes were on her from every window in the palace, Charlotte walked with the Duke as the sun set, and by the time they reached the stables she had accepted his proposal.

With one act of sacrifice Charlotte knew peace would descend upon Mirow. A remodel could begin on the building, a new roof could be installed, and she would assure the security of the family. All she need do was abandon these silly ideas of possessing genuine love, honest appreciation and well-deserved happiness.

Now, a month later, she was looking out the window, wondering what would happen if she hurled herself from it onto the snow below; a thought which made her chuckle when she considered that her mother would still marry her corpse to the Duke.

Charlotte idled over to the washbasin and looked at herself in the mirror above it. How inauthentic she looked to herself with the heavy white makeup painted all over her all the time. Dipping her hands in the cool water she washed every spec of it from her face using Sister Lena's lemon mint soap, then stared at her unadorned olive skinned reflection. If only she could be accepted this way. Then she remembered what Christian said to her at Sanssouci:

"I believe you are the most beautiful woman here…"

If only that were true. If only princesses and not sopranos were truly beautiful to him. If only there was no Lord Gregory. If only her mother was not a manipulating shrew. If only she was not a woman forced into a compromising personal decision. She thought about Anne, the African girl she met at Sanssouci, and the amulet she knew was somehow connected to her father's. It made her wish her mother hadn't robbed her of that inheritance.

Charlotte dried her face and went back to the window seat. Soon, she began to think about Jon Baptiste and how she missed their lessons together. Jon had gone back to his former life and they did not see much of each other anymore. Sometimes she went to the barn with books and was told Jon was in the village or working at the palace at Neustrelitz. It was almost as though they were being kept apart by some force, and she wanted to see him to reestablish their friendship.

Jon, too, wanted a restored relationship with the princess. He had equally missed their times together—those too precious moments when he felt like a human being, real royalty. He was sorry Charlotte was being forced into a loveless arrangement with the Duke of Anhalt and wished he could help. Then the day arrived when Adolph informed him he would be needed at Mirow for the engagement party.

Jon knew he would see Charlotte again. Perhaps he could make things right. If God would put the right words into his mouth maybe the circumstances of their estrangement could be reversed. Thus, on the day he arrived at Mirow from Neustrelitz, he beseeched his mother to prepare a special batch of Spatzen—something he knew Charlotte loved. Then he secretly stole a bottle of Rhine wine from the cellar.

As Sister Lena packed her son's burlap bag with the spatzen and wine she found she could no longer hold her tongue.

"Why do you need wine and spatzen for the Princess?"

"I want to do something special for her."

"Does the Grand Duke know about yer 'special' plans?"

Jon shook his head after which his mother balked.

"You not teachin' the Princess to dance now, so what's yer excuse? Or have you jus' forgot yer place again? I keep tellin' you, yer her slave—not her equal."

"Not with her, mama. We're past all of that."

"Past all o' that? How do you get past such a t'ing? I told you three months ago you was spendin' too much time with the Princess fer just dance lessons. Proximity like that brings trouble. 'Specially fer a slave."

Jon became angry. "Why do you constantly remind me I'm a slave? Remember, I take their demeaning slurs just like you. I scrub and clean out their stinking shit pots just like you! Why do you deny me those few precious moments when I can feel like a Lord."

"A 'Lord'? Boy you talkin' crazy."

"She called me 'Sir Jon' and she was teaching me reading and French. I liked it. She made me feel special, mama. She let me call her 'Lady' Charlotte."

"'Lady' Charlotte? Boy, don' never put your hat higher than your hand can reach. Big words and fancy French talk will not change a damn t'ing. Princess Charlotte calling you "Sir Jon" don't make you nothin' more than a fancy slave!"

"Mother, stop, dammit!"

Sister Lena's hand unconsciously went up to slap her son for insolence. But as soon as she raised it, she realized her behavior and lowered it. She had never acted so violently before. This was her son. They had been through much together, and here she was almost slapping him for his interest in bettering himself no matter how dangerous. Now both mother and son stood speechless in the stark reality of their conduct. Finally, Jon's mother pushed the burlap bag into his hands, her voice only a breath above a whisper. "If you wanna 'do somet'ing special,' get de princess to do somet'ing about slavery. That would make all this so called 'education' make sense." Sister Lena walked away. Jon stood there with myriad thoughts in his head. Finally he left to face the chill of the afternoon air.

Charlotte was still sitting in the window of her room thinking about her life when suddenly she caught sight of Jon standing on the outermost crest of the garden carrying his familiar burlap bag. She smiled praying her thoughts of him had actually made him materialize before her. After grabbing a shawl, she ran outside.

"Sir Jon," she called out as she ran toward him. "I haven't seen you in weeks. Where have you been?"

Jon turned toward the princess wanting so much to forget his mother's censure of him. But try as he may irritation rose within him and reality encroached. He grew cold saying nothing.

"What's wrong, Sir Jon?" the princess asked, sensing his vexation.

"Don't call me 'Sir' Jon anymore," Jon snapped. "It'll never be true. An' us pretending won't make it so."

Charlotte was stunned to disbelief. "Are you angry with me?"

"It's not you. It's what you represent!" Jon retorted as though a demon was unleashed. "I am a slave owned by your family—and the thought of independence or changing my status never crosses my mind—or yours. And me playing this silly game of 'Sir Jon and Lady Charlotte' with you, having a taste of what equality feels like, makes it worse. As long as I don't do something to help other slaves like me, I'll always hate myself, and you, for turning a blind eye."

Charlotte had never seen Jon so upset. He started off toward the palace but Charlotte followed quickly, concerned about him. "Jon, don't go like this. Let's talk. Don't be so angry."

But Jon kept going—which agitated the princess. "Stop I say!"

Jon instantly halted. Groaning with infuriation he turned back to the princess. "Because you *own* me, I'm forced to stop and do as you say. Now can you understand why the first thing I would do if I could, is to stop being a slave, and start being a man?"

"But I've done nothing to you," pleaded the princess, vulnerable in the face of his rage.

"You've done nothing but expose me to what I will never truly have—freedom. Genuine choice. One day I'm going to leave here and be a free man. Free enough not to have to serve drinks or brush horses. When we practiced dancing you treated me special. I was 'Sir' Jon. I was as good as you. But the truth is—I'm the valet. The stable boy. The one whose gonna sweep and shovel horse manure, and haul out piss pots 'til I die. *That* is why I'm angry." He choked back the hurt he was experiencing then started off again. Suddenly he turned back. "May I be permitted to leave, Your Highness?"

The princess finally nodded, after which Jon walked away.

Almost as though God ordained it, the weather betrayed me and the skies opened up. Snow fell in imposing flurries, and as I stood there watching Jon go, my body shook with disillusion. My eyes could not help but tear and disappointment carried me in a hail of agony into the palace, feeling a deepening resentment—not for Jon, my unwitting tormentor—but for my circumstances.

Thirteen

Baron Philip Adolphus von Munchhausen, the Hanoverian
Minister in London, had done part of his job as King George
requested. He had dispatched a letter of inquiry to Major von
Schulenburg, George's emissary in Germany. Von Schulenburg, a reliable
infiltrator who lived in Brandenburg, knew every royal living everywhere
in the Rhine. The letter was sent for the purpose of relaying preliminary
information on sixteen prospective princesses. Schulenburg had acquired
data and narrowed his initial list down to nine within a month. The list,
approved by Bute and King George, consisted of candidates from the
Houses of Hesse-Darmstadt, Brandenburg-Schwedt, Brunswick-
Wolfenbuttel, Anhalt-Dessau, Saxe-Gotha, and Mecklenburg-Strelitz.

It was now time for Munchhausen to personally interview the princesses. After being briefed by King George, he was dispatched on 19
March 1761. Arriving ten days later in Bremen, he rested for a day, then
set out to interview Princess Margaret of Anhalt-Dessau first.

Munchhausen was immediately led into the reception hall of the castle by Prince Leopold. He was served a strong tea, then waited. Finally,
the 15-year-old made her appearance. Princess Margaret, though congenial, was completely disinterested and stared out the window for most of
the time. Conversely, Prince Leopold talked incessantly as Munchhausen
took notes.

"I bless the day I met Margaret's mother, God rest her soul. I met
her when I was ill in 1743," he blabbered on. "She was the daughter of
the apothecary who filled my order for medicine. She was so beautiful. I

married her as soon as I was healthy again. And look at my little Marga-ret—as beautiful as her mother."

As Prince Leopold went on, Munchhausen's face went blanch. Did he just hear what he thought he'd heard? His head filled with a thousand questions but he kept a frozen expression on his face. As far as he was concerned, the interview was over and he wrote the fatal note to himself in his ledger: "Invalid pedigree. Mother a commoner" then drew a line through Princess Margaret's name. Neither King George nor the Privy Council would ever allow such a marriage.

Six days later Munchhausen traveled to Saxe-Gotha to seek out Princess Frederica Louise, whom he knew was also an unlikely candidate as she was Princess Augusta's niece. King George did not want so close an alliance with any member of his mother's family. The dowager Prin-cess of Wales had coerced Munchhausen to meet with the princess of whom people were disinclined to discuss. Munchhausen understood immediately upon greeting her. Princess Frederica had had smallpox, and had been left terribly marked by the disease. Her face and upper body unfortunately showcased remnants of her affliction, and she also had a limp, which, to his mind, ended all consideration, as well as the interview. In this instance he was actually relieved.

A fortnight later, Munchhausen was in the township of Branden-burg-Schwedt. Earlier, he had sent a message to Major von Schulenburg and asked if he would be helpful in obtaining any additional information on any of the princesses. Yet, when Munchhausen finally met with the Major and inquired about Princess Phillipa, von Schulenburg was less than forthcoming. In fact, it was like pulling teeth for von Schulenburg to respond to the question, "What do you think of the princess as a po-tential bride for His Majesty?"

"Well... the princess is handsome," Schulenburg stated nervously, "but...but she's...she's..." He could not continue, and Munchhausen became frustrated. "What is it which you seem constrained to tell His Majesty about her, sir?"

"Well...she is, how do you say...my English...is no too good. She is..." Finally he confessed and Munchhausen bleakly wrote down every word.

"Princess Phillipa is an opinionated, obstinate, rude, profane, and much unaccommodating female. She has far too many disagreeable qualities for a queen. She also refuses to marry a man she feels resembles…a frog."

Munchhausen was mortified and at that, thanked the Major, otherwise a thoughtful and judicious man, and left. The next day he saw for himself. Indeed Princess Phillipa was a beautiful creature, but she sent him running for his coach as she chastised him, throwing his hat after him, yelling, "You son of a pig's arse! I told that gutter snipe Major Schulenburg I will not marry that frog-eyed mother's boy King George! Now go! And don't send anyone else!"

Interviews such as this went on for another three weeks. Princesses were obese, infirmed, obdurate, standoffish, silly, hideous, suicidal or depressed. He had never seen such a motley assemblage of unsuitable, undesirable women of breeding in his life, and he prayed to God as to how he would inform the king. Yet inform him he must.

The baron rubbed his temples as he sat in an Inn in Brandenburg. Pulling off his wire-rim glasses he guzzled down two mugs of vintage ale in less than a minute, trying to formulate his words for the unfavorable correspondence to His Majesty. His head continued to throb knowing he had another five princesses to interview and hoped a proper candidate would emerge from amongst them.

The letter reached Bute at St. James, sending George's advisor into a tailspin as he read it to Augusta on their way to the king's robing chambers.

"Your Majesty, it is with deep regret that I write you regarding the first seven candidates. They are all unsuitable in the worst possible way. One princess was too progressive in attitude, another far too outspoken and sure of herself. The lunacy, incapacity and illnesses afflicting some would stun one's comportment. Attached on the second page of this correspondence are the specifics of each candidate's unsuitability for your assessment. I implore you to continue the services of Major Schulenburg to compile another list. At such time I will undertake it personally, interviewing each in the next month or two. Please accept my sincere apology for the state of these young women as well as my hope for better results in our next round. Yours faithfully, Baron Phillip Adolphus Von Munchhausen."

Bute's head shook as he paced up and down the hall with Augusta. "This is a nightmare."

"What was the problem with Princess Frederica?" Augusta questioned. "Did you not tell the Baron my niece should be favorably reviewed?

"According to this, she's disfigured from smallpox, has a hideous face, and a limp."

"Trivial details. George has said he does not require a beauty."

"Nor does he desire a troll." Bute was not in a humorous mood and Augusta glared at him as he knocked at the robing chamber door and entered.

George was preparing for a hunt and a decision was being made about two hats and three pairs of hunting boots as to which he would wear. Bute bowed, forcing himself to give the preoccupied king the letter. "Your Majesty, it appears I am the bearer of bad news. The first report from Germany has arrived. It's abysmal. None of the princesses are suitable. Munchhausen wants more time to gather names of other prospects to interview."

George read the correspondence and his shoulders drooped in frustration. Bute soon had second thoughts about offering up the second of his concerns, but knew if he didn't George would find out soon enough. "I have other news, Your Majesty. It appears Lady Sarah fell from her horse last Tuesday and broke her leg. She is recuperating at Holland House and won't be able to walk for several weeks."

George instantly removed the hunting hat he'd chosen and tossed it to his dresser. He went for the door, dismissing Bute and his mother. "I'm going to Sarah at once."

"George, this is business. I think you should reconsider Princess Frederica," Augusta called out after him.

"And I think I should reconsider Lady Sarah," George retorted, "as *your* suggestions have yet to work."

With that, off he went, with the door slamming behind him.

Fourteen

April, 1761

Spring had at last arrived and the grounds of Mirow Palace burst with cherry blossoms, wisteria and bougainvilleas. The event of the season was finally taking place: the engagement party of the Duke of Anhalt-Cothen and Princess Charlotte Sophia of Mecklenburg-Strelitz.

The theme of lilac and white was in evidence and everything glowed with candlelight and torches. A string quartet hired for the evening was playing gay tunes, and 250 members of German society filled the palace.

Duchess Elizabeth was ecstatic even as she struggled to hide her illness. Everything was working exactly as planned. Guests commented on the remodeled palace, the superb quality of the fabrics on the furniture, walls and draperies, as well as the lushness of the grounds. They also loved the cuisine, and though Sister Lena did not receive her deserved credit, she was proud of her contribution as she and several servants served hors d'oeuvres.

Charlotte and Lord Gregory danced under the vine-covered walkway with all eyes focused on them. Occasionally Charlotte glanced at Christiana and the two exchanged a solemn look. Christiana knew her sister was tortured, but nothing could be done.

Later, as Charlotte made her way through the crowd, she was continuously complimented on how beautiful she looked which made her feel esteemed even though she was painted as white as milk. Sir Alfred had fashioned her hair into an upsweep with soft ringlets falling around her face. But no matter how beautifully coifed or attired she was Charlotte was depressed. She did not want to engage in small talk with the guests and certainly not reside on Lord Gregory's arm. So as soon as the Duke noticed Wilhelm and took his daughter Helena over to force conversation between them for a second possible Frederick /Muldare match-up, Charlotte chose to disappear.

Excusing herself, she slipped down the hall into the parlor and sat in the window seat. She felt dead inside. Her impending marriage was one concern. Jon Baptiste was the other.

After their encounter in November Jon asked to be transferred to Neustrelitz Palace, according to Adolph. He never said goodbye and Charlotte had not seen him in months. All she could think about was their fight on the grounds and how much he hurt her with his comments. She thought of his desire to be "…free enough not to serve, sweep or shovel manure…" He deserved that freedom, she thought. He had been right about her family, too. None of them were doing anything toward a resolution to the Negro problem, and this bleak dilemma ensconced her in morose.

Jon had been depressed as well and regretted his actions. When he left Charlotte that day he went back to the palace and down to the kitchen where his mother was still making soap. Sister Lena could tell that her son was upset and when she questioned Jon he told her about his encounter with the princess and what he'd said. Sister Lena found herself vexed again. "Jon, how could you say such a t'ing to Her Highness?" It was all she could do not to throw the soap curd at him. "I can't believe that jus' cuz de princess help you read an' write, an' allow you ta teach her ta dance, that you t'ink you 'ave de same right as she do."

"But we *should* have the same rights. We need to stop thinking like slaves and be free."

"You don' say such t'ings to a princess. She's royal, boy. Wha' gon happen when she tell de Duchess? You want ta put us in danger?"

"No mother. That is not what I want," Jon muttered in exasperation. It just never occurred to me I couldn't say what was really on my mind to her."

"'Never occurred' to you?" Sister Lena mimicked in Jon's more re-fined attempts at the language, "My, my. We 'ave such style now, don' we? Such class an' sophistication. Well, let me tell you somethin', boy. Them Fredericks will sell you jus' as soon as you anger them, an' no amount of pretendin' give you the right ta jeopardize us. Now you go an' apologize. I know wha' it's like ta speak out of turn ta dem Fredericks an' be punished."

"But what do I say? Especially to *her*? Someone I have such... someone I feel...," Jon was unable to go on and moved to the soap curd to stir it. Sister Lena realized an awful truth.

"Boy, I know wha' happenin' here. You call her 'Charlotte' ta me. Not 'Princess' or 'Her Highness,' like she got yer heart in a twist. You got feelings fer de princess?"

Jon said nothing. He couldn't. He knew his mother's instincts were correct.

Sister Lena's face drained. "My God, chile, you can't. You gotta stop it now. They's t'ings you don't know 'bout her, 'bout dem." With a mixture of dread and foreboding Jon had never witnessed. Sister Lena rushed to her tarot cards to shuffle then display them. Once she was done, her hands went to her face and she shook her head in despair. "It's bad, boy."

Instead of asking his mother what she'd "read" in the cards, Jon poured the scented curd mixture into the soap molds. "Don't share your findings with me. I don't believe in your cards."

"Boy, these cards raised you. The power is in *me* believin'. Take heed. Apologize ta the princess as soon as possible an' remove dis cloud gatherin' over you."

"Mother, please, I..."

"Jon!" Lena snapped. "There's evil intent ta destroy you. Apologize ta de princess."

Jon walked out, never looking back at his mother. He never saw her tears. He never knew that what she saw in her cards—what she *always* saw in her cards for him—was death.

Unable to apologize to Charlotte, Jon asked Adolph if he could work at Neustrelitz permanently.

✠

Now, Charlotte was sitting in the window seat of the parlor while the merriment of her engagement party was on-going. She was enveloped in a veil of despair. Though she had made the decision freely to marry the Duke of Anhalt-Cothen, she was still frustrated. Here she was an aristocrat, a royal; someone at the summit of acceptability and prominence in society. But as a royal *woman*, she had no more freedom of choice than the enslaved population around the world from whom she, herself, was descended.

She was no different from Jon.

Soon, however, her thoughts were interrupted by the sounds of neighing horses and a carriage pulling up to the entrance of the palace. When she looked out the window she saw two well-dressed gentlemen, one carrying a satchel, approach the door. They looked familiar. Old James Baptiste opened the door to admit the men, taking their coats and hats before announcing them: "Herr Carl Emmanuel Bach and Herr Johann Christian Bach."

Surprise siphoned the blood from her face and she ran to the doorway of the parlor and opened it. There stood Christian, manifested before her like an answered prayer. The composer looked up and their eyes locked. Again, the world fell away leaving only them, and Emmanuel, knowing his brother's feelings for the princess, broke the spell. "Please forgive my tardiness, Your Highness," Emmanuel stated, "and congratulations on your forthcoming nuptials."

"Thank you, Herr Bach," Charlotte managed, her eyes still on Christian.

"My brother insisted I bring him as he is going away for a while," Emmanuel continued, noticing Christian had yet to say "hello" to Charlotte. "He would say so himself, but apparently he is incapable at the moment." Emmanuel bowed courteously and went to the Reception Hall where the other guests were.

This left Christian and Charlotte alone.

"Congratulations, Your Highness. I hope you and Lord Gregory will be very happy," said Christian, who finally found his voice and whose expression belied his true feelings.

"It has been six months, Christian," Charlotte started, her eyes nervously cast to the floor.

"One hundred eighty-eight days, actually," Christian corrected. "I wrote you three times from Milan, and again from Hamburg just last month. When I did not hear from you I assumed you had been cautioned against me. Then I heard about your engagement."

Charlotte frowned. "You wrote to me? I never received any of your letters."

"This is why I had to come. I had to know if there was some misunderstanding of how things stood between us. It all went by so fast at King's Ball I wasn't sure it happened at all."

Charlotte's finger went to his lips to silence him. She was already overwhelmed by his being there, but to know that he had written her and she had never received any letters upset her.

"I am marrying Lord Gregory. I made the decision myself. It has all been arranged."

"Do you love him? I need to know, for I saw no evidence of it at the king's ball."

"Christian, please," Charlotte pleaded. "You and I only had one dance together."

"Do you love him?" Christian repeated. "For I have not gotten that one dance out of my mind. Can you not say the same?"

Charlotte turned and hurried back into the parlor fighting back tears. But Christian followed her. Music from the string quartet could be heard quietly filtering through the walls as Christian closed the door and took Charlotte's hand not sure how to start. "We don't have much time." His voice softened to a whisper and his eyes searched hers. "I ask that you do not judge me for my forwardness but I leave tomorrow for Brussels. Three weeks after that I go to Vienna, then London. I will not return to the Rhine for years."

The sound of Charlotte's heart breaking was so loud even Christian could hear it.

"I have learned that feelings are best communicated before journeying as one never knows what the future holds," Christian lamented. "And if I do not say what is on my mind it will never be said." He pushed back the haphazard tendrils of her hair. "I love you." He stopped upon seeing Charlotte's eyes glazed with tears and he reached out to wipe them. "If you have feelings for your betrothed, so be it. I will understand. If, however, you have feelings for me—any feelings at all, I need to know. I need…"

Charlotte could not allow him to finish. Before she knew it, she impulsively kissed him. "I love you," she confessed, lurching back at the forwardness of her action, surprised at herself. But Christian drew her face back to his kissing her again. Charlotte had never experienced anything like it. Her body ached for more as his hands tenderly explored the back of her neck and shoulders finally finding her magnificent breasts to caress. As he pressed his body tightly against hers she came up for air emitting a sigh of ecstasy, then reclaimed Christian's lips with her own. They kissed until the need for oxygen and Charlotte's desire for answers to questions forced them apart.

"What is it, Charlotte?"

It took her a moment. "This is so wrong. The man I am engaged to is out there with all of our friends and family, and I am in here with you." She turned her back to him. "Christian, were I not royalty would you even care for me?"

"What a strange question."

"I am not your usual sort. I am not a soprano like the ones I hear you favor so much. I do not perform. No one thinks me beautiful or charismatic. What do you see in me?"

Christian took her gloved hand. "A kindred spirit," he said. "Someone with restless desire to leave the world better for having been here." He pulled off the glove to reveal her sun-kissed skin. "Someone who wants to show their *true* self to the world, but cannot. Remember, I knew you when you were eight. You were not hiding beneath quite so much chalk then."

The princess almost cried from his truths. "It's my mother. She insists on it."

"I, too, put forth a brave yet false face, " Christian continued softly. "People think because I am the son of J.S. Bach that I am rich. But I must make a living anyway I can, for my father did not leave any bequeaths when he died."

"Sebastian left no inheritances?"

"Only a clavier, three shirts and an enormous shadow out of which my talent will never take me," answered Christian, his head bowed. "I go day-to-day, month-to-month on the concert rounds—Italy, Germany, France, England—hoping for a better appointment because the one I have with Count Agostino Litta in Milan is so restrictive. Nothing but my music would have kept me from you, Charlotte. Nothing. Music is my mistress." Then Christian's voice softened. "As for sopranos, while it is true I keep company with a few, I am around. I am a composer.

Singers are the tools of my trade. But they do not govern my heart. You do, Charlotte."

Christian opened the satchel he brought and gave her a silver ballerina music box which, when wound, played J.S. Bach's "2 Part Invention."

"I love you the way I love my music," he continued to Charlotte. "I shall not see you for a long time. I wanted to give you something to keep me in your memory."

Charlotte smiled, listening to the music playing from the music box. "It's beautiful."

"Though I am but a poor composer, I have the heart of an aristocrat."

Charlotte turned from the object of her affection and held the music box to her herself.

"I do not care about such things, Christian. I only know that when I am with you, I feel joy. I feel accepted for being myself. I feel as though life has given me at least one special gift that is mine and mine alone, and I do not want to give it up." She turned back to him and took his hand. "Oh Christian. I cannot marry Lord Gregory. I will surely die married to him."

"But what can we do? We cannot run away and elope."

It suddenly struck Charlotte as though a chandelier had fallen on her. "Yes. We can. I can leave Mirow and denounce the impediments of my royal society. I want to be with you, Christian. I want to be *your* wife. I don't care that my pedigree will not allow it."

"Nothing would please me more than for you to be my bride. But life with me on the road, town to town, country to country is no place for a woman of royal breeding and birth."

"I do not care, Christian. I love you. Can we not find a way to be together?"

Christian thought a moment. Was it really happening? Did she truly understand what she would be giving up? Was it possible he could have the woman he desired and the career he so coveted in the same lifetime? Were the Gods blessing him with his dream?

"In three weeks I will be in Vienna. If you can get as far as Berlin, I will arrange to have you brought to me there where we can be married. Can you arrange it?"

"Yes," Charlotte answered quickly as a plan of action sprung into her head and came out of her mouth as though dictated from beyond her. "I can pretend I am not well and stay at home while my family goes into town for the Festival of the Equinox. I can enlist Jon's assistance to sneak me out with him and get me to the coach at Neustrelitz. By the time my family returns, I will be long gone."

"Then I will write you to confirm our dates and where to meet."

"Yes, yes. But send your letters in care of Lady Schwellenberg so I am sure to receive them this time."

They kissed each other. And as Christian's strong arms held her Charlotte felt safe and adored—perhaps for the first time in her life. "*Mrs.* Christian Bach," she murmured softly.

"I shall never forget tonight," Christian pledged.

Then from somewhere behind them they heard, "And I shall never forget it either."

Charlotte and Christian turned to find Lord Gregory, Duchess Elizabeth, Princess Helena and Wilhelm standing in the doorway. Lord Gregory marched over and slapped Christian's face.

"It appears, Herr Bach, that you cannot remember your place in regard to my fiancée."

Christian wanted to punch him, but couldn't. Lord Gregory was a Royal.

"Leave here at once," the Duke demanded, "or I shall be forced to challenge you to a duel—the consequences I assure you will have a detrimental effect on your hands, sir."

"Lord Gregory, you do not have authority in this house," Charlotte warned.

"But *I* do," Duchess Elizabeth icily snarled as she came over to Christian. "And I want Herr Bach to leave and take his brother with him." She turned to Christian with narrowed eyes, "Were it not for the high esteem in which I held your father, I would have you flogged, sir."

Christian bowed to the Duchess and Charlotte, then quickly left. Charlotte started after him but was halted by Lord Gregory's grasp. "I am of a mind to knock some sense into you. Your behavior is that of a petulant, wanton child, the likes of which I will not have in a wife."

"That is fine with me, sir," Charlotte admonished, finding a strength from deep within, "For I am convinced you are the last person on earth I can ever be insisted upon to wed." Charlotte removed her engagement ring, threw it at him and ran off with Christian's music box.

The Duke, taken aback, glared at Duchess Elizabeth. "I withdraw my pledge of 5,000 talers. I shall not appear a cuckold connected with such an unseemly incident as this. My apologies to our guests. Auf Wiedersehen."

Fifteen

Two days passed and Charlotte still lay in a disheveled heap on her bed. The engagement was off and she was in mourning for her life—a life in which she was forced to live with disappointment, loneliness and most of all, the loss of Christian Bach.

But as she had tearfully run from the parlor the night of the disastrous engagement party, she accidentally crashed into a servant with a tray of wine glasses. Both collapsed onto the floor. Coming to their rescue, of all people, was Jon Baptiste. Charlotte and Jon looked at each other for a moment and after he helped her up, she fell into his arms in tears.

Jon knew something had happened to cause the princess undue grief and despite himself he held her. "Don't cry, Lady Charlotte. I'm here. Jon is here."

"Thank you, Sir Jon," wept Charlotte.

It did not bother Jon when she called him "Sir Jon" this time. She seemed to need him and he wanted to be there for her. He walked her to her room and made sure she would be alright before he went back to serving. Charlotte, if nothing else, was his friend, and he would protect that friendship—even against the error of his own ways.

Charlotte locked herself in her room allowing no one in. If she could have stayed there undisturbed to collect herself it would have been a blessing. Alas no such luck. Duchess Elizabeth, thoroughly embarrassed at having to dismiss her guests and announce the engagement was called off, tore upstairs to Charlotte's room and banged on the door. She hurled invectives at her daughter the likes of which no other family member had ever experienced.

Charlotte never opened the door and the Duchess threatened to have it kicked in. The party and remodeling on the palace had cost Elizabeth a good sum of money which she could never recoup as Lord Gregory had now withdrawn his promise of funds. Charlotte threw a pillow over her head and played Christian's music box over and over to drown the sounds of the raving lunatic outside the door that was her mother. It took Adolph to finally remove the Duchess, now on the verge of a physical and mental breakdown, and take her to her room to put her to bed amidst charges that they were all "doomed to insolvency."

Eventually, Christiana convinced Charlotte—now disillusioned and weak—to open the door, and she was able to feed the princess some soup. Christiana never let her sister out of her sight for the next two weeks. Charlotte remained despondent. She had not heard from Christian since the engagement party and she hadn't seen Jon since their encounter in the hall. She also sensed that Sister Lena was avoiding her. The Jamaican woman rarely looked Charlotte in the eye anymore. If she was coming down a hall and chanced upon Charlotte she would find an excuse to turn around.

Order in the household was never regained, and Charlotte and her mother rarely spoke. The princess would take her meals upstairs in her room, and comforted herself with Christian's music box or Christiana's company, but her reason for living was destroyed and soon she imagined taking her own life.

Wilhelm, however, found his chance to step in and "save the family." He took it upon himself to go to Lord Gregory's estate in Anhalt-Cothen and pledge his undying love for the Duke's daughter, Princess Helena Muldare. With this move he would cull favor with his aunt, acquire a title, and build a nest egg for himself with the Duke's money. Additionally, he could still have Charlotte as a mistress, for she would be considered a dishonorable woman, and his life would be perfect.

Thus, he asked the aging Lord Gregory for Helena's hand in marriage and assured him there was no reason to expect a repeat of that which caused the Duke's untimely departure from Mirow in April. Lord Gregory, anxious to unload his homely, 27-year-old daughter, did not hesitate to make a contract with Wilhelm. However, he did not provide the same financial stipend he had offered the Grand Duchess. Instead of two notes for 5,000 talers, he offered one note for a total of 2,000 talers—to be delivered only upon the consummation of the marriage on their wedding night. This way he was assured of his daughter's future. He also offered Wilhelm the title of "Viscount" in the duchy, something Wilhelm was more than willing to accept as he had no title at all in the Frederick court of Mecklenburg.

Upon hearing this news Charlotte didn't know who she felt sorrier for: herself, for having no life and becoming the source of ridicule from her peers and family, or Princess Helena, who would be marrying her insane cousin Wilhelm—the Anti-Christ—and earmark herself to birth the child of the beast.

Yet, on a blissful afternoon one month later, a ray of hope pierced the cloud hovering over Charlotte. Just after tea, Lady Schwellenberg motioned for her to come into the hall. Charlotte excused herself and found her lady with a silver tray on top of which sat a single red rose and a letter. She winked at Charlotte and handed her the tray, then with a wry grin beseeched, "Tell me everything later."

Charlotte instantly knew it was from *him* and ran outside to her swing to read it in privacy. Her heart fluttered with anticipation as her fingers fumbled quickly to break the wax seal and read:

19 May, 1761
Her Serene Highness, Princess Charlotte Sophia Frederick
Mirow Palace, Mecklenburg-Strelitz, Germany

My Dearest Love Charlotte,

Happy Birthday, mon petit, and please forgive the tardiness of this letter. It has been two weeks since my departure to Brussels from Italy and my next stop is Vienna for three weeks, then London where my benefactor informs me I shall be staying for a year. Though I am composing better than ever, my thoughts are constantly of thee, I cherish our time at Sanssouci, and most importantly your home at Mirow last. I pray my coming there did not so stain and unfavorably impact your relationship with your family, for I would never be able to forgive myself. I had to see you, and if my thoughtlessness caused undue grief I shall be forever mortified.

Charlotte, I pray you have not changed your mind about our elopement. It is all I can think about. Without these thoughts I find myself a ship lost at sea without a rudder. I have contacted Herr Eldridge Chasin. He will be the one to come to Berlin to meet you and bring you to Vienna. All you need do is tell me you still wish to be mine in the sanctity of marriage. If so, he will bring you to the Rose Inn hotel where we will be wed in secret and become man and wife forever more. But I must leave Vienna by the 25th so please act with haste and let me know. Still, even if you have given the matter more thought and instead chosen not to act so rash and demonstratively I will understand. So please forgive the ramblings of this love-sick composer and know that I love you no matter who you choose in marriage, I am, and will always be, completely and forever thine own.

JCB

Charlotte read and reread Christian's letter all that afternoon. She smelled, fondled, and cherished it. Then she tucked it into her bosom next to her heart. Later that night she wrote Christian in return.

Herr Johann Christian Bach
In Care of the Rose Inn Hotel
Casamount, Vienna

Dearest Christian,

Your letter was received with much excitement. You see, I, too, was lost on life's ocean without rudder or direction until that same fateful day at Mirow. The blood rushed from my head as everything and everyone in the house froze to allow us our moment—a moment I think about every day. When I go to sleep I can feel your kiss on my lips. I think of it when I wake to the thrill of your touch in my mind's eye, and I go through my day with the memory of our hearts beating in unison when you agreed we should elope. Dear, sweet Christian, obviously I am no longer betrothed to Lord Gregory, and I am thrilled at the prospect of our marriage—no matter the manner. I have planned my escape even as I write this. So, yes, please dispatch Herr Chasin to Berlin where I shall be at the main hotel on the 15th. My plan is to leave here the day of the Feast of the Equinox and travel to Berlin with my friend and servant, Jon Baptiste. I pray our marriage will be a blessed one even though we are acting out of need, a desperate love and the immediacy of being together. This is our destiny Christian—to be in love and married no matter what. It is my dream to follow you to the ends of the earth if need be. So please do not question our decision. It is what I am living for.

God willing I shall be in Vienna by the 19ᵗʰ where we shall begin our life together. Wait for me, my love. Wait. I shall be there. Nothing can stop me for it is our fate to be wedded. Until then, hold on to the knowledge that I, too, am completely and forever thine.   Lotte

Thus began their epistolary relationship. Christian made good on his promise to write and the princess responded in kind. Lady Schwellenberg would stealthily deliver a letter, and Charlotte would give her one in return for posting. Charlotte cherished each letter, and when they became too numerous, she bound them in red ribbon and hid them in the bottom of her armoire.

☩

By the afternoon of the Feast of the Equinox celebration, Charlotte had reconciled with Jon and asked him to help her in her escape. He agreed for he was her friend and could never refuse her bidding. Everyone else had gone into the village to enjoy the festivities, including Adolph. Charlotte stayed behind feigning illness so she could make good her escape. Not even her trusted Ladies-in-Waiting were informed of her choice to run away and elope with Christian.

What a beautiful day, the princess thought as she looked out the window over the grounds. It was not too warm and there was just enough of a breeze to deliver the fragrance of Sister Lena's potpourri, placed in various rooms throughout the palace. Charlotte felt good as she packed her valise. Jon promised to take the support staff into Neustrelitz, an hour away, for the festival, then hurry back to Mecklenburg to deliver Charlotte to the carriage which would bring her to the "coaching inn" in Berlin three hours in the opposite direction. Knowing the family would not return until later that evening gave him enough time to retrieve them and have an alibi since he, as a servant, was supposed to wait with other drivers in the coach area of the festival.

After Jon left, Charlotte passed the standing mirror, stopping to look at herself. She was changing. She felt mature. Nothing could ever return her to the dark days of her mother's censure again. She was a woman now. She had the love of a man who wanted her the way she was as his wife. And it was this thought which drove her to the washbasin. She wiped off every trace of the powder and makeup she used daily to lighten her skin and had a good look at herself. Her lemon-olive complexion did not bother her any longer, nor did her broad nose or plump lips. This was who she was—the real Charlotte Sophia, and she liked her.

She then turned to her armoire—the vessel of her secret life and innermost passions—for she had an overwhelming desire to forage through her past. What should she take with her, she thought? Inside she found Christian's hidden letters tied in red ribbon, and the ballerina music box he had given her. Then she saw the pink chiffon ball gown, and it brought back memories of Sanssouci.

Suddenly Charlotte wanted to make those memories real again. The pink gown would be perfect for her elopement and she wanted to put it on again before packing it. As she slipped into the dress admiring the layers of matching crinolines, she went to the mirror and felt beautiful all over again. She remembered Christian's words the night of the King's Ball:

"... I believe you to be the most beautiful girl here—and I the luckiest man."

She wound up Christian's music box and let the music fill the air. She felt her body float like a cloud and she loosened her hair so that it fell long and coiled about her shoulders. Yes, it was her fantasy, but it would be the last one she'd have at Mirow. By nightfall she would be in Berlin and on to Vienna to become Christian's wife. An hour passed and though painful, Charlotte knew it was time to finish packing.

But when she turned to do so, it was then that she saw *him* and gasped.

Sixteen

Baron Von Munchhausen was crisscrossing Germany valiantly searching for a potential queen. He went to Baden, moved on to Württemberg, and then to Hesse-Nassau. Each princess received a negative rating. The Princess of Baden was blind and unable to bear children. The Princess of Württemberg's attention would wander and she would stare into space or mercilessly interrupt Munchhausen with long-winded stories. The Baron noted that she would "drive the king insane." Then, after meeting with the mother of the Princess of Hesse-Nassau and having several cups of tea and small talk, the princess was finally presented to him. Munchhausen was in shock. The Princess was but 10 years old and, though charming, the girl played with a doll throughout the interview. If it was not so ridiculous and insane, Munchhausen would have laughed in the child's face.

A fortnight later, Munchhausen made his way to Brunswick-Wolfenbuttel to inquire about Princess Elizabeth. Twenty minutes later he went fleeing from the palace. Princess Elizabeth was afflicted with a disagreeable condition which rendered her so flatulent that Munchhausen's kerchief stayed up to his nose as his stomach revolted. He was so odorously assaulted his nasal passages were still recovering three days later.

Thus, the Baron again took to his pen—and his ale. He had lost hope he indicated in his letter to the king, and, judging from the correspondence he received in response, so had the king.

Desperation was looming in the court of St. James. Eight months had passed since George had become king, yet no queen was on the horizon. All correspondence from Baron Von Munchhausen was dismal, and soon it was felt that their standards may have to be lowered. Apparently options were slim for eligible, young, amiable, blue-blooded, reasonably intelligent, marginally attractive, politically disinterested, child-bearing, Protestant princesses—who were not insane or infirmed.

Munchhausen was now down to two final choices, and as he arrived in the duchy of Hesse-Darmstadt his spirits were low. He knew the king was in his sexual peak and still physically desirous of Lady Sarah. If he did not quickly secure the proper princess for a wife, His Majesty would follow nature's course, and Sarah, knowing George was in love with her, would use the power of her feminine pulchritude to gestate a royal bastard, forcing a marriage.

Princess Caroline of Hesse-Darmstadt had come highly recommended by Major von Schulenburg's sister, who lived near the duchy. The drawback was that Princess Caroline had been the first-choice suggestion of the late King George II and young George had rejected the idea. Now that the choices were dwindling, Munchhausen had her placed back on the list.

But no sooner than the Baron was escorted into the parlor of Castle Darmstadt than he realized he'd made a terrible mistake. Princess Caroline was at least 300 pounds, far too obese and unattractive. Additionally, she was obdurate and standoffish, coupled with Munchhausen witnessing her father have a "vision" which put him in touch with the "spirit world."

The Baron's head fell into his hands. More familial mental deficiency would not be tolerated in the court of England. Not with Mary, Queen of Scots and King Edward VI, direct ancestors of King George, having been so afflicted.

His last choice was now the Princess of Mecklenburg-Strelitz, Charlotte Sophia. His concern, however, was that Von Schulenburg's report on her was found lacking. Her court was considered too small and insignificant, thus she might lack the social deportment necessary for a British queen. Also, Charlotte was not considered the most attractive princess of the lot. Munchhausen dispatched these reports to Bute as soon as he received them.

But Lord Bute answered the Baron immediately, telling him to interview Princess Charlotte Sophia with all haste:

"...The king is not as much in want of beauty as a queen who is capable of childbearing with enough intelligence to pass on to his heirs. As long as she is Protestant, of sound mind, not repulsive looking and has no interest in politics, she is to be considered..."

Munchhausen immediately contacted Major von Schulenburg to once again serve as emissary to make the proper introduction to Dowager Duchess Elizabeth and Grand Duke Adolph and pave the way for interviews with Princess Charlotte Sophia. He then crossed the Rhine Hills to make the two-week journey to Mecklenburg-Strelitz.

Seventeen

Wilhelm Albertina stood in the doorway of Charlotte's bedchamber, bullwhip in hand, staring at her with cold, drunken eyes. Charlotte was frightened. How long he had been there? Why was he there?

"So," he smirked with sinister inebriation. "P-poor, little Charlotte p-playing up here all by her so s-sick little self?"

Charlotte couldn't move. The horror of his unethical encroach-ment was frozen on her face.

"I t-thought you might like these as a 'get well' gift, cousin," he sniggered, pulling a packet of letters from his jacket pocket. "I intercepted them f-from Herr Bach a few m-months ago."

Charlotte was in shock. She immediately recognized them as Christian's letters, the ones she had never received. "*You* stole them. Give them to me!" she insisted. But as she tried to reach for them, Wilhelm held them high out of Charlotte's reach.

"I once t-told you I was g-going to knock you d-down a peg or two," he stammered, improperly touching the trim of the gown she was wearing, "Now t-take off that dress, Charlotte."

Had she heard correctly, she wondered, trembling and shaking her head. Yet it was as though her feet were affixed to the floor and her windpipe constricted with a dry wad. Wilhelm moved in closer with wicked thoughts running through his mind. "I said take off that dress."

Charlotte's breathing became sporadic and she was scared to death.

"Idiots. Adolph w-won't listen to any of my p-plans, the duchess ignores me until she n-needs something devious d-done. And you? You're just a w-whore in r-royal clothing."

"You're drunk and mad."

"You are the m-mad one—if you t-think I didn't see you and Bach turn the p-parlor into a b-brothel the night of your engagement p-party. I was there. D-do you think I h-haven't seen your lady b-bring you his letters?"

Charlotte's legs buckled beneath her and she began to lose strength. "No, we didn't…"

"…I s-saw him all over you m-myself. K-kissing you, touching you— and you, like a tramp, allowed it." Wilhelm crept closer, his face menacing, and his stutter more pronounced as he became more agitated. "I h-hated it. I always wanted the p-pleasure of your company myself. And t-today, I'm g-going to have it. You k-know why? B-because you do not w-want me t-telling my cousin t-that the stables of Mirow P-palace are a place to t-teach schwartzers to read." He narrowed his eyes. "Now, take off that dress."

Charlotte shook her head and tears rolled down her cheeks as Wilhelm unraveled the bullwhip. "Wilhelm, please…"

But Wilhelm popped the bullwhip angrily. "T-take the d-dress off now, dammit!"

Charlotte's eyes darted around looking for a way out. She was too high up to leap from the open window, and Wilhelm stood in front of the door so she could not run past him out of the room. She couldn't scream for no one was in the house. The princess cried in abject degradation and in one fast move, Wilhelm grabbed the front of her gown. When he yanked it, the beautiful dress ripped away in two torn pieces leaving Charlotte in only her bodice and under pantaloons. Crouching down she attempted to cover herself, crying openly.

"H-how does it feel, Charlotte? To be d-disrespected so. Doesn't feel g-good does it? Well, it's the way I am always m-made to feel. Adolph orders me around, my aunt orders me around, and you dismiss me. But today all that ends. You and that superior attitude of yours are g-gonna make up for all of that."

Charlotte found herself easing backward as her deranged cousin approached.

"You know you s-shouldn't consort with lower class lovers between your legs."

"No. Jon and I have never..."

But Wilhelm cracked his bullwhip. "Shut up! D-did I tell you to say anything? Did I?"

He grabbed the frightened girl's face. Charlotte managed to scream out. But the more she cried, the more maniacal Wilhelm became as he pinned the whimpering girl's body against the wall. Charlotte could smell his whisky-soaked breath as she tried to fight him off.

"Stop it, Wilhelm. Leave me alone, you bastard!" she screamed, finally slapping him hard across the face. Something snapped within him and Wilhelm forced her to the ground, ripping off her under-pantaloons. The fabric tore away like parchment paper as she sobbed hysterically. He forced Charlotte's arms back and fought her until she was completely out of breath. Sweat poured from her body as she heaved and gulped for air under his attack. Then Wilhelm unhooked his trousers and kicked out of them. Charlotte's head shook in disbelief. Wilhelm was going to ravish her. But would he kill her? Would she die?

"You—are going to be mine and m-mine alone. N-no more Christian, No m-more Jon. What I do t-today guarantees you will be unfit for consideration as any d-decent nobleman's wife. Then—*then*, you'll g-give me my respect and b-be all m-mine, cousin. Mine anytime I w-want," he spewed, grabbing Charlotte's breasts and kissing her like a savage beast until she was raw from pain and too exhausted to fight.

Her strength was gone and her breathing became difficult. She closed her eyes and prayed for it to be over quickly. But Wilhelm was possessed. He forced her legs open and tried to tear into her like an animal, pounding up and down on the girl for what seemed like eternity.

I was unable to look my stuttering assailant in the eye. I could only question God as to why this was happening and clench my fists hoping it would heal the swell of shame growing beyond my tears. I kicked then bit Wilhelm. But he slapped me so hard I ultimately submitted to his crazed lust out of sheer terror and bodily surrender—until all I saw was sweaty flesh on top of me blinding my guileless world. Until all I heard was Christian's incongruously cheerful music box echoing in my head along with the grunts and moans of Wilhelm's coerced copulation. Until all I smelled was perversion mixed with guilt and depravity. Until all I felt inside—was nothing. Nothing in my body. Nothing in my heart. Nothing in my soul.

Inexplicably, Wilhelm's body slumped on top of me, limp and enervated. He had failed to stiffen at the chance to deflower me, and his frustration was apparent. Finally he rolled off me sweating profusely. After a few moments, he angrily put on his pantaloons, went to my armoire, and snatched the packet of Christian's new letters.

"If you t-tell, I will have Jon Baptiste b-beaten and s-sold."

He started to go, then thought better. He turned back to me as I lay whimpering in a defiled pile of humiliation and pulled an object from his inside jacket pocket. When he showed it to me, my eyes widened, paralyzed by shock. "Incentive, d-dear cousin. I t-trust you'll heed my order for your s-silence, or you shall n-never, ever possess this which I know your heart yearns for—even more than your Mr. Bach."

It was the centuries-old gold amulet of my father—and Magragana ben Bekar. I stared at it as if it spoke to me in a language only we understood. It was a thing of beauty dangling from Wilhelm's fingers like a sunbeam from heaven. As he let it swing, I was hypnotized by the refractions of light bouncing from its surface. The strange symbols seemed to float off of it and swirl around me close enough to touch. But when I tried to, praying I could just hold it once more before I died, blackness descended and I fell unconscious.

In the end it would not be Christian, my kindhearted, sensitive, beloved, to whom I would have given myself freely and exclusively as his wife, but my mentally depraved cousin who violated my mind forever. My cousin, who warned me if I told anyone he would tell my mother I had fornicated with a Negro stable boy as well as Christian, who was deemed a commoner. My cousin who promised to have Jon sold into slavery, and threatened to reveal my correspondence with Christian as well as my planned elopement. And it was this same cousin who guaranteed my silence with his possession of the one thing that mattered to me beyond all understanding...the amulet. Thus hatred grew inside my once blameless heart...as did shame. The shame of violation and incestuous deviance.

They found Charlotte at seven o'clock that evening and realized she had been defiled. By then she had developed a high fever and her mother sent for Dr. Geisel. She floated in and out of consciousness and was so weak she couldn't move. Lady Schwellenberg sat with Charlotte all day, furious that she hadn't stayed with her on the day of her attack instead of enjoying the Feast of the Equinox as Charlotte had insisted.

Duchess Elizabeth was devastated. "What happened to her? How long will she be like this?" Charlotte heard her ask Dr. Geisel from her semi-conscious state.

"It appears she was molested. Bruises are all over her body, her neck, torso, thighs."

"Oh Lord, no. Please, no. Raped? Who would do such a thing?" the Duchess cried out. Then after a moment, she lowered her voice prudently. "She'll never be good for any aristocrat if she's ruined. No titled man wants a dishonored woman."

"I shall examine her more thoroughly once everyone leaves," Dr. Geisel informed.

Then Charlotte heard him—the voice which sent chills through her weakened, defiled body even as she lay there.

"I know w-what h-happened," said the familiar stutter.

"Tell me. Tell me this instant!" the duchess demanded.

Late the following day, two full days after her defilement, Charlotte finally awoke from her unconscious condition. Hearing noises on the grounds beneath the bedroom window she looked over and saw Lady Schwellenberg asleep in a corner chair having exhausted herself watching over her. The princess asked God for the strength to move from the bed so she could see the commotion. Struggling to get to her feet, she inched to the window praying not to vomit before getting there. But upon looking out, the scene on the lawn beneath her uncoiled every fiber of her being.

Jon Baptiste was tied to the whipping post. His feet were chained and his hands shackled above his head. Wilhelm mercilessly flogged him with his bullwhip as Charlotte's brothers, Christiana, aunt Albertina, the Duchess…and Sister Lena, in a state of hysterics, looked on. The sight was unbearable. Jon winced from pain. Each lash left an open slice of bloody flesh and each lash caused every servant watching this sadistic punishment to flinch in despair. Whap! Jon would cry out. Whap! More bloodcurdling screams.

"You black bastard," Wilhelm yelled. "I'll teach you to touch a royal woman again." Then Charlotte heard the bullwhip and Jon's screams until she couldn't take it. Jon was blamed for her violation. Yet the true transgressor stood as his accuser, administering the punishment.

"God, oh God, stop! He did not do it! He did not do it!" Charlotte cried out, beating at the window to get someone's attention, "Make them stop. Make them stop!" But no one could hear her from the upstairs window and it would not budge as she tried in vain to open it.

Then Charlotte heard, "I'll skin you alive!"

Sister Lena cried out. Finally, Lady Schwellenberg stirred awake. When she saw the princess at the window she panicked. "Your Highness what are you doing? You should not be out of bed." She leaped from her chair and tried to pull Charlotte away. But the girl found strength from some unknown source and pushed her Lady away. They both fell to the floor as Charlotte heard a barrage of cursing and verbal confrontation. She knew Jon was being brave, but surely he was terrified and in pain. But Wilhelm neither heard nor cared.

Suddenly a coil of fever and nightmares raged inside Charlotte. Her senses became clouded until she began to feel Wilhelm's bullwhip herself. She saw her own flesh rip open and bleed. Her screams obliterated reason as she envisioned her brothers, father, sister, mother, aunts, uncles, and grandparents standing with Sister Lena and every other Moor born under the African sun unjustly forced into secrecy, degradation or denial, take turns with the bullwhip as she was shackled, whipped and beaten like Jon.

All the sickening imagery and metaphors forced a pillow over Charlotte's head and her tears soaked through to the sheets but did nothing to blind her visions. It had to stop. She had to stop it. It had to be over. The whimpering of Jon's tribulations followed a dreadful silence, and Charlotte begged God to let her die that day. But she knew she would not. She knew as surely as she had been born a "blue-blooded Frederick" she would only awaken tomorrow and be forced into the pretense of 'All is well at Palace Mirow.'

Charlotte had to stop this cruelty. She pushed Lady Schwellenberg away and dragged herself up and out of her chamber door. She had just made it to the landing of the second floor stairs. "Hold on, Jon, I'm coming," she said, managing to walk down three steps without pain, "I'll tell them the truth. I'll tell them. It was Wilhelm. It was Wilhelm. It was Wil…"

But the world suddenly spun around her. The walls, stairs and banister became one enormous blurred jumble and her footing was uncertain. With one false move, she collapsed head first down the stairs like a rag doll, reeling, hurling, tumbling and striking every step until all there was left was total darkness, dead silence, and the twisted wreckage of her own body.

Eighteen

Anxious anticipation bubbled across Mecklenburg as news spread that the young King of England had dispatched Baron von Munchhausen to interview Princess Charlotte Sophia as a prospective choice for queen. Duchess Elizabeth's health was already on the decline since the horror of Charlotte's canceled engagement. Now, due to the stress brought on by her daughter's molestation, she was plagued with fever and dysentery. Yet, she gleefully received the news of Munchhausen's arrival by way of von Schulenburg's letter a week earlier. The Baron was due on 9 June, and Elizabeth was grateful she had spent what little money they had on the remodel for Charlotte's doomed engagement to Lord Gregory. Everything had to be just right.

The Duchess sent for Herr Byron Humbert, one of the best chefs in Germany, whose specialty was British cuisine. His instructions were simple—keep von Munchhausen's palate sated and his belly full. Elizabeth would not omit a single sensual pleasure if it meant her daughter would win his approval and her name be forwarded to the king with a recommendation.

In the excitement, however, no one bothered to consider the princess herself. Though her face still showed bruises from the fall and she suffered a sprained ankle, Charlotte's violation left her more scarred psychologically than physically. It was her mind attempting to mend the broken pieces of her soul that had not healed. She had planned to be with Christian by now, possibly married and traveling with him. But even as affectionate thoughts of Christian prevailed, others descended on her heart like a predator. She realized she could no longer envision herself with *any* man without seeing the malignant face of Wilhelm forever banishing her to the hell of her dishonor.

Then there was Jon Baptiste, who proved to be Charlotte's biggest regret. She remembered the day she opened her eyes after her fall. Most of her family was in the room. The first face she saw was Lady Schwellenberg's, then her mother, who was sitting on the bed caressing Charlotte's head as she held a letter in her hand.

"Charlotte, thank God you're finally awake. I received this letter and it's the best possible news..." started the Duchess.

"What day is it?" questioned Charlotte, still groggy and weak.

"It's the 25th. Oh Charlotte, this letter confirms that..."

But Charlotte was beside herself with despair. If it was the 25th she had missed meeting Christian before his scheduled departure for London. Now all was really lost.

"Oh no. Oh God no, I missed him. He's left Vienna by now."

"Who's left Vienna? What are you prattling on about? I have such excellent news."

Charlotte tried to stand but fell back onto the bed. "Where is Jon? I need to see Jon."

"Never mind him. This letter says that..."

"Where is Jon?" Charlotte insisted in a loud voice which irritated her mother. "Where?"

Elizabeth's expression tightened. "Gone...where he will never harm you again."

Charlotte tried to sit up, disbelieving. "Where did you send him?"

"To the colonies," she heard Adolph answer as he appeared in front of her with a leather pouch filled with German talers. "And for a handsome price I might add."

Charlotte was incredulous. "You *sold* him?"

"When Wilhelm told me of your violation by Jon, I, as ruler of this duchy, had him sold to a shipping captain in Anhalt who specializes in slaves bound for the colonies."

"You sold him to a slaver? To the colonies?"

"We had to," Duchess Elizabeth insisted. "We simply cannot abide a servant molesting a member of this family and remaining in our employ."

"But he did not molest me. Wilhelm did." She had finally said it.

"Wilhelm is marrying Lord Gregory's daughter, Helena. They will have their own castle and it will better align our family's finances! Now let us not discuss this unspeakable act again."

"Jon did *not* do this to me. He did not deserve to be sold. Wilhelm molested me."

"The subject is closed!" her mother snapped, coughing profusely. "Baron von Munchhausen, an emissary of King George III, is coming in one week to interview you as a candidate to be his bride. You'd be Queen of England," she insisted waving the letter in her hand. "This is what we have all waited, hoped and prayed for."

"You forever pray for money in return for my marital conquest. Last month it was for Lord Gregory. Now, it's for King George. I am not to be had just to satisfy this family's money crises."

"That is all you have to barter, foolish girl!" Elizabeth barked, "Thankfully, after a thorough examination we know you were not violated in such a way as to dishonor your virtue or candidacy."

"Dishonor *my* virtue or candidacy?" Charlotte echoed, her blood boiling. "Good Lord. The hypocrisy in this family is stunning," Charlotte spat. "Well, I've had quite enough. Enough of the debauchery, secrets, lies, insanity and discrimination in this family. Wilhelm molested me. Wilhelm. It was Wilhelm."

The princess fell back into the pillow, out of energy and spent from her tongue-lashing. She had infuriated her mother, and revealed her attacker as her cousin Wilhelm. She now realized that with this choice she might never see her father's beloved amulet again, and tearfully closed her eyes in frustration. Everyone stood in muted silence except Christiana who sobbed.

Charlotte anticipated being slapped. But Duchess Elizabeth, sitting in horror, finally forced a calm demeanor even though she did not know how to proceed. She wanted to strangle her daughter and prayed to God for the right words.

"Wilhelm...has an affliction which we all acknowledge and must help him through. It is the promise I made to my brother," she began. "But even with that, we all have our little secrets we don't wish others to know, so we don't discuss it. Charlotte, I have but one mission. I am forced to preserve this dynasty and its legacy. I also know that it is hard for you to accept the fate of most royal women—that of marriage to a man you do not know or care for. However, if you are lucky, you will come to love the man—as I did."

Duchess Elizabeth looked away for a moment wiping away just a hint of tears. "I was once in love with the Duke of Saxe-Gotha, but upon learning of my 'dark' lineage, he went fleeing. So when my father found a suitable candidate in Charles—who did not care about such things, my obligation to family dictated my plans." She finally looked back at Charlotte with a twinge of regret. "Now, obligation to family must dictate yours." The Duchess started for the door, then turned back. "You had better find a way to cope, and have on with your life."

I ceased to speak to anyone but my Ladies, and though I recovered well enough physically, an ill wind swept through me. Wilhelm was considered 'mentally afflicted,' a family blemish to be forgiven and helped. But Jon had been sold. Things would never be the same, and I began to feel the awful, haunting absence I experienced when father died. I recognized that any man I would come to love was destined to leave me, and I wondered if I would ever give my love to any man again for fear of losing them. This was underscored by the letter which Lady Schwellenberg brought to me that laid low my spirits and broke my heart.

The letter was from Johann Christian Bach with British stamps clearly affixed. Charlotte dismissed her ladies and sat on the bed to read it:

Dear Charlotte. Herr Chasin waited for you in Berlin for three days. When you did not show up he returned to Vienna where he informed me you were not coming. I stayed at the Rose Inn as long as I could before my departure for London became imperative. I can only hope that in changing your mind about our nuptials, you have not grown to disfavor me, or think ill of me for the suggestion of our elopement. I knew in my heart it would never truly happen, for you deserve a nobleman to love and be loved by. Still, my heart held out such hope for our future together. I do not think I will ever forget you no matter where I am. And I shall always love you deeply and forever. With sincere regret, Christian.

Charlotte felt numb, and it was a gestating mix of loss and apathy which prompted her to walk to the lake and seek an audience with God. She wanted forgiveness and to beseech his blessings. But, as if God ordained it, she took a different route, not toward Lake Ritouro, but toward the servants' quarters where she walked to the open door of Sister Lena's room.

Charlotte stepped inside and found the Jamaican woman rocking back and forth, staring into space. As she came closer the rocking immediately stopped and the princess came around the chair and looked at Sister Lena.

The Jamaican looked defeated. Her hair showed an inch of grey as though the trauma of Jon's departure had instantly turned it white. "What else you come ta take from me, chile?" she murmured.

"Nothing, Sister Lena. I'm so sorry. I couldn't get down the stairs in time to stop it."

Sister Lena lifted her eyes to meet Charlotte's; her stare stabbing through the girl's heart.

"You Fredericks all de same. You make a person feel dey kin do anyt'ing, 'ave anyt'ing. You put a dream in the mind, an' when you t'ink de dream come true, you Fredericks grind it up an' leave de pieces for someone else to handle. You, yer mother, an' especially yer father."

"My father? What does my father have to do with this?"

"Yer father de cause o' alla it!" Sister Lena snapped.

"How can you say that? He brought you, your mother and your brother James here to Mirow from the Gerhardt estate so you could be together and have a better life."

"Better life? You t'ink scrubbin', cookin', birthin' babies sun up ta sun down a better life? I was brought 'ere ta help wit you mother when she was havin' her time wit a baby. De baby die an' you mother was mean ta everyone. Next baby die, too. Your father do him best ta comfort that irritable woman, but de Duchess turned from him. An' when she do, he turned ta me."

Charlotte slowly reached out to the fireplace mantle to steel herself for support. She was shaking her head the whole while. "What do you mean 'turned to me'?"

Sister Lena pulled her tarot cards from her apron pocket. She began to arrange them on the table. Charlotte was incensed. "Tell me!" she threatened, "Or you'll never utter another word."

Lena shook her head and kept positioning the cards. "You nor you family kin hurt me, chile. My Jon be gone now—jus' like de cards foretol.' So you kin sell me, whip me, kill me. Sister already dead. Yer family 'ave taken my son from me—de onliest t'ing I loved. So you go tell you mother de sin of de father 'ave passed. Tell her she don' need ta hide her shame no more."

Sister Lena then turned over a card. It was the hangman's card, and it was upside down. For Charlotte this was inane gibberish and she couldn't comprehend what the conjure woman was trying to say. All she knew was that a chill ran through her body portending doom.

"What did you mean by 'turned to me'?"

"You not strong enough, Highness. You always had you father on such a high pedestal."

"I *am* strong enough, Sister. Your son showed me how much so."

"You mean yer *brother* showed you so!" Lena spat.

A horrible silence filled the room. Charlotte's throat constricted and she eased down on the cot. Lena placed the hangman's card face up on the deck and continued to position the tarot cards. "You father was a good man. But if him make a mistake, it don' matter, cuz it be taken care of. Jon was a mistake. But he loved Jon like he loved me—like all white, titled men love their blackamoors an' bastard offspring—only at night."

Charlotte shook her head in disbelief as Lena continued. "After you mother lose de third baby, she sleep in another room an' reject you father completely. He had put me in charge o' de kitchen an' laundry when I wasn't a midwife, an' sometimes he come down ta de kitchen fer food or drink himself. He always liked my spatzen an' I fix it whenever Charles wanted it."

Charlotte reacted to Sister Lena calling her father "*Charles.*"

"Sometimes he jus' wanna talk or have ale or wine. I listen. Then one day I read him cards. Dey say he have a secret. Charles tell me his secret— that he was given charge ta guard a great treasure, but de Duchess, she don't believe even though she herself have a secret almost as big. He ask me ta promise I never tell no one. An' I never did, til now. Charles tell me you mother's *real* father was a freed slave named Ibrahim Petrovitch Hannibal, a general in Peter the Great's army. He had been an Ethiopian prince abducted as a child, sold into slavery an' then freed as an adult. He have many mistresses, an' especially liked blond, German women. This man, Hannibal, used ta visit de Duchess' mother often, including nine months before de Duchess was born. An' *that*—was in addition to yer mother's descent from Magragana the Moor. Charles say fer years de Duchess' family cover it up an' pretend it was not de truth. So did de Duchess. That was her secret. Two lines of African descent—an' it eat at her. I promised ta keep this secret, an' de next day Charles 'ave a new dress delivered ta me. Next month, same t'ing. Den he move me from de room I share wit other servants—ta here. He knew I wanted my own hearth."

Lena wiped her eyes. The memory was so painful, and all Charlotte could do was listen for she *had* to know the whole story—the *true* story.

"Nineteen years ago, Charles come 'ere one night. I knew what was ta happen. I always knew cuz my cards tol' me. I was ta be his fer de takin'. Circumstances, trust, affection—all dese t'ings came together fer de moment. We never say a word—jus' a look sayin' I need you, if *only* tonight. He was so lonely, you father. All de children him 'ave. All de subjects him ruled over, yet he was like a thirsty man lost at sea, surrounded by de ocean, but not able ta drink de water. I step back ta let him in, an' de moment de door was shut—it happened.

Months later, I tell him I was to have him child. He was happy. He tell me he would make provisions fer me an' de baby. He say he make sure I could always have dis room an' my child would be treated well. But de night I give birth, he was not 'ere. Duchess, she announce she was wit child too, an' dey have a big party. My child come wit only de help o' a cook, my brother James, an' Joe Herford, the blacksmith—who say he always be 'ere fer me an' de baby."

Charlotte kept shaking her head. "No. I don't believe you. Not my father—and you."

"I lived in fear of reprisal—from de Duke if I tol' who sired my Jon—an' from de Duchess, who knew when she see my Jon have light skin...an' de mark o' Magragana."

Charlotte reacted to Jon having the mark, for it confirmed her father's actions.

"She come 'ere one night," continued Sister Lena. "She was eight months pregnant an' she barge in while I was feedin' Jon. She start hurlin' t'ings an' swearin' at me, tellin' me my child have de mark o' de devil, an' she gon kill it." Charles try ta calm her down, but de Duchess, she slapped me wit de back o' her hand wit a ring on it. She cut me bad."

Sister Lena touched the side of her face with the inch long scar on it. "De blood, make me furious an' I go ta speakin' in tongues. I hold out a finger an' I point at her an' say, 'You t'ink I don't know about Ibrahim Petrovitch Hannibal, or Magragana de Moor? Woman, fer de evil you do ta me today I curse you with yer worse fear what gon' come ta pass.'"

Charlotte sat spellbound as Sister Lena recounted that two months later, Elizabeth was in her time of lying in and as the midwives attended her she was screaming from the pain. Grand Duke Charles held her hand. But when the baby was born and presented to her, the expression on her face was of shock and dismay.

"She give birth to a daughter, an' dat daughter skin color come out brushed wit de Moor. De duchess never wanna accept de black in herself. But de baby's skin be darker than any o' her children. So she make de midwives take de baby away."

Charlotte's heart was skipping. "Me?" she asked in a small voice, knowing the answer.

Sister Lena nodded. "You everyt'ing she have been hidin' all her life. An' she hate you fer it. Still do."

Charlotte didn't know what to think about her father, her mother, or the lie that was her life.

"Yer mother abandoned you at first. So it was me who suckled you, me who raised you up like I done my Jon—like you was my own child. I knew you was one o' them. But you looked like one o' us...an' I loved you."

"And I have always loved you. You were always more like a mother to me than my own."

"It's why she still hate you. Hated my Jon too. She knew I possessed her husband an' her child in a way she never could. You father tell me one day that him would never send me or Jon away like de Duchess wanted, that he put it in him will that me an' Jon be here at Mirow as long as we live. I believed him. I never tell Jon who him father was—even though him grew ta look jus' like Charles. Every time I look at my Jon, I see Charles, an' I remember every moment of that night so long ago. So, I jus' let Jon t'ink Joe Herford was him father."

Sister Lena looked at Charlotte, whose face was drenched with tears. Charlotte remembered Jon's words from the first time they had a personal discussion, and it made her tremble now.

"…My mama usta say I was descended from kings…"

"Now my boy is gone. Sold off from 'ere t'inkin' him was in love wit you, an' dem t'inkin' he violated you. *You*—his own sister." Lena shook her head and cried.

Charlotte was overcome. She believed the story now and came over to take Sister Lena's hands. Both women were tearful.

"I don't know what to do. I feel so bad."

"You was put here fer a purpose having yer skin color," Lena added tearfully. "And no amount o' chalk, or wigs or hiding it will change anyt'ing. The moor in you cannot be denied. Magragana will not be denied. It's why yer father loved you most."

"I don't understand."

"Charles was vindicated wit yer birth. After all those years, spending all the family money tracing the truth of his African blood, and your mother rejecting it in her own, *she* was the one who birthed you. He didn't lay with *me* to make you dark. He laid with *her*—and you came out dark. You were his proof. God did it!" Sister Lena paused a moment and looked away. "But none 'o it will bring my boy back."

She snatched her hands away from Charlotte and went back to her cards. She turned over the High Priestess. Looking at it a moment her voice grew icy. "My boy *is* an aristocrat. According to yer own order o' precedence he should be 'Duke Jon Louis Baptiste Frederick.' But no." She pointed Charlotte to the door with an authority never exhibited before. "Go, now. Sister makin' plans."

Charlotte did as she was told. She slowly turned and walked away not knowing how to feel. Her beloved father had a mistress who bore him a child. Both lived beneath her mother's nose and were so different from them. The child became a man whom Charlotte counted on as a confidant and friend. That child was her half-brother. Suddenly hurt, anger and betrayal seized Charlotte's heart and hardened it. She could no longer trust—not the father whom she had loved since birth; nor the mother whose dispassion had pushed him into the affections of another woman. Nor could she trust that woman who was suffering the loss of her bastard son to whom Charlotte had introduced the concept of education and all its advantages, the most important of these being choice—the very thing Jon would never have now.

Charlotte hated that day. She hated everyone and everything about her life at Mirow. There could be no pretending that all was well. They were all guilty. They were all liars. She went back to her bedchamber and refused all food. It took Lady Hagedorn to force-feed her only because Lady Schwellenberg threatened to starve herself as well. Charlotte would speak to her sister and refused conversation with her mother or Adolph. Her mind became the fertile soil in which nightmares and vehemence germinated.

Four days later, Duchess Elizabeth came into Charlotte's room without benefit of knocking. She kept a handkerchief over her coughs and wildly gesticulated, "Get dressed. Our spies at Neustrelitz have informed us Baron von Munchhausen is expected here sometime this afternoon. Louisa, help Charlotte into the beige tabby. She looks good in that one," Elizabeth insisted, turning back to Charlotte. "Von Munchhausen is the King of England's emissary. He's going to interview you. It could mean a royal stipend for our family *if* you're chosen as queen." She narrowed her eyes. "I want you to do all you can to be charming and personable, do you understand? You are to arrest those farfetched notions you have about women, education, politics and any other such insanity and make yourself acceptable to his Lordship. If he asks you a question you are to *answer* him. That means you are to *speak*, Charlotte."

Charlotte only nodded as she had not spoken a word to her mother in days. Duchess Elizabeth moved in close to her daughter and added, "Lord Munchhausen has already interviewed the princesses of Brunswick-Wolfenbuttel and Anhalt-Dessau, who are far more beautiful than you, but for some reason were rejected, and at 25 your sister is too old. You have a chance, Charlotte. Make the most of it." Elizabeth turned to Lady Schwellenberg. "See to it she is in full paint for the interview. Apply it heavily, Louisa. I will not have Charlotte's swarthy complexion ruin things. Nothing must go wrong." The Duchess turned back to Charlotte pointedly, "*Nothing*, my girl."

After Elizabeth left the room Lady Schwellenberg looked at Charlotte who sat on her bed sadly. "Do not make yourself look so pitiful. Marriage to a king is not the worst thing in the world."

"Why should *I* be interviewed? Why cannot women choose?"

"But we *do* choose, milady," said Lady Hagedorn, "Every time we perform in coquettish ways to attract men, or smile demurely, or boost their spirits by telling them some innocent little white lie like how handsome they are when they look like frogs. Women have been ruling and subtly influencing men since Eve."

Suddenly, Christiana ran in crying hysterically. "Charlotte, come quickly. It's horrible. An awful, horrible thing."

I entered Sister Lena's room and my hand went to my face in disbelief. I had to hold onto Christiana to keep from falling. Sister Lena's lifeless body was hanging from the rafters, with one apron tie around her neck and the other around a beam. She had kicked the rocker from underneath her. How much pain must one be in to take their own life? I thought about Jon as I watched helplessly while his mother's body was lowered from the ceiling and taken from the room. I looked at her small table and saw the 'hanged man' tarot card still turned up—and upside down. Sister Lena had been used up by life and its discriminations. She had been hurt physically, emotionally, and socially, yet carried out the bravest, most powerful act: choice and control over her own demise. She chose to no longer be the property of we Fredericks and be her own human being. We had taken her life and her son's from her—and she had taken her own life back from us—and in that, I found her more courageous than anyone I knew. She had far more courage than I could muster, even with my travails. My eyes closed in prayer. If I was to die, I wanted to be like Sister Lena—and choose the day and method.

Inexplicably, in that moment, it came to me—the choice of my own death—marriage to an English king. It was the way I could leave Mecklenburg and the agony of my life. I thanked Sister Lena that day, and prayed for her soul, for she had helped me to kick the rocker of self-pity from beneath my cowardice.

Nineteen

"Get me dressed and ready immediately, Haggy," Charlotte instructed Lady Hagedorn in an insistent tone the moment she returned to her chambers. "My future depends on my skill as a thespian today."

Lady Hagedorn, in shock, turned to Lady Schwellenberg. "Who is this girl before us?"

Charlotte squeezed her Ladies' hands. "I love you both so much. You are the only ones who make me feel safe and protected. But I want to get away from here, and perhaps my doing well with this emissary from London will facilitate that."

"Are you certain about the reason you would want to go so far away to England if it happened?" asked Lady Hagedorn.

"I wish to leave for me," Charlotte finally answered. "For my own growth, for new experiences—and a chance to be happy."

Her ladies looked at each other. Though they knew she was lying, this was suddenly a new Charlotte, a more mature, determined Charlotte, and they understood. "Then let us do all we can to accommodate, my girl," said Swelly. "Let's get your performance polished. Shall we?"

✠

"Would you say you were generally a happy person, Your Highness?"

"I tend to be."

"And would you say you enjoy the company of family?"

"Very much."

Baron Phillip von Munchhausen wrote it all down, as well as his assessment of Charlotte's physical attributes, deportment, personality and the size and sophistication of the court of Mirow. Duchess Elizabeth and Grand Duke Adolph were also present in the receiving room as Munchhausen conducted his interview, and Elizabeth's coughs could occasionally be heard over the Baron's questions.

"Tell me about your spiritual life. What is your religious practice?"

"I am Lutheran. We are all Lutherans here."

"And the Lutheran doctrine consists of what?"

Charlotte was careful. One wrong word here could end it all. It had only been three hours since she'd seen Sister Lena's dead body hanging in ultimate defiance in her room, and two weeks since her molestation, fall, and Jon's sale. She desired to leave Mecklenburg no matter the circumstances. It was her paramount desire.

"Lutheranism is a branch of Protestant Christianity that identifies with the teachings of the 16th-century German reformer Martin Luther. We teach that salvation is possible because of the grace of God made manifest in the birth, life, suffering, death, resurrection, and continuing presence of the power of the Holy Spirit, of Jesus Christ." She saw Munchhausen's eyes glazing over, then smiled politely. "But, if any of this poses a problem, Lord Munchhausen, I am more than willing to join the Church of England if that is the king's desire."

Congenial and soft spoken, Charlotte answered the questions almost by rote, with responses she knew Munchhausen would relay favorably to King George. She had been rehearsed by Lady Schwellenberg and Lady Hagedorn, and was prepared for most of them. As for the others, she took her cues from her mother's slight nods or shakes of the head as Elizabeth was sitting just behind Baron von Munchhausen's left shoulder.

"Now then, Princess Charlotte, do you feel when a woman marries that she should be helpful with her husband's work?" Munchhausen continued.

Charlotte paused a moment to look at her mother. "Say the right thing" seemed to be the message given in Elizabeth's eyes as they narrowed.

"I do. I think providing a suitable home and hearth filled with his children, as well as an abundance of love, is what is most helpful to a husband's work."

Von Munchhausen jotted this down, smiling to himself. Elizabeth was pleased, as was Adolph. Charlotte was, of course, lying, but she no longer cared. If marriage to an English king got her out of Mirow and away from all this, she would say or do anything. Munchhausen was now the obstacle standing between her and the thing she desired—escaping Mecklenburg.

Soon Munchhausen walked to her and began to inspect her closely. Though her face was under heavy make-up, her neck and hands gave away her true color, and Munchhausen's eyes squinted as he perused her. "Rather dusky, aren't you?" he said, as though she were not there.

Duchess Elizabeth cringed, shooting a deadly look at Lady Schwellenberg, but quickly spoke up. "Our Charlotte spends far too much time at the Lake in the sun without her bonnet."

The Baron nodded, then looked back at Charlotte. "Is this true, Your Highness?"

"Indeed. It causes me to burn easily."

Munchhausen finished his tea and turned to Duchess Elizabeth, "Your Grace, I wonder if I may be permitted to speak to the Princess alone."

"Alone? Is that proper?" Duchess Elizabeth asked, somewhat taken aback.

Munchhausen was reassuring. "There are some delicate questions I must ask the Princess and, in my experience, sometimes the presence of others does not engender a spirit of honesty."

Duchess Elizabeth looked at Adolph, who nodded. She snapped open her fan and, with much chagrin, left the room. The others left as well.

Once the doors were shut, Munchhausen poured tea for himself and the Princess and sat across from her at the table. He studied her for a moment, and Charlotte did not shy away.

"Princess Charlotte," he started tentatively, "I am instructed to inquire on a number of personal subjects which may strike at your sense of propriety."

"Seek what you've come for, Lord Munchhausen," said the princess, preparing for the worst. "The quicker it is done, the quicker we shall both lose our apprehensions."

"Very well. Your cycle. Is it regular?"

From outside the closed door Duchess Elizabeth and Adolph were listening with their ears pressed to the wood. The fan Elizabeth had slapped to her face upon hearing the personal question thankfully muffled her gasp. Charlotte, meanwhile, took pause. She placed a hand over her heart as she voiced her realization. "I see. *These* kinds of personal questions."

Munchhausen nodded and kept his eyes downcast to his notebook.

"Yes. I am quite regular," the princess finally conceded. "You can set the seasons to me."

"And men. Have you... known a man yet? What I mean to say is...in the biblical sense?"

"No. I have not." It was true, and she said it with a straight face, for her violation by Wilhelm thankfully had not resulted in penetration.

Munchhausen wrote it down. "Do you have visions? Or talk to ghosts? Or does any member of your family seek audience with the spirit world?"

Charlotte frowned slightly. "No. I have no such affliction," she answered with confidence, "nor does any member of my family as far as I know."

"And do you feel compelled to know about the inner workings of government? Or wish women could be more of an influence or take part in the formulation of laws or policies?"

"Why you ignominious dunderhead." I wanted to blurt out to him, "Of course women should have more influence. We should rule most countries. Were I Queen of Prussia with the rights and power of sovereignty, do you think I would follow my supercilious sodomite cousin Frederick's example and hurl us into a war which has lasted some five years and left this country poorer in resources, reviled on the world stage, and unprogressive in industrial invention? Not to mention the loss of life. 'Tis the foolishness of men that causes them not to listen to the sometimes ingenious ideas of women, or rebuke their uncanny ability to use their intuitive natures which can make a man's life easier. You force us into the very cultural rituals that devalue and imprison our true personalities, then you deny us—the most valuable asset you have!

However, my true response was:

"I find the inner workings of government and politics and such things are better left to men. But speaking of influence, I do feel we women assert just the tinniest bit of influence…"

Munchhausen held his breath. So did the Duchess and Adolph from behind the door as they listened. Would this be Charlotte's undoing?

"…because we do cause men to fall in love with us. Do we not?" Charlotte mused.

Duchess Elizabeth and her son breathed sighs of relief. Baron von Munchhausen grinned, closed his notebook and stood. The Princess of Mecklenburg had answered his questions with such charm and wit he thought perhaps he was having visions himself. He humbly asked for a lock of her hair, which Charlotte obliged. Then, as he was on his way out, Charlotte's aunt Albertina gave the Baron a locket with a miniature painting of Charlotte's image inside. As Munchhausen said his goodbyes he was already formulating parts of the report he would later write to King George from Mecklenburg Manor:

10 June, 1761
His Royal Majesty, King George III
St. James Palace, London, England

Your Majesty,
    In my humble opinion we have at last found one suitable candidate in Her Serene Highness Princess Charlotte Sophia of Mecklenburg-Strelitz. While I agree that she is not the most alluring of the now twenty-eight princesses I have thus far interviewed, I must admit that I have the utmost confidence in her character and abilities. Thus I am including a locket with her image given me by her aunt, as well as a lock of the Princess's hair for your perusal.

When he finished and was satisfied with his correspondence, he placed the letter in an envelope and dripped the wax tallow onto it. He sealed the letter with his personal stamper which left an engraved "VM" in the cooling wax, and placed it on a stack of letters bound for posting.

Finally, von Munchhausen allowed himself to have the best night of sleep he'd had in months.

Twenty

As Munchhausen's letter made its voyage through the maze of protocol to the king, the sovereign himself was having second thoughts about marriage to anyone but Lady Sarah Lennox. While he stood at the window of the drawing room at St. James palace with Sarah on his mind, he was forced to listen to the blathering of his Prime Minister, William Pitt.

"Your Majesty, you have been king since 25 October of last year, and both the Cabinet and the Privy Council thought it best to postpone your coronation for when there was a queen," the Prime Minister droned. "You can understand that we are concerned that at this late date, there is still no candidate for queen, and we are also concerned that we have been left out of the elimination process. So we must set a coronation date and we have chosen 22 September—queen or no queen. We will make all the necessary arrangements and hope this date will be acceptable to Your Majesty."

George rubbed his temples, nodded, and with a wave indicated Pitt should go. The Prime Minister bowed and backed out of the room. Once Pitt was gone, George looked at the oak end table where the crown jewels sat. He intended to present the jewels to his new bride as a wedding present, hoping it would be Lady Sarah. Then he thought about all he'd gone through to acquire them. The collection included a diamond stomacher, several rings, bracelets, and the queen's crown once worn by Queen Anne herself. It had been the property of his grandfather, King George II, whose complicated English and German wills resulted in his only surviving son—George's uncle, William Augustus, Duke of Cumberland—receiving one half of the jewels, and young George the other. But the Duke of Cumberland had recently found himself ill and in debt, and because he was unmarried, he allowed his nephew to purchase his half for £50,000. George now owned the entire collection of crowned jewels, and he envisioned Lady Sarah dressed in them.

The crown would be on her head, and her bosoms would be heaving under the large diamond necklace gleaming on her cleavage. He fantasized her coming toward him with her arms outstretched for his embrace, her mouth moistened by his kisses. He could taste her tongue caressing his while her silken skin melted under his touch. Then he undressed her except for the jewels and made love to her on the settee with reckless abandon. God how he wanted her. But when he opened his eyes from his fantasy, Lord Bute was standing there with a letter in his hand.

"Your Majesty, it is the best possible news."

George took the letter and read it. Showing no outward signs of emotion, he handed it back to Bute. "Very well. It shall be the Princess of Mecklenburg." He turned from Bute with a look of resignation. The decision was made. His life would be in keeping with English law. The matter was now past.

Bute knew this was the right resolution for the king, yet he saw great sadness in George and felt for his charge. "Your Majesty, you do not appear pleased about this decision."

"I am not pleased, Lord Bute. But one does what one must." George then reached out and patted Bute's shoulder. "Do not worry. I shall be happier when the queen is actually here. Alert Colonel Graeme and have my mother plan the announcement party."

Bute left as George went back to the window, gazing at the beauty of his gardens. He closed his eyes and prayed for a way to live with his decision…and without Sarah.

Ten days later, Augusta arranged a most elegant announcement party. A string quintet played as George stood with his mother, siblings, Lord Bute and his wife Baroness Bute.

"…French Plenipotentiary Minister Chevalier Charles Louis D'Eon and the Countess of Yarmouth…" announced the palace crier as handsome Minister d'Eon escorted Lady Yarmouth over to the king. He bowed while Lady Yarmouth kissed each of George's cheeks.

"Your Majesty, thank you for inviting me and for sending your grandfather's bequeath so quickly. It allows me to remain here in London and to enjoy his memory for the rest of my life."

"You're most welcome, Lady Yarmouth,," George replied with a nod to d'Eon. As Lady Yarmouth and d'Eon moved on, Augusta leaned in close to George with gossipy delight. "Foolish woman. Had she been more clever she could have been queen."

The crier announced other guests: "...Sir Henry Fox, Lady Caroline Lennox-Fox, Lady Susan Fox-Strangeways and Lady Sarah Lennox of Holland House..."

George looked over and suddenly everything moved in a slow blur. All eyes were on Sarah since every courtier at the palace knew the king was now betrothed to marry anyone *but* her. George could not take his eyes off of her, and Sarah had expressly designed it that way. She made sure the fullness of her form would be revealed by her dress, she doused herself in French perfumed oils and powdered herself with the finest silk powder. Her makeup was perfection: her eyelashes were beaded black and her lips were pouty and glistening with rouge. Sarah intended to drive George mad, so no matter what choice he made for a wife, she ensured her lingering on his mind for all eternity.

Her plan was working. She floated to George just as she had done in his fantasy—and she was beautiful. But after her deep, respectful curtsey, her eyes narrowed upon meeting his.

"Your Majesty, I am so delighted you have at last found the 'proper' woman to marry," she said with words dripping in sarcasm, "May you have all the happiness you so justly deserve."

George knew she was still hurt by his decision and the way he announced it to her last winter. The image of her storming out of the palace heartbroken, maligned, and in a fit of betrayal was ingrained in his soul, and he understood every bit of her derision toward him. Still, he loved her. He missed seeing her at court, and his longing for her was deeper than ever. He wondered, as he perused her beautiful face, if he could truly ever give her up.

"Thank you, Lady Sarah," he said, aware he was the object of focus. "How is your leg?"

"Mended—much like my heart."

George flinched slightly. The swipe hit its mark. Sarah nonchalantly glided away to a chair at the head of the dancers' bench, which allowed any eligible gentleman of the court to dance with the eligible ladies seated there. Sir Henry Fox, standing with his wife Caroline, his sister Susan, and Sarah's sister Lady Emily, admired the antics. Still incensed with the king, Sir Henry was enjoying every bit of his sister-in-law's performance and smugly grinned while Lady Sarah danced with Sir Alfred Newcastle, with whom she feigned ease. As far as Sir Henry was concerned, the king deserved whatever he emotionally experienced for subjecting Sarah to derision and humiliating social ridicule. It was high time George discovered for himself what it felt like to be made a fool of, and Sir Henry deduced the king was feeling just that.

He was right. Though George continued to greet other guests, his attention constantly pulled to Sarah. She, too, looked at him from time to time, yet turned away continuing to dance.

George began to fume. "Bloody son-of-a-bitch," he murmured to himself as he watched the couple dance until the music indicated a change of partner. He watched as Lady Sarah allowed Sir Thomas Charles Bunbury, a Member of Parliament, to dance with her twice, further exacerbating his frustration. Six months ago he had ruined both their lives with his decision. Now he was without her. Five times he tried to see her. Five times she refused. He wrote letters professing his undying love. She never responded. Soon, George began drinking the port. After three glasses in rapid succession, Augusta motioned to Bute who went to him.

"Sire. Your vexation is palpable," Bute whispered furtively to George.

"Fucking Bunbury. He's taking full advantage of my feelings."

"No. Sarah is, and do not allow it to consume you. Everyone is watching."

But upon seeing Sarah dance four times with Bunbury, George could no longer control himself. He angled toward Sarah despite Bute's admonishments, and stood in front of her, his expression unyielding. He held out his hand commanding she dance with him.

Sarah used the moment to full advantage, eventually flipping open her fan and curtsying coyly when she was good and ready. George's look to Bunbury burned like fire, suggesting he leave. The MP, realizing he was being dismissed, moved away out of respect. Courtiers raised their fans, whispering and pointing discreetly as George pulled Sarah to him and they danced. Halfway through, his fingers laced through hers as he looked languishingly into her eyes.

"Why will you not see me?" he whispered.

"I do not wish to, Your Majesty," Sarah retorted trying to stay composed.

"Sarah, please, I need to see you. You know I still have the deepest affections for you."

"I have no interest in your affections, deep or otherwise," she snapped. "But if you would like, you may go and share them with the German bitch you chose."

George reacted, and had to force himself to maintain his composure. Sarah, realizing she was not capable of a civil tongue, started to leave, feeling her emotions welling up inside. But George held her tighter still, his grip nearly bursting a blood vessel in her forearm. "No. I shall not let you go. You're no good for any man but me. You know that."

From across the room, Sir Henry Fox leaned in to his wife upon observing the tête-à-tête.

"I do believe the king still shows the slightest regard for our dear Sarah."

"It would appear so," Lady Fox resolved. "Could it be Sarah still has a chance?"

But the moment the words were spoken, Lady Sarah wriggled out of the king's grip and maneuvered out of the room into the nearby salon to collect herself. George, far too intrigued and stiffened by her withdrawal, excused himself and, despite stares and whispers, followed her. The moment he entered the room Sarah tried to hurry away, but George rushed toward her taking her arm. She held out her fan for him to stop and tried not to sob in front of him. "Please stop, George. Do not come any closer less I burst from emotion."

"Sarah. I cannot bear it. Why do you refuse my letters, my requests? I have told you, what I do, I must do for England."

"And I have told you I loathe and despise you for your decision. You are king. You can determine your own destiny. Yet you allow Bute, your mother and any other privy council to control and advise you. It's precisely why I hate you, George. I hate you."

George was overcome with emotion, turning Sarah to him. "No. You love me."

"I loathe you."

"You love me. Tell me you do." His mouth covered hers with kisses. "Tell me!"

But Sarah slapped him. George, though stunned, kept after her, forcing her mouth to his, kissing her again and again. Sarah slapped him again, trying to struggle from his kisses until the fight left her body. She collapsed in resolution and began returning his kisses. Her fingers dug into his flesh from tearful surrender until she drew blood. George winced, feeling her emotional resignation and the pain her fingernails engendered. But still he held her tightly.

"I do love you. God help me," Sarah cried hopelessly. "But I cannot allow myself to be your mistress. I deserve better. I deserve to have someone committed to me, George. *Me*."

She then pulled away, glaring at her beloved. "I have decided this very night to marry Sir Thomas Bunbury. It will be to *him* I willingly give myself and *his* bed I will gladly share." She cupped her breasts and hurled a final blow. "And it will be *he* who can ravage and enjoy every morsel of *these*, which you so willingly sacrifice—for England."

Sarah wiped her eyes, pointing her fan at the king. "And do not forget the rules of Precedence dictate that at your wedding, the bride must be attended by the highest-ranking unmarried lady in the land. As there are no unmarried princesses, it means the eldest unmarried daughter of the highest-ranking duke who has any unmarried daughters. That is the 2nd Duke of Richmond, which means, dear George, that *I* become the queen-to-be's maid of honor at your wedding." Sarah laughed with icy satisfaction. "I shall have the supreme delight of watching you cast your eyes upon your bride wishing she were me, whilst I witness it first hand."

At that, she smoothed her gown, forcing some semblance of composure, and curtsied. "Good evening, Your Majesty." Then she turned and left the room.

When George regained his repose, he returned to the drawing room and discovered that Lady Sarah had called for her coach and, together with Lady Susan, was departing the palace, leaving everyone sated in suspense. For the rest of the evening, King George had to make do with small talk and subtle glances while the object of his desire cried her eyes out in her coach.

Twenty One

Just after midnight on the evening of the 24 June 1761, there came a loud pounding at the door of the ducal residence of Mirow. The dogs began barking, causing Duchess Elizabeth, nauseous and frightened, to fumble for her over-robe and call out to Old James. Adolph ran down the stairs fearing the worst, as only bad news arrived at such an ungodly hour.

"Who is there?" Old James bellowed.

"Colonel David Graeme of the Scottish Brigade, in the service of the United Provinces," answered the voice in an official timber.

Adolph motioned for Old James to open the door. There stood a tall, ruddy-faced man with bushy whiskers, holding official correspondence bearing the seal of the King of England. "I carry a letter from the Princess Dowager of Wales to the Duchess Dowager Elizabeth Albertina Frederick. I have been instructed to place it in the hands of the Duchess herself."

"I am Grand Duke Adolph Frederick," responded Adolph. "The duchess is unwell. I shall take it up to her with haste."

"I am sorry, my Lord Frederick, but my instructions are clear. I must place the letter in the hands of the duchess dowager personally, in the name of the King of England."

"It's all right, Adolph. I shall accept the letter," said a weak voice from behind them.

Duchess Elizabeth somehow managed to struggle down the stairs to the landing. Adolph assisted his mother as she painfully went to the door.

"I am Duchess Elizabeth." She then motioned to Graeme. "Step inside, Colonel. The air is too chilly here in the doorway."

Graeme bowed and came inside, then handed the Duchess the letter. When she read it she clutched her breast. "Good Lord," she exclaimed, finding the nearest chair to sit upon. "It's a marriage contract. Our Charlotte is the king's choice."

Having heard the commotion, Charlotte eased out of her bedchamber and stood at the top of the stairs. She could not believe what she heard. Of all the princesses in Germany, she was the King of England's choice as his queen. She knew she would have to accept this appointment for, unlike Lord Gregory, this would be a much more powerful, influential servitude, but servitude nonetheless. Charlotte's mother and brother had conspired and planned her life with a man she had never met and didn't love. They were sending her to a country where she did not know the language or customs. She had been bartered away the same way they bartered Jon's life away—for money. It was just another form of prostitution where a woman traded her dowry in return for childbearing and the security of home, hearth and companionship.

Charlotte thought about how lucky her sister was to be beyond the age of acceptance as a wife. She could come and go as she pleased without the encumbrance of wifely duties.

Adolph showed Colonel Graeme into the library and instructed the nurse to assist his mother to a chaise near them. While Adolph poured brandy Graeme continued his business.

"I have been empowered to make clear that the king's final decision rests on the duchess' response to certain points in the letter of negotiation. First, the king insists the marriage take place quickly, by proxy, and that the official wedding ceremony be conducted in London prior to their coronations. Will that pose a problem, Your Grace?"

"It will not," the Duchess responded, coughing profusely.

How dare they, Charlotte thought. Was she not even allowed to meet her future husband before she married him? No. She was to be the handpicked vessel—the royal portal—through which the king's future *assets* would flow. What if he was a repulsive, violent man given to beating women? What impudence, Charlotte felt, growing angrier and angrier as she listened.

"...And the princess can only bring two femmes de chambres to attend her as England will not accept foreigners to appointments in the court of St. James," Graeme continued.

Fury rose up within Charlotte again. To add insult to the scheme, they were negotiating how many assistants she could take with her to a place from which she would never return.

Charlotte had enough. Before anyone could respond she walked into the room and, with a newfound confidence gleaned from God knew where, she informed them of her own decision.

"Colonel, I must insist upon one or two conditions of my own."

They all turned to her with shocked, perplexed expressions, the likes of which were worth the price of admission. Adolph rushed over, surprised Charlotte was out of bed.

"Charlotte, we have wonderful news. This is Colonel David Graeme in service to King George III. *You* are the King's choice. *You* are to become Queen of England. Isn't wonderful?!"

Charlotte was gracious, but firm. "I am pleased I'm the king's choice, but I must insist upon bringing Sir Albert with me in addition to Lady Schwellenberg and Lady Hagedorn."

Adolph and her mother were as stunned as Colonel Graeme; and the look on Charlotte's face was resolute. For the first time in 17 years she had a strength of will.

"I am most insistent upon this point and will be discomforted by *any* other arrangement."

The Colonel cleared his throat and stammered. "I—I am certain your request will be taken under consideration, Your Highness."

"You will place it into the marriage contract if indeed the king wishes for there to *be* a marriage." Charlotte responded emphatically, "After all, this is a negotiation, is it not?"

"And I would like to inquire about the amount of our stipend," the Duchess added.

"Six thousand talers." answered Colonel Graeme cockily.

"They will accept nine," responded Charlotte with equal cockiness.

The Colonel nodded slightly and wrote it down. Duchess Elizabeth and Adolph actually smiled at Charlotte who curtsied politely and left the room. This allowed her mother and brother to finish discussing the rest of the contract. At least she would have what she wanted—friends she trusted with her on this uncharted journey.

When she reached the top of the stairs Christiana was there and hugged her. "Charlotte! What you said, how you said it, it was magnificent! I am so proud of you!" Then she said something that put the experience into perspective for Charlotte. "Maybe you can utilize your position to alter perceptions about women. You will be a queen, Charlotte."

Charlotte took solace in Christiana's words and held them as motivation, for she would receive the last and final indignity the next morning after breakfast. The princess was brought into the reception hall to find the Colonel and another gentleman. Her entire family was present. Adolph led her to Colonel Graeme and the gentleman. The Duchess was too ill to rise. "Charlotte, you have already met Colonel Graeme. This is Doctor von Stockmar," said Adolph. "He will be your physician and accompany you to England. He will also examine you today for His Majesty's assurance you are still intact."

"Intact?" Charlotte repeated, her heart pounding hard enough to appear visible through her dress.

Baron von Stockmar, an older man with thinning hair and thick glasses, offered clarity.

"His Majesty must be confident his bride is virtuous and...unknowing...of the carnal aspects of men."

"'Unknowing of the carnal aspects of men?'" Charlotte repeated in her head. Why could he not just say it? A virgin. All any man was interested in was carnal pursuits, yet they placed such a premium on virginity with their perspective wives. Charlotte's nostrils flared and indignation stained her cheeks. This was the ultimate humiliation—an examination of her private person to prove her physically worthy for a sovereign who had yet to meet her. Was *he* intact? Was *he* a virgin? Suppose she was interested in a man unknowing of the "carnal aspects" of a woman?

Charlotte was trembling. But as she grabbed Christiana's hand she thought of her words from the previous night, *"You could change things, Charlotte,"* and she found not only her voice, but her resolve. "I am afraid an examination shall have to wait."

Everyone froze. Dr. Stockmar looked at Colonel Graeme, who shook his head in agitation as Charlotte continued. "I, as a woman, would be far too uncomfortable in such a delicate situation of propriety as this without my *own* doctor present." She turned to Adolph. "Send for Dr. Geisel. Tell him to hurry. The next Queen of England requires his assistance."

Charlotte made them wait until Dr. Geisel arrived some three hours later. They retired to Charlotte's chambers where she was subjected to the impersonal and degrading probing of Doctor Stockmar, whose fingers were as cold as his bedside attitude. This time she was squeezing Dr. Geisel's hand, praying for it to be over. When the doctor finished his examination of her womb, he looked at Charlotte's mother, sitting weakly on a nearby settee.

"The hymen is intact, Your Grace," he said with cool professionalism, "She is virtuous and capable of childbearing thereby satisfying our requirements for marriage."

At that, Dr. Stockmar left without further comment to Charlotte. Her own Dr. Geisel patted Charlotte's hand thoughtfully. "As I shall not see you again, I wish you a safe journey, a good marriage, and perfect, healthy children." He bowed and left. Duchess Elizabeth came over and gave Charlotte a kiss on the forehead. Though she began to cough profusely, she, too, left my room without further comment. Once she was gone, Charlotte fell into a hail of tears. Dear Lady Schwellenberg held her lovingly. "There, there, It's all over."

Two weeks later, Charlotte stood before a minister performing the *By-Proxy* wedding ceremony. She was is in full make-up and wearing a hastily designed white gown. Standing next to her was Colonel David Graeme, standing in for the king; and on the other side of her was her brother Grand Duke Adolph who was giving her away. All of the Frederick family members were present—including Wilhelm. Christiana was teary-eyed as she stood serving as a bridesmaid.

Duchess Elizabeth sat on a nearby chaise for she was too ill to stand or participate. She looked piqued but was satisfied. Her daughter had saved the family. She was becoming Queen of England and all was right with the world.

Soon, the minister closed his bible and bowed to Charlotte as did Colonel Graeme. "La Reine," the Colonel declared, "Your marriage to King George is complete and solemnized by proclamation. God save the Queen!"

Everyone bowed in reverence, then declared in kind, "God save the Queen!" and in 45 minutes Charlotte had gone from Her Serene Highness Charlotte Sophia Albertina Frederick—to Her Royal Majesty Queen Charlotte Sophia Frederick Hanover, of Great Britain and Ireland.

Though Charlotte felt no differently, she immediately noticed how her eminence as Queen affected everyone else. Suddenly Lady Schwellenberg and Lady Hagedorn no longer referred to her as "My girl," or "Charlotte," but "Your Majesty" and they constantly bowed in supplication to her. After a week Charlotte gave them permission to maintain their colloquial natures with her when they were alone. She did not wish to be so exalted she no longer had genuine friends or truthful, trustworthy companions. Though they were in service to her and she wanted their respect, she had chosen them to accompany her on her journey to England because they had a shared history.

While Charlotte's valises and boxes were being packed the princess tried to learn all she could about Britain, its policies, and the language.

As she was practicing some basic English sentences one evening, there came a knock at the door. It was Adolph, who was forlorn. "Charlotte, it's mother. It won't be long now."

The princess immediately rushed to her mother's bedchamber where Christiana, Ernest, Aunt Albertina, Charles, George and Wilhelm had surrounded her bedside. After exchanging faint words of goodbye to each of her children, the Duchess motioned Charlotte forward.

Charlotte knelt by her mother's side, taking her hand. The Duchess' voice was barely above a whisper, but definitive. "You are now queen, and it is all I could form to myself as satisfaction. You have exceeded all my expectations, and are anything but ordinary."

A compliment? Had Charlotte lived long enough to hear one from her mother? She was in shock as she watched the Duchess motion for Adolph to fetch a package in a nearby armoire and give it to her. When Charlotte opened it she found two beautiful red leather diaries with blank parchment pages.

"Keep a journal. Your father kept one. It is how I discovered his feelings for...she, who is no longer here." She stopped a moment to collect herself and not become angry about Sister Lena. "Write, my dear. It will help you through times when the hardness of your new position becomes untenable." She then looked at Charlotte's un-powdered face. "And do not forget your paint, dear girl."

Charlotte nodded and promised she would not. Her mother motioned to everyone else.

"I need...to speak...to Charlotte alone, please."

Everyone quietly left. But the Duchess stopped Wilhelm. "Except you. You...stay."

Once her family was gone, Charlotte's mother held out her hand to Wilhelm. "Give it... to me. I know you still have it. And I know what you do... to our servant girls, you pig."

An expression of guilt enveloped Wilhelm's face as the Duchess' fingers waved threateningly at him, beckoning him to comply. Wilhelm grunted, then removed a handkerchief from his pocket which seemed heavy and gave it to the Duchess. Charlotte watched her fragile mother open the handkerchief out of which fell...

...The gold amulet.

"Now get the chest from the vault," the Duchess ordered. Her cousin stared at her yet dutifully moved the armoire back revealing the wall vault in which sat the other object of Charlotte heart's desire—the carved wooden chest. Wilhelm brought it to the bed and started out of the room. Charlotte stopped him. "Wait. Where are my letters from Christian?" she demanded.

"Burned," spat Wilhelm who left without further word.

Charlotte was crushed. Her mother sighed through her pain, "We cannot help who we are as a result of our birth." She caressed the amulet then looked up at Charlotte. "He kept secrets from me, your father," she said indicating the amulet. "This has been a source of consternation all my life, and his. It was handed down...through my family for over a millennia...and the reliquary passed down through his. Our genealogies connected three generations ago." The Duchess put the amulet into Charlotte's hand, wrapping her fingers around her daughter's. "Good or bad, right or wrong, these are yours now. Your father's journals are in there. They will answer your questions, for you can no longer plead ignorance upon knowing what is there."

"Mother. I know about Ibrahim Petrovitch Hannibal," Charlotte confessed quietly.

The Duchess developed a resigned look on her face Charlotte never forgot.

"Then Lena told you everything you shall ever need to know. Rightly or wrongly."

Charlotte's mother then sank onto the pillow and closed her eyes forever.

On 2 July 1761, my mother, Duchess Elizabetta Albertina Frederick, age 48, was buried in the cemetery of the old Parish church. As I stared at the mound of dirt under which mother would reside next to my father for eternity, I clutched the amulet proudly.

Out of respect, King George waited for three days after mother's funeral to dispatch Lord Simon Harcourt to escort me and my cortege to England. For this duty, Lord Harcourt would become my Master of the Horse, an honored position at court. The king also dispatched two British women to accompany me—the Duchess of Hamilton, and the Duchess of Ancaster. They, too, would receive special appointments in my home once we arrived safely in London.

On 10 August I looked from the window and saw the official Hanoverian state coach sent by His Majesty pull up in front of Mirow. Along with it were six covered chariots to transport my cortège and luggage to Stade. From there we would embark on our journey across the North Sea, then down the Thames aboard the HMS Royal Charlotte.

Christiana, who was standing next to me, kissed my cheek. "I shall never see you again," she sighed, her eyes watering.

"No, no. I shall see you again. I promise."

But Christiana knew better. "No, Charlotte. You will be the consort of the most powerful sovereign in the world. You can no longer come and go as you please."

We hugged, then Colonel Graeme escorted me to the carriage, where I had father's carved chest placed safely on top. I said goodbye to my brothers Charles, Ernest and George, and kissed Aunt Albertina. Then I reached out for Adolph, who came over and presented me with father's favorite sword, intricately adorned with red Templar crosses. I thanked him and we, too, hugged. "I'm going to miss you terribly," he whispered as I wept in his arms. "I will write you every month."

"And I shall write you back. I promise," I replied.

We lingered in our embrace for an eternity. "Just remember what I told you months ago," he grinned. "Should you find yourself neglected, or bored or unhappy, take a lover." Though I chuckled, Adolph kissed my forehead and added: "Have a good life and accomplish something worthwhile."

I smiled at my brother for it was he I would miss the most. Then I climbed into the carriage with my ladies and Sir Albert. Once the door was safely closed I glanced out of the window and saw Wilhelm in the distance staring at me. I refused to react to him. I simply reconciled myself to the knowledge that everything I had known to that point in my life was behind me—and my new life ahead was now prologue.

Thus, when we took off down the road, I never looked back...not at the palace, nor at my family, nor at my past. I left my country with my memories securely in my mind, and hope for the future in my heart. Later, aboard the HMS Royal Charlotte, after a 21-gun salute, I gave myself permission to adopt my new country of England. I watched as Germany become a speck on the sea, and it was that day I began these diaries as Queen Charlotte—utilizing the beautiful red leather journals mother gave me on her deathbed. Perhaps now I could finally open my heart again, and chart my own destiny.

My own future.

Part Two

QUEEN CHARLOTTE

London, England
1761 – 1770

"…All things are subject to interpretation.
Whichever interpretation prevails at a given time
is a function of power not truth…"

Friedrich Nietzsche

5 September, 1751

Dearest daughter Charlotte,

By the time you open the reliquary and receive this letter,
I shall be a part of the dust to which we must all resign
ourselves in time. My child, some things can only be
entrusted to your safe keeping for you and I have always
had a special understanding, and you bear the marks.

As you know, I have not been well of late and these last few
months I have gathered and placed in this chest all that was
of importance to me except my most precious commodities
my children. However, it is for you, Charlotte, that I feel
most compelled to unravel an explanation for your existence.
I want you to claim for yourself all that you are entitled to,
and it falls upon you to guard the contents of the reliquary
for the contents are sacred, undeniable and cursed.

Within it you will learn the truth of our existence; six wood
cylinders containing Magragana's own words and language;
and four papyrus scrolls which my grandfather insisted
are codices but have yet to be deciphered as such. I have
spent my life attempting to unravel the mystery
surrounding them without causing undue attention to
myself or to their existence for they contain the secret.

your father ✝

Twenty Two

18 September 1761, Aboard the HMS Royal Charlotte

I am on the vessel sailing me to my new life in England, and I am nervous. A storm is raging outside causing queasiness in my stomach, and I cannot help thinking of the tempestuous sea which swallowed my sister's betrothed. As for my own betrothed, I have yet to meet him, nor do I know what lies ahead. I am far too familiar with the wretchedness of a past I long to forget, and have prayed I could change who I was—so I could accept who I am.

A cacophony of lightning strikes preceded the crash of thunder, and the skies darkened around her. Sails on the *HMS Royal Charlotte* flapped angrily against the wind straining to keep the ship steady on the North Sea. Seconds later the sky unleashed a deluge of rain. The ship's crew of eighteen rushed about frantically securing cargo and attending to the safety of the voyagers bound for London.

Charlotte closed her brand-new red leather journal into which she had been jotting her thoughts and looked up at the angry skies nervously caressing the amulet. As the rain became more forceful it pounded on the Queen's face until her heavily applied make-up began to streak away revealing her wheat-colored skin beneath.

Ever protective, Lady Schwellenberg saw this and quickly replaced Charlotte's black velvet hood over her head. "We must get you below," said Charlotte's lady, glancing about to make sure no one saw the princess exposed. "Your make-up, my girl."

Charlotte nodded and gave her quill and inkpot to Lady Schwellenberg. Both quickly went below-deck to her quarters where she placed her diary on the writing table. As the ship swayed, Lady Hagedorn unhooked Charlotte's wet dress and helped her into a dry one. Lady Schwellenberg found the jar of white make-up in the exquisitely carved wooden chest and heavily reapplied it to Charlotte's face.

"A storm on these very same waters swallowed my sister's betrothed causing her madness," Charlotte said to no one in particular.

"Do not worry," Lady Hagedorn replied, "You shall not suffer the same fate. You are far too valuable to the British throne."

"Perhaps," Charlotte murmured, then with a wave dismissed her ladies. "Leave me."

The two ladies nodded obediently and left. Charlotte went to her chest and fingered the intricate patterns for a moment. Lifting the lid, she retrieved her silver ballerina music box, wound it up, and placed it on the deck floor. Her mouth curved into a smile of enchantment as J.S. Bach's "2 Part Invention" played.

She sat with the chest a while running her fingers over every gorgeous groove, carving and symbol. She looked at the five-pointed star inlaid on the top, and upon opening it marveled at the faded red velvet lining, which still felt sumptuous after so many generations. Her father had been a collector of unusual things such as swords from the 13th century, and buckles and shields from the 15th century. The chest had its own special history. She remembered her parents arguing over it, with her father insisting it be hidden behind the armoire in a section of wall to be cut out for its safekeeping.

Her mother was afraid of the chest the same way she feared the amulet. Something about both unsettled Duchess Elizabeth, which Charlotte never understood. But her father adored the history and meaning of the chest, and she was sure it still held the treasure the Grand Duke promised her. It was her entitlement, she thought, one that reminded her of herself—a wood exterior which when opened revealed a soft truth and knowledge not obvious to others.

After removing her makeup containers and the pink chiffon dress she had brought on the trip, Charlotte began to feel around the base of the chest, her fingers examining every nuance and crevice, for her father had told her to look inside the bottom for the treasure. But even when she gently tore at the velvet lining to lay bare the wood underneath, she could find no opening. She picked up the chest and shook it. There was a slight rattling indicating something was still inside it. But as she examined the outside of it again, she could not find any indentation or keyhole.

The chest had been carved from one solid piece of wood from a Kauri tree known to last thousands of years. Its hinges were secured using a unique mortise and tenon joint, an ancient joining method used in the Giza pyramid complex, built to last for centuries. But try as she may, she could not find a way into the bottom of it.

Then she noticed another small five-point star symbol carved on the bottom of the chest angled slightly to the left. The same carved symbol on the right side was straight. Charlotte had never noticed it before. Why would one symbol be carved askance this way? Both sides felt identical—the inlaid symbols had the same depth of serrated edges and signatures. How odd that this tiny section was off.

Suddenly Charlotte became obsessed. She looked closer and saw a slightly darker line around the symbol on the left, but no line around the symbol on the right side. She thought for a moment, then went to her writing desk and got her quill. Using the nib she stuck it between a groove in the carved crevasse and the five-point star symbol itself and forced pressure downward. Magically, it moved. She kept turning it and the section twisted in a circle until—surprise!—the small section fell off in her hand and there was a click. Seconds later, a secret drawer comprising the false bottom of the chest popped out.

Charlotte was shaking, her mind a mixture of hope and anxiety. With fingers trembling, she pulled the drawer forward. From the sound and smell, it hadn't been opened in ages—easily the nine years since her father died. The treasure, she thought, the promised treasure awaits and she remembered her father's words: *"There is great wealth inside", "A great treasure."* But her expression dropped in disillusion. Instead of tangible wealth or riches, what lay before her was peculiar. There were four round wooden containers corked and waxed closed; two brown leather-bound volumes of her father's diaries which she recognized; some graphs, charts, and a sealed letter on top, addressed to "Her Serene Highness

Charlotte Sophia Albertina Frederick" in her father's handwriting. Instantly, she opened the letter and read:

10 June, 1752

Dearest daughter Charlotte,

By the time you open the reliquary and receive this letter, I shall be a part of the dust to which we must all resign ourselves in time. I have requested the chest and amulet be delivered to you the moment I am declared thus. I pray your mother will obey this appeal and grant you the protection you will need as the owner of this reliquary. My child, these things can only be entrusted to your safe keeping, for we have always had a special understanding. You also bear the mark.

As you know, I have not been well of late and these last few months I have placed in this reliquary all that is of importance to me except my most precious possessions—my children. However, it is for you, Charlotte, that I feel most compelled to unveil an explanation. .

You are descended from many great kings whose bloodlines eventually merged to create your lineage. You are descended from the proud, great Moors as the fourteenth great-granddaughter of King Magrem of Faro, Portugal. But you are also descended from an even mightier king—one whose descendants included the Knights Templar. I want you to know about your own being, to not be afraid of it, and to claim for yourself all that you are entitled to, for you are as unique in your orientation as I am in mine. It falls upon you now to guard this reliquary and the amulet, for they are sacred and undeniable. Within it you will find my journals, and six wooden cylinders containing Magragana's own words that have yet to be deciphered. I have spent my life attempting to unravel the mystery and truths surrounding them without causing undue attention to myself or to their existence. Take heed with them, for there are those who would do us, and now you, great harm for those truths. Protect the secret and yourself, my daughter, and may Magragana keep you safe. Your loving father.

Charlotte touched the symbol her father had drawn at the end of the letter. She knew it as the Lorraine cross—the Templar cross—with a circle drawn around it. But what did her father mean by *'The secret?'*

'Protection you will need as the owner of this reliquary?' And why did he call the chest a *'reliquary,'* a word she knew to mean a housing for religious relics or artifacts?

She then picked up the one of the wooden cylinders. The wood on each had been burned with roman numerals. Using a lit candle Charlotte melted the age-old wax from the end of the one marked "I" and carefully pulled out its contents. There were several parchments rolled up inside, etched with text which she thought odd. She became frustrated for, like her father, she could not speak the language thus would not be able to understand what she had or what it meant. As she gingerly unwound the scroll she could tell its age from the musty, embedded dust particles it emitted, and by the way in which the scroll did not want to unravel easily, underscoring its antiquity.

She examined the strange writing inside.

ⲚⲀⲈⲒ ⲚⲈ Ⲛ̄ϢⲀⲬⲈ ⲈⲐⲎⲠ ⲈⲚⲦⲀⲒⲤ̄ ⲈⲦⲞⲚⲌ
ⲬⲞⲞⲨ ⲀⲨⲰ ⲀϥⲤⲌⲀⲒⲤⲞⲨ Ⲛ̄ϬⲒ ⲆⲒⲆⲨⲘⲞⲤ
ⲒⲞⲨⲆⲀⲤ ⲐⲰⲘⲀⲤ ⲀⲨⲰ ⲠⲈⲬⲀϥ ⲬⲈ ⲠⲈ
ⲦⲀⲌⲈ ⲈⲐⲈⲢⲘⲎⲚⲈⲒⲀ Ⲛ̄ⲚⲈⲈⲒϢⲀⲬⲈ ϥⲚⲀ
ⲬⲒ ⲦⲠⲈ ⲀⲚ Ⲙ̄ⲠⲘⲞⲨ ⲠⲈⲬⲈ ⲒⲤ̄ Ⲙ̄Ⲛ̄ⲦⲢⲈϥ
ⲖⲞ Ⲛ̄ϬⲒ ⲠⲈⲦϢⲒⲚⲈ ⲈϥϢⲒⲚⲈ ϢⲀⲚⲦⲈϥ
ϬⲒⲚⲈ ⲀⲨⲰ ⲌⲞⲦⲀⲚ ⲈϥϢⲀⲚϬⲒⲚⲈ ϥⲚⲀ
ϢⲦⲢ̄ⲦⲢ̄ ⲀⲨⲰ ⲈϥϢⲀⲚϢⲦⲞⲢⲦⲢ̄ ϥⲚⲀⲢ̄

Charlotte recognized many of the symbols from her amulet and the chest. Quite a few of the words were fading, and she worried that whatever information was contained on the scroll would soon be lost to history if not translated. But to whom do you charge with such a task if the objects themselves have been entrusted to you as a secret to protect? And why didn't her father or his ancestors have them interpreted in all this time?

Suddenly she remembered something. Her father had said *six* scrolls, yet she had only found four. Charlotte reached her hand as far back as she could into the secret compartment only to realize there was nothing more to be found. Perhaps her father was mistaken. She also remembered something else. Following her father's funeral, she witnessed her mother and Wilhelm burning papers and precious items from this chest. Perhaps the other scroll had fallen victim to their indiscriminate destruction.

Tina Andrews

In a state of bewilderment, Charlotte paced restlessly around the room. All these years she thought there was a vast *understandable* treasure in this chest. But what she actually had were ancient, undecipherable volumes of claptrap. There wasn't even a treasure map. What a cruel joke, for until the documents were translated, she had absolutely nothing...

...except her father's diaries—which brought joy to Charlotte's face. The diaries would be in German—comprehensible and intelligible. So she rushed back to them, untying the leather binding of the first one.

Though several pages were torn from it, others were ripe for reading. The future queen also found genealogy charts written there in her father's handwriting. One page showed her immediate family tree, and as her finger traced her father's lineage, she discovered her mother had been right. Her father's descent from Magragana was indeed through illegitimacy. His grandmother, Antonie Sibylle, had an affair with her mother's grandfather, Count George Ludwig I of Erbach. So when her father's mother, Princess Christiane Emile Antonie, was born, there was controversy over her paternity which became clear upon the discovery of her birthmark.

But on her mother's side, Charlotte's descent from Magragana ben Bekar was clear: Magragana the Moor and Portuguese King Afonso III begat Martin Afonso Chichorro, who begat Martin Afonso Chichorro II, who begat Vasco Martin de Sousa Chichorro, who begat Affonso de Sousa, who begat Mencia de Sousa, who begat Margarita de Castro de Sousa—the famous Moor from the Portuguese de Sousa dynasty, who begat Ferdinand de Neufchatel, who begat Marguerite de Salm-Dhaun, who begat George III Von Erbach, who begat George Albrecht I, who begat George Ludwig I, who begat Sophia Albertina, who begat Charlotte's mother, Elizabeth Albertina Frederick. Even her mother's possible father, Ibrahim Petrovich Hannibal, the slave, was signified by dotted lines. Now Charlotte understood it was these inter-marriages of Moors, mulattos, slaves and mixed-race ancestors that provided her dark color.

The genealogy chart continued on to the next page and the one after that, until Charlotte's heart raced at the discovery of a far more ancient lineage—lines of descent on both sides which reached further back from Magragana and her Moorish, Muslim blood, to France and Israel.

Charlotte gathered the wooden containers and placed them back in the false bottom of the chest. After winding up the ballerina music box again, she sat with her father's diary as the storm rocked the ship. She did not know whether to be frightened, curious, or remain blissfully ignorant.

And yet, Charlotte had a seeker's heart. As the voyage to London would take another six days, there would be ample time for more reading. She knew she would never be able to stay away from her father's writings, for they might provide answers to questions she'd had for years.

She thought about what awaited her in England—an impending marriage, coronation, new language, and new friends. Music from the silver ballerina music box caused her to think about Christian and the fact that she would never see him again. All she had left of him now was his gift, and the music echoed all around her. Then she looked at the diary—her father's gift to her as well, and emotions caused her to think about her father's words that day before he died: *"I want for you the gift of knowledge, independent thought, and power so long denied women."*

So, as thunder rolled around her and the sky beyond her porthole remained blackened with rain, Charlotte lit another candle and began reading. She read for most of the entire nine-day trip across the North Sea except on rare occasions when she went on deck to comfort those afraid of the rising squalls.

She learned so much about her father and his quest, and certain passages within his diaries stayed with her. Many of those passages Charlotte committed to memory; but three in particular she committed to memory.

9 June, 1725

Today, mother gave me two familial possessions held in secret for centuries. One was an intricately carved wooden box. The other was a gold amulet. She told me of their history. She said Count Ludwig I of Erbach was, in fact, my blood grandfather and not Prince Christian Wilhelm, as I had believed all this time. Count Ludwig was a member of the Order and mother was adamant I join. She said the amulet was given to her the day she was born by her real father—because she had inherited Magragana's mark, as have I. She insisted it be given to me despite the illegitimacy inherent in her being.

Mother explained there were nine similarly designed gold amulets created for Hugues de Payens, André de Montbard, Payen de Montdidier, Geoffroi de Sainte-Omer, Archambaud de St Amand, Geoffroi Bisol, Gondemare, Rosal, and some say Count Hugh I de Champagne, who were the nine founding members of the Knights of the Temple of Solomon. They became known as the Knights Templar, and Hugues de Payens was the Order's first Grand Master...

15 April 1726

Through my friend and fellow Mason, Francois Antoine Gaston, the Duke de Levis-Mirepoix, I now know I am descended from Geoffroy de Charny, Preceptor of Normandy and the last Seneschal of the Knights Templar. Wisely, de Charny was not wearing his amulet the day he and Grand Master Jacques de Molay were burned to death in 1307. De Charny instructed his important belongings be given to his extended family because, as a Knight, he could not have a wife or children. His amulet and other relics went to his nephew named 'Geoffroi' de Charny.

Among the objects Geoffroi de Charny inherited and protected was the carved reliquary and its mysterious contents, which included several scrolls and another item sacred enough to keep the de Charny family and our own united for three centuries. It was the linen Shroud of Edessa, known in ancient texts as the Sydoine. It was the herringbone linen cloth purchased by Joseph of Arimathea who wrapped Jesus in it after the crucifixion. It is now known as the Holy Shroud mysteriously imprinted with the image of our Lord not made by human hands. The Shroud was brought to France by de Charny's ancestor, Otto de la Roche, who acquired it suspiciously.

Upon de Charny's death in 1356, the Shroud and reliquary passed to his widow, Jeanne de Vergy, then to her son, another 'Geoffrey,' then by Geoffrey's daughter Marguerite. She had the carved box redesigned so it contained a secret compartment to hide the Shroud. Now, I am on a quest to have my familial scrolls transcribed.

6 February, 1735

Today, as a wedding present, my parents gave me a Templar sword from the 4th Crusades, circa 1250. It is a magnificent thirty-six inch heavy rapier with razor-sharp steel carved with symbols of the Templars and Egyptian hieroglyphs. Mother said it once belonged to Geoffroi de Charny. But I have yet to know what is in the scrolls.

I married Princess Elizabeth Albertine of Saxe-Hildburghausen, who was chosen for me for many reasons, not the least of which is we share the same incredible genealogy. Though she, too, is descended from Magragana, she does not subscribe to the notion that those of us with the mark must carry forth a mission, for she has no such birthmark. She does not believe nor accept what I am culling from our collective roots—that our bloodline is an amalgam of Christian, Semetic, Muslim, Templar, Merovingian, Desposyni...

...and Moor.

Twenty Three

King George was nervous. He had been all morning. He had changed clothes three times, picked out two different wigs yet chosen none, and had not eaten. His stomach was queasy and his palms sweated with excitement for it was Monday, 7 September 1761. His new queen was expected that afternoon, and by midnight he would be the officially married sovereign of Great Britain.

Lord Bute and the king's mother Princess Augusta came into his quarters and Augusta presented him with an early wedding present. It was his father's initiation uniform pin, which she attached to George's vest and kissed him. George and Bute shook hands.

"Tis a glorious day, Majesty," smiled Bute. "All is right in Britain this day."

Bute was correct. Everyone in the country was jubilant anticipating Charlotte's arrival. Windows had been washed, rugs and floors scrubbed, streets swept clean. Fresh flowers in vivid color and variety exploded from clay pots large and small in shop windows, churches and homes across England. All anyone could discuss was the fabulous royal wedding at St. James Cathedral and the coronation to be held at Westminster Abbey. Everyone was joyous...

...except for Lady Sarah Lennox.

She had not moved from the chair in front of her dressing table since dawn. Inexplicably still in denial and incredulity, she felt dead. There was no feeling in her spirit knowing she may never be happy again. Even at this late date, she pitifully hoped George would denounce his choice of wife and come to her in his true desire to marry her. As she stared at her reflection in the mirror all she saw was failure, loss and the horrible knowledge she would have to stand as maid of honor to the woman who won her lover's decision.

✣

After a rough nine-day journey from Cuxhaven to Harwich, the *HMS Royal Charlotte* had made its descent down the Thames with its sweeping vistas and ruined medieval castles. Now the ship had been towed into the port of Gravesend, and the gangplank was rattling down into place. An orchestra hired for the event played processional music, and there was great fanfare quayside. Hordes of British people waved flags and cheered the arrival of their next queen.

Below deck, however, Charlotte was a bundle of nerves, having become deeply affected by both her arrival and the information she had read in her father's diary.

"You're shaking, my girl," Lady Schwellenberg cautioned, as she hooked Charlotte's introduction dress. "Do not allow the English to see that the king's German consort is unready for her duties. Whatever you are reading must not cause you introspection and humility now—of all times. Shoulders back, head high. You are to be their queen, dammit. And the new Queen of England is a fiercely proud woman."

Charlotte nodded and hugged her lady and friend. "Thank God I have you, Swelly," she said, turning to look at herself in the mirror. Throwing her shoulders back, Charlotte felt assured.

It was true. Though nervous about her reception in England, Charlotte *was* proud. She had learned much the last few days and could not contain the esteem she was experiencing. She knew the pedigree from which she was born, and the purpose for which she now derived motivation, for that morning, before dawn, she had finished her father's second journal and savored his last entry:

9 March, 1752

Finally, there has been news. After years attempting to locate a translator for the reliquary documents, I received a reply from my friend and fellow Mason, the Duke de Levis-Mirepoix. The Duke is fluent in Greek, Latin, Hebrew, Aramaic and the Coptic languages and agreed to decipher whatever he could for me. Two years ago, I sent him three pages of text I copied from my scrolls. Yesterday, I received a coded letter from Duke Francois informing me that the text was in Coptic. He said it was part of an ancient codex of grimoires, or book of magic spells, which means these words are banned and therefore heretical. Thus I am even more curious. I want to know what exactly it is I am protecting within the texts of these scrolls. As there are issues of propriety surrounding them, I must travel to Mirepoix myself to have them translated."

Charlotte was stunned. *The Duke of Levis-Mirepoix?* Was this why Duke Francois asked her if her father left any instructions for him when she was at Sanssouci at King Fredrick's Ball? She knew if her father could have made the trip to France he would have. But he did not live long enough. He died four months later in front of her. Was Duke Francois the answer to her questions and her father's?

She had to know. Upon reading the last of his words, knowing his quest and concerns, Charlotte decided to continue her father's mission whatever it was. With her power and access as queen perhaps she could find out exactly what was in the entire scroll and the others she inherited from her father.

Soon, there came a knock at Charlotte's door. Lady Hagedorn answered it admitting Captain Anson, Sir Albert Papendiek, Lady Hagedorn, the Duchess of Hamilton and the Duchess of Ancaster who were wearing their best clothes.

"Are you ready, Your Majesty?" asked the Captain. "All of England awaits you."

With her shoulders back and head high, Charlotte smiled confidently, "Quite ready."

Amidst a flurry of applause, Captain Anson came down the gangplank, followed by twenty members of his crew. Sir Albert and Charlotte's two British ladies in waiting emerged and came down. Finally Charlotte, Lady Hagedorn and Lady Schwellenberg appeared at the top of the gangplank. Citizens quayside broke into thunderous applause shouting, "All hail the queen." Charlotte and her ladies held each other for dear life as they looked around this strange new country.

England was nothing like Germany to her. It smelled different, its panorama and landscapes looked like none other she had ever seen. Even its colors were different. The docks of Gravesend were bustling with merchants, sailors and crew members, which overwhelmed her. As she squeezed Lady Schwellenberg's fingers, Charlotte's face outwardly radiated an appreciation for the affection the British people exhibited.

But as the next queen slowly made her way to the port walk, a foul odor wafted in the air, becoming more pungent. Charlotte held a handkerchief to her nose as Lady Hagedorn tapped her shoulder and nodded Charlotte's head in the direction of a ship docked two berths away. It was then Charlotte saw strange leg and wrist shackles being washed of blood and feces by crew members, and the stench had permeated the dock. At the bottom of the gangplank nailed to a signpost nearby was an advertisement:

"Saturday! 140 SLAVES FOR SALE! Bristol and Liverpool. All offers considered!"

Charlotte was disquieted, yet kept her gaze forward, determined to make the best of whatever this new life had to offer.

Sir John Wilkes and Sir Horace Walpole, two Members of Parliament, were present for Charlotte's arrival, as was the Lord Mayor and the Alderman of Harwich. Walpole took notes on the young queen's deportment and physical attributes as she disembarked. Also present was an impeccably well-dressed aristocrat who moved to the young queen and bowed.

"Welcome to England, Your Majesty," said the aristocrat with a handkerchief occasionally pressed to his nose, "Permit me to introduce myself. I am Sir David Harcourt, the king's Master of the Equerries. His Majesty sent me to take you to your new home at St James."

Charlotte nodded respectfully, then drew in a deep breath of English air despite the odor. Still squeezing Lady Schwellenberg's hand, she turned to Captain Anson and thanked him for her safe arrival despite the stormy days. Captain Anson bid the next queen safe passage to St. James, then nodded to Sir David to take over. His job was now done, and he would enjoy the new commission the king would grant him for ensuring Charlotte arrived unharmed.

Sir David led Charlotte and her entourage to a striking burgundy and gold coach drawn by two pairs of magnificent stallions. Charlotte made sure her father's reliquary was loaded atop her carriage and protected her and her father's diaries personally as she did not want them far from her.

As the cortege passed by, Sir Wilkes shook his head, disconcerted. "I say," he grimaced to Walpole, "Our new queen is quite…" He fumbled, looking for the right word finally settling on, "…'swarthy,' wouldn't you say?"

Sir Walpole agreed. "She does have just a hint of the mulatto, doesn't she?" he mused, writing boldly in his notes: "Wide nostrils, swarthy, mulatto appearance…"

Lady Schwellenberg, overhearing the comment as she walked behind Charlotte's retinue, hurried to catch up to the new queen. Upon entering the carriage she moved in close to Charlotte so no one else could hear and whispered, "We must re-powder you at once."

The pallor of Charlotte's skin gave rise to murmurs throughout the crowd as well. Those close enough to view her frowned suspiciously behind their fans. One spectator remarked loud enough for Charlotte to hear: "My word, she's tawny." Another commented that it was a shame her "nose was so pug" and that her mouth had the "same fault."

Soon, those lining the future queen's route began yelling their own one-word assessment. It became so persistent that Charlotte, overcome by curiosity and not totally understanding the English language, turned to Lady Hagedorn and questioned, "What means 'pug'?"

"Never you mind, my girl. No attention should be paid to them." At that, Lady Schwellenberg closed the drapes inside the carriage, reminiscent of Charlotte's mother, and reapplied the chalk-white powder to Charlotte's face. Thereafter Charlotte's coach toured the rest of the way without disturbance.

After dinner and an overnight rest at the estate of Lord Abercorn in Witham, the royal coaches left for London the next morning. Charlotte, though powdered to perfection, was uncomfortably dressed in a scratchy quilted jacket that was up to her chin and down to her waist. Every few minutes Lady Hagedorn asked if she should loosen the collar or waistline. Charlotte demurred, but felt itchy nonetheless. Sir Albert Papendiek was not happy with his work either. Charlotte's hair was in unattractive *tete de mouton* knots with an odd coif-piece on top. He regretted all of it as they rode along, yet it was too late to change it.

Finally, at a quarter past three in the afternoon the team of six horses came to a halt in front of St. James Palace. Lady Schwellenberg and Lady Hagedorn stuck their faces out of the window and grimaced. Charlotte shook her head in disbelief. Though it was imposing, visually St. James palace was the dullest, most unattractive palace Charlotte had ever seen. Instead of a grand limestone and marble showplace with beautiful gardens, fountains and cobblestone walkways, St. James was a completely unremarkable palace sporting plain brown brick, architecturally uninspired clock towers, and a bland dirt courtyard adorned with voluminous, malodorous leavings from the myriad horses in and out that morning.

Sir Lyndon Childs, an effeminate valet, opened the door for the arriving party. Everything he did was larger than life, aided with flourishes of his hands. He bowed in respect to Charlotte. "Your Majesty, Sir Lyndon Anthony Childs at your service. I am the king's Valet de Chambre. I trust your journey was a pleasant one?"

"Very much so, Sir Lyndon."

The valet, with his bulbous nose in the air, reached into the carriage and took Charlotte's hand. He instructed three other male servants in dark uniforms to attend to the thirty-five chests, suitcases and hat boxes, snapping orders and directing which chests should go where. Charlotte insisted her father's carved chest should follow her, as she did not want it out of her sight. After smoothing her dress, she and the 45-year-old valet went ahead into the palace. Within seconds the other valets appeared to graciously assist Ladies Schwellenberg, Hagedorn, and the Duchess of Hamilton from the carriage and welcomed them to London as well.

Upon entering St. James, Charlotte was met by Lord William Cavendish, a smug young gentleman whose family had been intertwined with the Hanover's from George the II's reign. Cavendish clicked his heels and bowed to Charlotte.

"Your Majesty, Sir William Cavendish, 4th Duke of Devonshire. I am the king's Lord Chamberlain. Permit me to introduce you to the royal family. This is the king's mother, Princess Dowager Augusta Hanover; the king's sisters, Princesses Caroline and Augusta Matilda; the king's brothers, Princes Edward, William, Henry and Frederick; and the king's uncle, the Duke of Cumberland."

As Cavendish introduced Charlotte to her new family, each bowed or curtsied respectfully and Charlotte smiled to each, repeating, "I am most pleased to meet you." She was then whisked away to the awaiting staff. As she passed, Princess Dowager Augusta leaned into her daughter Caroline, shaking her head, "Odd-looking thing. So much makeup for one so young. And such a strange pug nose."

Charlotte, still within earshot, overheard the remark, and since this was not the first time she'd heard the phrase "pug nose" upon arriving in England, she steeled herself against its uncomplimentary definition. Cavendish escorted her across the black-and-white checkerboard floor to the grand staircase where several people were gathered. "These are members of your personal and household staff," he indicated.

Charlotte gasped. The number of employees waiting to meet her was astounding. It reached up the stairs to the second floor and beyond. Each member would bow or curtsey, and Charlotte nodded in response as Cavendish, in a slow delivery, introduced them all.

"This is Lord Robert Montagu, 3rd Duke of Manchester. He will serve as your Lord Chamberlain. You know Mary Bertie, the Duchess of Ancester, and Elizabeth Campbell, the Duchess Dowager of Hamilton, as they traveled with you. They shall be your Mistress of the Bedchamber and Mistress of Robes, respectively. The Honorable Deborah Chetwynd is your Mistress Laundress, Seamstress and Starchier; the Countess of Pembroke, Elizabeth Spencer, and Lady Elizabeth Wells are your ladies of the bedchamber; Sir David Harcourt, whom you also met, is your Master of the Horse; the Honorable Catherine Elizabeth Herbert and the widow Dashwood are your Necessary women…"

And so on, ad infinitum.

My neck became numb as I nodded to each of the sixty-six members of my support staff. I met two vice-chamberlains, an Attorney General, a Treasurer and a Treasurer's clerk, four pages of the backstairs, an operator of the teeth, six ladies of the bedchamber, a necessary woman of the queen's private apartment, a clerk of the stables with six assistants for horses, two equerries, two pages of the presence chamber, five coachmen, five postillions, two apothecaries, two physicians, two surgeons, and various others too numerous for me to fathom or remember.

Finally, Lord Cavendish nodded to Charlotte's Lord Chamberlain, Sir Robert Montagu, who escorted Charlotte, and Ladies Hagedorn and Schwellenberg to the third-floor apartments. Along the way Montegu showed them eighteen elegant rooms decorated to showcase the Hanover dynasty's obsession with Palladio architecture. Though plain on the outside, the interior of St. James palace was a vast improvement in Charlotte's opinion. Silk walls, painted ceilings, gold gildings and tapestries dominated. But the real delight was evidenced by one room.

"Your personal apartment, Your Majesty," said Montagu as he opened the door. "It is across the hall from Lady Schwellenberg's suites and down the hall from Lady Hagedorn's."

Seeing that the presumptive queen was delighted, he smiled. "The king had all the furniture shipped in from Paris. He hoped it would please Her Majesty."

Charlotte was awestruck as she visually took it all in. The apartment was dazzling in matching brocade drapes and bed covers swathed in ornate rococo ornamentation. To the left was an oak dressing table replete with a silver trimmed comb and brush set and crystal perfume bottles set atop lace doilies. To the right was a large oak armoire.

Four attendants placed the queen's luggage in the room, including the reliquary, then left.

"Your Majesty, His Majesty will send for you shortly. Until then, should you require anything else I am at your service." Lord Montegu pointed to a long velvet rope shining from wear. "Simply pull that rope and it will alert me of your need. I shall be here with haste." He placed one hand over his heart, bowed and backed out of the room, closing the door behind him.

The moment he was gone, Charlotte and her ladies screamed like children. Charlotte's hands covered her mouth as she looked around the great rooms, one leading into another. Lady Schwellenberg threw back the brocade drapes and let in the light. "Goodness. It's three times the size of the master chambers at Mirow," she squealed.

"It's the size of the reception hall at Neustrelitz," Lady Hagedorn exclaimed.

Charlotte touched the bedding, smelled the soft scent of the cut lilies in vases, and then looked at the garments which lay on top. It was her bridal gown and accessories, including shoes. She looked back at Lady

Schwellenberg who gave her a dazzling smile in approval, and they both giggled.

"Beautiful, is it not? The palace is very old, very grand, very expensive..." they heard someone say in a clipped Scottish accent from behind them, "...and all very boring."

When Charlotte and her two ladies turned, there stood one of the beautiful ladies in waiting Charlotte had met earlier who eased into the room uninvited and began to unpack the luggage. She leaned in, her voice dropping to a whisper. "It all arrived this morning a hair's breath before you, Your Highness."

"I'm sorry. I have forgotten your name. There are so many to remember," Charlotte replied.

The woman curtsied. "Lady Elizabeth Wells, Mistress of the Bedchamber, at your service. But if it would please Your Majesty, I would like it very much if you called me 'Lady Lizzie.' As there are ten 'Lady Elizabeth's' in service to you, I suspect we shall all die of confusion."

Charlotte nodded. "Lady Lizzie would be fine."

"I have been sent by His Majesty to dress you for your introduction." Lady Lizzie smiled as she set about hanging Charlotte's meager gowns in the armoire next to the window. Charlotte watched her a moment. Elizabeth Wells was a petit woman with dark hair and eyes, and as cheery a personality as Charlotte had ever experienced. Each word was punctuated with a hand gesture or bob of her head, and one could tell her inner thoughts from the curl of her lip.

"Lady Lizzie, how is it you've come to attend me?"

"I asked for the appointment, Your Majesty. Begged for it, in fact. I could not think of a more honored, important position as taking care of Her Majesty's wardrobe or personal self. 'Tis quite an honor. One which seven other candidates are livid not to have received."

"Then I applaud your success and your enthusiasm. Now will you pick out something appropriate for me to wear? I wish to fit in with the English style of things."

"I am a Scot, Your Majesty. England has no style of her own," Lizzie quipped. "Style, I'm afraid, belongs to the French. What England does have, is power, influence and magnificent greed, which allows us, or shall I say *men*, to conquer and indulge themselves in excess. Curiosity in you will also allow Your Majesty to set new and hopefully better standards for British style."

Charlotte smiled, allowing the dark-haired lady to go through her dresses. But Lizzie grumbled at every gown. "Abominable, ghastly. These are terrible, Your Majesty." She turned to Charlotte, dumbstruck. "Is this everything you brought? If so, we shall have to order from Paris. Though the English abhor the French, the French do have such unyielding good taste, don't they?"

Charlotte looked at her ladies, who shrugged, not sure if they agreed or misunderstood her. Finally, Lady Lizzie pulled out Charlotte's yellow brocade sacque dress. "Well, the gods prevail. This one will do...for now." She motioned to Lady Hagedorn and Lady Schwellenberg. "We must order for the two of you as well. You are both far too attractive and cut too fine a figure to wear such dull blues and grays. Tis a new day, ladies. A new day!"

All the women chuckled as Charlotte was fitted into her introduction gown. Lady Lizzie placed a rose in Charlotte's hair and marveled. "Your Majesty, you are ready to be received."

"Thank you, Lady Lizzie." And the four women left the royal bed chamber and entered into a candlelit corridor which led down to the second-floor apartments and parlors. Diffused sunlight beamed in from the stained-glass cathedral windows falling gently on the royal portraits. Charlotte found herself looking at the gallery of exquisitely painted women and stood mesmerized by the third portrait.

"Who is that stunning creature?"

"Lady Yarmouth. King George II's famous mistress," answered Lady Lizzie. "They are all mistresses in point of fact."

Charlotte gasped. "Do you mean...?" She couldn't finish.

"Yes, Your Majesty. Courtesans, concubines, wives and lovers of the various kings who lived here at St. James." Lizzie pointed to another portrait that intrigued Charlotte. "That was Anne Boleyn...*before* she lost her head for King Henry VIII—literally."

Charlotte snickered. Then a voice boomed from behind them.

"Do you always keep your betroths waiting?"

Charlotte turned to find King George resplendent in his introduction clothes. He came forward and took Charlotte's hand, kissing it gently. He bowed. "I am George Frederick Hanover...your unofficial husband."

Charlotte curtsied. "Charlotte Sophia Albertina Frederick Hanover... your unofficial wife."

She beheld him. He was not unattractive, even though his eyes were so large she thought him ill from gout. She liked that he was tall with well-formed shoulders, had a clear complexion, and his hair was thick and bountiful. She smiled awkwardly and lowered her eyes.

George found his new bride somewhat plain, but reports which preceded her did her no justice. He liked her face—especially her smile, and her personality was engaging. Perhaps in time he could even care for her—not like his love for Sarah, but a respectful, affectionate love.

"They told me what you lacked in feminine pulchritude you more than made up for in intellect. You must be brilliant, for you are not hard on the eye."

Charlotte blushed, becoming somewhat timorous before George.

"I see Lady Elizabeth was giving you the St. James scandal tour." George grinned.

"She was, and frankly, I am fascinated."

"Well then, allow me to show you the rest of the palace and grounds." George motioned to Charlotte's ladies in waiting. Lady Lizzie, with the subtlest of looks, indicated to Lady Hagedorn and Lady Schwellenberg that they had been dismissed. The king took Charlotte's hand and they walked through the palace, making their way to the gardens. "The palace was originally built by Henry VIII as a hunting lodge. His second wife, Anne Boleyn, stayed here the night after her coronation. Oh, 'tis grand history and tradition you are moving into, Charlotte."

The two ventured outside to the gardens. Though they were small, Charlotte marveled at the flowers in full bloom in the heat of this early September day. Charlotte turned to George with an enchanting smile which George found impossible not to return. Together they walked arm-in-arm through the roses, irises and geraniums and began to get to know one another. George's manner appeared obliging, and his comportment genteel. Though he was just the tiniest bit awkward, he had his own charm to Charlotte, who prayed they would make a good match and that she would come to love him, and her new country.

Twenty Four

That afternoon, bells tolled all over London. England was awash in excitement, for King George III was officially marrying Princess Charlotte Sophia of Mecklenburg. The streets outside the Chapel Royal at St. James Palace were filled with people anxious to get a glimpse of the wedding of the decade.

It was a spectacular event. Thomas Secker, the Archbishop of Canterbury, would formally marry the couple. He stood at the altar next to King George in a dazzling gold and white ermine mantel, a formal white velvet waistcoat, and his gold and royal blue velvet sash. The royal family, in the first two rows, turned as processional music announced the bride.

Charlotte Sophia came up the aisle escorted by George's brothers Prince William and Prince Frederick. She looked beautiful. Sir Albert Papendiek had spent two hours on her hair intent to not make the mistake he'd made with her introduction hairstyle. Charlotte's tightly coiled hair was hidden under an elaborate auburn wig fashioned into a mountain of intertwined silk ribbons and curls. Her face and arms were covered in heavy white makeup, and her head was held high despite the extraordinary weight she was carrying.

The wedding gown, designed by couturier Sir Phillip Motley, was so heavy it severely restricted Charlotte's movements. She could barely walk. Six hundred thousand bugle beads were sewn onto one hundred yards of satin and chiffon. Twenty yards of white velvet and ermine mink were draped onto a cape resting on her shoulders, and under all of this was a burdensome breastplate, diamond stomacher, corset, a whalebone under-hoop, and silk stockings. Her feet were tortuously stuffed into pointy white satin English-made shoes that were so tight she could only tiptoe in pain. Then, to underscore her eminence as Queen of England, Charlotte was wearing the leaded crown jewels. In all, 152 pounds of excess were heaped on top of her 112-pound frame.

Ten bridesmaids helped maneuver Charlotte's heavy, purple velvet train up the aisle. On the left, positioned in order of precedence, was Lady Susan Fox-Strangeways, whose sister-in-law Lady Sarah Lennox, the maid of honor, led on the right, trying to contain her emotions.

Meanwhile, in the Royal Banquet Hall, Franz and Fritz, twin waiters, meticulously set a lace-covered table with the finest china and linen in St. James's dining hall. The late King George II's salons at St. James had been renowned for their resplendence. There was always fabulous food, and the eclectic mix of guests who discoursed there were second to none. Young King George III, however, was far different. More frugal and simple, he thus far had the most boring salons of any king to reside in the palace. But tonight was different. Lord Nicholas had convinced the king to allow him to present the wedding party in a manner the occasion required.

Lavender-scented candles hung from candelabras. Rarely a glass was empty before champagne was proffered and poured and a string quintet played until the music was interrupted by the sounds of applause. The young king and queen had now entered the grand ballroom. The musicians launched into "God Save the King" and George greeted each guest with a smile. His arm was looped through Charlotte's and he exuded pride as he presented his bride to his friends.

Charlotte, however, was dying. She stood awkwardly under the weight she wore as she was presented to British aristocracy thinking, *When will all this be over?*

"Your Majesties," announced Lord Montagu, "I present Sir John Wilkes and his daughter Mistress Polly Wilkes."

The older aristocrat and his 10-year-old daughter bowed and curtsied respectfully. Charlotte noticed right away that Sir Wilkes was no fan of the king's as he quickly turned his attention to her, smiling in approval. "Your Majesty, England is ever grateful for your presence," said Wilkes with only a cursory glance to George as he and young Polly moved on.

"Mister Josiah Wedgwood."

Charlotte nodded respectfully to the distinguished gentleman. "Mister Wedgwood, your exquisite pottery has reached us even in Germany. I look forward to seeing more of it."

"I shall have several pieces delivered to you on Monday," said Wedgwood proudly, moving on.

"Presenting Lord and Lady Bethany of Liverpool," Montagu heralded.

Following Wilkes was a familiar face which brought joy to Charlotte's own. Though it was the aristocratic Bethanys who stood before her offering their bows in respect, it was their maid, Anne Josef, the Ethiopian Charlotte had met at Sanssouci, whom she fondly remembered and to whom she smiled. Anne was again wearing her amulet, the significance of which Charlotte now understood and wondered if Anne was as aware of its meaning. At least this distracted her from the weight and pain of her clothing. Anne, conscious of her place in this world of royals and courtiers, remained behind Lady Bethany. Mindful she was in service to her mistress, she still managed to acknowledge Charlotte's smile with one of her own as well as a slight curtsey.

"Baron Philip Adolphus von Munchhausen," announced Montagu.

Charlotte smiled. "I know the Baron very well. I made his acquaintance in Mecklenburg."

Munchhausen bowed, smiling at the acknowledgement. "More than anyone, I am delighted Her Majesty… *is* Her Majesty."

Then another introduction was made. "…French Minister, Charles Auguste Timothee d'Eon."

D'Eon, dressed handsomely in his Dragoon officer's uniform, stepped forward, smiling broadly, and Charlotte allowed him to kiss both cheeks. "Comment faites vous, Votre Majestè?

"Tres bien, merci," smiled Charlotte, happy to see him, and grateful he spoke a language she knew well. "Do allow me to apologize for that most unpleasant dinner in Mecklenburg."

"It was forgotten as soon as it ended," assured the French Minister, who then turned to the gathering, holding his glass aloft in the air. "Let us toast our most beautiful new queen and her safe arrival in London. To Queen Charlotte Sophia Frederick Hanover. May she be blessed with long life…and many children."

The audience applauded echoing back "Here, here," all but Lady Sarah, who, with some discretion, found her way to a food table without notice—except to George. Charlotte modestly acknowledged d'Eon's toast and the gathering with a wave and smile. King George was pleased, nodding to d'Eon. Charlotte, also pleased with d'Eon, added, "We shall be good friends you and I."

After an hour of introductions, Charlotte finally looked around the room at the sea of painted, bejeweled humanity. She had never seen anything like this in Mecklenburg or at Sanssouci—the palace considered to be the finest in Germany.

From the sidelines, Sir John Wilkes and Sir Horace Walpole stood together, observing all the intrigues of the evening. Noticing Charlotte's fidgety discomfort in her wedding attire, Walpole grimaced to Wilkes. "The heaviness of the queen's gown pulls the front so far down we guests know as much of her upper half as the king himself will tonight." The two chuckled. Then they witnessed the aging Earl of Westmorland who, upon seeing Lady Sarah's beauty and style, mistakenly paid homage to her as queen to which Lady Sarah reacted. "Sir, you insult me. I am not the queen!" The Earl had to be forcibly removed and Wilkes could not stop laughing. "Indeed she is not. Can he not see her beauty is unmistakably superior to the actual queen?"

Other disparaging comments were made. Though ladies of the court curtsied to the queen as they were presented, from behind their fans they reproached her appearance. Charlotte overheard some of these comments and felt demeaned.

Dowager Princess Augusta saw this and started to make her way over. But as George's mother approached the new queen she noticed something on Charlotte's left shoulder which startled her—the birthmark. It was faint, but definitely visible through the queen's makeup. Augusta collected herself, after all she was in front of every member of her royal society. Yet her heart was racing. "Geniessen Sie die Festlichkeiten Ihre Majestät? Augusta asked Charlotte in German.

Thrilled to have conversation in her native tongue, Charlotte turned and smiled. "Ja, ich geniesse sie sehr. Yes. I'm enjoying it very much. Except for my feet. I'm afraid I shall never get used to English shoes. High arches I suspect."

"I, too, was brought here from Germany—to marry George's father," remarked the dowager in German, "I had to learn English ways, English laws, eat English food—all the protocols required for British royal society. And you will too. But I do miss Germany," she sighed. "Especially German shoes." Augusta pulled Charlotte aside and dropped her voice. "I shall have three dozen pairs delivered to you. Just keep my son's mind on British politics...," she then indicated Lady Sarah, "...and off that Irish blonde." She patted Charlotte's shoulder where she had seen the raised birthmark before she moved off.

Charlotte looked over and saw Lady Sarah in conversation with George for an eternity. When Sarah moved away, George's attention was still on her. Charlotte glanced back at Augusta, who gave her a knowing look. The queen moved toward a chair. Both Lady Lizzie and Lady Schwellenberg saw her, but Lizzie gestured that she would handle the queen.

"Forgive me, Your Majesty. It appears your feet hurt," said the Scottish lady.

"I'm seconds from hurling these shoes out a window."

Lady Lizzie grinned, then helped Charlotte sit down, whispering, "Give them to me and go barefoot. Who will know under that heavy gown?"

The queen smiled and eased out of her shoes. Lady Lizzie furtively hid them under the folds of her pettiskirt. "Imagine, all of this fuss for strangers," sighed Charlotte, rubbing her throbbing toes together under her gown. "There are so many here I will never get to know."

"Or ridicule," quipped Lady Lizzie.

Charlotte's expression was so quizzical, Lizzie had to chuckle. "It's just that so many of these people present a false self here at court, when their private lives are as dramatic as anything at Drury Lane. For instance," the queen's lady pointed to a trio of elegantly dressed people to their left. "See those two women there, standing with the man in the black broadcloth?"

Charlotte nodded.

"The man is the Prince of Brussels. The older woman is Lady Kent who came with him. The pretty younger one is Countess Yasmina. The countess and Madame Kent praise the virtues of the domesticated woman, yet are anything but. They're lovers, unbeknownst to the prince, who sleeps with Lady Kent while his wife is in Prague awaiting the birth of their first child. It's the most scandalous ménage-a-trois. And French Minister d'Eon, the one who made the adoring toast to you? Some say he is actually a woman with a penchant for men's clothing and that he frequents pubs dedicated exclusively to sodomites."

Charlotte's fan went to her mouth in shock as Lady Lizzie continued. "And he's not the only one. Sir Horace Walpole over there with Sir George Selwyn in the corner? They, too, are lovers—two closeted old fairies—one of which—Selwyn—is fascinated by necrophilia."

"What is that? It sounds sinister."

"It's one who's carnally intrigued with dead bodies, caskets, skeletons—that sort of morbidity. They say he dresses up like a woman to go to executions," Lady Lizzie mused. "I tell you were it not for hypocrisy, we'd have no aristocracy. They are all actors—and St. James, a theatre."

Charlotte was astounded by all she'd heard, but as she glanced over her shoulder she saw George still spellbound in conversation with Lady Sarah. "And who is the beautiful woman opposite the king in the green taffeta? My maid of honor who was mistaken for me?"

Lady Lizzie looked, then grimaced slightly. "Were you not introduced, Your Majesty?" she asked in a small voice, which annoyed the queen.

"Of course I was. I am asking who she is to the king?" snapped Charlotte with a tone.

"She's a… she is his… 'special friend,'" Lizzie stammered.

"I see." Charlotte took a moment to accept what she had already surmised from George's mother. The king had a mistress; someone there before her. Why should it surprise her? He was a man, and she was learning that men—especially men of royal bearing—had mistresses and lovers as though they were rights of passage. Christian Bach had his sopranos, her father had Sister Lena. Did she expect her new husband, who was also a king, to be the lone exception?

"Perhaps we should hang her portrait next to the other 'special friends' on the third floor," Charlotte mused to Lady Lizzie.

Lizzie chuckled, after which Charlotte held out her hand to be helped up, "Find my ladies and tell them I'm ready to go up now."

Lady Lizzie curtsied and angled through the crowd, searching for the queen's ladies. It was then that Charlotte saw Lady Bethany chastising Anne, who kept trying to please her mistress. The gesture annoyed Charlotte. *Different kingdom, same music*, she thought, and after feigning exhaustion she begged forgiveness and had her ladies show her to her bedroom chambers.

✠

As Princess Augusta watched Charlotte ascend the stairs she went to George and pulled him aside. "She is Merovingian, your wife. I saw the mark myself. She may be a de Sousa, too."

George grunted at his mother. "You know I do not believe in all that."

"You should. Your father certainly did. It's why he joined the Order. Pay attention, son."

George clenched his jaw in an effort to hide his displeasure at his mother's obstinacy. "I'm going up now."

"For the evening? You know we must gather the others for…"

"No!" George held up his hand to her. "I am dispensing with all of that in my reign." He excused himself from his guests and went upstairs, leaving his mother aghast.

Twenty Five

Charlotte entered her chambers and pulled off her crown, heaving in pain. "Get me out of this dress at once," she demanded of her ladies. "It weighs as much as me." Lady Schwellenberg and Lady Hagedorn quickly unhooked the heavy gown.

"I do not understand these people. Is 'pug' the only word the British can use to describe my nose?" Charlotte lamented, "If so, what on earth were they calling it in Germany?"

"Unique, I hope...," they heard from behind them.

Charlotte turned to find George approaching her with a small velvet box. "...for I'm sure the citizens of the Rhine were far more expressive in their assessment of beauty."

Charlotte blushed. Her new husband was a charmer she thought as he held out the box.

"A wedding gift," he offered.

Charlotte was touched as she opened the box. Inside she found pearls and a locket with George's image. The king showed her his matching locket, which had a lock of her hair inside.

"Thank you, Your Majesty. I will cherish it always."

"You're welcome. But as we are now husband and wife, do you think you can concede to calling me 'George'?"

Charlotte smiled warmly. "Yes, George."

George put the pearls and locket around her neck and noticed the amulet, which had been hidden in the bosom of her gown.

"A childhood gift...from my father," Charlotte offered without prompting.

"It's as lovely and unusual as you."

The queen smiled nervously as George traced her throat lightly. Then, her chalk-white makeup came off on his finger, and he frowned. He took his thumb and rubbed the side of her face harder. This time the makeup came off completely, revealing Charlotte's olive complexion.

George was perplexed, took a step back, then went to his water pitcher. He wet his handkerchief then approached the queen and rubbed her face vigorously. Soon the realization his new bride was a woman of color brought a redness to his face and he motioned to Charlotte's ladies.

"Remove her wig, bathe her completely, then bring her to my chambers undusted. I want to see what *exactly* I have acquired for a wife." He left the room without further comment.

After a few moments to access the situation, Charlotte came to an understanding and turned to her ladies. "Let's have on with it. If I, with my abominable German wardrobe, large German feet, and pug nose, am to be sent packing back to Germany, sooner is better."

An hour later, Charlotte was presented to George bathed, perfumed and dressed in a peignoir by her ladies. Her own hair was in its natural mass of auburn curls, and she was scrubbed clean and devoid of make-up revealing her true golden complexion.

George perused her a moment, then gestured for her ladies to leave. After a hug to each, Charlotte's look assured them she would be all right. Lady Schwellenberg and Lady Hagedorn curtsied and left. Charlotte turned back to George nervously, her head bowed.

"Remove your gown," George commanded quietly, his stare burning into her.

Charlotte's eyes welled with tears as she slowly reached up to undo the ribbons supporting her peignoir. Instantly it dropped to the floor. She stood before her husband naked—her hands covering her private parts, her head still bowed. George, not displeased, remained expressionless as he walked around. Seeing her birthmark he remarked. "So it's true. You *do* have the taint of Moor in you?"

Charlotte nodded slightly. George lifted her head. "And the mark of the Merovingians?"

Charlotte said nothing, keeping her eyes down. How could he know this, when she had only learned it herself on the ship?

"Look at me," George requested.

But his wife's eyes remained cast down and her tears were falling. She felt herself trembling and chanted *Calm down, Charlotte, calm down* over and over in her head.

"Look at me," George demanded again.

Charlotte's eyes finally rose to meet his. The king touched her birthmark, frowning slightly. "I have spared you the humiliating custom of the entire court at our bedside watching us consummate our marriage. Believe me, my mother is not happy about it," he informed her. "I have very few rules, the most important being that you are never to be alone with my mother, Charlotte. She's an artful woman and will try to govern you."

Charlotte did not know how to react.

"Your Moorish blood can remain our secret. You may continue with the subterfuge of powder and paint, and I shall make sure you have the most comfortable and privileged of lives. I shall give you everything, Charlotte, everything you require for your happiness," he stated flatly, "except my heart."

Charlotte's countenance dropped as George covered her with her peignoir. "You are my queen, Charlotte. And as such, you need only provide heirs to continue the Hanover line to the throne. Please find it in your heart to extract contentment from that." George lifted Charlotte's head when it fell again. He smiled, "So. First things first—heirs."

George took his bride to the bed flinging off the sheets. They did not make love. They merely had sex. Charlotte's first time actually submitting to a man had none of the fireworks or craved lust she always dreamed there might be with Christian. Instead, it was the rote and complaisant obligation of two people forced to perform that which had to be. Charlotte's eyes remained open throughout, and she counted 317 cracks in the ceiling paint as George lowered himself onto her, entered her body, and used it without emotion, care, and most certainly without love. She wondered if it would have been different with Christian.

Minutes later, the king rolled over onto his right side, leaving Charlotte to ask herself if this was all there was to it. An hour passed and George, embarrassed by his performance, turned to his sleeping wife and stroked her hair. His new bride's closed eyes seemed so sweet in repose. But inevitably, his mind wandered off to Sarah. He had disappointed two women in this one night. Both with the decision he made for the sake of England. Could he be happy with Charlotte for the rest of his days? Or would he succumb to the nature of the Hanover men and always keep a mistress for his pleasure? And what would it do to Sarah, being at his beck and call merely for carnal gratification? Could he do that to her simply because he was king?

He and his new queen had just consummated their marriage, yet his mind had been on Sarah the whole time, however short. All England was now his and he had to rule wisely, but what of his truest, deepest affections? Would they ever be for Charlotte? Having to settle it, at least in his own mind, George eased out of bed and put on his night jacket. After a brief moment's pause, he crept out of the room and hurried down the hall and up the stairs to the apartment which had been assigned to Lady Sarah for the evening.

The urgent knocking on the door awakened Lady Sarah's lady in waiting, who answered in her nightdress. She was shocked to see the king.

"Leave us," demanded George as he stepped inside the room without invitation. The lady hurried away leaving Sarah, also in a nightdress, trembling upon seeing the king.

"Your Majesty, what are you doing here?" she wondered aloud, curtseying in reverence.

George said nothing. He barged into the room and scooped her into his arms, kissing her uncontrollably. She struggled a moment before pushing herself away from his amorous advances.

"Are you mad? This is your wedding night."

"My heart is still yours. It will always be," he said, pulling her to him again. "I need you."

"Your needs no longer concern me, sir. Remember, you have a wife for that—a woman you married less than ten hours ago."

But George kissed her again, urgent, passionate, unrelenting. Eventually Sarah's heart lost the battle with her head and she yielded, returning his kisses and pressing herself into him with abandon. Finally, she found the strength to turn her head, tears building with regret.

"You have to leave, George. This is not honorable."

"Honor be damned. I love you, Sarah,"

Lady Sarah crossed herself, sighed, and looked at her beloved. Despite everything, she still loved him, too. Thus, without even realizing it, the king's lover closed and bolted the door. She never again thought about the new Queen of England—George's new wife—who was sleeping just two floors below.

As for the queen, unbeknownst to George, her eyes had opened the moment he rose from the bed. She turned and looked at the place where his head had been just minutes before, knowing he'd left her bed for Lady Sarah's. This was to be her fate now. Though she had allowed herself to be manipulated into a loveless marriage, the time for self-pity was long gone. Charlotte had to make peace with the situation and continue the mission she promised herself on the ship. Either that, or do as her brother Adolph suggested: *"Take a lover."*

> *Our official coronation took place a fortnight later. George and I were crowned King and Queen of England, anointed with holy oil, and received our scepters at Westminster Abbey. My life as a queen began. But oh what a lonely, unrewarding existence it became. Though my new world was vast and gilded, I felt enslaved. I was in a foreign country, struggling with the language, and worse, the cuisine. Even though Lady Hagedorn, Lady Schwellenberg and Sir Albert genuinely comforted me, I felt alone. George was content to leave me abandoned and spent his time hunting or reading while I wrote letters to my family and cherished the ones I received in return. George's mother was true to her word and delivered several dozen German-made shoes within months of my arrival. But I still had no connection to family except the heirs I was expected to gestate. So, I accommodated my new husband and country and did my job.*
>
> *On the 12th day of August, 1762, nine months to the night of my wedding, I delivered England her future king. From the birthing chamber, as I sweated from a nine-hour labor, I watched as Doctor Hunter took my newborn from my arms and brought him to the window to present him to the British people. In his deeply northern brogue he announced: 'It is a boy!! The Prince of Wales and future king—George Augustus Frederick*

Hanover!' I heard cheers from the crowd, and then fell into a long sleep and recuperation.

The king, I discovered, had three constants in his life: his prized collection of forty-five clocks which rang out at the same time causing my head to explode. His raging headaches and illness which in '62 kept him waylaid from January until July from fever and insomnia…

…And Lady Sarah Lennox. He continued to see her whenever he could, forcing me to take it in stride. This was the deal I had struck—my choice of death.

And I accepted it.

Twenty Six

*I*n the intervening two years I wrote six letters to Francois Antoine
Gaston, Duke of Levis-Mirepoix asking for his help. I explained
to him I was the daughter of the late Grand Duke Charles Louis
*Frederick from Mecklenburg for whom years ago he had translated a few scroll
passages. I told him that we had met at Sanssouci at King Fredrick's birthday
ball and that I now understood what he meant when he asked if my father left
me with instructions for him. I wrote that I wanted to invite him to London.
But I never received a word. So, until father's scrolls or the words on my amulet
could be deciphered, there was nothing to do regarding my search for truth but
wait. As queen, my comings, goings, incoming and outgoing mail were
monitored. So for propriety's sake I dispatched my letters through Swelly.*

*Meanwhile, through the tutelage of Doctor John Majendie, a canon of
Windsor, I learned English well enough to have conversations with the palace
staff and George's family without too prominent a German accent. I also read
the newspapers Swelly snuck in for me. From them I learned that George had
a great deal of enemies. A year after our marriage he appointed his friend and
long-time advisor John Stuart, the Earl of Bute, as Prime Minister. He did it
to diminish the power base of the Whig party, who dominated Parliament,
and he hoped Bute could help him bring about peace with France now that
the Seven Years war had ended.*"

Charlotte went out of her way to please George as well as find positions
for members of her family in Mecklenburg. But she was perennially
disappointed. She was unable to offer her brother Adolph a vacant Knight
Companionship in the Order of the Garter. Instead, she stood next to her

husband as he removed his sword from its sheath and knighted Lord Bute into the Order.

Charlotte always thought Bute's appointment as Prime Minister was a terrible misstep. Like George, he was a Tory. But he was also a Scot which made him greatly despised. Both Houses of Parliament felt he was too inexperienced and disagreements arose concerning Bute's attempts to extend the power of the monarchy. This dissention was orchestrated by George's arch enemy, Sir John Wilkes, an opponent of George's policies, and instigated by Henry Fox, still bitter that George didn't marry his sister-in-law, Lady Sarah. Members of Parliament felt George was manipulated by Bute, and on every occasion George addressed the Houses the prevailing innuendo was that he was regurgitating "a Bute idea or theory."

Charlotte tried her best to intervene suggesting George ask for Bute's resignation, even though she liked the Prime Minister. George swatted the idea, reminding the queen of her place.

"You are a consort. Not the sovereign," he would say.

This foreclosed the issue and Charlotte tried to stay out of George's affairs. Living with him was especially difficult as each day of contention between George, Bute and the Whig party infuriated Fox and Wilkes. Wilkes was so enraged, he created a newspaper called *The New Briton* entirely for the purpose of deriding George. Caricatures and essays on the king's "latest mistakes" always sent George into shouting spells, particularly at the cartoons of the married Bute and George's mother—which alluded to their affair. Each of George's screaming sessions inevitably landed at Charlotte's feet and the queen somehow became the cause of all his ills. Charlotte, of course, understood why. She was not Lady Sarah, whom George wanted, and at who better to vent than the woman who could do nothing but accept his behavior and stay silent. If Charlotte voiced anything remotely political, George harangued her and she would be forced to apologize or endure his wrath for days. As this was never worth it, the queen learned to keep her opinions to herself…

…Until one night.

Charlotte and George were in their coach returning from King's Theatre. There had been a fire on the main road, so their coachman used a detour past the St. Giles in the Fields section of the city. This area was clearly unfashionable and Charlotte noticed several poor Negroes begging in the streets. There were also Caucasian women prostituting them-selves for any gentleman passers-by, purse snatchers plying their trade, and children hungry on the street. George paid no attention, but Char-lotte did not like what she saw. It reminded her of what she'd seen be-fore arriving at Sanssouci palace years earlier.

"These people are suffering."

"You can't allow it in," George countered. "Poverty exists every-where in the world. That is the way of things." He reached over her to draw the curtains. But Charlotte stopped him refusing to accept such a dismissal as she had before. "George, these people are in a bad way."

"Most of them are Negroes or slaves," George snapped. "What do you purport we do, leap from this coach and feed them from our privy purse? All twenty thousand of them?"

Charlotte was in shock. "My God. Are there twenty thousand slaves in London?"

"Why do you care?"

"Why do you not?"

The king said nothing. At first Charlotte thought she had been too vocal and overstepped her boundaries. Then, an explosion from somewhere deep within erupted like a volcano. "What is your position on abolishing this practice? Do you not see its inhumanity?"

George was initially incredulous, then belligerent. "Slavery is part of the economic survival of the empire. If Britain ceased the trade France would merely pick up the spoils and become even more powerful. The outcome for slaves themselves will not be different. Why would I be foolish and end the one enduring commercial enterprise which sustains us against our debt." He reached over the queen and pulled the curtains anyway. "I knew it was only a matter of time before the Moor in you would rear its ugly head and charge me like a bull. Who have you been listening to—idle chit-chat courtesy of Sir Wilkes? Or perhaps the footmen and servants below-stairs who are pining away for freedom from the drudgery and cruelty of their lives suffered in the splendor of the Palace?"

"I listen to my heart, George. The same heart you do not seem to mind having a son with—a son whose heart, by the way, beats with that same *Moorish* blood."

"Enough!" bellowed George. "Be silent, or you will be sorry."

There. She had been dismissed by the king's tone which demanded he not tolerate any more insolence from his wife. Ergo, she remained quiet for the rest of the trip back to St. James. She knew there would be hell to pay that night. George would have a glass of brandy to fortify himself, then let loose the dogs of rage upon her. She did not have to wait long. While Charlotte was in the nursery kissing little Prince George goodnight, the king thundered in and so cruelly dismissed the governess that she looked upon Charlotte hoping the queen would survive his wrath. With as much confidence as Charlotte could muster, she asked the governess to stay with the baby as she, Charlotte, would be the one leaving instead. When the queen turned to go, George took her arm in protest. "Are you leaving the presence of your king without so much as a 'By your leave'?"

"Yes," snapped Charlotte yanking her arm away. She then left the nursery and ran upstairs to her chambers. But George was hot on her heels, raving like a lunatic. "How dare you disrespect your king in this manner. I could have you…"

"…Shot?" Charlotte spat back, continuing to the second floor. "Beheaded like Anne Boleyn? Sent to the Tower? Hanged? Must you endure the humiliation of me turning my back against your insufferable verbiage as I have at the hands of your continuing dalliances with Lady Sarah? Or your dismissal of my heartfelt opinions regarding slavery, given not in anger, but in truth and esteem for you?" She opened the door to her chambers struggling against a tide of tears. "You claim a want of respect, Your Majesty? Show some." She slammed the door.

George entered immediately. "You shall not speak to me this way. I am king."

"And I am queen, dammit!" She sat at her dressing table and began brushing her hair without the aid of Lady Lizzie who, upon seeing the king's attitude, fled from the room. The brush fell to the floor and Charlotte did not retrieve it. Instead, her head fell into her hands in despair.

George became curiously quiet and, after a moment, wandered over to her. He quietly picked up the brush and in an unexpected move knelt down to her as a curtain of gravitas enveloped him. "I am sorry, my dear," he said softly. "In our two years together you have never done anything improper except have my child, suggest ideas for the betterment of England, and care for me." He wiped her eyes. "You deserve to be happy. I just wish I could make you so."

Charlotte had already said too much for one evening, and thus remained silent. Finally, after some thought, he kissed her. His look was the saddest, most unresolved expression she had ever seen. Then he left the room with no further comment. The queen turned to her reflection in the mirror and stared at it for some time. After a moment, she took her beloved silver ballerina music box from her chest and wound it up. As the familiar music filled the room, she allowed herself to think about Christian. She wanted to remember *his* kiss, *his* words to her that last day at Mirow: *"...I want you to be my wife...for I love you like I love my music..."* As far as love went, all she had was yesterday, and the ocean of secrets in a woman's heart were best left there.

Charlotte and George said very little to each other for the next several days. At mealtimes even his family noticed it, and one day his mother pulled the queen aside to inquire about it. Charlotte told Princess Augusta that George had not been feeling well. Augusta knew better. She knew her son, and her look to Charlotte suggested she "tow the line" as a wife.

Charlotte never refused her husband's desire for marital congress. But each time he touched her, it always felt perfunctory, and when he was done, he would roll over and fall asleep.

Then one Friday, while planting tulip bulbs in her small garden enjoying her one true pleasure, Charlotte saw it for herself. George was at the side gate furtively spiriting Lady Sarah out of the palace to a carriage. She seemed upset, prompting Charlotte to curiously hurry to the side of the building, attempting to hear them if she could. Lady Sarah was frustrated.

"I have told you I cannot and will not play the king's mistress," she lamented.

"Sarah, what would you have me do? I cannot rid myself of my wife for no apparent reason. She has given me a son and the country loves her," George responded.

"Then I have your answer. You have your hereditary heir for a Hanover succession, and I have my self-respect and pride. Goodbye, Your Majesty."

Sarah got into the carriage and it sped away leaving George flustered. Witnessing their interaction broke Charlotte's heart.

A fortnight later at the king's Friday evening drawing room, Charlotte was chatting with Sir Allan Ramsey, the royal portrait painter. Generally, the king's levees began at noon, but George was having another in a series of bad headaches and was late that day. Charlotte came down without him. Two hours later George arrived, and the queen kept her distance. This however, was not unusual because guests were presented to them from separate sides of the room. Charlotte remained with Sir Allan engaged in conversation, and promised him she would start posing the following week for an official portrait. Sir Allan introduced two of his friends to her—a fabulously dressed, confident and opinionated French woman named Madame Lia de Beaumont who appeared to be in her forties; and Chevalier Joseph Boulogne de Saint-George—a brilliant violinist and swordsman of mixed African ancestry who had enthralled all of Europe with his virtuosity. Charlotte asked Saint-George if he would grace them with a performance. Saint George replied that he had not been invited to. Charlotte told him she would personally remedy the situation at their next levee and found him gracious.

But there was something about Madame Lia, something in her eyes which was familiar and engaging, and she was instantly drawn to her. Straight away they exchanged confidences, and Mme. Lia complimented the queen on how beautiful she thought Charlotte's complexion was with the amount of makeup she was wearing. Charlotte dared not tell her it was to hide the pallor of her skin tone, but just receiving flattery from anyone took her aback. She appreciated it. Mme. Lia said she had a shipment of facial potion coming in from France which would keep the queen's skin radiant and offered to bring some as soon as it came—if Charlotte so desired. The queen told her she would be delighted to receive such a gift. It was then she also learned that Mme. Lia also knew the Duke de Levis-Mirepoix. "I adored his father Charles-Pierre," said Lia. "But his son, Francois is such a joy. What a shame the poor man is in such wretched health."

Charlotte was surprised. "Duke Francois is ill?"

"Oh yes. They don't know what is wrong. Do you know him?"

"Only in passing." Charlotte confessed in a small voice. Now she understood why the Duke had not answered her letters regarding her father's diary claims. As they chatted, Charlotte's eyes wandered over to Lord and Lady Bethany and their maid, Anne. She watched as Lady Bethany asked something of Anne, who frowned and shook her head. Lady Bethany pulled Anne into the hallway, verbally abused her again, and this time slapped the girl's face so hard her amulet jerked from its hiding place and fell across her shoulder. Anne began to cry.

Charlotte became angry. She had experienced such behavior with her own mother at Sanssouci and knew the humiliation of it. When she and the Ethiopian caught each other's eye Anne looked away mortified. Something came over Charlotte and she excused herself. After dismissing Lady Bethany with a look connoting her eminence, she took Anne aside and asked if she was content working for Lord and Lady Bethany. After a cursory glance to Lady Bethany, Anne informed the queen she had food, shelter and a fireplace. "I am their slave, Your Majesty. What more can I say?"

Charlotte stared at her. Anne had spoken the words, *"What more can I say?"* but her unconscious, desperate look into the queen's eyes spoke misery in volumes. Charlotte returned to Mme. Lia as St. George regaled everyone with his story of being born a slave in Santo Domingo and his white colonialist father taking him to Paris where he learned to fence, play the violin, and compose music. During his story Charlotte looked back at Anne.

"Imagine if all Negroes had such a chance," she whispered.

"Or women," Mme. Lia added pointedly, looking at Charlotte as if to remind her that she had the tiniest modicum of power. Charlotte looked at Mme. Lia, nodding in agreement, and smiled—for instantly she had an epiphany.

✠

"Lady Bethany, would you be interested in parting with your maid, Anne Josef? The queen has very much become attached to her and wishes her to be employed here at St. James."

There was a long pause as Lady Bethany looked at Lord Robert Montagu aghast. *Ah*, she thought, so this was why she had been summoned to the palace so soon after the king's levee. She was to be negotiated out of her maid. Shaking her head she replied, "But, sir, Lord Bethany and I own Anne. We require her services at Epps House and cannot do without her."

Lord Montagu moved in closer, narrowing his eyes. "Lady Bethany. Am I to understand that your queen requests of you the services of your maid and you refuse?"

"Not so much as refuse, Lord Montagu. I...I mean to say Lord Bethany and I paid good money for Anne, and we need her. We do not enjoy as many maids and persons of service as Her Majesty. We cannot afford to let her go with no…remuneration of any kind. Surely the queen can find it in her heart to, perhaps, mortgage or barter for the girl in some way?"

Now Lord Montagu understood what was going on. The Bethanys needed money. They were obviously another in a long line of royals who were rich in titles yet poor in liquid assets.

"I am prepared to offer £400 from the queen's privy purse to purchase her. Is that 'barter' enough for Your Ladyship?"

Lady Bethany tried to contain her pleasure with an outward expression of acquiescence. "Yes, Lord Montagu. I am sure Lord Bethany would accept that as incentive."

"I should hope so, for Lord Bethany's. Especially since the king's memory goes in and out as regards to his support and good graces— especially when constantly badgered by the queen."

Lady Bethany understood. "I will have the girl delivered to Her Majesty tomorrow."

The next afternoon Charlotte was in the reception hall sipping tea in the window seat, reading a newspaper Lady Schwellenberg had snuck in to her. A notice caught her eye announcing that "Orione," a new opera by Johann Christian Bach, starring Anna Lucia de Amicis, would be opening at King's Theatre that February.

The queen's heart leaped. Christian was in London and would be at King's Theatre. It meant the royal couple would be attending the first performance. How would she react to seeing him? He would be so near—close enough to touch.

These thoughts, however, were soon interrupted by Lord Montagu who announced the arrival of Anne Josef. The African was nervous, and all her humble belongings were tucked away into a lone valise. When she was brought into the Presence Room before Charlotte she instantly dropped into a deep curtsey, keeping her head down. Charlotte slipped the newspaper behind a pillow in the window seat, then motioned Montagu away. When he was gone she waved Anne forward. "Do you know why you are here?"

Anne kept her head lowered. "I was told you have purchased me— that I am to start working for Your Majesty and live here in the palace from now on."

"That is correct."

Anne looked up, her eyes flashing humility. "You have always been kind to me—even respectful. I shall die happily in service to you, Your Majesty."

"You shall die in no one's service, happily or not, but your own."

Now it was Anne who frowned in confusion as the queen continued. "You are free now, Anne. I offer employment here. You shall be paid proper wages of twenty-four guineas a year for your labors." Charlotte reached out to touch the amulet around Anne's neck. "And you will have regular time off for your own pursuits."

Still, Anne was not sure what she had heard and her grimace remained puzzled.

"Did you not understand what I just said?" asked Charlotte.

Anne shook her head slightly. "You… you spent money to buy me from Lady Bethany, yet you're freeing me only to pay me more for my services?"

"Yes. Everyone has a right to their own opinions, pursuits, comings and goings. It should be the same with Negroes. Now, the king and I have a difference of opinion on this issue, so I dare say he will be bothered by my decision regarding you. Nonetheless, you will be in service to me should you choose to work here. And if you do not wish to work here, you are free to go."

Now Anne was really disconcerted. "Do you mean I don't *have* to work here for you?"

"Not if you don't wish to. That is an option free people have."

Again Anne fell into a curtsey radiating appreciation. "It was foretold that the God of David would favor me in this way. I would be most delighted to work for you. I will do anything this humble servant can for Her Majesty with all my heart for the rest of my days."

The queen nodded. "Very well. You shall operate as my eyes and ears here at court, and you shall have the same rights and privileges as all my other staff. Your services shall be most valued and we shall be good friends, you and I." Charlotte rang the bell on the sideboard, then added, "And, one day we shall have a talk…" she pulled her own amulet from her bosom to show Anne, whose face registered utter amazement, "…about our respective secrets."

Anne curtsied as Lord Montagu came in and the queen nodded to him. "Show Miss Josef her room and have uniforms made for her."

Montagu left with Anne, who smiled appreciatively at Charlotte before going. Charlotte turned to the window, grateful for small miracles. *Good. One less slave in Britain*, she thought. She was wondering about the other 20,000 Negroes in the Empire as Lady Schwellenberg tapped on the door, then entered. "It's time to dress you for dinner." She noted Charlotte's mood. "Your spirits are at a low ebb, Your Majesty. They have been for some time. What is wrong?"

"My life is so routine here, Swelly. I have my books, my children, my diary, but no genuine inspiration to help enlighten or engender purpose."

"How does one acquire inspiration?"

"I haven't the foggiest. But whatever it is—I shall never find it here in England."

"What about your music? You used to play the piano-forte all the time in Mecklenburg."

"*You* played, remember?"

The two women chuckled. Charlotte then thought, "Tis a foolish person who cannot find contentment in their present and can only forage through their past for nuggets of happiness."

"Your Majesty, you had more than nuggets of happiness in the Rhine," said Swelly. "You had your music, your sister and favorite brother. You had Jon, Sister Lena, and you had…"

"…Christian?"

There was an uncomfortable pause as the obvious became apparent. Charlotte removed the newspaper from under the pillow and showed the story to Lady Schwellenberg, who read it, regretting she'd brought up the subject. "What will you do?"

"I don't know," answered Charlotte.

"Do you still have feelings for him, my girl?"

Charlotte fiddled with her amulet and finally nodded. She could not lie anymore—not to herself, and not to her lady who knew her too well. "How could I not, Swelly? There isn't a day that goes by that I do not think about him, or wonder what he's doing, or who he is with, or if he is in love. Every time George touches me, I close my eyes and pray that when they open it will be Christian touching me. In those precious few months in Mecklenburg I felt more loved and desired than I had ever been, or will be again." After another moment of silence, Charlotte stood and patted her lady on the shoulder. "Come, Swelly. Let's get me dressed. Try to make me as lovely as you can, for something tells me after what I've done today, George will be cranky."

"What did you do?"

"I freed Anne Josef, the Bethany's former slave. Then I employed her here a moment ago."

"Oh," Lady Schwellenberg mocked. "*That* requires your green brocade."

The two chuckled and left the Presence Room, buoyed by their longtime friendship. Little did they know that Lady Lizzie had been listening just outside the door and craftily hid in a doorway as they went upstairs to the queen's private chambers.

An hour later, Charlotte was dressed in the green brocade dress, having her first-course soup with George, his mother, brothers Edward, William, Henry, and Frederick, his uncle William, and two sisters Augusta and Caroline. A tense hush had consumed the room and everyone was eating quietly for, indeed, the king appeared rankled.

Charlotte ignored this and remained cheerful, complimenting Fritz on the food. Immediately after he served her a second helping of mutton and potatoes, she offered conversation bored by the silence.

"I hear there has been some contention in Parliament regarding the Colonists. I understand they are upset over something called a 'Stamp Act'? What is that, exactly?"

George's mother shot Charlotte a cold look, as though her daughter-in-law had conjured up Lucifer himself. Everyone looked at George, whose eyes turned blood-red in attack.

"And it is my understanding you made an acquisition today."

Charlotte was prepared and chose a different strategy from their other arguments. "Yes," she responded gaily, "I purchased a person using my privy purse—my own private financial allotment. Then I felt badly about *owning* a human being, so I freed her. And because I like her, I gave her employment here at the palace." Charlotte then jested, "These potatoes are divine."

"Charlotte…"

"…George," Charlotte interrupted, "I shall have no ugliness this evening when *you* can do something to keep me happy—which you said two weeks ago you didn't know how to do."

George was embarrassed by his wife's reference. "And what would make you happy?"

"A new harpsichord."

Everyone looked at Charlotte as she became more confident and authoritative. "A new harpsichord, a music room, and the services of a music master," Charlotte continued. "I want concerts and artists performing here at St. James. This palace is devoid of inspiration. We had better entertainment at Mirow Palace, which I have heard you thought was a small, unfashionable court. Also, ask the gardeners to bring me a better selection of floral bulbs for larger gardens. I enjoy gardening. It's one of the few pursuits you allow me other than reading. And, by the way, I want more books for the library, and to have an occasional friend to come and visit. I shall not be imprisoned here."

"To what do we owe this sudden burst of interests?" said George, raising an eyebrow.

"You have your 'diversions.' Now, I am claiming mine," Charlotte answered pointedly.

Princess Dowager Augusta grinned behind her napkin, for her son could say nothing.

Twenty Seven

On 15 February, in the Royal Box under the cavernous arch of King's Theatre, sat George and Charlotte. It was opening night of "Orione," the new opera by Johann Christian Bach, and everyone who was anyone in British aristocracy was in attendance. Lady Sarah Lennox was there seated next to Sir Thomas Bunbury and the famous actress Sarah Siddons.

As the young king and queen listened to an aria sung by Anna Lucia de Amicis, George glanced at Lady Sarah and Bunbury holding her hand. He was oblivious to Charlotte's feelings as his own were divided between annoyance with Sarah and enchantment with the soprano.

Anna's voice was magnificent. Her gestures and theatrical presence were polished, and on several occasions evoked tearful emotion from the king. George was also impressed with the story of the opera, and leaned into Charlotte remarking on how wonderful it was. Charlotte, too, acknowledged how much Christian had grown as a composer, but, more than anything, she worried about how she would react upon seeing him in person.

George had planned a special King's Levee for Christian and members of the cast at St. James after the performance. As Charlotte had not been consulted in the planning of the levee, she was informed of it the day before, and was not emotionally prepared. Though she had been experiencing pain in her side, it wouldn't be appropriate to plead illness and hide in her room all night—not after attending the performance. So she would have to be there, and she would have to be the consummate actress and submerge her emotions.

An hour later, the curtain rang down and when it rose again the entire cast assembled onstage. After applause for the tenor and baritone, thunderous cheers echoed throughout the theatre for Miss Amicis. Then she and the other cast members stood aside and gestured upstage, where Johann Christian Bach appeared and came forward. Tumultuous applause rose from the audience, and the composer looked up to the box seats and bowed reverently to their Majesties.

Charlotte's heart stopped as she nodded in acknowledgement. For just a moment their eyes locked and a myriad of thoughts flooded her mind. Was it possible that Christian had become *more* handsome and self-assured? She soon admonished herself. *Stop this fantasizing, Charlotte. You are queen for God's sake. Remember what your mother once said. Christian is a 'mere musician—there to entertain the masses.'* Then she chastised herself for daring to diminish Christian and his accomplishments. He was now one of the most renowned composers in Europe—a feat to rival Handel, and she applauded along with all of Christian's admirers because she was, in fact, his biggest one—the one whose heart would always be his.

The opera started promptly at five o'clock that evening, and by seven-thirty, despite the winter's snow, St. James Palace was a cornucopia of MPs, celebrities, aristocrats and opera lovers. The well-dressed guests chatted and danced to music provided by a string quintet. They also enjoyed free-flowing wine, canapés, hors d'oeuvres and candied fruits served by Franz, Fritz and Anne Josef. Anne volunteered her services, for she wanted to experience this levee from the perspective of a palace insider, as opposed to Lord and Lady Bethany's ill-treated slave. The first moment she handed punch to her former masters gave her such pleasure she thought she would burst.

"Orione" had been a resounding success, and members of the cast moved easily through the drawing rooms with the royal guests. Charlotte and George were on one side of the room conversing with French Minister Charles d'Eon, elegantly dressed in his Dragoons uniform, and Colomba Mattei, the aging manager of King's Theatre. Opposite them were Prime Minister Bute and Princess Augusta, trying not to be obvious but having difficulty ignoring each other while Bute's wife chatted with other courtiers.

Across the way stood Sir Henry Fox and Sir John Wilkes hungrily perusing the room for intrigues like witches in a Shakespeare play. Their hunger was quickly sated when the crier announced the arrival of "...Lady Sarah Lennox 'Bunbury' and Sir Thomas Bunbury." Charlotte turned to catch George's reaction.

The king could not mask his disbelief as the two came through the reception line, and soon infuriation took residence on his face. He had to accept that Sarah meant what she had said—that she would no longer be "the king's mistress" and that he had lost her.

"Congratulations on your nuptials, Lady Sarah," George heard himself utter, knowing the entire court was aware of his affection for the woman in question. "I pray for your happiness."

Liar, Charlotte mused to herself, watching the drama unfold with a smidgeon of satisfaction as the king and Lady Bunbury thereafter avoided each other. She was not alone. From their perch across the room, Lord Henry Fox was just as amused and reveled in the king's consternation as did Sir John Wilkes.

Finally, the guest of honor arrived and was announced. "Your Majesties, Lords and Ladies, Mr. Johann Christian Bach and Miss Anna Lucia de Amicis." Applause exploded and everyone turned to greet Christian and the lovely 23-year-old opera star clinging to his arm like a crutch. As they made their way through the crowd, Christian looked around valiantly for the queen, finally catching a glimpse of her with George up ahead. He composed himself while offering "hellos" and "thank-you's" to well-wishers along the way. Sir William Cavendish brought the two over to the sovereign and queen's reception line and introduced them. Anna de Amicis dropped into a curtsy, while Christian bowed covertly glancing at Charlotte—who averted her eyes.

"Mr. Bach, never have I heard a more entertaining and heartfelt performance than this evening's. Bravo," George praised cheerfully, turning to Miss Amicis. "And you, my dear, are a delight. Blessed with the voice of an angel."

Anna was so overcome by the king's compliment she became tearful. All she could manage was "Thank you, Sire."

She and Christian then turned to the queen. Charlotte, knowing Christian's penchant for sopranos, canvassed Anna's face a moment. The singer was a beauty without a doubt. She possessed luminous pale skin, and her large gray-blue eyes radiated tenderness and vulnerability —all things Charlotte knew men loved and of which she felt dispossessed. Even at this moment, when she was impeccably dressed, powdered to perfection and her hair fabulously fashioned by Sir Albert, Charlotte still felt unworthy in front of this woman and Christian.

She extended her hand. "Miss Amicis, I share my husband's praise of you, for your voice is most remarkable."

Anna took the queen's hand and curtsied, thanking the queen as best she could overwhelmed as she was by emotion. Finally, Charlotte had to turn to Christian. After a moment, she extended her hand, looking at him directly now. Her gaze into his eyes caused constriction in her voice. "It was…a w-wonderful opera, Herr Bach," she stuttered. "I enjoyed it immensely."

"Thank you, Your Majesty," responded Christian, kissing Charlotte's extended hand and lingeringly looking into her eyes. "It's lovely to see you again after so long an absence."

George reacted. "I did not realize you knew each other."

For just a moment Charlotte appeared guilt-ridden, but found her voice again, never breaking eye contact with Christian. "Yes. I-I knew Herr Bach as a child in Mecklenburg. His brother Emmanuel was my music master and Herr Bach visited my family on rare occasions."

It was a good answer, yes, but not wholly the truth. But how could I tell George the truth? There I was staring at the only man I had ever loved and the pull was still evident between us. I could not take my eyes off of him as I struggled to keep my face set with no discernible trace of emotion. In the four years since last I saw him Christian's features had deepened. His eyes had become more magnetic. He was not the thin, boyish man I remembered, but a sturdy well-formed celebrity with a worldly, aristocratic bearing. When he kissed my hand I found that it took all my resilience to control myself.

"How fortuitous for me," smiled George, motioning to Christian, "I shall have some words for you later, sir."

Christian bowed in acknowledgement, yet glanced at Charlotte. The quintet segued into a lively tune, and George turned to Charlotte. "This is a Betty Blue. Do you know it?"

Charlotte almost laughed aloud. The Betty Blue had been taught to her by Jon Baptiste—whom she hadn't thought about in years—and all for the express purpose of dancing with Christian at Sanssouci. "I do indeed," she smiled, whereupon George excused them from Christian and Anna, and promenaded her to the area where people were dancing—including Lady Sarah and Sir Charles Bunbury. George bowed, Charlotte curtsied, and the king and queen danced—something they rarely did.

Charlotte found herself enjoying this levee more than any other they'd held at St. James, and for just a moment her mind moved away from Christian, his obvious new paramour Anna, and any arguments she'd recently had with the king. She and George were actually laughing, and it felt good to be with him. Since the Betty Blue interchanged partners, George soon found himself dancing with Sarah Siddons; Lady Dunston, and in an unexpected turn of coincidence, Lady Sarah.

George and Sarah could only look at each other feeling regret for what might have been. To speak to each other would create far too much scandal to be acceptable, as anyone watching knew that the king wanted nothing more than to wring her neck—or kiss it.

Charlotte exchanged several partners as well, including Minister d'Eon, the Lord Mayor of London, and, in her own twist of circumstances, Christian Bach.

Both Christian and Charlotte remained silent, as neither knew what to say, yet conveyed all their emotion with their eyes, just as George and Sarah were forced to.

Across the room, Princess Augusta sipped a glass of punch as she and Prime Minister Bute watched George dancing with his new partner, Lady Grenville. Eyeing Christian a moment, Augusta smirked. "Mr. Bach has most attractive legs. Almost as attractive as yours, John."

Bute smiled. "No one's legs are as attractive as mine, Madame." They chuckled, then Bute leaned in to Augusta and furtively patted her bottom. "Now, duty calls, my dear." He excused himself and went over to his wife, who was standing with other ladies of the court, and asked for her hand. The two then went to the dance floor to join the other dancers.

Across the way, Sir John Wilkes caught the action between the Prime Minister and the king's mother and grinned slyly. He reached for another glass of wine, musing to Sir Henry. "It appears there are more unfinished intrigues playing out this evening than at King's Theatre."

"How so, sir?" asked Fox.

Wilkes pointed around the room for emphasis. "Poor Baroness Bute is pining away in the corner forced to endure the constant cozying of her husband and the king's mother. Meanwhile, the king is still flummoxed by the sudden marriage of your sister-in-law to Sir Bunbury, while his queen entertains herself with a certain celebrated composer. It's perfect for the paper. It's all so salacious and divine."

"Also seditious, Wilkes. Tread carefully."

"I always do, dear sir. It's my evil twin '*Mr. North Briton*' who must be cautioned. Just you wait for *his* next installment. Number 43 will expose more machinations and schemes than all his volumes put together." Wilkes chuckled, then reached for his daughter Polly's hand. Leaning in to Fox he advised, "Now, dear boy, I suggest you find your wife and join the intrigues on the dance floor lest we be left out."

As the Betty Blue progressed, Christian found himself with Charlotte once again. This time he had to say something. He had waited three years and could not let things go unsaid again.

"Forgive my not contacting you sooner. I thought you would not wish to see me."

"On the contrary," Charlotte responded furtively, "I had no idea you were in London."

"Surely you received my opus congratulating you on your marriage."

"I did. But I assumed you had sent the music from Italy."

Then after a pause, Christian looked at her directly. "I waited three extra days in Vienna."

But the partners changed again, and Christian had to wait a full three minutes before he and the queen were in proximity to each other again. But it was the king who was Charlotte's partner for the rest of the promenade, and when the Betty Blue ended, Charlotte was escorted by him to their chairs.

For the remainder of the evening Christian had to pretend all would remain right in his world now that he had seen Charlotte again.

And the queen had to do the same.

Twenty Eight

After a multitude of excuses and false starts, Charlotte was finally sitting for Sir Allan Ramsey to have her official portrait painted. It was, in fact, her third sitting that week. But today the lappets on her collar were scratching the queen's neck, yet she dare not move for today Sir Allan was painting her facial image. As she posed perfectly still, her mind ruminated over the events of the last weeks: freeing Anne, Lady Sarah's marriage, the scathing indictments of George and Bute in issue #43 of the North Briton, and seeing Christian again.

Charlotte tried to consign these thoughts to the far reaches of her mind by conversing with Sir Allan. She liked the Scottish rococo painter whose renderings of previous sovereigns she had admired. From the moment she met him at her coronation there was something comforting about him. They chatted easily without regard for rank or caste, and in particular she enjoyed their conversations about the affairs of the day for they agreed on a great many subjects. It never occurred to Sir Allan that a woman should not be involved in politics, nor did he know the king had forbidden Charlotte to engage in such discourse in which the queen took pleasure.

"Is it true Sir Wilkes writes most of the North Briton under a nom de plume?" Charlotte questioned, holding her head as steadily as possible and suppressing the desire to scratch herself.

"Yes. And everyone knows it," Sir Allan responded in his soft Scottish brogue. "No matter the name ascribed to a story, the words of the text match Wilkes' own sentiments exactly—down to the wording, innuendo and accusation. Yet, if he claimed authorship, especially of the disparaging remarks he constantly makes against the king and Minister Bute, he would be arrested for sedition, libel, or both."

"As he should be," snipped Charlotte. But after several more minutes of irritation, she held up her hand. "I'm sorry, Sir Allan, we must stop. These lappets are far too itchy."

Sir Allan paused and watched as the queen unloosened her collar. When she scratched her neck, he saw the heavy white makeup come off on her fingers and her tanner skin showing beneath the red, irritated scratch marks.

"It's just as well, Your Majesty," said the painter, using the moment to great effect. "I cannot seem to get your color pallet just right and I'm annoyed with myself."

Charlotte rubbed her throat, taking in a much-needed deep breath, then posed again, holding herself still as Sir Allan went back to his easel. Moments later the painter frowned again. His hands went to his hips and he shook his head. "Your Majesty, perhaps we should turn you toward the window where the light may be better." Sir Allan moved the queen 90 degrees to the left toward the open window. But upon returning to his easel it still wasn't right. He went back again and looked at her face, inspecting her makeup. "Perhaps it is your face paint which is causing the problem. I cannot get the light right because your face reflects an unnatural gray base no matter where I place you. May I touch your face?"

Charlotte appeared slightly nervous, yet acquiesced. Sir Allan softly touched her chin and her heavy white chalk came off on his fingers. He went back to the easel and got a towel for her.

"Would you mind taking off the excess chalk?"

"I will not. You will paint the queen as she has presented herself."

Now certain this was a personal issue for the queen, Sir Allan stepped back to his easel and tried to paint again. How could he make her understand that he was acting in her best interest? That he knew what was underneath her makeup and had much admiration for his queen.

"Your Majesty," the painter timorously began, praying for absolution should he offend, "You and I have a marvelous opportunity. Together we can present you authentically in a way which would..." he paused and then thought, "celebrate the 'totality' of your...heritage."

Charlotte stared at the painter whose face contorted with nerves and unspoken apology. Yet his demeanor appeared genuine, and again he slowly eased toward her with the towel. "Majesty, may I be permitted to touch you?" He tenderly reached out to touch her cheek. Charlotte remained as still as stone and allowed his touch. Sir Allan looked at his fingers stained with white chalk. Though his voice was soft, it was resolute, which Charlotte appreciated.

"What lies beneath is too beautiful to hide. Please think about my suggestion."

But before the queen could react, Lord Montagu, her Lord Chamberlain, entered the room. "Your Majesty, the king has sent a coach for you. Lord Cavendish is downstairs waiting as he is to accompany you to meet the king."

Charlotte was surprised. "Meet the king? I thought His Majesty was hunting today."

"I am just following orders, ma'am. Now, what shall I tell his Lordship?"

Charlotte gathered her thoughts. "You may tell Lord Cavendish I won't be a moment."

Montagu bowed and left. Charlotte rose from her posing chair in confusion. She turned to Sir Allan. "Obviously we must leave it there for today, Sir Allan." She started to go, and then turned back after a thought. "But...I shall give some...consideration...to your suggestion."

Ramsey bowed as Charlotte left the portrait studio, thanking God that his intentions were positively received.

Forty-three minutes later, two royal coaches crossed St. James's Park and pulled into the courtyard of a beautiful, large limestone manor with more windows than usual for an estate in London. Charlotte was inside the first coach, awed by the formidable elm and lime trees which lined the street. "What was George up to?" she wondered.

Two footmen opened her coach door and Cavendish helped the queen inside the main house where, upon her approach, she could hear hammering and smelled the distinct odor of fresh paint. Inside the grand house, floors were covered by drop-cloths and the interior was being worked on by masons, wood carvers, painters and plasterers. Charlotte carefully stepped over bags of nails, tools and lumber haphazardly strewn about as foremen shouted orders to workmen.

"Good Lord. What on earth is going on, Lord Cavendish? Where is His Majesty?"

"Here," they heard.

George emerged from one of the rooms and angled toward the queen with arms outstretched.

"Welcome to Buckingham House, my dear, your new home."

Charlotte was rendered mute. She looked around the large, impressive estate and immediately imagined what it could be. It was not at all palace size, not by St. James or Windsor standards, and reminded her favorably of the intimacy of Mirow Palace she always loved. At the same time, she was befuddled by George's choice of surprise. "New home? My word."

"I've had my eye on it for quite some time—as did my grandfather and great-grandfather. But the price or the circumstance was never quite right. A week ago, after years of negotiations, Lord Buckingham's grandson, Lord Sheffield, finally agreed to a figure I could live with. For £28,000 pounds I now own it, and I'm giving it to you." George smiled as he continued, "It is my surprise for you—especially after your goings-on about bulbs and gardens and music rooms."

Charlotte held her heart and walked with George through the remodeling. "I love its proximity to St. James," George continued, "and I thought perhaps you would like it as your own estate—to get away from those things which irritate you about court life. Perhaps you would consider bringing up the children here as well."

"Such attention to detail," Charlotte marveled, still in shock. "It's magnificent."

"The main house here will be livable by late spring, complete with your requests for several large gardens and a supply of as many flower bulbs as you require. I am also having a few hundred books delivered in a few weeks." George then pointed to a room just off to the left on the first floor. "Now. Let me show you the room you requested, which is ready at present."

They entered a charming, well-appointed room with crimson velvet drapes and a fire already flickering in the fireplace. Charlotte's face burst into a grin when she saw the lovely harpsichord with a marble bust of Handel sitting on top. Nearby were three music stands, a violin and a crimson velvet settee for relaxing. "This harpsichord is my most prized possession. It once belonged to the great Handel himself. I had it brought from Balmoral to fulfill your wish."

Charlotte was overcome as she looked around joyfully.

"I want you to be happy here at Buckingham. Choose whatever you wish for furnishings and have it decorated as you desire." George motioned to Sir William Cavendish, who appeared with a bottle of champagne and three glasses. George poured two glasses, giving one to the queen. "We have Father Jean Oudart and Dom Pierre Pérignon to thank for the invention of this most excellent drink, and thus I wish to make a toast." George held up his glass, as did Charlotte. "To Buckingham House, which from this day forth shall be 'Queen's House.'"

The two tapped their glasses together and sipped the champagne. Then George gave Cavendish a knowing nod, and his Lord Chamberlain left the room. "Now for the coup d'grace. I was most fortunate to engage some very special services for you and, later on, the children."

George stepped aside and Charlotte heard footsteps approaching. When she looked in the direction of the door she saw Lord Cavendish motion someone in. A moment later, a well-dressed figure adorned in black entered from the shadows, and when Charlotte focused on his face she froze upon recognition: Johann Christian Bach.

Christian smiled knowingly at Charlotte and bowed. "Your Majesties."

"When I discovered Mr. Bach's brother had once been your music master, a bell went off in my head. I approached him and insisted he stay in London to serve here at Queen's House as your music master," George smiled patting Christian on the back. "He agreed so quickly I thought perhaps I had offered him too much," he said, turning to Charlotte. "Are you pleased, my dear?"

Charlotte couldn't speak. She was shaking so much the glass slipped from her fingers, shattering into a thousand chards on the floor. As Cavendish hurried to find someone to clean up the glass, Christian reached out to kiss the queen's hand. "When His Majesty told me of your desire for musical instruction, I told him I could not think of anything better than to please the Queen of England," he grinned wryly.

Charlotte took back her hand and held it, and herself, with the other. She cleared her throat and found her voice finally. "And for that, I am grateful, Herr Bach."

As he sipped champagne from the third glass Cavendish presented him I was on fire inside. George, completely unaware of our previous relationship, babbled on about his hopes that music lessons with the illustrious Bach would occupy my time at the new palace. No doubt he was praying this transparent ploy would help him continue his political duties at St. James without vocal interference from me. But as Christian beheld me I did not care. I knew we were still hopelessly in love with each other. Christian knew he had to maintain decorum as a gentleman. I, too, was reverential in front of George and we conducted ourselves with utmost restraint. But it was difficult. Waves of desire lay waiting for the moment a tide of passion would engulf us. And the moment George left us alone that day, our resolve was tested.

"Your Majesty, you asked me to remind you when it was two o'clock," said Cavendish.

"Ah," groaned the king, as he turned back to Charlotte and Christian, "Legislation to sign, scurrilous scandalmongers to indict, dunderheads to raise to the position of Paymaster."

"Sir Henry Fox is being raised to Paymaster?" Charlotte frowned.

At first George was surprised Charlotte knew to whom he was referring—then he corrected her. "'*Lord*' Henry Fox, Paymaster—in an hour. His help with the Peace Treaty with France forced the appointment. Now if only I can rid myself of Wilkes with an arrest for sedition as swiftly, but…" George grunted, then nodded to Christian, "I'll leave you to your music lesson. Good to have you with us, Mr. Bach."

"Your Majesty," Christian bowed reverentially as George started out. But Charlotte stopped him. "George, thank you for all of this. It was so unexpected…and generous."

George smiled pleased with her response and left with Cavendish.

The moment the door shut Charlotte's pulse raced. She squeezed her fingers trying to hold herself together. Christian came closer and after a few moments broke the silence.

"I instantly gave up my position with Count Litta in Milan, the planning of two more operas, and a series of concerts here in London when the king made his offer. I could not bear to refuse him." Christian's voice dropped to a fervent whisper. "All I could do was count the agonizing moments until I could see you again."

"All as you wiled away said agony with so beautiful a diversion as Miss Amicis."

Christian came around to the queen to look at her face. "Charlotte, I waited in Vienna until I had to go. I never heard from you. I sent so many unanswered letters I felt you had either not received them, like before, changed your mind about our elopement, or abandoned me. Anna de Amicis means nothing to my heart. She is merely a friend."

"I didn't abandon you or change my mind about our being married. My world fell apart."

Christian indicated her surroundings. "Pray, how? You are Queen of England, the British people love you. You have a beautiful son and heir. You have security."

"You are correct. I have no right to complain. But I do wish I still had the letters you sent me instead of the memory of them being stolen from me, along with my virtue, by my cousin. Or that I had not been negotiated into a loveless marriage to a man, who only recently was seeing someone else." She reached out and touched Christian's face, unable to help herself. "Or could have wed the man I loved without regard for pedigree or privilege."

Christian took the queen's hand, kissing it desperately. Yet he dare not go further for fear his want would overwhelm him. Charlotte's eyes spilled forth tears which fell onto his fingers clasped over hers. She, too, chose not to pursue the desires of her heart.

"Christian, we cannot return to the past. We can only go forward. Let's try to fondly remember that innocent time when we meant more to one another and not torture ourselves with what might have been."

Christian bowed in acquiescence. He knew in his heart he would have to struggle with this decision. Charlotte was married, a mother, and the Queen of England. Nothing could ever come of his affection for her. Thus, he motioned toward the harpsichord. After all, what else could he do but give the queen a music lesson as dictated by his employment.

Twenty Nine

*C*hristian and I met every Tuesday and Thursday. It was wonderful to
have music in my life again. As we had promised each other to not
put pressure on our feelings but to enjoy each other's company and
confidences, I found that before long I had confessed quite a few of my
opinions and interests beyond those of a confined wife and mother. He
shared many of them—most particularly my interest in the condition of
Negroes in Britain. Christian was a well-read, well-traveled man, and he
informed me of the plight of Negroes in other areas of the world. Soon, our
conversations deepened and he felt more comfortable expressing his own
opinions and sentiments, and I found him a satisfactory conversationalist.
Although I failed to tell him about my father's diaries or my descent from
Magragana and the Templars, I did find in him a kindred spirit.
Christian Bach was one of the most advanced-thinking men I'd ever
met…"

✠

"Do you know Chevalier St. George?" Charlotte asked one
afternoon as she and Christian took a break from her lesson at Queen's
House.

"Yes. He is one of the most renowned violinists in Europe."

"He was a guest at one of our levees in January. He's of mixed ex-
traction, as you know, and told us his moving story. It made me think of

Jon Baptiste, one of our slaves at Mirow," Charlotte answered, emotionally unable yet to reveal that Jon was also her half-brother. "He and I became good friends. In fact, it was Jon who taught me the Betty Blue in Mecklenburg so I could dance with you without embarrassment at Sanssouci. Despite our friendship, he was sold away for a molestation he did not commit merely because he was black. That, and other considerations, is why I have an affinity for the plight of enslaved people, I suppose."

"I admit I have the same affinity," Christian offered, sipping his brandy. "I have seen with my own eyes atrocities committed against blacks which are sickening. Here in England there is so much poverty, especially in areas they populate," he lamented. "And to exacerbate matters, Britain is the largest exporter of slaves to the Colonies and West Indies."

"I was unaware."

"So much money is in that business. Nearly every member of Parliament is a plantation owner who utilizes slaves in their Caribbean cane fields."

Charlotte was shocked. "Really?"

"It's a world-wide industry," Christian continued. "The French profit from the trade as much as Britain, and for the same reason— sugar, cotton, coffee and tobacco gleaned from the West Indies and the Colonies."

Christian's passion for the subject took hold of him. "We have a system, all perfectly sanctioned, by which we steal human beings from their native land and carry them off against their will so we can sell them and work them to death for the fruits of British mercantile and colonial expansion. And we do it because they are darker-skinned and therefore 'less than' and not entitled to their liberty. We even force them to accept Christianity, as if they did not have a belief system of their own."

"All to assuage guilt from the barbarous behavior exacted on them based on our inflated sense of superiority," Charlotte commented, realizing Christian's sentiments matched hers.

"Queen Elizabeth once said, 'If any of the Africans are carried away without their own consent, it would be detestable, and call down the vengeance of Heaven upon the undertakers,'" responded Christian as he sipped his brandy. "But even *she* turned a blind eye when it came to the economics of Britain's coffers." Christian shook his head and sighed.

"My goodness. I'm beginning to sound like Ramsey—like some raving abolitionist spouting anti-slavery rhetoric at every turn."

"Sir James Ramsey, the minister?" Charlotte inquired.

"Sir Allan Ramsey, the portraitist."

"Sir Allan Ramsey…is *my* portraitist."

When Christian saw Charlotte's reaction, his voice lowered. "Then I implore you to keep it secret. All such persons are in danger of their lives from your husband, the king."

Now it all made sense, Charlotte thought, Sir Allan's comments to her about presenting herself more "authentically" and "in a reality which would 'celebrate' the 'totality' of her heritage," had come from an agenda. Her court painter was an abolitionist, and as an artist with a trained eye, saw right through her ethnic cover-up.

"Were I you, Christian, I would not concern myself with pronouncements resembling others, but whether they are *your* truths. More than anyone, I understand. Only by the grace of God go I."

"What do you mean?"

Charlotte was cautious as she poured a cup of tea for herself, "I know what it's like to feel 'less than' and I did one small thing recently, so someone else wouldn't experience it…"

Christian's brow furrowed as he waited for Charlotte to continue.

"I bought a slave," Charlotte confessed. "I freed her. Now I pay her to work for me."

Christian smiled. "Are things better for her now? What do you know of her life?"

Surprisingly, Charlotte could not answer. She sipped her tea and began to play a few notes as a distraction as Christian stared at her.

"I see. You know about the lives of your ladies-in-waiting for they've been handpicked by the king. They come from your own society," Christian denounced. "But is it not as important for you to know about the life of this woman whom you so valiantly freed, or did you do it merely to prove that you could—to mock the king, or infuriate her former owners?"

"The queen does not make it her business to 'ask questions of' nor 'become intimate with' her household staff. I have sixty-six such people in service to me between St. James and here."

"Yes. Sixty-six people in service to *your pleasure*, Charlotte."

Charlotte continued playing the harpsichord, hoping to drown out Christian's truth—until he took her hands away from the keys, forcing her to look into his eyes.

"Can you not take this woman into your confidence as you once did Jon? Or is she 'less than' in your eyes as well?"

Charlotte knew in her heart she had intended to talk to Anne for two months but was not sure how to proceed. She had freed Anne partly because of the treatment the girl received from the Bethanys, but she also freed the African out of her need to know about Anne's amulet. Now she was embarrassed in front of Christian to have this bubble of truth burst so blatantly.

"I shall be more mindful," Charlotte finally confessed in a small voice.

"I know you will," smiled Christian kissing her hand—which excited her enormously.

✠

The following month, Charlotte entered the portrait studio devoid of her normally overdone chalk makeup. She sat in the poising chair and, after a few moments, announced her decision. "Sir Allan, I have considered your suggestion, and I wish for you to paint me in whichever fashion you deem suitable."

Allan Ramsey was stunned. "You changed your mind, Your Majesty?"

"No. *You* changed it, sir. It has come to my attention you are an…," she searched for the appropriate word, "…'advocate' for the betterment of the conditions of the darker race."

"Well," Sir Allan managed, flabbergasted by her knowledge. "I must commend you on the quality of your spies, Your Majesty."

"Then it's true?"

"I believe quite strongly that God meant for all of us to be independent persons of free will," said the painter, choosing his words carefully. "For far too long there have been those who have allowed human 'servitude' to degenerate into a vile and repugnant institution solely for the profitable crops of tobacco and sugar cane. It is a system of injustice which only serves to elevate the continued arrogance and perceived superiority of the white aristocracy and degrade and humiliate the black oppressed."

Charlotte smiled slightly. "Identifying the problem is one thing. Acting on it is quite another, is it not?"

Sir Allan picked up his brush and dipped it into several colors until he mixed just the right faintly tan oil paint for Charlotte's complexion.

"Indeed. That is why I, as a God-fearing Christian man, occasionally meet with other like-minded members of British society who would like to form an association toward ending not only the slave trade, but slavery itself."

"Are you aware that your words could be construed as treasonous in some circles?"

"I am. But you asked my opinion, Your Majesty," he responded, "Now, shall we begin?"

Charlotte acknowledged this and sat still as he began to paint over his earlier portrait of her. As he worked, he had no idea the queen was nervous about her decision. Even though she had just given him permission to paint her realistically, she wondered if he would create too ethnic a rendering of her to be considered either an official portrait or an attractive likeness. Yet, since her conversation with Christian, the queen was feeling more inclined to allow herself to *be* herself. This also included learning about the minions who served at her pleasure.

"Sir Allan, tell me about those of you who want to form an anti-slavery association."

Sir Allan, again surprised by her interest, steadied his brush. Obviously the fact that the queen was allowing him to paint her with an eye toward her Moorish roots was merely the beginning. "We feel there is a lack of Christian goodness in owning another human being," he started. "Throughout history, every world power, every society where slavery was a component, failed—Egypt, Assyria, Rome, Greece. Whenever one group held another in bondage, ultimately there were uprisings and revolts which always ended in defeat for the persecuters." The painter stopped a moment to work out his thoughts, mindful that he was in the presence of his queen. "I have met many others who share this view, and on occasion we gather and talk."

"Do you and your compatriots feel sugar, tobacco or tea can be harvested without a slave workforce? Most of the plantation owners in the Indies and Jamaica are members of Parliament," Charlotte offered almost paraphrasing Christian's words.

"We know, and we've talked about the idea of a sharecrop system. But any discussion of this is far too ahead of the basic, moral issue—that no one should own another human being."

Charlotte also knew this was the problem, and she remembered Christian's plea a month earlier. "Well, Sir, should you and your associates find you need a 'friend,' I would be happy to support your cause." She then lowered her voice. "Secretly, of course."

"Thank you," the Scotsman said graciously. "Your support would be most cherished—even if it doesn't include the king's."

There came a knock at the door and Charlotte removed herself behind a panel to reapply her makeup as Lord Montagu entered.

"Your Majesty, you have a guest."

"Am I expecting someone, Sir Robert?" Charlotte called out from behind the screen, frowning in the realization that she may have forgotton an appointment.

"Not at all, ma'am. It's Madame Lia de Beaumont. She said she was not expected, but has gifts. I put her in the reception room until I checked with Your Majesty first."

Charlotte grinned and nodded, "Ah. Tell Mme. Lia I shall be there presently." Montagu left and Charlotte turned to Sir Allan. "To be continued—as always."

Charlotte left the studio and made her way downstairs to the Reception Hall, where she found the impeccably dressed, beautifully coiffed Madame Lia de Beaumont waiting for her.

"Thank you for seeing me on such short notice," said Lia in her distinctive French accent.

Charlotte was delighted to see her friend. "Goodness, Mme. Lia. It's been months since the levee. I thought surely you'd forgotten about me."

"Never. And I never forget a promise—especially to so deserving and beautiful a queen. My shipment finally arrived today and I went to the docks to receive the crates myself," Lia grinned, opening her large bag and removing several jars and bottles of perfume. "These are jars of that fabulous face cream I promised Your Majesty. Your skin will love me for this."

Charlotte turned into a gleeful child, rushing to the jars as though it were Christmas morning. She opened one and smelled its contents. "Oh my, it's heavenly."

"Use it twice a day—morning, and at night before bed. There is enough here for a year." Lia handed Charlotte an intricately designed bottle of perfume. "You will love this. French perfume. It's a divine fragrance," she prattled. "I call it 'Majesty' in your honor. She dabbed a bit behind Charlotte's ears and on her wrists.

Charlotte smelled the fragrance and swooned. "It's wonderful."

"Now for the pièce de résistance." Lia retrieved a gorgeous piece of red fabric from the bag. "This is the finest spun silk from Asia, which would make the most wonderful gown for Her Majesty."

"How on earth do you do all of this?" Charlotte asked as she twirled around in the fabric.

Mme. Lia winked. "As long as I have the best vineyard in Tonnerre, I have friends all over the world who will do anything for bottles of it."

"You have a vineyard?"

Mme. Lia pulled two bottles of burgundy from her bag. "Indeed. The best in France. Over 200 acres. Now try this, Your Majesty." She went to the sideboard, where several wine and cordial glasses stood, along with decanters of brandy and sherry. Lia poured two glasses of her exquisite red wine. "This is a Vin Rouge de Beaune. Very rare, uncommonly good vintage, and ridiculously expensive." She handed a glass to Charlotte. "My estate is in the Burgundy region. It has made me quite popular with the Brits. I import so much wine to London your Prime Minister has threatened to impose taxes on me."

"My dear, our Lord Bute threatens to tax anything these days…birds, horses, bridal girdles…"

The two chuckled, then toasted each other. They sipped the vintage.

"Delicious. It's all so wonderful," Charlotte exclaimed.

Lia was pleased. There was a quiet pause as they savored the wine.

"Tell me Mme. Lia, since you are French and go back and forth to Paris all the time, what is your official affiliation with France these days, as there is such tension between our two countries?"

Lia was somewhat evasive. "Let's just say I adore everything about England, but one simply cannot do without French clothes, French perfume—or French wine."

They both laughed. "Well put, Madame," said Charlotte.

Mme. Lia paused a moment to canvass the queen's face. Charlotte had grown a tad haggard in the last several months, she thought—far too plain for a 19-year-old with a once vibrant personality. But Lia was a wise woman who knew her place and station as a courtier of the palace. She knew she could not ask the Queen of England if things were all right with her for she valued this budding friendship too much. She would have to be patient if she wanted to be taken into Charlotte's confidences.

So Lia and the queen were content to spend a lovely day just talking and getting to know each other. It was satisfactory for each.

Thirty

Over the next two months Lia would visit St. James when George was away—especially since the king did not encourage outside influences. Sometimes they talked, other times they played whist or cricket with Lady Schwellenberg, Lady Hagedorn and Lady Lizzie. On other occasions they would take a turn around the grounds, where one day Lia introduced Charlotte to snuff. The queen would sniff the fine tobacco into her nostrils and kept a kerchief tucked in her sleeve for the resultant sneezing. Charlotte loved snuff.

Lia would listen to Charlotte play the pianoforte. They would share books and enjoyed riding their horses. They came to discuss many topics which were of importance to the queen—slavery, the second-class status of women, and the unrest of the Colonists. But one day in the library at St. James's, as the two were enjoying Lia's Chardonnay, the queen bent forward to retrieve her glass of wine and her amulet fell from its secret place in her bosom. Mme. Lia saw it and marveled. "How gorgeous your necklace is. Is it a talisman? It looks old."

Charlotte panicked, but recovered well. "Yes. It is quite old. An heirloom handed down in my family for years." She quickly shoved the amulet back into her bosom.

"Were it mine, I would never hide it—especially in such fabulous bosoms as yours," at which Charlotte blushed as Lia continued, "Goodness. The lovers you must entice with them."

"No. No lovers," hastened the queen in embarrassment.

"No lovers? My God, I have three," admitted Lia shamelessly. "Having only one is far too insufficient for me."

"Three lovers?" Charlotte gasped, "Do you not want to be married?"

"Good lord, no. Why would I legally bind myself to the smug and proprietary attitudes of a man's nature when I know myself to be superior?" Lia mused. "They arrogantly think they are wiser, wealthier, savvier—and definitely wonderful lovers, when they're anything but. That is why they all want virgins—a woman who knows nothing about the finesse and intricacies of lovemaking. That way the woman has nothing to compare her bloke of a husband to."

Charlotte blushed from embarrassment. "My goodness, Lia. Such a subject."

"Well they don't. And if you do not know the difference because you've never had a good lover, you'll think they're wonderful. But in fact, the average man will just hoist himself on you, do his business—leaving you wanting, then turn over and snore, thinking he's been God's gift."

Charlotte laughed. "Now that is true."

"That is why a woman should have a husband, and if he's insufficient in the bedroom, oh, bloody hell, even if he is fabulous in the bedroom, she should have a lover as well." Lia smiled, looking the queen in her eyes. "Even *you*, Your Majesty."

Charlotte stared at her friend, outdone. "Me? A lover? My goodness. You sound like my brother who made the same suggestion years ago in Mecklenburg."

"Don't tell me you have not thought about it."

"Never," Charlotte lied.

Mme. Lia narrowed her eyes. "Come, come. Not even with your music master? Now *there* is a most agreeable man."

"That will be all, Mme. Lia," Charlotte cautioned.

"I did not mean to strike at your sensibilities, Your Majesty," Lia mused. "It's just that it must be wonderful to have such a lovely distraction available all to oneself with just a pianoforte as witness. Think about it. If His Majesty can practice the 'Divine Right of Kings' and have a mistress, why should you not have a lover? Call it the 'Divine Equity of Queens.'"

Charlotte was struck mute. Could Lia see through her? Did her friend know she thought about Christian ceaselessly? Perhaps she should be more careful and not show any emotion where Christian was concerned lest she be found out for certain.

Soon there was an urgent knock at the door, followed by Lady Schwellenberg, who was in an emotional state. "Your Majesty, I must speak with you…," she glanced at Lia and back at the queen. "Alone, please."

Mme. Lia understood that her visit with the queen was over. She curtsied to Charlotte and kissed each cheek. "We shall see each other again soon to…continue our discussion?"

"Trust me, dear lady. *That* discussion has concluded," Charlotte grinned.

The moment Madame Lia de Beaumont left the library, Lady Schwellenberg was unable to contain herself. She offered up a letter hidden in her sleeve. "It came. The letter you've been waiting for from Mirepoix, France. It came addressed to me just as you requested."

Charlotte excitedly took the letter. "Finally, after all this time." She and Lady Schwellenberg then hurriedly ran up the stairs to Charlotte's chambers. Anne was inside cleaning, and when Lady Schwellenberg saw her she looked at the queen with alarm. Charlotte was reassuring. "She's harmless. She can stay."

Though Anne heard this, she continued her work as Charlotte undid the wax-sealed enveloped addressed to "Lady Juliana Schwellenberg." Inside was a handwritten page in English. But the contents contained strange words that did not belong and seemed oddly out of place.

22 June 1762
Lady Juliana Schwellenberg
In care of Frogmore House, London, England

Dear Lady Schwellenberg,
I trust you will deliver this message to Her Majesty and beg her for-giveness that I could not write sooner. vs lbh pna qrpvcure guvf zrffntr, Unfortunately, my father passed away two years ago, and sadly, cyrnfr oevat gur qbcbzragf lbhefrys haqre ybpx naq xrl, I have been ill and my health precludes my be tvir gurz gb fbzrbar lbh gehfg sbe genafcbegngvba.

ohg cyrnfr traveling to London. or pnershy. jung lbh chffrff vf qnatrebhf. gurer ner gubfr jub jbhyq qb lbh unez she gurve chffrffvba. I have always wanted V gbyq lbhe sngure the fnzr guvat orsber lbhe sngure qvrq. to visit Great Britain. fb she fnsrgl naq cevinpl fnxr, And although I cannot go there, I would be delighted to welcome and entertain Her Majesty any-time here in Mirepoix. sebz abj ba cyrnfr fraq lbhe pbeerfcbaqrapr gb zr va pbqr.

Yours faithfully,
François Antoine Gaston de Lévis
Duc de Lévis-Mirepoix

Charlotte crumbled the letter into a ball and hurled it to the floor. She slumped onto the window seat in frustration. The queen's obvious disappointment concerned Lady Schwellenberg who went to her, "What did it say, my girl?"

Charlotte shook her head in disgust. "It's gibberish. Two and a half years I've waited, and all I can discern is that Duke François' letter is no more than a benign invitation to visit Mirepoix. The rest is undecipher-able."

"May I see?"

Charlotte indicated the letter was on the floor and she stared out the window. Lady Schwellenberg picked it up and unrumpled it. After reading it she, too, sighed. "What on earth are these indistinguishable words in the text?"

Charlotte threw up her hands. Lady Schwellenberg put the rumpled letter on the desk, then poured water for the disillusioned queen. "Per-haps he does not speak English well and that was the best he could man-age," said the lady as she brought the water to Charlotte. "Or perhaps he sincerely wants you to visit him in Mirepoix."

"There is no possible way the Queen of England can go to another country without suitable explanation. I need the Duke's assistance, but how on earth will I obtain it when I do not understand what is in his let-ter?"

"It's a cipher, Your Majesty," they heard from behind them.

Charlotte and Lady Schwellenberg turned to find Anne reading the rumpled letter. Charlotte frowned at the girl, mystified by her assertions. "What did you say?"

"It…it's a Caesar cipher," Anne continued, nervously.

Lady Schwellenberg snatched the letter from Anne. "How dare you read the queen's mail when it does not concern you. I had no idea you even knew *how* to read."

"No, Swelly," Charlotte insisted, "give it back to her."

Lady Schwellenberg begrudgingly handed the letter back to Anne as Charlotte waved the girl forward.

"What is a Caesar cipher?" asked the queen.

"It's a coded way to send correspondence to someone that cannot be deciphered by anyone but the receiver—in case of interception or theft. At first I thought it was an Atbash, but it is clearly a Caesar cipher. It substitutes the alphabet by a particular number of places—in this case thirteen. That means A becomes N, B becomes O, and so forth. It's said Julius Caesar used to write to his friends using it so his letters would not be disseminated to his enemies."

It took Charlotte a moment before she could speak. "Show me."

Anne took the pen from Charlotte's inkpot. She began writing the alphabet on a separate sheet of paper. "The first word of gibberish has the letters 'L' and 'i.' If you count thirteen letters from the letter 'L', you get "I,' and thirteen letters from the letter 'i' is 'f' making the word 'If.'

"So what does the letter say?" Charlotte insisted, sated with suspense.

It took Anne a few minutes to write down the cipher and then she read it aloud:

"If you can decipher this message, please bring the documents yourself under lock and key, or give them to someone you trust for transportation. But please be careful. What you possess is dangerous. There are those who would do you harm for their possession. I told your father the same thing before he died. So for safety and privacy sake, from now on please send your correspondence to me in code."

"My God," Charlotte gasped. Then suddenly the air became stifling and Charlotte could not breathe. She grabbed her stomach as the room swirled around her, and before she knew it, she had fainted away.

An hour later, Dr. Hunter wiped the queen's forehead and patted George on the back as Charlotte lay in bed. "Her Majesty is breeding. I would say the baby is due next August or September."

"Thank goodness," George declared in relief—even though a headache had him in the throes of consternation.

"Just let her have a little broth tonight. It will help her fever. I'll look in on her in the morning." Dr. Hunter then frowned at the king. "Sir, I am concerned with the frequency of your headaches. Should I send Dr. Baker in?"

"Don't bother. By tomorrow my malady will have subsided."

Dr. Hunter bowed to the royals and left the queen's chambers. George sat with Charlotte. As she rested, he stroked her face tenderly. "We are going to have another child, my dear, and I could not be more pleased." As his fingers gently touched her cheek Charlotte's eyes opened and she smiled at George.

There came a knock at the door. Lady Schwellenberg went to answer, admitting Anne into the room. The African bowed to the king. "I came to see if Her Majesty was all right." Anne looked at the queen's pale face. "She fell so hard I was concerned she'd hit her head."

"Her Majesty will be fine," said George. "Please bring the queen some warm chicken broth and a bowl of caudle. Her Majesty needs her strength."

Anne dutifully obeyed. Then George kissed Charlotte's cheek and left, still rubbing his temples.

Lady Schwellenberg and Lady Hagedorn sat with Charlotte until Anne returned with a tray of broth, tea and caudle. After her ladies helped the queen sit up, Anne placed the tray on her lap and started to leave, but Charlotte stopped her.

"Anne, one moment, I wish to speak with you alone."

The African turned back. Charlotte motioned for Ladies Schwellenberg and Hagedorn to go. After they left, she patted the bed.

"Sit here, my dear."

Anne sat at the foot of the bed with her eyes cast down in reverence to Charlotte.

"How do you like it here at St. James so far?" asked the queen.

"Very much, Your Majesty. The other staff are very nice to me."

Charlotte perused Anne's face. Her skin was the color of the tea in Charlotte's cup, and although her eyes were large and equally brown, they turned up at the corners as though a hint of Asian was in her blood. Her hair was still fashioned in shoulder-length, tightly coiled ropes, and she looked well suited in her blue uniform with its crisp white collar where Charlotte saw her amulet parked discreetly. "Tell me about yourself—about your family and background."

Anne was both surprised and nervous. "Your Majesty, you would not be interested. It is a mundane and typical story—not worthy of repeating to one so exalted as yourself."

"Nonsense," Charlotte mused, sipping her tea. "The queen is most interested in every aspect of a life which includes knowledge of several languages, the intimacies of various aristocrats, an ability to decode ciphers," then, with pointed frankness, "and the possession of a sacred Templar amulet."

Anne now understood what the queen wanted to know and why. It took her a moment to gather her thoughts, then she looked at Charlotte.

"I was born Anajuhari Josef Tsoji in Ethiopia in 1743. I am the daughter of an Ethiopian woman and a Dabtara priest. My father possessed the arcane, esoteric knowledge of the Dabtaras and the Essenes, and he acquired the gift of the sixth finger, which he learned from his forefathers going generations back to King Solomon."

Though part of Anne's story was beginning to sound familiar, Charlotte was still puzzled as she sat up in bed. "What is the 'gift of the sixth finger'?"

"It is the gift of healing and seeing into the future with the laying on of hands," Anne replied. "My father's duties as *Akomo*, the Chief and High Holy priest of the tribe, was to guard various sacred relics which arrived in Ethiopia through Menelik, son of Solomon and the dark Queen of Sheba. He also was given charge of other treasures which were stolen from King Solomon's Temple by the Knights Templar in the eleventh century. Only one priest—a Dabtara, knew the location and was allowed to guard and protect these items. When that priest died he was replaced by his son and so forth."

"Unbelievable," Charlotte amazed aloud.

"This amulet was designed for one of the Templar Grand Masters to be handed down to the next Grand Master or Seneschal." Anne offered as she caressed her amulet. "After the Templar arrests and executions, nineteen of their ships left France with their treasure, and seven of the nine amulets left as well. One ship came to Ethiopia and I was told that my amulet was placed with the 'Protector priest.' Eventually, that protector became the High Holy priest—my sixth great grandfather. Eventually the tradition fell to my father."

Anne poured Charlotte another cup of tea. "But my father was unlucky. He did not have sons as was Dabtara law to pass down the sacred, mystical gnosis of the Essenes, or this amulet. When I was born, he already had ten daughters and realized he may never have a son. I also possessed a mark upon my body which, had I been a boy, would have guaranteed my inheriting the amulet and the position of Akomo..."

Charlotte sat enrapted. Did Anne have Magragana's mark?

"...So my father committed an unbelievable, scandalous act," continued Anne. "He raised me as a boy and my name was Juhari. I never knew about my own secret history until much later when I could read. I was quiet and stayed to myself, and I studied with the other boys. I learned every language of the peoples with whom we met and traded, and was considered a valuable asset destined to ascend to the status of Akomo. When I became older, and realized I was growing breasts and did not possess the appendage which identifies boys from girls, my father told me I was to continue as a boy in order to receive "the gift," and because any revelation of my truth as a girl would bring about a curse. So, I continued as a male." Anne smiled at the memory for a moment. "The more I developed breasts I bound and hid them under loose clothing. I learned more as a boy than I ever would have as a woman and I cherished that bonus. I received respect and consideration simply because of my perceived gender.

But soon, my time as a woman began. During a *Choipat,* a class for young male leaders, an elder saw that I had bled through my trousers. Soon they realized I was not injured or sick, but a female. I was cast out and a curse was placed on my family. But it was the tribe that suffered reversals. No crops yielded that year or the next, and many unexplained illnesses and deaths occurred." Anne's eyes filled with tears at the memory. "One day my father came to me with this amulet and told me the story of its history and journey, and why I had to protect it. He said he just learned his time on earth was short and I had to assume my duties as Akomo, even though I would never actually become one. He told me to quickly gather my belongings, that some members of the nomadic tribe of Vendas would come for me near the river. He had made a secret pact with their chief to ensure my safety and my life. I did what I was told. That night, my father, mother and nine of my siblings were killed for father's conspiracy.

But the Venda chief, instead of honoring my father's pact with him, sold me to a white trader. I did not want the amulet stolen from me and knew because it was gold it would have been confiscated. So I hid it in the only place they would not check—my womb."

Charlotte was shocked by this and put her cup down to listen intently.

"We traveled for three days, picking up other stolen or runaway Africans from various tribes. Then one day we were placed on a boat and chained together. I was 14, and fortunate—for no one molested me on the ship. My amulet was safe, even though I was in constant pain. We sailed for two weeks until we reached Bristol. There, I stood on the docks with the other slaves for sale. I saw Lord Bethany point to me, and that is how I came to be in this country with the Bethanys."

Anne went on explain that when she arrived at the Bethanys' she secretly removed the amulet from inside herself, cleaned it, polished it, and secretly painted it to hide its gold gleam. She understood she was now the Bethanys' property and, as before, did not want the amulet unjustly taken. So she strung it low so it fell well down inside her clothing. The only time it slipped was at King Frederick's ball, when she accompanied the Bethanys to Germany. That was the evening Charlotte saw Anne's amulet and recognized it.

"Life with the Bethanys was difficult. Lady Bethany was kind at first, then less so when she discovered Lord Bethany with me against my will." Anne stopped, wiping her eyes a moment. Charlotte reached out her hand and took Anne's as she continued. "So many times I had fought him off and so many times lost the battle. Even in my time of confinement, he would still come to my quarters to have his way with me."

"Time of confinement? You have children?" Charlotte asked in astonishment.

"Yes, Your Majesty. I have a daughter, Mary, for Lord Bethany."

Anne wiped her eyes and gathered her resolve. "She is eight now. And with the money you pay me, I shall try to find her and buy her out of bondage." Anne indicated her amulet. "And later I will give her my amulet when the time comes, for it will rightfully be hers."

"Why do you say it will be hers?"

Anne ladled another bowl of soup for the queen. "She possesses the mark, too." The Ethiopian stopped a moment and thought. "My father gave me this amulet to keep me safe and give me meaning and purpose. I intend to do the same and give mine to my child. "

Charlotte caressed her own amulet. "I was given this one for the same reason." She looked at Anne and smiled, "Apparently we are kindred spirits in purpose."

Anne helped the queen sit back on her pillow. It was then she saw the queen's birthmark. Charlotte saw Anne's reaction. "What is wrong?"

Anne trembled. "Your Majesty. Y-you bear the mark of a 'Daughter of David'," she stammered. "The king's mother bears it as well."

"How do you know the princess dowager has this birthmark?"

"When she was being fitted for a new gown I went in to change her linen. I saw the mark for myself. It's the same one, in the same place as yours," Anne answered, unhooking the collar of her uniform and pulling it to the side. There on her right shoulder was a small red, raised birthmark. "The same one I have."

Charlotte was now in a state of shock as the Ethiopian continued. "There is a prophecy amongst the Dabtaras that says: 'A Daughter of David will lead the children of darkness to the light.' I thought perhaps it was me. But now I see it is you, Your Majesty."

Charlotte's breath caught in her lungs in incomprehension. She was too mystified by all she had learned in the last few moments: Anne had the mark, Princess Augusta had the mark. Prophesies, children of darkness, Daughters of David? Suddenly it all came flooding back, and she remembered what her father had said the day he died so many years ago:

"…*You must be older in order to fully understand it. But for now, realize that as a girl with the mark, you are a 'Daughter of David' who will one day wear the amulet…*"

Charlotte, beleaguered by all this information, needed time to put some perspective on it. She set her face with authority and nodded to Anne, "Thank you. That will be all."

Anne nodded and collected the dishes, then left. Charlotte looked at her amulet and thought about its long journey. Holding her stomach, she made her way over to her armoire, where she had hidden the wooden chest from view, with rugs and fur pelts atop it. Upon unlocking the armoire, she opened the secret bottom drawer of the chest just so she could touch the precious wooden containers once again—almost to assure herself they were real. After closing the reliquary, Charlotte went to the writing desk and took out her diary. With fingers still trembling she picked up the quill and wrote all night.

Thirty One
April, 1763

The new Buckingham residence, called "Queen's House," stood as a beacon of enlightenment when it was finally finished. Charlotte's exquisite new chambers were large and comfortable, and though she was not expecting George to be a permanent tenant as he so loved St. James, she welcomed his company, especially now that she was expecting her second child.

Charlotte's confinement kept her in bed for long hours at a time where she had little to do but read and think. She fretted about who she could trust to deliver her scrolls to the Duke of Levis-Mirepoix for translation.

Would she ever really know what she had?

Yet, no matter how curious she was, dare she approach Augusta about the dowager's birthmark? And what if the dowager princess had seen Charlotte's birthmark? If it were true that Augusta possessed a similar one, surely she would have said something to the queen by now. Thus, Charlotte remained silent, and neither she nor Anne spoke of their conversation again.

Fortunately, there were two occasions when she found abandon from the burden of her thoughts. She spent a good deal of time with Lia de Beaumont, whom she adored. Mme. Lia, who was also a bibliophile, snuck books and pamphlets into the palace for the queen's private reading. One pamphlet was Anthony Benezet's "*Observations on the Enslaving,*

Importing and Purchasing of Negroes," which Lia bought on the black market. Charlotte was so moved by the author's searing indictment against slavery that it served as further motivation.

She also had the distraction of her music lessons with Christian. But as much as she yearned otherwise, her time with him always passed too quickly. Christian would arrive promptly at 11 o'clock and play until she arrived. Upon her arrival, the queen would dismiss her ladies and the guards outside the door, and then the two would begin. Sometimes it was a harpsichord lesson, other times a singing lesson, and sometimes they would just have a talk with tea. Their talks were the best part of seeing him. When finally she told Christian she was to have another child, he was happy for her, as it was his desire to have sons himself, even though he had yet to find their potential mother.

"Well it's not because you haven't tried, sir," Charlotte chuckled. Christian then regaled her with his plans for court entertainment. He had found a boy virtuoso named Mozart whom he wanted to bring to London with his family to perform. "Perhaps next season I can have a series of concerts with Saint George, and this wonder of a boy."

"Sounds heavenly," Charlotte responded, brimming with expectation.

Then the two looked at each other and a flood of emotion rushed a blush of scarlet to the queen's cheeks, and she looked away from Christian and stood. "I'm afraid I won't be able to have another lesson until after my lying-in," she fabricated. "The good news is you'll have plenty of time to finish your new opera and rehearse it until the baby is born…"

"Charlotte, why do you do this every time we find ourselves close with no words to express save what's in our hearts?"

Charlotte moved away, looking at Christian with a measure of regret. "We'll speak no more of this." She left the room, blindly rushing past Lady Lizzie who, frowning in interest, came to the opened door of the music room and saw the maestro holding his head in anguish. As Charlotte headed up to her chambers, her Lord Chamberlain ran to her. "Your Majesty, His Majesty wishes you to remain inside the residence until further notice."

"Why, Sir Robert? What is going on?"

"There is some agitation in the streets. I've been instructed to inform all that no one can leave."

In the music room, Christian was placing music pages into a valise when Sir Robert came in. "Mr. Bach, His Majesty wishes you to stay here at Queen's House this evening. He has instructed everyone to do so. There is unrest in the streets and your safety cannot be guaranteed otherwise. We are readying an apartment for you now."

"What sort of unrest?" asked Christian, now concerned.

✠

Prime Minister Bute's driver was having difficulty steering the coach and horses. Bute was in fear for his life. For five months anger had been building because of the authorized taxes imposed on the people, who were already financially stretched to the limit. Now Cider Taxes, another levy, had alienated citizens and members of Parliament. The people had enough and tension festered into riots in the streets. Though Bute was principally responsible for the "Peace of Paris" which officially ended the Seven Years War, he was still criticized as having compromised the government, and the masses hated him. Especially Sir John Wilkes who, under a pseudonym, attacked Bute in issue after issue of the *North Briton*. Now an angry mob was protesting and the unrest was uncontained and spilling forth near St. James and Queen's House. MPs were stoned and effigies of Bute were burning across London.

As Bute perilously made his way to Queen's House, which was far closer than his own residence in Hampshire, furious dissidents attempted to terrorize his carriage. Thankfully, he was protected by a bodyguard, for he lived in fear. Finally, he reached the front entrance of Queen's House and was immediately taken to the king after inquiring if George was in residence.

"Your Majesty, an irate mob is on its way. I hardly made it," Bute informed the king.

"Yes, my guards alerted me earlier. You must remain here. I made certain the queen and my son are safe, and everyone is ordered to stay in the residence until the crisis abates."

"Where is Princess Augusta?"

"Upstairs. She and my sisters were brought over from Carlton House."

In the second-floor guest apartment, George's mother was crying at the window where she had witnessed her beloved Bute disparaged in the streets. Signs held aloft in the air touted, "No Scotch Rogues" or "No Butes!" She saw depictions of Bute as a he-goat riding Augusta as a she-goat to hell, and it upset her. But it was when she saw the wagon hauling Bute burning in effigy that Princess Augusta turned from the window in tears and collapsed onto the settee.

Finally, Bute knocked at the door and entered. Augusta ran to him, burying her head in his chest. "Oh John, thank God you're safe."

"I don't know if we can weather this, Augusta," Bute lamented. "I may have to resign."

"You mustn't. They will win if you do," she cried.

Bute held her close. "They already have. The newspapers are rife with insult. They're calling me 'the Northern Thane' referring to Macbeth, and 'Sir Pertinax MacSycophant.'"

George was not immune either. A man had jumped into his sedan-chair and tried to stab him as he was on his way to Carlton House to visit his mother the day before. Equally vexing was the current issue of the *North Briton*. In issue #45 Wilkes, under his own name, had discredited the king's government by calling it the most "abandoned instance of ministerial effrontery." He criticized Bute's peace treaty as a "corrupt shambles without honor" and accused the government of being "mendacious and not functioning in the country's best interests."

Now George was at Queen's House with his family and guests like a prisoner. That evening, Charlotte and George tried to dine with Christian, Bute, Augusta and the king's siblings as sounds of the unrest echoed in the distance. The king insisted the best way for them to cope was to go on with normal conversation as long as they did not discuss politics.

Unknown to him, however, was the tension permeating between Charlotte and Christian, who could hardly look at each other. After dinner the king suggested they all play music together. "We can have an impromptu concert. I can play my flute; Christian, the violin; and Charlotte, the harpsichord."

So, for the next hour and a half they entertained each other while Augusta, Bute and George's family enjoyed themselves. Eventually, Charlotte excused herself citing an upset stomach and left the room. Her ladies followed suit, leaving the men.

"Despite the ongoing dissent outside, the new side gardens are now open and are a thing to behold," said the king to Christian as they drank brandies. "Especially at night with the torches lit and the moon shimmering off the reflecting pond. Avail yourself of them before you retire, Mr. Bach." George then apologized for the dissent outside and Christian's inability to leave, but insisted he had to speak to Bute alone.

Christian bowed as George and Bute left the music room, no doubt to discuss what must be done to quell the rebel savages beyond the gates. He wasn't sure he wanted to tour the gardens under these circumstances as he was unsure he wanted to be in the same location with Charlotte, who he knew was irritated with him. But after reconsidering, he found himself wandering in those very gardens with his brandy.

Upstairs, Charlotte lit a candle and went to her desk to make an entry in her diary. The room was stifling and she opened a window, placing the candle in the sill. The maelstrom in the distance seemed to be waning, yet the tempest of her thoughts showed no sign of abating. All she could think about was what to do. Since her conversation with Anne she found herself rereading her father's diary, searching for any clues she could have missed. But there were none, and perhaps it was this frustration which made her overreact to Christian earlier, something she now regretted.

From the flower garden below, the unexpected flash of candlelight startled Christian as he sat on a stone bench near the reflecting pond. He looked up and saw Charlotte as she settled into the window seat. The light flickering from the candle accentuated her figure, most particularly her nose and voluptuous mouth, which always seemed primed to be kissed. As she put her diary aside and stared into the riotous night sky, Christian closed his eyes and prayed she would see him out there in the dark and come to him, or beckon him to her private quarters. He could hear his own heartbeat throbbing in his ears, and his breathing was in unison with his heart.

But when he opened his eyes again, Charlotte had moved away from his private view and was gone. He chastised himself. Here he was, one of the most famous composers in Europe, desirous of the one woman in the world he could not have. He shook his head in frustration for he needed to abandon these childish fantasies and get on with it. Thus, upon finishing his brandy, he turned to go back into the palace.

But there in front of his view…was Charlotte.

She had on a robe and just stood there. They looked at each other for an impenetrable moment. Christian eased in closer, never losing eye contact with her, and Charlotte did not back away. His fingers caressed her face, which eased into his palm with such desire for his touch.

"Charlotte…" Christian whispered.

But a finger touched his lips. "Shhhh," Charlotte cautioned quietly. Christian's mouth found hers wanting as he pulled her into the cradle of his arms. It was the kiss of which they had dreamed, which they had long craved. Yet, when finally their lips parted, Charlotte had regrets.

"I understand," said Christian. "I just had to know if there was still any feeling left for me."

"So much so I cannot stand it," whispered Charlotte, "But I am *his*. His child is inside me."

Christian bowed and allowed Charlotte to return to her chambers. When she had gone, he could at least take solace in the fact that she cared for him and he still loved her—enough to let her go. Now that he was reconciled he went up the stairs which led him to the room assigned to him for the night. On the way he passed the library, where George and Bute were talking.

George's head was throbbing as he chatted with Bute. "How do you expect me to accept this after all you've meant to my reign and my happiness?" he said, rubbing his temples.

"I must free you from ridicule, Your Majesty, for the good of your government, and for the people's sake. I'm under too much pressure. The archangel Michael cannot govern England."

"It's Wilkes and his damnable newspaper. This is why you're leaving."

Bute set his brandy aside and placed his hand on the king's shoulder. "Wilkes's newspaper is the tip of an iceberg of grievances the people have against you and me. As it is, I cannot travel the streets without a disguise of hats and wigs. I'm in danger for my life at all times," he sighed. "Sire, I am expendable. Allow me to be such and resign."

The king shook his head. He couldn't speak. Bute was conciliatory, hoping he was more of a comfort to George than to his genuine feelings. "I have always said I would stay in office only until peace with France was achieved. That has been accomplished. So, do not worry about me.

I'm relieved, frankly. You'll find another Prime Minister to form a government in your name. One capable of less dissent."

George looked off a moment. It wasn't as though this was unexpected. Even Charlotte had suggested he ask for Bute's resignation two years ago. Finally, the king turned to his friend. "John, we've been together so long, sometimes I do not know how to function without you."

"If it's any consolation, I shall ever remain your trusted advisor, and I have no intention of abandoning our friendship. You're too much like a son to me," prided Bute.

George offered his hand. Bute shook it, and there was a long, awkward pause. "I shall hold you to that, old friend," said the king.

After another moment's pause, John Stuart, third Earl of Bute and former Prime Minister of England, left the library and went to sleep at Queen's House Buckingham a private citizen.

Six days later, on 30 April, general warrants were issued for the arrests of Wilkes and the publishers of the *North Briton*. They were charged with seditious libel. Wilkes was taken to the Tower of London jail, where he vowed retribution from King George III.

By the summer of 1763, the people were thrilled with Bute's resignation. But it was Sir John Wilkes' arrest along with forty-nine other people associated with the North Briton, that created an angry flurry of commentary in the newspapers and on the streets. George, who felt publicly maligned by issue #45 and thought no one should speak out against government, was pleased that Wilkes was receiving just recompense, but with each day of incarceration Wilkes kept gaining support.

His trial went before Chief Justice William Mansfield, another of his hatred adversaries, and his anger at my husband was palpable. Sir Wilkes vowed that the king would feel the full wrath of his anger. When Lord Henry Fox visited Wilkes in the Tower of London jail, they discussed their collective hatred for George, Bute and me. Wilkes vowed that if he was ever released he would continue to print whatever damning information he could find on George who, according to him, 'could not govern without a puppeteer.' Because he was an MP, Wilkes did have executive privilege from libel or sedition, and was released from jail. His followers chanted his name in the streets, and Wilkes returned to demonizing George.

However, Bute—the accused puppeteer—acting on the king's behalf as a private citizen, spoke to a Tory friend and supporter in the House of Commons to put forth a motion that a member's privilege from arrest should not extend to writing and publishing seditious libel. A week later, Parliament voted on the motion. It passed. Another warrant was issued for Wilkes.

But before Wilkes could be arrested again, a group of his friends, led by Lord Fox, spirited him out of the country. Wilkes boarded a ship bound for Paris under the subterfuge of 'visiting his daughter.' Lord Fox promised revenge for Wilkes by 'gathering gossip, scandal or dirt' on the monarchy. I learned years later that Fox suggested they find a suitable spy to help them, someone who could infiltrate our personal lives and collect information. Wilkes suddenly had an idea for such a person, and Lord Fox helped him facilitate it. Once he got to Paris, Wilkes decided not to return to face prosecution. He was tried in his absence and found guilty of publishing seditious libel against George, and pronounced an outlaw.

As for me, during those four months of contention, George's headaches were worse than ever, making him difficult to live with. And yet, my thoughts were always of Christian and that one glorious kiss we shared in the garden the night of the riots. I relived it over and over in my mind, and it occupied my every waking moment right up until my time of confinement ended.

✠

"Born this 16th day of August, 1763, Prince Frederick Augustus Hanover, the Duke of York!" Dr. Hunter announced.

It had been an easy labor and a quick birth, considering the arduous lying-in the queen had. Charlotte sat up in bed, half dazed in the sweltering summer heat, watching as George held their second son up to a cheering crowd below. Afterward, the king gave the baby to a midwife as Dr. Hunter gave Charlotte a bowl of caudle and some tea. The king came to the royal bed and kissed his wife's forehead. "Well done, my dear," he said to Charlotte, squeezing her hand in appreciation. "We have an heir and a spare." They both chuckled, then it settled. "When you've rested sufficiently we'll go to Bath to take the waters. It'll do us both some good."

Charlotte nodded, then asked George about his recurring headaches. After assuring her he was all right, he touched her face sweetly then left the room, allowing his mother to sit with the queen a while. Augusta had a book with her, and as she sat she wiped the perspiration flowing profusely from her brow.

"My God, this heat. It's the hottest August I can remember," she lamented, handing the book to Charlotte. "I brought you a gift. Something to read as you regain your strength. I know you love books, and this is quite an adventure tale written a while back by William Dafoe."

"The man who wrote Robinson Crusoe?"

"The same. This one is 'The Fortunes and Misfortunes of the Famous Moll Flanders.' And since I know you have just the tiniest streak of the independent female in you, I sent Lady Lizzie out to fetch a copy for you."

"Thank you, Your Highness. I shall cherish it," Charlotte smiled gratefully, then motioned to the midwife to bring little Frederick over. "Here is your newst grandchild."

As Augusta turned to receive the child, Charlotte saw it. It was right there on her right shoulder, clearly showing just below the collar bone. The birthmark. It was smaller than Charlotte's, but still red, raised and cross shaped. Clearly Merovingian and hereditary.

Charlotte leaned against the pillow. Anne had been right. Now Charlotte needed answers. She watched as Augusta played with her newborn son, trying to formulate a plan by which she could talk to the dowager about what could perhaps be their extraordinary common past.

It took Charlotte another two weeks to gather the courage to speak to George's mother, and her reticence reminded her of how long it took for her to approach Jon Baptiste about dance lessons in Mecklenburg. Nonetheless, the perfect opportunity afforded itself after a family breakfast one morning at Queen's House. George and his brother William decided to play a game of chess, leaving Charlotte with the dowager and George's sisters Augusta and Caroline Matilda.

"Augusta, may I speak to you...privately?" Charlotte asked the king's mother.

The dowager nodded and the two left the dining hall and went into the library for privacy. After Charlotte closed the door, she turned to her mother-in-law and pulled over her collar, revealing her birthmark. Augusta remained silent, trying not to react as Charlotte came closer.

"I understand this is a very unusual birthmark. I understand it is specific and hereditary."

Augusta remained outwardly unemotional, but was quivering inside. "It is. I saw your mark the day of your wedding. I told George of it. He, as is his way, dismissed me out of hand."

Charlotte processed this information, then continued. "Is it true *you* possess this mark?"

Now Augusta reacted. "What do you know about them?"

"It is my understanding they have come to us from the Merovingian kings."

"Is that all you know?"

"I'm confused about them. Is there is a connection to the Templars?"

"We do not speak of that. It is unconfirmed," Augusta interrupted. "Who told you about your birthmark?"

Charlotte was cautious. She purposely did not mention Magragana, and if Augusta knew about Charlotte's amulet, her father's diaries, the scrolls, or Anne, the dowager would probably explode into flames. "My father told me things before he died. Some of it he wrote down."

"Do you still have this written information?"

"No." Charlotte hated lying to Augusta, but she had to protect herself and her secrets.

Augusta just stared at the queen, not sure if she was telling the truth or was sincerely curious about who she was. She began circling around Charlotte. "Your Majesty, why have you waited until now to approach me about this?"

"I…I only just saw your birthmark when you were playing with the baby. There has always been such myth and legend surrounding mine and I thought perhaps you would know more about its meaning."

Augusta took her time to respond, as she had to decide if she should reveal all she knew or withhold some. "George's father, Frederick, became a Mason. He was, in fact, one of the first royal Masons in Britain to be initiated at Masonic Hall. He did it so he could be a part of a secret society whose sacred assignment was to protect some information he knew, but chose not to entrust to me. I only discovered it after he died."

"What was it?"

There was another long pause as Augusta stared at Charlotte. "We knew that somewhere in his family ancestry there was a Moor of Davidic descent who left scrolls of her life story and genealogy. But Frederick was only successful in going back eight generations." She stopped a moment to steady herself. "My ancestry, however, goes back quite a bit further."

"How far back?" inquired Charlotte.

George's mother turned back to the young queen, and when she did, Charlotte had taken her amulet from its place of protection inside her dress and had it out to show Augusta.

"Good lord. Y-you have an amulet," gasped the Princess dowager. "But how?" She reached out with fingers trembling to touch the talisman. Awestruck, she looked into Charlotte's eyes and confirmed the queen knew more than she'd let on. "Do you know what this is?"

Charlotte nodded silently. At this, the princess dowager instantly went to a desk and wrote something on paper. When she was finished she folded it carefully and sealed it with wax. She called to the page and handed it to him. "Have Lady Worthington deliver this quickly."

The page nodded and left. The princess dowager turned to Charlotte. "You will do as I ask, Your Majesty," she commanded so definitively Charlotte instantly nodded. "The significance of your amulet is deeply profound. I don't think you realize how much so."

"I have been informed of my descent from Margarita de Castro y Sousa and Magragana ben Bekar before that," Charlotte whispered. "I'm told it's one of the reasons I have darker skin and that I was chosen for a purpose. But I do not know what that purpose is yet." Suddenly Charlotte became quiet. She dared not reveal Anne's amulet.

"Were you told of your descent from Margarita's husband Count Jean II of Neufchatel, or the Daughters of David?" Augusta insisted.

Now Charlotte was trembling. Obviously Augusta knew about all of it. "You're frightening me. Tell me what I need to know."

"Tomorrow morning, you will come with me. We must go to a place where you will have a deeper understanding of your amulet…and yourself. But you must not tell George."

Thirty Two

The next morning Charlotte eased out of bed and Lady Lizzie dressed her for travel. She had eggs and porridge with Augusta, who then called for her coach and not Charlotte's. Augusta explained that Charlotte's official coach would attract too much attention where they were going, and that Charlotte should remove jewelry and any accoutrements identifying her as the Queen. Minutes later the page returned and indicated Augusta's coach was ready.

"Should the king ask, tell him the queen and I have gone to visit my sisters," Augusta informed the page who nodded and left.

The queen struggled to keep George's mother from seeing how uneasy she was while they traveled more than three hours across the countryside. Mister Harvey, their driver, seemed to know where they were going as they shuttled over craggy hillsides and suffered through the bumpy, rural terrain along London Road. Augusta reassured Charlotte they would be fine and squeezed the frightened queen's hand.

At noon, their carriage reached the city of Hertfordshire, north of London. They were taken to #42 Fore Street near Market Square. The building was a beautiful stone structure flaunting high arches, intricately carved wood cornices, and a lead roof—the kind of design commonly employed by 13th-century architects. Augusta suggested Charlotte keep her head low, and as they walked up to the side door, Charlotte's palms were moistening. There was something odd about it as Augusta stealthily looked around to make sure no one was watching. Upon reaching the entrance she knocked three times in a distinctive manner on the ancient door. Charlotte noticed there was no sign; nothing to indicate this side door was in fact the main entrance to the building. Nothing that is, except a small symbol carved onto it, a triangle with what looked like an eye at the top.

Soon, they heard three distinctive knocks in response to Augusta's. The dowager knocked once. One knock came in response. A male voice was soon heard from within asking the question: "Whom do you represent?"

"God, and the three lesser lights," Augusta responded.

"What are those three lesser lights?"

"The Sun, the Moon, and Master of the Lodge."

"How are they explained?"

"As the Sun rules the day and the Moon governs the night, so does the Worshipful Master use his endeavors to rule and govern his Lodge with equal regularity."

The door swung open. The man behind it was large and wore the hooded robe of a monk. Charlotte could see he had limpid blue eyes, a somewhat left-sloping nose, and sparse hog bristles of hair. He was a frightening figure. Charlotte kept her head low, trying to be inconspicuous, but she was fascinated. Upon entering, Augusta announced herself to the monk as "Sister Augusta Hanover, widow of Brother Frederick Louis Hanover," then she bid him to make sure the "Sisters" had gathered. The monk nodded, then pointed them toward a door to their left.

The interior of the building featured a black-and-white checkerboard floor and was well lit with candles in gothic candlesticks. The walls were adorned with paintings of men resplendent in sashes and white aprons who were of obvious importance. Some of the symbols on the painted ceiling were oddities, and there many drawings of pyramids, some with an eye at the center top, much like the symbol on the door. The furnishings were sparse. When they entered the designated room, Charlotte realized it was actually a hall. Augusta led her down two more long hallways, one of which dead-ended at a stone staircase. They traveled down several flights of limestone stairs until they found themselves in the building's foundation. To their right was a massive wooden door with a complicated system of locks and bolts, and an ominous guard wearing a white apron and a regal-looking sash. The man held out his hand. The dowager curtsied, kissed his ring, then shook his hand in a distinctive, familiar way which Charlotte recognized as the Lion's Paw.

Her father had once instructed her to remember it, for it would indicate a true friend. The secret handshake resulted in the man speaking to the dowager in Latin:

"Es Davidis filiarum sectatrix?"

Augusta nodded. "Ego sum a Filia quod eo per a Filia quod an phylacterium habitum."

The man bowed, unlocked the various locks and bolts, then opened the large door. He handed each of them a lighted torch. Augusta took Charlotte's other hand and led them into the darkness, which seemed to swallow them.

"What did you say to the guard?" Charlotte inquired, her voice a fretful octave higher than usual.

"He asked me if I was a Daughter of David. I answered that I am a Daughter and travel with a Daughter and an amulet holder."

They walked for what seemed like half a kilometer. The large tunnel before them had the putrid smell of stifled air, mold and inactivity. Charlotte's eyes, large and curious, welled with curiosity as she tried to see into the shadowy darkness—the torch unable to illuminate beyond a few feet. On the walls as they passed were painted symbols and graphs. Some she recognized from her amulet, others were similar to writings she had seen on her father's prized chest.

Finally they could see glimmers of light appearing before them, and Charlotte knew they had reached their destination—whatever it was. Easing under the portcullis which hung over the gated entrance, they approached a dimly lit cavernous room which smelled of pungent oil. In the middle of the room between two large but uneven pillars was a statue of four women from ancient times. At the foot of the statue was a marble bowl filled with oil and three candles burning in the center. A mural had been painted on the center wall depicting six boats, one without oars, drifting at sea. In the first boat was an older man holding a box with a halo around it accompanied by four women: one with a halo around her head, and one who looked young and was dark-skinned.

"What is this place?" asked Charlotte, almost afraid to know the answer.

Princess Augusta went about lighting the various torches to better illuminate the area. "We are in an ancient labyrinth beneath Hertford Castle. It is one of many underground tunnels which connect to various buildings in Hertfordshire—Bayley Hall, the old Priory, Salisbury Arms. These tunnels and the vault were created by the Templars so they could assemble, as well as easily access their British treasure, in several locations beneath the city."

Augusta went on to explain that the vault complex had remained untouched and sealed until the time of King Henry VI when an amulet was discovered in the old Priory around the neck of a dead Cistercian monk. "Father Asul was working on a translation of his amulet from diagrams drawn by Bernard, the Abbot of Clairvaux, for whom the Knights swore allegiance. It is said the monk was killed for his translation. Supposedly it was a map to the location of the sacred treasure of the Cathars in France. Little did they know his amulet itself held the secret."

"Who killed him?"

"We do not know for certain. But we do know many myths and secrets exist about the Templar treasure, and there are those who would kill for information as to its locations even now. Fortunately, Father Azul's work was not in vain."

George's mother showed Charlotte other artifacts in the room: scrolls, coins, gemstones, jewelry, and another gold amulet which made Charlotte gasp. "Yes," she said. "We have Father Azul's amulet. It had been designed for Andre de Montbard, one of the original nine Templars. So, you see, we have one amulet here in England. With yours, there are now two here. We also know where an amulet is in Scotland, and in Spain. That makes four. Two others are purportedly in France, one in Ethiopia, and one is in the Colonies. We do not know where those are with certainty, and we are missing the location of the ninth one, but when intertwined together, the nine amulets reveal the locations of the Templar vaults where they hid their treasure and scrolls."

Charlotte trembled for she knew Anne had the Ethiopian amulet.

"How can you tell for which Knight an amulet was originally designed?"

"They possess the initials of the original Templar brother for whom it was created." Augusta showed Charlotte the back of the amulet on the table. "AdM. Andre de Montbard."

Charlotte removed the amulet from her bosom and looked at it. But when she turned it over she did not find any initials. Augusta reached out and looked at the amulet again. Her hand went to her mouth in shock. "Oh my. Why did I not see it before," she exclaimed. "Your amulet appears to be the oldest, most significant of the nine. It may be the one King Solomon himself owned—the model upon which all the others were designed. This one was used by Hugues de Payen, the original Grand Master." Augusta pointed to certain symbols. "This is supposedly the word for God and these five words are purportedly invocations of some sort—all are deemed a heresy to say aloud. King Solomon had it designed after carvings on the Ark of the Covenant."

I began shaking. "Do you want to collect all of the amulets and place them here?"

"Some time in the future, there will be a reckoning. The nine amulets will come together as one and reveal their secrets. When that happens, the Church of Rome will be shaken apart."

"Why?"

"The Vatican has hidden much over the centuries they do not wish for the faithful to know…documents, relics, information which runs contrary to their dogma and doctrines. In addition to great monetary treasure, the Templars found and hid books, scrolls, charts and codices of apocryphal writings—gnostic healing techniques, magic, and knowledge of the Essenes, who utilized sacred geometry and the principles of alchemy. It is why the Templars were arrested, executed and driven underground. King Phillip of France wanted their vast wealth and knowledge."

The dowager went to the wall mural of the six boats drifting at sea and the old man holding a box with a halo around it. She pointed to him. "The man with the box is Joseph of Arimathea, our ancestor. Inside the box is the Holy Shroud, which he brought to France in AD 37, then transported it to Glastonbury here in England. It was handed down in our family for hundreds of years." Augusta went over to a stone box sitting on the shrine with the statues and the oil in the center. With reverence she opened it and removed a small bundle of fabric, which she brought back to Charlotte.

The queen stood silently as Augusta unfolded the material, out of which she drew a small, ancient piece of linen cloth. "Christ's blood was collected in the head band of one of his linen burial cloths." She placed the cloth respectfully on a table. There on it was the faint image of a familiar face. "It is the image of Jesus," said the king's mother. "Six or seven pieces of cloth were used in a traditional Jewish burial. But we know Jesus was buried hurriedly for the Sabbath was nigh. Matthew, Mark and Luke's writings refer to the larger linen cloth as a 'Sindon,' meaning Shroud. John refers to it as the Othonia, and in the Gospel bearing his name it said that after the body of Christ disappeared, '...*Peter went into the tomb and he saw the linen cloths lying there, and the handkerchief that had been around his head, not lying with the linen cloths, but folded together in a place by itself...*'" Augusta indicated the small cloth on the table. "This is the *Soudarion.* The handkerchief John referred to in his Gospel that was placed over our Lord's head. This along with the Sindon, were found in the tomb of Jesus." Augusta paused a moment. "*This* is one of the Grail pieces the Templars were accused of worshipping."

Tears streamed down Charlotte's face and she turned her back on the cloth. It could not be true. It could not be the real cloth with the genuine imprint of Christ in the hands of her mother-in-law.

"Turn around. Look at that which you are pledged to protect!"

Charlotte shook her head. "It's blasphemous. No wonder the Templars were arrested."

"Then your family should have been too—for they secretly hid the reliquary containing the Holy Shroud for three centuries."

Charlotte's body doubled over and her stomach wretched. She knew this to be true from her father's diaries, and she had to sit anywhere she could.

"Your Majesty, I am the Worthy Grand Matron of this, the Order of the Daughters of David," declared Augusta. "We are a secret guild of females in the Masonic Order with the same rights and privileges as the Order of the Garter, or the Knights Templar. We have used this location as our assembly site for over 500 years. It is where we women of Merovingian and Davidic ancestry meet to initiate new members and keep our records current. You possess the mark, and your amulet directly connects you to me, and to the Shroud family. You, George and I share a common ancestor—Templar Seneschal Geoffrey de Charny, who was burned at the stake along with Grand Master Jacques de Molay in 1307. We have the genealogy. I checked into yours when I first saw your birthmark. Since you are also an amulet holder, you are here for a reason," she said. "To be initiated."

I was trembling so badly the torch fell from my fingers. Augusta re-lit it and placed it into a holder. She moved to the oil at the foot of the statue, dipped a finger into it, and rubbed a small amount onto my wrist in the sign of the cross. "In nomine Patris, et Filis, et Spiritus Sancti." Suddenly ten women came into our tunnel, all carrying lighted torches, and all dressed in white with white aprons, sashes, and veils were over their faces. They formed a circle around me.

"These are the Daughters of David, soon to be your sisters. Each of them represents one of the four women depicted on this statue."

I asked Augusta who the women of the statue were. She told me they were Mary Magdalene, and Jesus' sisters—Mary Salome and Mary Jacobe, along with Saint Sarah—known as Sarah-la-Kali, or Black Sarah, the Egyptian servant who, along with Joseph of Arimathea, brought the three Mary's to Gaul—now known as Provence, France. It is said they were adrift in a boat without oars.

I walked to the altar and looked up at the statue. The eyes of the women seemed to follow me as I circled it, their gaze assuring me that I belonged, that I was worthy of inclusion in this sisterhood. Augusta took me to an ancient stash of papyrus papers, leather-clad books, and scrolls. She pointed to the papers. "These are our records. We Sisters can each trace ourselves back to a Templar or to King David, and we are each sworn to protect the sacred relics and the treasure of the Templars, for they are one and the same, and powerful in their usage." Augusta motioned to Lady Covington, one of the "Sisters," who came over and began unhooking my dress. "Now it is time to accept your destiny and be reborn." I timidly stepped out of my dress and was then blindfolded. I was assured I had to endure the same initiation performed on countless masons, knights and Sisters down through time.

And what followed unnerved and stayed with me ever since.

Thirty Three

When Charlotte and Augusta finally returned to Queen's House, Charlotte was still shaking. She hurried past George without uttering a word and went up to the nursery, for she had to see and hug her children then find a place to think. George was perplexed as he watched his wife run up the stairs and turned to his mother.

"What happened?"

"I took her to see my 'Sisters.'"

George's expression dropped dramatically. "You took her to Hertfordshire? Why? Anything could have happened there so far from our protection. It was unconscionable."

"You know we are protected there. We have our allies."

George tried his best not to chastise his mother. For years this issue had been a source of ongoing consternation between them, and there would be no resolving it tonight. "Mother, it is too hard for me to cope with the enormous pressures I have with the Whigs, France, and the Colonies, *and* concern myself with whether the Queen of England is galavanting in dungeons and caves protecting phantom relics and legends. Do not take her there again. I forbid it."

"Forbid all you wish, but your wife is one of us now."

Augusta poured herself a glass of port. "We have been blessed, George. Of all the women you could have chosen, your bride is the link connecting us to our divine past," said his mother, "I misjudged her. My desire for my niece to reign as queen overshadowed my ability to see Charlotte's value. Do not make the same mistake."

George became quiet and just looked at his mother. Finally, he sat down and stared off. This was exactly why he detested the meddlesome nature of women in political affairs. They were relentless, insistent, grated on the nerves—and were mostly correct.

"I adore you, son. But the fact that neither you nor your siblings received the mark does not preclude you from accepting who you are. Despite your choice not to believe it, your father's blood connects you to your own Moorish roots, mine connects you to King David, and all of it connects us to the Templars and the protection of their secrets."

"Do you not understand. We cannot forage this terrain. Should this information fall into the wrong hands it could lead to the same dissent Henry VIII faced when his actions seperated England from the Roman Catholic Church."

George unfolded his arms and stood; his head was beginning to throb as the day's events were affecting him. "I have too many enemies—Wilkes and Fox foremost and I will not divide this country with gossip and unsavory allusions to controversies. I refuse to countanence a connection to anything or anyone deemed divine. It is pretentious and divisive. And do not think Charlotte's involvement in the Order will force my hand. That kind of thing is fine for you, or my uncle, or my father when he was alive, but not me." He started toward the stairs, then turned back. "And hereafter, I will not countenance your taking Charlotte to Hertfordshire again. That is my final word."

Meanwhile, Charlotte had retreated to her chambers after kissing two-year-old George and baby Frederick. Having satisfied herself that each was well and happy, she now laid across her bed rummanating over what happened earlier. Did she actually have the experience, or was it all a dream? Was she enlightened today? Or was it all a hallucination? But when she looked at her index finger bandaged with a strip of white linen she knew it had actually happened.

Lady Hagedorn came into the room after seeing that Charlotte was in a "mood" in the nursery. She asked if Charlotte required anything. Charlotte shook her head. "Am I mad?"

Not knowing how to respond, Lady Hagedorn wondered what had Charlotte so tightly wound. Generally when the queen was emotional like this it was because the king had hurt her feelings or she just had an encounter with Christian. But this was different. Charlotte was trembling as she lay across the bed, and on top of this she did not want supper, which was unusual. Whatever happened that day, wherever she had gone, caused her to question her sanity.

"Of course not, Your Majesty. You just had a trying day."

Charlotte sat up. "Fetch Anne to me."

Lady Hagedorn left the room just as George appeared at the door. The king and queen held each other's stare a moment before Charlotte looked off at a loss for words. George sat on the bed, searching his heart for what to say, and for a few moments there was a deafening silence. Finally the king cleared his throat slightly.

"I have been told the events of your day. I know what you discovered—or think you did."

Charlotte was unable to verbalize her thoughts. George finally took her hand. The gesture touched her and she returned his look with a measure of resignation. "We have adopted a policy of silence on the subject of relics and gnosticism, or the Templars and the innuendo of Moorish descent here," George informed her. "Such knowledge and activity performed by a royal would be considered heretical and construed as against God and the Church of England."

"How is the 'innuendo' of Moorish blood heretical, George?" Charlotte wondered aloud, feeling as though she was standing before her dead mother's equal disregard. "You knew who and what I was on our wedding night. I pledged to you the sacrifice of genuine love from you in exchange for a good life here, and you 'overlooking' the subterfuge of my 'powder and paint' disguise. Those were your words."

"I shall tell you what I just told my mother. There will be no discussion of this matter. No more travel to Hertfordshire, no more searches for relics, Grails, artifacts, manna from heaven," he pulled the amulet from her cleavage, "or mystical talismen," he firmly insisted. "You are to remain here—where I can keep you, and us, safe."

"A prisoner…in my own home?"

It took George a moment, but he softly kissed her on her forehead. "Charlotte…"

Charlotte interrupted. "I want to be alone for a while."

The king nodded and, after a pause, left quietly. Charlotte sat up on the bed, thinking. She was overwrought with questions. How was she to deal with what she experienced today? Who else could she be expected to share it with but George's mother? After a few moments trying to process it, she stood in front of her armoire. She unlocked it and threw off the rugs and fabric to reveal the hiding place of her father's precious chest and caressed it. She sat on the floor. Was this truly the reliquary for the burial garments of Jesus? She thought about Herford Castle and the image of the head band with the face of Christ in blood.

Charlotte thought about her initiation into the Sisterhood, and the humiliation she felt at the rituals forced upon her. She wrapped her arms around herself as the memory flooded back.

✠

The queen had been stripped naked and was moved to a candle-lit altar blindfolded. In all her tan-skinned glory she was asked to repeat certain phrases. "Sister, to you the secrets of our Order will be unveiled," she heard Augusta say. "A brighter sun never shone luster on your eyes. Prostrate thyself before this altar and do not shudder."

Charlotte knelt. She could feel the warmth from the several dozen candles on her face.

"Have confidence in every virtue. Let these thoughts inspire you with noble sentiments. May you feel the elevation of soul that shall scorn a dishonest act. Sister, what do you desire?"

Charlotte was told to respond, "Light," which she did.

"Sisters, stretch forth your hands and assist in bringing this new-made Sister from darkness to light," Augusta commanded.

Charlotte could hear the members form a circle around her, and then she felt her index finger being cut with a knife and she flinched in pain. As her blood flowed her finger was pressed against the index finger of each of the ten women there until their blood co-mingled. Soon she was raised to a standing position and felt a sash placed over her naked shoulders and an apron tied around her stomach.

"Sister, I now present you with the sash and white apron, emblems of innocence and the badges of a Mason," she heard. "They have been worn by the potentates of the earth, and it is more honorable than the diamonds of kings, or the pearls of princesses. You have shared your blood with the blood of your Sisters who in turn have shared their blood with the Brothers of the Order back through time to the ancient Order of the Knights of the Temple of Solomon. As a Daughter of King David, you are now required and charged to protect the secrets of this Order and to continue the quest for the sacred knowledge."

Charlotte was asked to repeat the Acceptance Creed of the Order of the Daughters of David, which she did. Following this, the queen felt the tip of a sword placed at her left breast and Augusta's voice become demanding requiring her to repeat:

"I hereby most solemnly and sincerely promise and swear, that I will always hail, ever conceal, and never reveal any part or parts, art or arts, point or points of the secrets and mysteries of ancient Free Masonry, which I have received, am about to receive, or may hereafter be instructed in, to any person or persons in the known world, except it be a true and lawful Brother or Sister Mason. And I bind myself under no fewer penalties than to have my throat cut, my tongue torn out, and my body buried in the sea. So help me God."

Charlotte then heard Augusta declare: "God said, 'Let there be light' and there was light."

The blindfold was removed and Charlotte saw all the faces of the women gathered seemingly glowing brightly as if on fire. The illumination from them seemed to crescendo into a blaze of fire and Charlotte didn't know whether she was hallucinating or having a divine vision. Finally her eyes adjusted and the sight before her diminished into normalcy. She began to sob until two women came forward and put her clothes back on over her new white sash and apron. Then she looked down, and gasped.

Shaking uncontrollably Charlotte fell to her knees in prayer, for there, imprinted on the cloth in her hand—like its sacred counterpart, the Soudarion—was the faint image of Charlotte's own eyes. Eyes which looked back at her with the haunting gaze of revelation.

┼

Now, seven hours later, Charlotte was sitting on the floor of her chambers with the reliquary and the linen blindfold she had just removed from her pocket. The image of her eyes had vanished but her memory of it had not. She looked at her index finger, which had been cut and was now encased in a linen bandage. She unwrapped it only to find the faint glimmer of a scar, a near miraculous healing. At that moment there was a knock at the door, then she heard:

"Your Majesty, it's Anne Josef. You sent for me?"

"One moment Anne." Charlotte quickly hid the bandages and blindfold in the armoire then covered the reliquary. "Come in."

Her servant entered.

"Please help me out of this dress," Charlotte commanded.

The Ethiopian nodded and undid all twenty hooks. Charlotte disappeared behind her dressing screen to slip out of her dress. In the mirror the queen received further confirmation of the day's events. She was wearing the white sash and apron she had received at her initiation. It wasn't a dream. The queen took off the Masonic regalia and put on her robe. Remembering her blood oath to the Order, she hid the sash and apron behind the dressing panel and emerged. She then asked to see Anne's amulet again. Anne removed the talisman from her neck and gave it to the queen, who inspected it until she finally found what she was looking for—the initials "GB."

"Your amulet originally belonged to Geoffroi Bissol," she said giving the amulet back to Anne. "Take care with it. I was somewhere today that made me realize its importance. I can't give you any particulars, but there is a concerted effort to collect all of the amulets for their cumulative secrets. They know where four of them are for certain. Yours makes the fifth, but I did not reveal you have it."

Anne nodded a grateful "thank you," not knowing what to say otherwise. Charlotte hoped she was doing the right thing and continued, "I need your help."

"Anything, Your Majesty."

"I want you to help me compose a coded letter and send it to the Duke of Levis-Mirepoix. Tell him I have two amulets—one perhaps is the Solomon amulet. Impress upon him I need to have some scrolls in my possession translated as soon as possible so I can understand the significance of them. It is of life and death importance."

Anne frowned. "My amulet too?"

"Yes, my dear. Your amulet is of great significance."

Thirty Four

*A*nne and I took our own blood oath that night as amulet holders. She composed the letter and I had Lady Schwellenberg post it. At my request, Anne sewed pockets into her uniforms to keep her amulet safely hidden inside as opposed to dangling around her neck. Meanwhile, I had an opening with a locked door constructed into the wall behind my armoire similar to the one my parents had installed in their chambers at Mirow, and I hid the reliquary within it. My mind slowly accepted what happened to me that day in Hertfordshire, and I knew I was now a part of something much larger than myself or my father's quest.

During the next three months, nothing of consequence transpired, and I went about my usual days. I gardened, played with my children, attended our levees, visited with Mme. Lia, and played cards with Swelly, Haggy and Lady Lizzie. George and I took long walks and sometimes went riding in the mornings. A few times a week I posed for Sir Allan so he could finish my coronation portrait, now two years in creation. Once I'd given him permission to paint me more authentically our conversations became more enlightened. I gave him license to speak freely and his abolitionists leanings emerged with passion. We had healthy exchanges about what should be done regarding emancipating slaves here in Britain, and I relished being taken seriously for my opinions and not dismissed as a 'mere woman' even though I was queen and his superior.

Then there was Christian—the man I had been avoiding since the night of the April riots, Wilkes' arrest, and the birth of my son. The man I had allowed to kiss me. The man I could not get out of my mind—despite my desire to know the truth of my amulet.

✠

At breakfast, three days after the New Year, 1764, Charlotte wore a dress made from the red silk fabric Mme. Lia de Beaumont had given her the previous spring. George barely noticed. Augusta, however, took pleasure at the sight of the queen, acutely aware she and Charlotte had not had a meaningful conversation since the trip to Hertford in early September. She wanted to reestablish their relationship. "Your dress is lovely, my dear. Is it new?"

"It is, Your Highness. Thank you for noticing. I had it made from material given me as a gift," Charlotte gratefully acknowledged.

Augusta noticed George's complete absorption in the headlines of the *Gazette*, oblivious of his wife's presence. "Do you not think the queen's dress is lovely, George?"

"What I think...is that the bloody Colonists are insane," George snipped.

Everyone looked at him. He was clearly in another of his moods. "In their anger over the Stamp Tax, they have now rejected the use of stamps altogether. How are we expected to pay for our war debts and the protection of the Colonists themselves from invasion by Indians? With only our domestic taxes? The sale of tea? Profits from the trade?"

Charlotte reacted. When young George and baby Frederick had finished eating, the queen instructed their governess to take them to the nursery. Though she was aware of the others at the table, she still addressed the king with a measure of ire. "Do profits from the trade mean more to you than the human lives lost and ill-treated in their gain?"

"Please. Not another of your rants on slavery. It's too early, and my head is fitful."

"No, answer me, because I do not understand..."

"Charlotte," George lowered his voice, forcing himself not to shout. "I will not discuss the subject while our country is embroiled with concerns of budget and conflicts with the Colonies. It would be impolitic."

Charlotte forced composure. "I've recently read Anthony Benezet's pamphlet on slavery. It's enlightening. Perhaps you should read it too, since apparently *I* am too 'impolitic.'"

Augusta's head fell into her hands. All hell would be unleashed now as George looked at Charlotte as if she'd contracted leprosy.

"Where did you acquire such reading material?" he asked with a furled brow.

"From our library," Charlotte lied.

"No you did not. I would not have such contemptible material in the library."

Charlotte said nothing regretting that she had brought it up. George now launched into a tirade. "Who gave it to you? That woman who visits you? The one who gives you fabric and French wine? The one whose loyalties we cannot confirm? This is why I forbade you to have friends I do not know. They are always undue influences. You are not to see her again."

"Why don't you just lock me in the Tower where you put everyone who disagrees with you?"

George tossed his napkin to the table and stood. "God save me from petticoat politics," he grunted, leaving the room with the newspaper.

Charlotte looked at the rest of her family. Duke William, the king's brother, said nothing while finishing his eggs. Augusta finally leaned into Charlotte and whispered: "Learn not to verbalize your opinions in political matters to George. He abhors it. A woman's place is not in Parliament's chambers, but where she can do more good."

"And where is that? In His Majesty's bedchambers? Because I'm there every night, and not much good it does me, save for having more 'heirs.'"

The queen excused herself, leaving everyone to ponder her state of mind.

Two hours later, Charlotte was having a music lesson. Christian complimented her on how beautiful she looked in her new red dress, but Charlotte, though flattered, still played with neither energy nor interest. Christian knew something was wrong and, before long, stopped the lesson. "What's bothering you?"

Charlotte sighed in frustration. "I have two children, a husband who loves another, and I feel trapped in this gilded cage called 'Queen's House.' My comings and goings are monitored, and other than my ladies from Germany I cannot have any friends. Even Mme. Lia's days are numbered as of this morning." Charlotte wandered to the window, perusing the grounds of her vast impound. "Christian, I am too young to feel as though I am marking time until I die, accomplishing nothing along the way. I have such ambition to do more, to be of service, to love and be loved. But I have no way to move past my present condition."

"You can have anything you want, Charlotte. All you need do is want it badly enough."

"If only that were true."

"But it is. You can do much more about the things that matter to you—about women, slavery, poverty, but you must do it with stealth. You can lend your influence and status to causes dear to you, and the king would never know. But you must be cunning." He came over to her. "You can have love. All you have to do is take it. It's been here for you all the time."

Charlotte turned to him crying out for his touch, but she was afraid.

"I do want love in my life—genuine, complete, unadulterated love. But all that is available to me is the clandestine, sullied, dishonorable kind, and I do not want that."

Christian was hurt and turned away, biting the inside of his cheek.

"Christian, please understand."

"I do not." Christian turned back in anger. "All we have…is what we have now. And however brief, I would have it in a heartbeat. Do you know how hard it is to see you every other day knowing you accept the itinerant disregard of a king who will never love you? Do you know how frustrating it is to recount over and over in my head our last evening in Mecklenburg, or our letters, or what happened in the garden here last April? How can you be so pitiless as to toss away so casually one who has only the deepest regard for you, and admonish that regard as 'clandestine, sullied and dishonorable'?"

Charlotte's eyes began to tear as Christian took her face in his hands. "I love you, Charlotte. I do not know how not to. And I know you love me too. Even before you were my queen, you were my love."

He kissed her. Charlotte tried to stop him, but he kissed her again. She used all her strength to push away from him, and finally rushed off.

"You lie—even to yourself!" Christian yelled after her. But Charlotte was gone.

"…At that moment I knew I was doomed to be forever unhappy…or an adulteress…"

Outside the door, Lady Lizzie saw Charlotte running up the stairs, upset. But Anne saw it as well—including Lady Lizzie's observance.

For the rest of the day, Charlotte refused to leave her room or eat with the king and his family. She played Christian's ballerina music box over and over, unable to sleep. Mme. Lia and her brother's words kept repeating in her head: *"...Take a lover."*

Anne continued to be loyal to her queen. Occasionally she would look at Charlotte praying the queen was all right. She knew Charlotte was bedeviled by her present—marriage to an indifferent, intemperate king— and by her past. The Ethiopian vowed to assist her queen through whatever trials her life brandished, and to keep an eye on those who would do Charlotte harm—even those right under the queen's nose.

✠

That Friday, a snow storm nearly incapacitated London. Most people could not leave their homes or businesses for two days. George, Bute and Augusta were snowed in at St. James. Christian felt lucky. He had arrived at Queen's House an hour before the snow morphed into a blinding blizzard. Lady Lizzie took his wet overcoat and hat, Lady Hagedorn prepared him a cup of hot tea, and he waited for the queen in front of the fireplace.

Soon Christian began to pace, acutely aware of the ticking clock above the mantle. He was not sure after Wednesday's events how Charlotte would receive him, or *if* she would receive him at all.

On the other hand, Charlotte was not expecting Christian—not with the weather. So upon Lady Hagedorn's announcement that he was downstairs, she had to prepare herself. She looked at her reflection in the mirror above her bureau and instructed herself to stay strong. Her plan was to steel herself against his classic good looks and tender countenance, and it was this course of action in play as she entered the music room focused, prepared and vigilant. She would not allow Christian to distract her today.

Then she saw him in front of the fire, sipping his tea bearing an intense expression. When Christian realized the queen was in the room, he stood. Her defenses evaporated. Their eyes locked while unspoken passion and unrequited longing was masked with royal deference.

Charlotte and Christian went to the harpsichord, pretending nothing had happened two days earlier. Christian was formal, and Charlotte regal. This dance went on for twenty minutes. Then Charlotte began having difficulty with a musical passage and humorously mimicked Emmanuel Bach's high-pitched voice:

"Your Highness, your fingering is too sluggish. It is why you keep missing the b flat..."

Christian chuckled. "You do my brother so well."

"I should. Swelly and I endlessly joked about him. We called him 'Old harpy Bach.'"

"Oh my. If Emmanuel was a 'harpy,' what, pray tell, did you call me?"

Charlotte became coy. "Let me see. There was 'divine,' 'fetching,' oh, and my personal favorite, 'incandescent manifestation.'"

Christian so wanted to kiss her. But that action always led to confusion and reprisals, so he began to play a familiar melody.

"I know this," Charlotte exclaimed. "You played it for me at Sansoucci."

"Yes. It's finished. It's the aria from my newest opera, 'Artaserse' which I've dedicated to you."

Charlotte was moved. Before she realized it her fingers touched his, and ever so slowly he eased her into his powerful arms. Soon they could not help but give in to the raging passion which had them possessed. Christian's body pushed hers onto the harpsichord while he lifted layer upon layer of pettiskirts. Charlotte neither objected nor recinded. Rather, she accepted the inevitable, relishing it as the most exciting, sensuous experience she had ever had with a man. This was indeed different. Better. It was not the cruel, beastly corruptions of a demented cousin, nor the perfunctory, obligatory act of an uncaring husband. Every moment of this was thrilling.

They made love everywhere that day—the settee, the window seat, the floor. In one sublime snowy afternoon, years of forbidden, pent-up frustration was finally released.

In the aftermath, as they lay in front of the fire, Christian became introspective as he held his beloved. "For so long I've thought of nothing but this moment. And now that it's done, I fear that is all it will ever be—one fleeting, luminescent moment."

Charlotte turned to Christian kissing him softly. Her body tingled with sweet sensations. "Then let us have our moments as they come— one at a time."

She collected herself, tipped to the door and opened it. After making sure no one was watching, she looked back at Christian with liberating urgency, suggesting he follow her. Christian's common sense betrayed him, and they eased up the stairs to her private chambers.

At the end of the hall on the second-floor residence level, Lady Schwellenberg saw them and watched as the door to Charlotte's chambers closed behind the two. She smiled, knowing what would come next, and how long they had waited for it. So when Anne came down the hall with fresh linen and towels headed for the queen's chambers, Lady Schwellenberg stopped her.

"Not now, Anne. Trust me, the queen is deliciously indisposed."

Thirty Five

he next morning, it had stopped snowing and everyone began the long process of shoveling London out from under its white blanket of winter. From the comfort of my window seat I watched as several dozen servants dug a path so horses and carriages could reach the entrance of Queen's House, and it seemed all would be right with the world after all.

Christian had stayed the night in my chambers, and I had now taken him into my keeping. There would be no retreat now unless I deemed it, and I was filled with mixed emotions. Was I wicked? Should I have remained loyal to my king? Should I be judged an ungrateful Jezebel who surrendered to a moment of genuine happiness?

I had already made a deal with the devil by way of my marriage. This was now a new deal—one of my own choosing—and I chose to take my precious moments..."

✠

"I want every incredible detail or I swear on my sainted mother I will never serve at your pleasure again," Lady Hagedorn entreated Charlotte the moment Christian left Buckingham.

"Me too," asserted Lady Schwellenberg. "I am even more invested than you, Haggy."

"Now, now ladies. Don't fight," Charlotte chuckled, pulling her two friends into the music room. "After all, it is indecorous to discuss intimate details of one's connubial relationships."

"Yes, but...," insisted Lady Hagedorn.

"And to do so constitutes a most undignified breach of etiquette..."

"But...," insisted Lady Schwellenberg.

"...It was the most divine experience I have ever had in my life," confessed Charlotte, which caused her ladies to sigh with envy. "The sensations I felt must be against the law. The things he did to me, things I allowed him to do which I could not help, oh my sweet Lord—divine. When I tell you I never thought it possible to undergo so rapturous a jolt throughout one's body and not feel amoral, I tell you... it was a religious experience. I saw God."

Ladies Schwellenberg and Hagedorn stood with their mouths agape in shock. "You *enjoyed* it?" Lady Hagedorn uttered in astonishment. "I never knew any woman who actually enjoyed it..."

"...Who wasn't depraved," Lady Schwellenberg added in jest.

Charlotte smiled wickedly, taking her ladies hands. She now felt qualified and wise. "My dears, I know now that a woman's enjoyment of the experience is solely up to the man. If he is proficient in the matter there is no doubt of its being a most satisfactory event for both." She winked at them and departed the room, leaving Lady Hagedorn and Lady Schwellenberg aghast.

"...Christian and I spent any time we could together. He would come to give me a lesson, we'd practice a while, sometimes talk, sometimes play chess. The one thing we did not do—was discuss my escapade to Hertford or what transpired there. I kept that a closely guarded secret, shared only with Anne and Augusta.

What Christian and I did do, however, was what nature demanded, even though we knew it could not last. It was wrong, yes. But the time we spent with each other was of such quality and meaning it obliterated the reality of committing the sin of adultery."

☩

The following spring, despite the ongoing tension between the Colonists and Britain, Charlotte and George held their usual levees. Christian always arranged the entertainment, fascinating the courtiers with such performers as Sarah Siddons, who gave theatrical readings, and one of Charlotte's favorites, Carl Frederich Abel. But it was at the king's ball in May where, as promised, Christian delivered two extraordinary musicians for the king and queen—Chevalier Saint George, who thrilled everyone with a virtuoso violin performance, and a special concert by Christian's protégé—Wolfgang Amadeus Mozart, a child prodigy at age eight. Accompanied by his father Leopold on violin, young Wolfgang electrified the gathering playing several sonatas he had composed on both the harpsichord and the king's organ.

As the boy played, Charlotte was stunned by his musical prowess and looked over at Christian, nodding her approval. Eventually Christian moved over and stood near her.

"He is unbelievable," Charlotte whispered.

"The most amazing creature of nature I've ever encountered," Christian responded, and then stealthily caressed her back with one finger, "save you."

Charlotte smiled and eased away. Christian watched her go, unable to take his eyes off of her, not realizing that a few courtiers in attendance had witnessed the encounter. One of them was Mme. Lia de Beaumont, who had received a vicious tongue-lashing from Lord Bute about her frequent visits and undue influence on the queen, after which she promised to keep her distance. But Lia still kept a furtive eye on Charlotte and Christian throughout the evening, and in so doing noticed Lord Bute taking note of the closeness developing between the queen and her music master.

George was, of course, oblivious. He was thoroughly mesmerized by young Mozart's performance, and enraptured by the presence of Lady Sarah Lennox-Bunbury, who had ceased coming to court soon after her marriage. He noted her expectant belly and her beautiful albeit sad face, and his mind wandered back to what he believed were his happiest times when a future with Sarah shined with possibility. She was unforgettable; and the sigh in his heart resounded as loudly as Mozart's music.

Lady Sarah felt George's stare burning into her and turned. When their eyes met she quickly gripped her husband's hand tighter. But George noticed Sir Bunbury's attention to his wife was strained tonight as he removed his fingers from hers. Sarah looked at him with pleading eyes, but Bunbury moved away and stood near a buffet table by himself. After consuming a glass of wine to calm his nerves, he finished watching Mozart's performance.

George moved through the crowd until he was near Lady Sarah, careful not to exhibit too much emotion lest there be gossip. "Good to have you back at court, Lady Sarah," he said in a low voice. "I see you are well…and with child."

"Yes. Charles and I...are expecting in August," she responded, keeping her eyes forward.

"If there is anything you need...or shall ever need, you have only to let me..."

"Charles and I are fine, Your Majesty," whispered Sarah abruptly, and she tried to move away, but George's hand grabbed hers, then he dropped it quickly. "Sarah..."

"Charles and I are fine," she repeated stridently, then walked away.

George watched her go to her husband, taking her place at his side. But as Mozart concluded his performance, the king's head began to throb. From across the room, Charlotte caught the exchange. Unbeknownst to her, Mme. Lia and Lord Bute observed it also, as did Lady Lizzie, now more curious than ever. They all took note as George shifted through the crowd to the young composer and his father to join the queen in adulation of the boy's abilities.

Leopold Mozart praised Christian for his influence on his son. Charlotte promised to sponsor the young Wolfgang's next London engagement and the boy promised to write a sonata for her. After George complimented Christian on providing the palace with the most transcendent entertainment he had ever experienced, he begged off citing a pain in his temples growing worse by the second. He glanced back at Lady Sarah, which Charlotte and Christian noticed, then left the ball.

Lia chose that opportunity to approach the queen. "Your Majesty, a moment, please," she asked after a nod to Christian and Saint George. Charlotte acquiesced, and the two moved to a buffet table out of earshot of others. Franz served them each a glass of sherry, and Charlotte held her wrist out to her friend. "I'm wearing that exquisite perfume you gave me. It's my absolute favorite." Then Charlotte saw Lia's concern. "What is it?"

"Take heed within your house and your private person. Conspiracies abound to thwart your happiness. Lord Bute is no friend to you, and neither is Lady Sarah Bunbury. One hides the fact the other still maintains the interest of the king." Lia then took a moment. "At the king's behest, Lord Bute warned me not to visit you as often as I enjoy if I wished to remain at court."

"Oh no."

"It is all right. I shall come every other month and bring you all the things you enjoy, but I will not compromise our friendship by provoking the king's ire. I value it too much."

"As do I, Mme. Lia. Nothing brings me more pleasure."

Lia grinned. "No? Apparently, there is one other person here who brings you greater pleasure." She looked over at Christian, then back at Charlotte, who blushed. "Have fun, Your Majesty. You deserve every happiness—especially under your present circumstance."

☩

Charlotte was not to see Mme. Lia for two months, and was contemptuous of George for denying her access. Yet, she wasn't lonely or unoccupied. She continued to enjoy her "music lessons" with Christian, and she took consolation, however brief, in the fact Sir Henry Fox was forced to resign as Paymaster after his books failed to balance and public funds were missing. He became the most reviled politician in London.

However, it was not long before Charlotte found her anger at George's censure of Lia and her glee over Sir Henry's resignation waning. The king's headaches had increased in intensity to the point where Charlotte had become worried. He was having stomach pains, fever, coughing, and was losing weight. He began vomiting and his urine turned as purple as an eggplant. Dr. Baker was summoned, who brought in other experts. All were baffled by the king's malady, which had escalated into inexplicable attacks lasting weeks.

One evening, Ladies Hagedorn, Schwellenberg and Lizzie and the staff were awakened as George removed his clothes and ran down the halls naked, screaming obscenities. Dr. Baker called upon two pages to help remove George downstairs to the bowels of the palace, where the king was placed in a straitjacket and locked up. There, George began screaming for hours.

In the next two months the king was blooded many times. Prime Minister Grenville, who succeeded Bute; George's family, personal advisors and Charlotte were all concerned about his ability to govern. A Regency Bill was suggested in case of permanent ailment or his untimely death.

"It must be proposed without raising suspicion that the king is ill," Charlotte cautioned, and they all agreed. However, she still had concerns. Who would become regent? Their eldest son, Prince George, was only four, and there was no one Charlotte or George could trust. Grenville suggested the queen become regent in the event of George's incapacitation and Charlotte only agreed if everyone else did unanimously. All advisors were in accord, and the bill was proposed before the Commons.

Day after day Charlotte hoped to hear from the Duke of Levis-Mirepoix with no such luck. Night after night she tearfully sat with George as he traveled in and out of clarity. Dr. Baker thought the king should go to Bath to heal in the therapeutic waters there. The rest of the medical staff agreed, and George was spirited away for a month under cover of darkness.

The Regency Bill passed, but still Charlotte was concerned. She knew the bill would arrive for George's signature while he was in Bath having treatment, and Parliament would know for certain that something was wrong if it was not signed in a timely fashion. Great care had been taken to shield the dire state of the king's illness.

So there she was, two weeks later in George's office at Windsor, worried. As expected, the bill was presented for signature in the usual manner: It arrived in the red leather box by the Sergeant-of-Arms from Parliament and was given to a page, who brought it inside the office. The page put the box on the desk, then went back outside and stood by the door. Charlotte began to shake. Should she be truthful and disclose George's absence or how seriously ill he was when the country needed leadership? Lord Bute was standing near her almost at attention and, upon the box's arrival, chose to leave and wait outside the door. It was almost as though he approved of Charlotte doing an illegal, yet necessary act. She thought about Magragana, and what she might want the queen to do under this circumstance. After all, she was an amulet holder— whatever that meant—and perhaps the dark "Daughter of David" was supposed to commit this small act of treason.

Suddenly, Charlotte acquired strength and knew what to do. She opened the box and looked at the bill. Her pulse was racing. Finally, she picked up the pen and, with a determined stroke, forged George's signature on it. Then, after a deep breath, she realized it was too late for regret. The deed was done. She folded the document, melted the wax, used the king's official seal for imprinting, and placed the bill back in the red leather box. With unchallenged authority Charlotte summoned the page to enter and handed the box back to him. He in turn handed the box back to the Sergeant-at-Arms for transportation to Parliament. Then the queen clutched her precious amulet through her dress, and prayed she had done the right thing.

Moments later, Lord Bute entered and they exchanged a knowing look. Though he was no longer Prime Minister, he nonetheless remained the king's private advisor and protector. He came over to the queen as if to say "thank you," but Charlotte couldn't respond. She hastily left George's office with her mind suddenly racing. All she thought of was if anyone discovered her transgression both she and Christian could be tried for treason and the idea of this unsettled her. Plus, she had signed a bill, functioning as a sovereign, and all to keep George's health a secret.

Yet, it wasn't her only secret. The queen had begun to experience stomach pains and morning sickness again. Having had two children, she did not need Dr. Hunter to tell her she was breeding again. But this time, and more importantly, she knew she'd had a lover—someone she feared could have fathered her child—and the thought of this made her tremble. She prayed that if George recovered she would do everything she could to make him happy. She prayed to God to take away her feelings for Christian and return to a life of honor and righteousness.

Miraculously, George's condition seemed to improve, but he had little time to fully recover before receiving unsettling news. At the next meeting of the Privy Counsel he listened to his advisors warn of an impending war with America. The Stamp Act had provoked more furor with the Colonists, and in protest they refused to buy British goods or use paper products. When George came upstairs to join Charlotte in the apartment, he felt and looked far older than his 26 years.

Charlotte watched as he laid the petition on a table nearby and asked her if she wanted to play a game of chess. As they played, Charlotte became concerned and asked her husband if he was all right. Though he insisted he was fine, she knew better, so they played in silence while Charlotte waited until he was ready to speak his mind.

"Your prowess at chess reveals cunning," he said, taking her pawn with his knight.

"Does it surprise you I have any?" Charlotte mused, taking his knight with her bishop. She could never tell him her training was at the tutelage of Christian Bach.

"Few things surprise me about you these days, Charlotte. For instance, it takes a certain shrewdness to forge the king's signature on a bill providing the queen becomes regent in the event of the king's death or incapacitation."

Charlotte froze. How did George know this? Then, almost as though he'd read her mind George rose to pour himself a glass of brandy, "I still have friends who are devotedly loyal to me."

"Would you have preferred Lord Rockingham or Lord Pelham be appointed in my stead?" Charlotte retorted, positioning her queen within two moves of a checkmate. "Men who cannot be controlled or guided by your 'devotedly loyal' friends?"

"No. You were right to protect me and the line of succession."

She could see the imprint of pain on his face, and although checkmate was imminent she remained silent. Finally, George could see no way of winning and stopped playing.

"The Colonists are raising an army to protect what they feel are their rights. They insist that if we are going to unfairly tax them, they should have a delegate or some representation in Parliament." He rubbed his head. "They've adopted a *Declaration of Rights and Grievances,*' and written letters of protest to me and Parliament. They have acquired detailed knowledge of our strategic outposts, our tactics, and they've been talking to the French about support should they choose to separate from us."

"How do they know such things?"

"We suspect a spy from here is feeding it to them."

"A spy?"

"We have reason to suspect French Minister d'Eon. We believe King Louis sent him here to gather information about British plans all along—especially Colonial unrest."

"But I know Minister d'Eon. He is an old family friend. How valid are your suspicions?"

"A letter was intercepted bearing the Dauphin's seal. It was on its way to d'Eon recalling him officially, yet privately asking him to remain in London pending further orders."

At first it surprised Charlotte that George was so forthcoming with political matters. Then she found herself concerned about the spy being d'Eon. "I find the timing of all of this suspicious, especially since France is where Sir Wilkes absconded to. Are you sure it isn't Wilkes?

"We can be sure of nothing. All we know is d'Eon hasn't been seen in weeks," George commented as he brought the grievance over and handed it to his wife. "So you see, this is what loyalty has brought me."

Charlotte read the petition...but as she went through the various points in the grievance, she found herself on the other side. "Actually George, the Colonists are quite justified in wanting a say in how their tax monies are used. Remember, they owe the same allegiance to you and Parliament as all Britons. And according to this they feel '...*entitled to all the inherent rights and liberties of natural born subjects.*' There is something to be said for that."

George became irritated. "It costs Britain £350,000 annually to maintain an army just to protect the Colonists from the Indians. Add to that the cost of the Seven Years War—which depleted our coffers. Ten months ago you suggested we abolish the slave trade. How will we pay the expenses of our country with your suggestions?"

"I would repeal that Stamp Act and consider the Colonists' grievances," Charlotte offered even though she was more than a little annoyed. "For if they, in fact, acquire France's help in rising against you, England shall sink, and you, my dear, shall be remembered for far more than this foolish decision. You shall become America's last king, who was both insane, incompetent and a dunderhead!"

A knock sounded at the door, blessedly interrupting them.

"What!" bellowed George.

The door opened and George's chamberlain entered. "Your Majesty, there is news from the Colonies," said Lord Cavendish. "It is not good, sir."

Thirty Six

February, 1766

George tried to control his emotions. He had been informed that in the Colonies, a large crowd marched to Hanover Square in Boston, hung an effigy of the Distributor of Stamps for Massachusetts Bay on an Elm tree, then burned it for effect. Two days later the mob tarred and feathered six tax collectors and burned the home of the Lieutenant Governor of Massachusetts. Colonists, thoroughly opposed to the repressive policies of Britain and its Stamp Act, were poised to riot. Today the Stamp Act had been repealed.

The king tried in vain to convince the Privy Council that the Stamp Act was necessary—even as Charlotte's words to the contrary kept rummaging through his head. After much debate in Parliament, Lord Rockingham, George's second Prime Minister in two years, insisted it be banished and put forth the motion. The repeal passed in the Commons, and today, the House of Lords, thus making the entire matter a fait accompli.

When Rockingham entered George's office to deliver the news, the king shook his head and declared: "England and America are being governed by a mob. War is eminent."

Whenever these setbacks occurred, George usually retreated to his private chambers and sulked for days. But today he was more rankled by an article he read in the *London Chronicle*. After gulping down his second brandy he instructed his chamberlain to summon Sir Henry Fox.

Sir Henry had not had a private audience with the king in three years, and promptly arrived later that day. George showed the former

Paymaster the newspaper and pointed to the article. "Have you seen this commentary, Sir Henry?" inquired the king.

Fox looked at the item and nodded.

"Is it true?" George pressed him.

After a moment laced with personal anguish, Fox nodded again and told George the whole sordid story. "Yes, Your Majesty. Lady Sarah's marriage has been failing for some time. It was bad enough her conduct and gambling made her fodder for salacious gossip, but now she's taken up with Lord Gordon, boldly doing so in front of her husband whom she's now left."

"And the baby?"

"I am afraid Lord Gordon is the child's true father and Sarah had the gall to name her Louisa 'Bunbury.' Two weeks ago, Lord Gordon spirited Sarah away, leaving their bastard baby with her husband, who was willing to pass her off as his own. I must say, the whole unholy business strikes at the fiber of one's morality."

"Where are they now?"

Fox hesitated a moment, then lied. "Sarah and Lord Gordon have vanished."

George circled Fox narrowing his eyes. He did not believe him.

"Vanished? Lady Sarah is your wife's sister. You must know where they are, Lord Fox—and you will tell me, for I am concerned about her."

Fox could not contain his ire. "Your Majesty, were you genuinely 'concerned' about Sarah, she would be queen and a happy woman today. Instead, her heart was broken and she never recovered. Nothing she does surprizes or upsets me for the genesis of it—is abject rejection by you, sir."

Guilt thought long suppressed into the recesses of his past emerged within George. "It has been five years, Sir Henry. High time we all adjusted to what is."

"Far easier for you, Your Majesty. Sarah is the broken woman. You, sir, are king."

"A king with feelings. Despite my duty to country, I am still a man."

There was an uncomfortable pause as both men considered George's last statement. Finally, Fox sighed and found another tact. "Let us say I *did* know Sarah's whereabouts. What could I expect in return for such information? Especially in light of personal travails since my forced resignation as Paymaster."

"Ah yes. You took public money, invested it in your own pursuits, and now you're desperately trying to replace the money or go to Tower jail." George grinned slyly. "And let us suppose I knew that you had amassed a small fortune for yourself, and the only way the charges and scrutiny can all go away is by a Royal decree. Now, of course, such salvation can only come from the king—and I assume you would want to take advantage of my one-time generous spirit."

Fox, ever the politician, understood. "Sarah is in Southampton on Hockney Road under the name 'Gore.' She's lost everything—her good name, her husband, her illegitimate daughter, and the protection of her family. All for the sake of that rake of a man, Gordon."

George nodded. "Thank you. You will have six months to make up the accounts of the Paymaster's office and all indiscretions will be forgiven." George paused a moment to review his offer, adding, "And, I will allow you to keep the wealth you've thus amassed."

Fox bowed gratefully and left, passing Lady Lizzie in the hall. Lizzie had eavesdropped and hurried away. But at the other end of the hall Anne saw her, making a mental note.

After a change of clothes, George summoned his carriage and directed his driver to take him to Southampton. Upon reaching Hockney Road he found the small, elegant, country home with manicured lawns and a delightful rose garden. As he approached, the name "Gore" was indeed on the front door and he had his driver knock.

Footsteps from within could be heard approaching and in seconds Lady Sarah answered, looking dowdy yet proud. She was shocked to see the king standing there.

"What are you doing here?"

"I should ask you the same question," George replied, stepping inside without so much as an invitation.

"I live here now—as if it's any of your business."

"I am your king. You are my subject, which means everything about you is my business." He removed his hat and looked around.

The house was plainly decorated as the home of a soldier's would be; sparsely furnished with only a few rugs on the floors. "Will you ask me to sit?"

"You are my king," retorted Sarah smugly, after which she motioned him to a chair in front of the fireplace. "Will you have tea?"

"Have you any?" smirked the king. Lady Sarah grunted aloud then went into her tiny kitchen. Moments later she returned with two cups, saucers and a pot of hot water which was already prepared and placed them in front of the king. George looked at her, knowing he was being cruel, but he couldn't help himself as a rush of regret overtook him.

"Speak your mind, Your Majesty. Why have you come?"

"Is it true? Have you abandoned your husband and child, and taken up with a lover?"

"Yes," answered Sarah matter-of-factly.

"Why? How could you do it?"

"My husband, Charles, is a bore. He's routine and predictable. Life with him was a constant chore. I only married him because I had been so publicly humiliated by you and therefore wanted revenge. But then I met Lord Gordon. There was excitement and real passion again. He was funny and enjoyed my company." She paused a moment, her eyes studying the floor. "But the price is high. I'm unwelcome in polite society, a social outcast because of adultery, I live in sin, and my bastard daughter resides with my husband so she won't suffer my sins without merit. Is that what you want to know?"

"But you did not need to resort to this."

"Why do you care what I resort to? What possible difference can it make to you?"

"Because...I still...care for you...care about what happens to you. I cannot help myself. It will never truly be finished for me."

Lady Sarah stared at him, eyes welling. "Then it should be. Two children you have. The queen is expecting another. Yet you say it will never be finished? Well, it's finished for me. I have found love again, George. Real love."

"It cannot be real love. Not with the level of hurt the situation has created."

"'The amount of hurt'?" Sarah stood fixated by his effrontery, veins in her forehead rising. "Sir, you don't know what hurt is. This is not the first time I have been ostracized and mocked by my own society. Witness what happened after my public rejection."

"Sarah…"

"If you came here to torture me, you have succeeded. Now go."

"Sarah…"

"Let me go, George.

"I cannot. I still…"

"…Do not say it." Sarah wiped the tears from her face betraying her resolve and walked toward the door. "That time is long past. I'm doomed to divorce and scandal." As she opened the door, the February cold rushed in. "There is nothing here for you, Your Majesty. Please do not return."

George stood there a moment. It was his fault—all of it his fault, and he couldn't handle it. He turned to Sarah whose tearful, bewildered eyes were red and swollen. His fingers reached out, touching her cheek. She did not recoil as his thumb caressed it softly. Then, before he dare become more beleaguered, he left the house and did not look back. In so doing, he never saw Lady Sarah Lennox-Bunbury sink to the floor in a puddle of repentance.

Thirty Seven

*S*he had a stirring voice, this soprano of his. But then, Christian always had perfect taste when it came to opera singers. They gathered to him like mosquitoes to still water—and with as much irritation to me. This irritation's name was Cecilia Grassi, a beautiful twenty-two year old Italian soprano who was Christian's latest protégée.

At the king's Friday evening levee the following week, our music master played the harpsichord while Miss Grassi sang the aria. As she performed, I watched Christian's reaction to her. He was enthralled by her, and vice versa. But why it infuriated me this time I'll never know. Perhaps it was because I could have been carrying his child, and he had the temerity to bring yet another soprano to Queen's House for George and I to approve. Well, not this time. Not this soprano. I would not be made a fool of. I would not sit by and allow him to flaunt his new interest in my face.

So, when the aria was completed, instead of joining the king and others in high praise for Miss Grassi's performance, I stood where I was stone-faced and taciturn. Then, after making sure Christian saw my look of consternation, I walked out of the room passing Lady Covington, a Sister in the Order of the Daughters of David.

Christian was perplexed. When he saw Charlotte leave the levee he could not understand what was wrong. After he and Miss Grassi accepted their kudos from the gathering, he slowly moved through the crowd toward the door, following Charlotte. He was not careful enough in his movements, however, as he was witnessed by Bute, Lady Lizzie,

Sir Henry Fox—and Lady Schwellenberg, who went to Lady Hagedorn concerned.

Once upstairs, Charlotte absently wound Christian's silver ballerina music box. It played gaily as the queen sat in front of the fireplace and gazed into the flames. Flickering bright colors illuminated the concerns etched on her face and she thought about everything: the reliquary scrolls, the secret of her amulet, the Daughters of David of which a Sister was downstairs, and most especially her affair with Christian and its possible consequences as a baby grew inside of her.

Soon there came a soft knock. When she looked over, there was Christian standing in the doorway. The two shared a long, intimate moment before Charlotte's gaze returned to the flames.

"Why did you leave?" asked her lover.

"You have your adoring fans and a lovely protégée downstairs. What more do you need?"

"So that is what's bothering you? Cecilia Grassi?" he queried, wandering toward her. "A year ago it was Anna Lucia de Amicis. At Sanssouci it was Maria Monticellini. Charlotte, you must stop these foolish notions you have about me and the sopranos I work with."

Charlotte thought a moment, looking back at the flames. Her heart was aching, but her mind was sharp and dictated what to say. "The only notion I have is this: we must end this. It is better we do not see each other privately anymore. I must consider another music master."

"No!"

"We must! Je suis enceinte. It could be *yours*!" Charlotte bemoaned, knowing that telling him put her at risk.

Christian was stunned. It was one of a million emotions which cataloged across his face. "*My* child? What will you do? What will *we* do?"

"Nothing—and it shall be done."

"You would raise my child as his?"

"Am I expected to tell the King of England, my husband, that I carry our music master's child? No. This is a sign from God to end it. Let us remain friends and keep what we have in the sanctity of the past."

Though acknowledging her words, Christian demurred. "I cannot," he whispered. "I love you." He took her head into his hands. Effortlessly he outlined her eyelids and nose with his lips. When he reached her trembling mouth, neither of them could suppress their feelings, and Christian kissed her desperately. He slowly undid the hooks supporting her dress and kissed her belly, where all his love for Charlotte was growing inside her, awaiting birth.

Downstairs in the drawing room, George began to search for Charlotte. When he could not find her, he saw Lady Schwellenberg near the sideboard having punch with Lady Hagedorn and angled toward them. Both curtsied.

"Where is Her Majesty?"

Both of Charlotte's ladies blanched with guilt. "I-I have not seen her for a while," stuttered Lady Hagedorn.

"Perhaps she is in the water closet, indisposed," Lady Schwellenberg offered quickly.

George looked at each with skepticism. As their expressions belied the truth he raised an eyebrow suspiciously. "Is not your job to be with Her Majesty when she's 'indisposed'?"

The ladies looked at each other knowing this was accurate. "Yes, Your Majesty, but Her Majesty mentioned she was just going upstairs for a moment," answered Lady Schwellenberg. "I took it to mean she did not require us."

The king nodded a look of dismissal. The two women curtsied and quickly removed themselves from his presence. He perused the room for Christian or Mme. Lia. Neither could be found. Finally, he saw Lord Bute chatting with Augusta and Sir Horace Walpole and made his way over to them.

"Lord Bute, a word."

Bute bowed, excusing himself from the others, and followed the king into the library, sensing that George was irritated. The moment the door was closed, this was confirmed.

"Where is Her Majesty?"

Bute swallowed hard and didn't speak right away, further aggravating the king, who was unused to so much silent insolence from so many in his charge. "Where is she?" George repeated.

"She...," Bute hesitated until George's look commanded him. "She is with *him*. I saw him follow her out. I presume they are...in her chambers."

"I see. And by '*him*,' I take it you mean Mister Bach?" George stated, feeling hurt and vulnerable.

Bute nodded.

"How long has it been going on?"

"A year. Perhaps eighteen months."

"Eighteen months? And you felt it unnecessary to inform me of it?"

"Majesty," Bute started nervously, trying to gather his thoughts for an appropriate response, "it has been my experience that these things go away on their own without damage to the primary relationship. We—you and I—have had our …'other pursuits'…which, in the end, have not unduly compromised our marriages."

"Your 'other pursuit' is my mother, Bute," George snapped. "And in case you did not notice, it compromised everything you and I did in government. That is why you resigned and to hell with what it did or did not do to your marriage!" George went to the sideboard near a window and poured himself a glass of brandy.

Bute realized he had overstepped his boundaries. "I am sorry, Majesty, I did not mean to—"

"Please," George threw up his hands in apology. "It is done." He looked outside, deep in thought. A light rain was falling, clouding his spirits. Bute did not know what to do for the king, his friend, so he stood there patiently as George spoke to no one in particular.

"It is entirely my fault. I've ruined her life, Sarah's life, and my own with indecision and compromise. I drove Charlotte into Bach's affections as I did Sarah into Lord Gordon's." The king somberly tossed back another brandy. "My indifference, absences, intolerance on issues important to her… I do not believe I showed her any affection from the first." He paused to further assess. "And there was my continuing attachment to Lady Sarah, even though the affair has long ended."

"But does Her Majesty know it has ended?" Bute asked blithely. "I personally witnessed how hurt she was at the last levee, when she saw you still in pursuit of Lady Sarah's attention."

After a moment of acknowledgement George nodded. "It's over with Sarah, Bute. I saw her just two weeks ago and she is in a terrible situation. She is completely alienated from her society and family, and lives with her lover in sin. Somehow, I thought my appearing at her door would rekindle any…latent feelings she may have yet had for me, but…" George stopped to collect himself. "…I cannot lie. I did feel a certain surge of emotion again. But as I traveled back to the palace I began to think about Charlotte and my behavior toward her these last years. It made me feel terrible."

"Then I suggest you tell her how you feel. Such a confession is bound to end it with *him*."

George patted the former Prime Minister's shoulder and managed a smile. "Thank you, Bute. As usual you've been a good friend despite the harsh reality of your words."

Bute bowed and left George at the window with yet another brandy, searching his heart for a course of action. Could he correct the situation? Or had he lost Charlotte forever?

Meanwhile, Charlotte was dressing quietly while Christian still lay in bed looking at her. She was feeling guilt all over again and he could see the angst on her face.

"I hope the baby looks like you," he smiled.

"No. I want it to be beautiful...like you," she insisted, turning to look at him. "But it will be George's child. Do you understand?"

Christian got out of bed and went to her. "Don't push me away. I will not give you up."

"I am not yours to give up."

"Yes you are, Charlotte. I've claimed you for myself."

Charlotte resolutely stared at her lover. "I cannot be claimed. I belong to this country. Do not forget that."

Christian made tiny circles around her birthmark with his finger. "No," he countered determinedly. "Like this birthmark, I have placed a mark on your heart—same as the one you've etched on mine. You belong to *me*, Charlotte, as deeply and wholly as my own body." Christian kissed her, got dressed, then left the room as the unbearable silence between them remained.

It took Charlotte a moment to move after Christian had gone. She found herself touching her stomach, rubbing the area with a tenderness which rendered her melancholy. Absently, she wandered to her standing mirror and gazed at her reflection. What a disappointment she was to herself. She'd had every intention of breaking it off with Christian, yet lay with him under the nose of her husband, who was but two floors below entertaining their guests.

As she gazed upon her image, feeling the tarnished recriminations of a harlot, she wondered why she attracted men like Christian who had either an unrelenting; or in the case of her demented cousin Wilhelm, a lamentably ribald, obsession with her. These thoughts disconcerted her for Wilhelm had not been on her mind in five years, and she hated herself for allowing memories of him to invade her spirit after her actions with Christian had disheartened her. She had to shake these thoughts, for in the end they would destroy her. So she forced herself to straighten her dress, fix the rumpled strands of her hair, and put on a cheerful face so she would be presentable when she returned to the levee. But as she turned to go, she looked over and gasped.

George was there, his arms crossed. He was drunk and Charlotte had never seen this look on his face before.

"I looked everywhere for you downstairs," he stated flatly.

"I did not realize I'd be missed."

"Of course you were missed, Charlotte. You are the queen. Everyone was asking for you, wondering if you were all right since you were ill at the last levee." Then his bulbous eyes narrowed with suspicion. "So imagine how lucky it was for me to find Mr. Bach on his way back downstairs after, what, 'nursing' you back to health up here?"

Charlotte quivered but said nothing, realizing George knew. She panicked as to his next move as he inched in closer, finally standing directly in front of her, staring wildly. Charlotte could not look at him and cast her eyes to the floor. George lifted her chin with an agitated finger. "I had become concerned these levee illnesses were due to your pregnancy," he swiped with a voice laced with cynicism, "until I realized our music master is smitten with the same illness each time you are."

Charlotte turned from him feeling like a hunted animal. This was the very thing she feared—his reprisal. "Say what you've come to say."

"You will stop seeing Bach and send him away. Do you understand? Because if you don't, I will. And my method, I assure you, will not be as congenial as Her Majesty may deem appropriate. My method will include the Tower."

"You will do no such thing!" raged the queen. "I've found a little happiness in this gilded compound you consigned me to and it does not give you the right to jail a man who has only shown me affection in my neglected, loveless life."

"Shown you affection? It is my understanding Bach has shown you a great deal more."

"What are you saying?" Charlotte demanded.

"I am saying I was sick last fall—not stupid. We did not have conjugal relations during the time I was being treated. So how have you conceived a child? Immaculate conception?"

Charlotte's arms folded around her waist. "How long have you known?"

"Long enough. I suspected when I saw the two of you together in the courtyard last summer during the riots, then again tonight at the levee."

"And you said nothing?"

"A harmless flirtation is meaningless. But when it turns into a lustful 'affaire de coeur' resulting in bastards, or me appearing the cuckold, I must step in."

"'Affaire de coeur'? You self-righteous son-of-a-bitch. What were you and Lady Sarah? Was I not the cuckold there? And what about *her* bastard child?"

"Never mind her."

"Never mind *her*? You men are amazing louts! Lady Sarah is the cause of it all. Your lust for her and neglect for me!"

George forcibly grabbed Charlotte's arm. "You listen to me. I don't want any man touching you! Do you understand! You are my queen. You belong to me, dammit!"

Something snapped inside of Charlotte and she pulled her arm free. Without thinking she hurled a glass figurine at him barely missing his face by centimeters. "Everybody feels they own me—that I 'belong' to them. Well, I will have you know I belong to me, George! Me! You only 'possess' me when it's convenient for you. You have never told me you love me. I have never been made to feel special or desired, or cared for in the way every woman deserves to feel by the man she's married to. And why? Because you are, after all this time and circumstance, still in love with Lady Sarah, a woman who has fallen from grace. You've forced me to deal with her from the second I arrived in London. You told me on our wedding night I would never have your heart. So do I not deserve to have love in my life ever? From *anyone*? Even a small portion of it reserved solely for me? Did it ever occur to you I may be homesick for Germany or lonely or unhappy?"

Like a madwoman Charlotte unhooked her gown in a complete rage. It was as though the person she knew vacated her body and sat on a shelf watching the lunatic attacking George as though she were disconnected from her. "Very well. You want to treat me like a possession? One of the object d'art's you own? Fine."

Charlotte undid the ribbon supporting her pettiskirt. It dropped to the floor and she stood before George half-naked with her arms outstretched. "Here I am! Your Moorish property! This unfeeling, inanimate part of your exotic collection who's here only to deliver heirs to the throne! So go ahead, possess me! Or are you afraid Christian has shown me real love! Because he has!"

George slapped Charlotte who held her stinging face. "Damn you!" He was enraged yet aroused and grabbed Charlotte's face and in an unexpected turn, kissed her. Soon, dark forces overtook him and his kiss became forceful. Charlotte fought him hard until she could no longer. She succumbed, and George heaved her onto the bed. All she could do was close her eyes and pray as she throttled back tears. "Please, don't hurt me," she finally managed, wondering if Christian's scent permeated her body highlighting her dishonor.

George found himself confounded by his actions. "My God, what am I doing?" he muttered to himself as he moved off of her holding his head in embarrassment. "I'm so sorry, Charlotte" he bemoaned. "I do not know what's gotten into me. Forgive me." George held her desperately and began to sob. "Forgive me."

Suddenly Charlotte winced feeling a stabbing pain. Soon after something warm and wet trickled down her legs and when she looked she saw it: blood, so much blood. George rushed a sheet over his wife's body and ran to the door calling out. "Help! Someone help! The queen...!"

╬

When Charlotte awoke and her surroundings cleared from the fuzzy images she initially saw, she realized she was in her private quarters. Though feeling dizzy she tried to sit up and found she could not sustain herself. She fell back upon the pillows. Lady Schwellenberg quickly came to Charlotte's aid, placing a wet cloth to her forehead.

"What happened?" the queen whispered.

"I'm sorry, Your Majesty. You lost the baby."

Her words stunned Charlotte. The baby. Christian's baby. The child not of her husband. She'd lost it. Charlotte sank further into the pillow in despair, knowing this was God's punishment. Soon, she thought about George and their last encounter and it all came rushing back. It was retribution.

Charlotte was only awake a short time before George softly rapped at the door. He entered carrying a basket and dismissed her ladies. The queen heard faint yelping noises and George opened the basket. Inside was a puppy. "It isn't a baby, but I did not think you would resist," he said with a modicum of contrition handing her a Pomeranian no bigger than the palm of Charlotte's hand. The puppy instantly knew she was its mother and lovingly licked Charlotte's face. This made her feel better despite the circumstances. George stroked the puppy a moment while looking at his wife as she played with it.

"Thank you. I shall name him 'Petoe,'" Charlotte said quietly.

"You were out all night," George consoled, "I was worried to death. But Doctor Hunter assures me that you should be fine after a few days rest. He suggests you go to Bath and if you would like, I shall go with you." He took Charlotte's hand, then glanced off as she played with Petoe. "I owe you an apology, my love. I've been the most unrepentant ass. I have not allowed myself to see what an angel I was given when you became my queen." He turned her face to his. "But I will make it up to you. I promise. As God is my witness, I promise."

Could it be a second chance, I thought? Some unexpected, albeit divine salvation for George and me? Could I put it all behind me? Could I put Christian behind me and start anew? I had to try. I had to hope. And most of all I had to pray. Because most of all, I wanted peace.

CS

Thirty Eight

Time went by quickly in the months following Charlotte's miscarriage. George, true to his word, did his best to be with his wife as much as possible and Charlotte enjoyed their time together. They played chess, took long walks, and occasionally played with their children as Petoe cavorted nearby. Slowly their relationship mended and morphed into the marriage Charlotte felt was more appropriate than ever in the past. Even Sir Albert Papendiek, the queen's long-time hairdresser, commented on the queen's mood. "You appear almost as happy as I," he mused one day. "And I have just been blessed with a daughter I named 'Charlotte' out of respect for Her Majesty. One cannot be happier than I." Charlotte was touched.

But the king and queen had a difficult discussion about Christian Bach's role in their lives. George vowed to forgive the maestro his transgressions as long as the queen renounced their relationship and Christian would function purely as music master. Though the queen missed her friendship with Christian, she understood she could not have both he and George. So she made the appropriate decision and summoned him one day.

Christian knew what a summons from the queen meant. He was either to be relieved of his duties or his access to the queen limited. He had felt her pulling away emotionally ever since that night at the king's levee in April. It was the last time they had made love. The next day he heard she had lost her child and wondered if anything he did was at its core. He had so wanted Charlotte to have the baby for he knew it was his and that his connection to her would be forever. Even if they could never be together just knowing that his blood flowed through a child being raised in the palace by his beloved could be enough for him.

But Charlotte had lost the child and for days she was ill. Then when she felt better she began to limit their meetings to just her music lessons. To add frustration to the mix they were never alone. Lady Hagedorn always attended the lessons or King George accompanied them on his flute so his presence put an end to all speculation of any possible affair. Then in June Christian was instructed by Lord Montagu that since Prince George was now five years old he should teach the boy music as well as three of the other princes. Painfully Christian had come to the realization that any personal time with Charlotte may have reached an inevitable conclusion.

Now he was standing before her; his heart filled with love for her as she sat on one of the tufted chairs in the music room. They were alone for the first time in seven months yet her face was stoic and devoid of emotion.

"Christian, we must talk. I have had a lot of time to think about..."

"...I've had time to think as well," Christian interrupted, "Seven months of agonizing, frustrating, exasperating time to wonder why you will not let me see you alone."

"That is why I wished to see you today. We must make some alterations to our...friendship however difficult. We cannot do or be what we've been in the past. We have to end it. Cleanly."

"But Charlotte..."

"It must be over. God ended the pregnancy for a reason. As punishment. My sin created a life within me to be a constant reminder of not working harder on my marriage. Please help me honor my original vows—to God and to George. Please."

Christian searched her face for some sign of regret or uncertainty but found none. Charlotte looked away as his heart broke into a million fragments. He bowed then started out. Moments later he turned back. "Your Majesty, I do have my hopes that you will continue your fight for the rights and privileges of those less fortunate than the titled members of your world. I speak of course of Anne Josef and other brownskinned people for whom I know you care."

"I shall, Christian. Thank you."

Christian bowed again and left. The moment he was past the outer door he sat on an outside bench with his head in his hands trying to make sense of what had just occurred.

For her part Charlotte sat motionless in her chair for the next hour staring into space. She felt wretched and drained of joy but knew she was doing the right thing. It would take everything in her to keep moving forward, and she appreciated Christian reminding her of her ultimate mission. She then thought about Anne and the plans she had for her. At least she'd have some satisfaction, however secret, for it would take her mind off of Christian and the future they would never have. At least she could help one person she cared about.

In all this time Charlotte had still chosen not to discuss her amulet, the reliquary, or her scrolls however lore-filled or divine with the king. She knew George was still unwilling to accept his diverse or sacred background, and Charlotte was unwilling to risk his censure nor discuss it with his mother anymore. Equally, Dowager Princess Augusta stayed clear of any discussion of Hertford Castle or its below-ground activities with her son as she, too, had been cautioned by him. But Augusta also had other concerns. She was developing an abscess on the side of her neck which doctors feared was a slow-growing tumor inside her throat. She had difficulty swallowing on occasion and resorted to sipping liquids. Most times Augusta would not leave Carlton House because she was too weak.

But tonight Charlotte decided to visit her mother-in-law prompted not only by Christian's advice but a request from Sir Allan Ramsey to see her portrait which was now finished. When she entered into the portrait studio and gazed upon her image she was overcome. Her depiction was beautiful, regal in repose, and revealed her actual wheat-like coloration.

"No one has ever captured my authentic likeness in such a distinguished, agreeable way," marveled Charlotte.

Sir Allan bowed. "Thank you, Your Majesty. You pay me high honor indeed." He then went to his easel drawer and retrieved a small jar of pinkish beige crème and handed it to her. "Now, if your Majesty will permit, this chalk face paint offers a far more realistic color choice. It is designed to cover that which you are trying to 'disguise' without appearing too artificially white. I blended it myself without the use of lead. Her Majesty's skin is too beautiful to debase with lead."

Charlotte was grateful. She placed the makeup in the pocket of her over-jacket then turned back to the painting. "I believe this to be my favorite of all the renderings of me thus far. I shall insist George hang it in the gallery at Queen's House, that every day I may gaze upon it and remind myself who I genuinely am."

Sir Allan thought a moment as he began cleaning his brushes with rags. "There are those of us who understand the queen's 'dilemma,' and are here to serve she who honors our cause."

"You are far too cryptic, Sir Allan. Speak your mind clearly."

It took the painter a moment. "I believe the 'authentic' you would be interested to know that we have found a permanent meeting place at Phillips Printing Shop where we informally gather every second Tuesday. We discuss a variety of subjects: war, taxes—the slave trade."

Charlotte's brow rose. "And what should the queen do with this information?"

"Whatever Her Majesty deems appropriate. It's just something to be mindful of, for due to slavery and its tentacles even freed Negroes are kept from the promise of their potential."

Charlotte said nothing then looked back at her image. "Have the painting delivered to Queen's House tomorrow." She then left the room.

Once she returned to her chambers Ramsey's words kept traversing her mind: "...due to slavery and its tentacles even freed Negroes are kept from the promise of their potential." Her half-brother and former friend Jon Baptiste came into her thoughts, having been sold into slavery, he could be dead by now. Then she thought about Anne, whom she managed to save from a similar fate. But Anne, for all the help she had provided the queen, was another Negro not allowed the promise of her own potential. She, like Charlotte, was an amulet holder and as such should be entitled to the same privileges as a Daughter of David like Charlotte or Augusta. So with these thoughts the queen sought an audience with the dowager princess.

Upon admittance into the receiving room that evening Charlotte found Augusta knitting in front of a fire. Though she was weak and thin the dowager was in fine voice and spirit and motioned the queen to the chair next to hers. Charlotte offered her the gift box she had brought then watched as Augusta opened it. Inside were six handmade linen handkerchiefs embroidered with Augusta's initials.

"How lovely these are. What exquisite detail," Augusta marveled.

"Thank you. My maid, Anne Josef, has a wondrous gift for such intricate work."

"I understand you are with child again," the dowager noted, tucking one of the handkerchiefs into her sleeve.

"I am, Your Highness," answered Charlotte, who accepted a cup of tea presented by Augusta's maid. "But I have come to request something of you." She waited until the maid had gone to continue. "I wish to return to Hertford castle for another initiation into the Sisters."

Augusta frowned. "But you have already attained the rank of Apprentice. There is no..."

"...It is not for me but for someone else," Charlotte interrupted.

Now Augusta's interest was piqued. "Our mandate is quite clear. A candidate must possess the mark of the Merovingians or be of Davidic or Templar descent. We have compiled lists of potential candidates throughout the world. But they cannot request. They must be invited."

"This candidate fits the criteria, but would never make your list."

"Who is she?" Augusta insisted with slight irritation.

Charlotte swallowed hard. "My maid."

The dowager's eyes bulged as her brow rose to an indignant arch. Removing the knitting basket from her lap to the floor she took umbrage with Charlotte. "The African? Surely you jest."

"Yes. The one who created your handkerchiefs."

"Your Majesty, such inclusion into our Order would be unacceptable for so many reasons. Ours is an organization of patrician blood. Our charter is clear."

"Anne is of Davidic descent. She bears the Merovingian mark, and owns an amulet."

Augusta was in shock and sat back in her chair. The reality of this hung in the air like smoke from an ill-vented chimney.

"I want her inducted," demanded Charlotte. "It is her right and our obligation as Daughters of David. I need your support, Augusta."

"And if the sisters reject her claim?"

Charlotte knew this question would be broached and she was prepared. With absolute resolve she challenged the dowager's integrity while championing her ancestors.

"Then I shall reveal my African ancestry and the king's to anyone who will listen."

At first light the following Thursday, Charlotte left for Hertford Castle with Anne in tow. Dowager Princess Augusta was not with them. Instead, she sent notes ahead to prepare the Sisters for an initiation ceremony, citing poor health as cause for her absence. Charlotte informed her Chamberlain she would be having a music lesson later and that she was sending Lady Schwellenberg to Brighton to visit her sister.

Lady Schwellenberg, well versed in their various subterfuges in the past, exchanged clothes with Charlotte, dressing the queen in a cotton sacque dress appropriate for one in service to an aristocrat. The only jewelry Charlotte wore was the amulet residing far down in her cleavage, hidden by a buttoned up under-chemise. The queen put on a large hat with a veil and with it pulled well down over her face she and Anne left Queen's House before Christian arrived for their music lesson. The queen had thought of everything. Christian was asked to give Lady Schwellenberg a music lesson for the day and her lady, dressed in Charlotte's royal accoutrements, waited in the music room for Christian. No one was the wiser as the entire palace heard the musical ruminations of she they assumed to be the queen.

Meanwhile, Charlotte and Anne absconded to Hertford. Anne was hesitant about being initiated as a Daughter of David. Two nights earlier, after Charlotte informed her she was to become a secret mason, she had a dream portending doom. In it, she was abducted and harnessed by her ankles. When Anne arose that morning her right ankle was red and sore for no apparent reason. She approached Charlotte about it and the queen promised nothing would happen to her as she was under the protection of the royal household. She instructed her maid to hide her amulet and prepare to give explanation of her Templar background.

At 11 that morning their coach arrived at #42 Fore Street. Since Augusta first brought her there Charlotte had only been back once—to induct Lady Dunston who kept Charlotte up-to-date whenever she saw the queen at a levee. No new sister had been initiated in two years, and it was important that Anne became part of what the queen felt was her birthright.

The two made their way to the intricate oak door and Charlotte, after making sure no one was looking, knocked three distinctive times. Moments later she and Anne heard three distinctive knocks in response. Soon the male voice from within asked: "To whom do you represent?"

"God, and the three lesser lights," Charlotte answered, and the coded verbal mantra she had learned from Augusta began through the door—until it swung open.

The same monk appeared. Charlotte announced herself as "Sister Charlotte Sophia Frederick Hanover, daughter-in-law to Sister Augusta Hanover, wife of the late Brother Frederick Louis Hanover." She told the monk she was an amulet holder as was Anne. The two were permitted in whereupon Charlotte instructed the monk to assemble the Sisters.

I held Anne's hand through the experience for she was frightened. Descending the stone stairway into the tunnels reminded her of the bowels of the slave ship which brought her to England and it unsettled her. When finally Anne was presented for initiation the Sisters refused to even entertain the idea for her ethnicity was unacceptable. Even upon the realization she was genuine after hearing Anne's story and genealogy, they half-heartedly tried to create a subset for her known as the 'Sister of Sarah la Kali' after the Egyptian servant of Mary Salome. This would be a segregated group and I would not allow it. Arguing ensued that could have gone on all day until finally we were shocked by the weak, but definitive admonishments of one Sister who suddenly emerged from the darkness into the light.

It was Dowager Princess Augusta who hobbled over and, with a pointed finger, glared at every sister. "Here in this place, we Sisters do not and will not suffer the same discrimination and bias of men and whites created above ground. We are special here, we are divine, and we are One. All of us! I am Worthy Grand Matron of this order, and I thought it important enough to be here to see that this woman receives her due as an equal Sister, and she shall have it. Any objections?"

There were none and Anne was finally accepted and initiated into the Order of the Daughters of David as a full and official 'Sister.' I hugged Augusta proudly and asked how she got to Herefordshire in her weak condition. The Princess said she had her Chamberlain bring her and swore him to secrecy. "Now, allow me to return before I die in this damp place."

I insisted that Augusta travel back to London with us. Anne was curiously quiet for most of the trip back. When I probed her, she couldn't believe what had happened to her, and of what she was now a member. She prayed to locate and buy the freedom of her daughter Mary so the girl could know her birthright—especially since Mary also possessed the mark. I, more than anyone else, understood Anne's desire, and promised I would do all I could to help.

We continued on our way. Then, almost as if God had ordained it, our driver had to make a personal stop to relieve himself. While he was gone, I looked up to see a row of elegant shops and my eyes widened in shock. There, not twenty feet away, was Phillips Printing Shop. Of all the streets we could have turned onto, we were on George Lane, and once again Sir Allan Ramsey's words echoed in my heart:

'...Those of us who understand the Queen's dilemma serve she who honors our cause...'

Thirty Nine

In the wee early hours of 21 August, 1765, Charlotte gave birth to her third child at Queen's House—a son named William Henry Hanover who was made Duke of Clarence. George had fretted about this birth as Charlotte had lost the previous baby and he prayed for things to go smoothly with this birth. They did. And so did the queen's next birth the following September, 1766 to a daughter, Charlotte Augusta Matilda—the Princess Royal. No one was more pleased than the king that his family was growing and seemingly happy.

Charlotte was happy too even though at times during her lying-in's, she wished there had been some word from the Duke of Levis-Mirepoix. She was also concerned about the dowager princess whose health continued to decline. George, worried about both his mother and impending war with the Colonies, had a health crisis similar to the one in 1763. As with the earlier malady his urine turned purple, stomach cramps weakened him, and madness descended upon his mind. He took to having conversations with trees and dueling with statues in the garden. He even ravished Lady Hagedorn's breasts one day, which sent the woman screaming into the queen's private quarters from which she would not leave. But Charlotte stayed at his side, tending him with care and concern.

The next year she had another child, a son named Edward, born 2 November 1767.

But even with all her children and the king now emotionally available to her, Charlotte still felt she was missing purpose in her life, and the pull of knowing that abolitionist meetings took place at Phillips Print Shop every other Tuesday was hard to ignore. One Sunday afternoon, the queen asked George if she could travel into London to "visit friends." George was adamant.

"There is no one or nothing out there that cannot be brought to you here, my dear."

Charlotte realized she had to put the plan she had been brewing for two years into effect. As it required help, she invited Mme. Lia de Beaumont to visit Queen's House. While they played cards with Ladies Schwellenberg and Hagedorn, the queen gathered her resolve and asked Lia to take her on a trip, which would not be in an official capacity. "I want to experience London not as a royal, but as a commoner. I feel disconnected from what is going on by virtue of the life I live. And I have a place in mind I wish to visit."

"Where?" asked Lia, who pulled out a packet of snuff, taking in some herself, then offering it to the queen and her ladies.

Only Charlotte partook of it. "Phillips Printing Shop," she answered.

Lia was skeptical. "Why Phillips Printing Shop? Are they distributing contraband?"

"Not at all. Something far more vile and salacious."

"Pray, what?" asked Lady Hagedorn.

"There are discussions held there every other Tuesday by abolitionists and their sympathizers regarding the slave trade."

Silence abounded as the three women looked at the queen in astonishment.

"And *you* wish to partake in these discussions?" queried Lia.

"I do."

Madame Lia placed her cards down on the table and stopped playing. "'Tis a valiant and heroic idea, Your Majesty, but how on earth can you leave Queen's House for such an endeavor without anyone's knowledge—particularly the king. And what about your safety?"

Charlotte mused. "Oh, Lady Schwellenberg and I know quite a bit about planning adventures, safe or otherwise. Don't we Swelly?"

Lady Schwellenberg chuckled in agreement.

╬

On the second Tuesday of that May, sounds from Charlotte's harpsichord lesson with Christian Bach echoed throughout the palace as Mme. Lia's carriage arrived. Lia was dressed casually as she entered Queen's House. Moments later, from the side entrance, Lia emerged with Lady Schwellenberg and a large picnic basket. The carriage took off. The harpsichord music continued along with Christian's instructions, and everything was routine at Queen's House…

…except it was not Lady Schwellenberg in Madame Lia's coach, but Charlotte in her lady's clothes. In the music room Lady Schwellenberg, dressed as the queen, was delighted to be taught music by the handsome, renowned Bach. And Christian, who would do anything for Charlotte's renewed favor, agreed to the subterfuge.

Charlotte and her French confidant rode through the streets of London, and it was as though the queen was seeing the city for the first time. London was bristling with activity. Shopkeepers swept in front of their stores, bakers set out fresh goods, and new buildings were being erected.

Just outside the Tower of London they witnessed a public hanging. Four male bodies dropped to their deaths as people cheered, and Charlotte's stomach turned. Then they journeyed to the city's east end, where many impoverished Londoners lived in squalor.

Finally, they arrived at their destination—Phillip's Printing Shop, where they entered and were directed to a back room. There they found Quakers, business men, nobles and working folk gathered. But they also noticed that women primarily sat in the back of the room.

Soon, after some congenial conversation and the consumption of drinks and hors d'oeuvres the meeting began with an introduction of the main speaker given by Sir Allan Ramsey himself. The young orator was Thomas Clarkson, an abolitionist who spoke with authority and passion.

"It is a triangular route. British-made goods go to Africa to purchase slaves, then the slaves are transported to the West Indies and the Colonies. Then the slave-grown products of sugar, tobacco, and cotton are brought back here to Britain. This practice represents 80 percent of Britain's foreign income. Our British ships dominate the trade. We supply French, Spanish, Dutch, Portuguese and the British colonies, and carry 40,000 African men, women and children across the Atlantic in horrific conditions," Clarkson lectured. He went on to explain that of the

11 million Africans transported into slavery, almost two million have died during the voyage. He also noted that for the last two years he had researched, documented, interviewed 20,000 sailors, and even obtained the hideous equipment used to control the enslaved aboard these slave ships.

Clarkson illustrated his point by showing this equipment to the gathering: leg shackles, handcuffs, thumb screws, instruments for forcing jaws open, and branding irons. Everyone present was revolted by the sight—especially Charlotte who, in her mind, envisioned Jon Baptiste being tortured by such instruments. Clarkson's vehemence engulfed the room, sweeping the crowd into fervor as he urged them:

"Develop a network of interested people to help us organize. We need documentation, testimonials and witnesses to the inhumanity. We need a petition. We need the world to know England will take the necessary first steps to draft a bill and pass a law to end this monstrous institution!"

The crowd cheered, Charlotte included, and when the basket was passed for contributions to the cause, she made a large one.

Later, as Charlotte and Mme. Lia traveled back to Queen's House, both were silent for most of the way fraught with emotion. Finally Lia turned to the queen. "Why did you go there? What was the purpose?"

"I've thought about this issue of ending slavery for a very long time. But nothing could prepareme for what I saw today. I feel as though I should be doing something."

"Convince the king of the importance of emancipating these people," said Lia.

My people Charlotte thought privately as the carriage came to a rest at the side entrance of Queen's House. With this, she suddenly understood it to be the cause for which she was born, and with that, the course of her life would change.

Madame Lia and I snuck out to Phillip's Printing shop on the second Tuesday for nearly six months even though it was dangerous. I would dress as Lady Schwellenberg while my real lady pretended to be me at Queen's House with Christian. I was sickened by the disparity between the wealthy aristocracy and the huge underclass of poor, of which Negroes were the worst off.

Each speaker motivated me, and I found I needed these meetings to feel I was part of something important.

On the second Tuesday of November, Charlotte listened to guest speaker Grandville Sharp, an attorney who described the case of a former slave he represented who escaped his master and came to London. Sharp had taken the slave master to court, successfully winning the slave's freedom. A man in the crowd caught Charlotte's attention, as he had been staring at her. After the meeting the man judiciously moved toward her, and upon closer inspection Charlotte realized it was Sir John Wilkes.

She panicked. Wilkes had been spirited out of the country to Paris with the help of Lord Henry Fox. Now, apparently, he had returned to England and was planning many grievances against the king and his policies, slavery being among them according to statements he delivered at the meeting.

Charlotte moved away quickly. But Wilkes, a notorious womanizer, soon found his attention aimed at Madame Lia. He went to her, introduced himself, and blatantly flirted. When Lia rebuffed Wilkes' advances he patted her on her derriere, chuckled and moved off, glancing back at Charlotte with a frown of seeming recognition.

The queen grabbed Lia and insisted they leave immediately. Inside their carriage, Charlotte told Lia she couldn't venture out again. "It's too risky. Sir Wilkes was a whisper from recognizing me and eventually others will too. Besides, I'm breeding again."

"That scalawag Wilkes. No wonder he is so reviled," Lia groused.

"But he appeals to the people's sense of personal freedoms—except for a woman's—from the blatant way he patted your backside. My concern is it's the king Wilkes hates."

The two hugged and Mme. Lia told the queen to send her a note when she needed a friend. Charlotte slipped back into her chambers, thinking about what had transpired. She worried Wilkes' return could surely trigger problems.

And it was true. When Charlotte saw Wilkes he had been back in England for four months. Living extravagantly in France in self-imposed exile for five years had rendered him financially insolvent. Desirous to pay for his daughter's expensive education, he snuck back into London even though he had been found guilty of liable in his absence. One of the first people he visited was Sir Henry Fox who, at this time, was ill and had not left Holland House in a month. Wilkes told Fox, "I have so staunchly thought of nothing else but revenge against the king that just last week I imagined I saw the queen at an abolitionist meeting."

Wilkes discussed plans to bring the *North Briton* back with a vengeance. This time, more careful of slander charges, he would provide hard evidence of his accusations, telling Fox he had found the perfect spy to infiltrate the king's inner circle, someone who could provide him everything he needed by way of proof. Fox advised Wilkes to "Push the idea that the people need to read the truth without writers fearing arrest."

After a few months gathering support, and creating a social platform, Wilkes boldly wrote to the king asking for a pardon. George could not stop laughing and ignored the request. The following week, assured he would not hear from the king, Wilkes publicly announced his candidacy to become a Member of the House of Commons.

By this time Charlotte had given birth to another daughter on whom she doted. Princess Augusta Sophia, the most beautiful of Charlotte's children, was born on 8 November 1768. She brought much happiness to the king and queen. Unfortunately, their happiness was not to last for the bottom of England's economy plummeted. Unemployment escalated, workers went on strike, food became scarce, war was threatened...

...and Sir John Wilkes rose to unprecedented power.

Part Three

✠

REVELATIONS

Queen's House
London, 1772 - 1818

*"...Nothing is hidden that will not be made known,
or secret that will not come to light..."*

Jesus Christ - The Q Gospel

No Liberty
No King!

Forty

The body of Dowager Princess Augusta Hanover lay in repose at Westminster Abbey. She had died peacefully from throat cancer at six in the morning with her children, Augusta, Caroline Matilda, George and myself at her side. She was honored with a full-court funeral, and George ordered all palace flags flown at half-staff.

As we sat in the crowded Abbey—me, large and expectant, George tearfully somber, and Bute sobbing softly despite his wife's presence—we could hear the unfortunate sounds of an angry mob outside. Sir Horace Walpole, outraged by the disrespect accorded the king's mother, moved from his pew and went to a chapel window. Through the leaded glass he saw a crowd surging toward the Abbey doors and the black mourning cloth stripped from the platform. They refused to leave poor Princess Augusta alone—even in death.

Much had happened in the intervening three years. Since the mysterious reemergence of Sir John Wilkes in London, there had been a resurgence of bad press concerning Augusta and Lord Bute even though their relationship had become but a loyal friendship. It upset Augusta, and finally on 7 February 1772 she succumbed.

George mourned for months despite his mother having become egregiously cruel to him in her last years. The very next year he lost his brother, and began grieving all over again. By then, my little dog Petoe had died, and I had three more children. I began to worry. Whenever George was under immense stress he lapsed first into thunderous, inexplicable headaches, then finally into "the illness." These maladies lasted from a week to several months, and there was no telling what his behavior would be. Each time it happened, his doctors and advisors spirited him to another palace, where he could be secretly treated without the knowledge of Parlia-

ment or the people. Once recovered, he would make a very public appear-
ance somewhere and no one was the wiser. Except for Sir John Wilkes,
the bane of our existence."

John Wilkes won election to the House of Commons by a huge majority. His popularity was fueled by common people who declared
"Wilkes and Liberty!" or "Freedom of the Presses." Upon his election,
he surrendered to authorities. He was sentenced to King's Bench Prison
for twenty-two months and fined £1,000—a punishment he gladly accepted because prisoners were allowed to purchase the right to move
around within a three mile radius. As an MP, Wilkes took advantage of
the privilege and continued his personal attacks against the king in his
newspaper.

At St. James, George and Charlotte were shocked by the huge
crowd of Wilkes supporters who amassed at St. George's Field next to
King's Bench prison.

"How is it that Wilkes can be a condemned man serving a sentence,
yet is *still* allowed to function as a Member of the House of Commons?"
decried George as he descended the stairs in preparation for that day's
session of Parliament. "I shall have Lord Grafton put forth a motion to
remove him."

"Wilkes is an elected official. There is no rule he must forfeit his
seat if arrested," Charlotte asserted.

"Then there should be!"

Yet the king's plan was derailed by a headstrong mob rampaging
through the streets. They broke windows—including those in Lord
Bute's home, and demanded citizens illuminate their homes to support
Wilkes' release. Thirty thousand "Wilkites," as they were known, converged on St. George's Field, chanting, "No liberty, No king." Fearing
the mob would attempt to rescue Wilkes, officers ordered troops to fix
bayonets. The crowd went wild, hurling insults and invectives at the soldiers, who immediately responded by firing upon them.

Seven people were killed and countless others injured. Anger at the
'Massacre of St. George's Field' led to rioting all over London. The unrest
lasted for days forcing George to consider abdicating the throne. I needed an-
swers. So I asked Mme. Lia to visit Wilkes in jail.

Madame Lia de Beaumont arrived at King's Bench prison and spirited through a private entrance under the queen's seal. Wilkes had flirted with her at Phillip's Printing Shop and the queen hoped he would forget himself and open up to Lia while in her presence. To help the situation, Lia brought a bottle of her finest burgundy and a dozen smoked tongues to an unsuspecting Wilkes. She told him she was a huge fan—one who agreed with his revolutionary ideas. She even told him she had writing ability and a desire to write for his newspaper.

"I would be agreeable to using the name 'Mr. Peter Sussex.'"

"Why so?" asked Wilkes curiously.

"I am but a wretched woman—born to be a slave to that Lord of creation called man."

Wilkes, impressed with her intelligence and wit, confessed she looked familiar. Mme. Lia reminded him of their brief meeting at Phillips Printing Shop. "But I must say you were a hair more cheeky than you are today."

Through the bars Wilkes stroked her arm suggestively.

"That is because we have the impediment of these bars separating us, my dear."

Lia looked around at his prison compartment. "I should have such an 'impediment.'"

It was true. Wilkes' accommodations at the prison were generous. His first floor cell had a sumptuous view of St. George's Fields. When she arrived, Lia witnessed two female supporters leaving him after what could only be described as an apparent sexual tryst. At a time of food shortages in England, cases of ham, ale, cheese, wine, and tobacco filled his cell from devoted fans. Political associates freely came and went, meeting there to run his campaign and bring envelopes of money which poured in to help his debt of £20,000. Finally, Lia turned back to him. "Sir Wilkes, why do you hate the king so? Others have disagreed with his policies, but none vilify him to the degree you do."

Wilkes' expression became strident and his flirtatious visage disappeared altogether. "Do you know the king has issued instructions demanding that the governor of Virginia assent to no law by which the importation of slaves should be prohibited or obstructed. That says to me the king is intractable, unfit to govern, and, I have it on good authority, insane. Who, but a mad man, places the continuance of the slave trade to the colonies above the representation of those same colonies in Parliament? It's no wonder the queen is having an affair with her music master."

Lia, shocked by this revelation, forced herself to maintain a composed demeanor.

"How do you know such a thing? You would not print it without proof, would you?"

"My proof of it is not solid enough for publication. Without confirmation from my source who, as yet, will not go on public record, I cannot print it. But suffice to say, I have determined to find another way to provide my readers with the truth." He then winked. "So worry not, my dear. As you and the queen are dear friends, you may tell her she is safe. For now."

Lia was nonplussed and rushed away as Wilkes chuckled. Later that afternoon she returned to Queen's House and reported her conversation with Wilkes to the queen.

"The blackguard knows all about you...and Bach."

Charlotte's face went blanch. "How would Wilkes know about my private world?"

"Someone is informing on you to Wilkes' camp. Someone close to you," Lia warned.

Just then Anne came in to light the candles. Mme. Lia noticed her, then turned to the queen with a raised eyebrow. "I once told you to be very careful, Your Majesty. *Everyone* around you...is potentially a spy."

Charlotte looked at Anne as well. Knowing Anne's quest for her daughter could make her vulnerable, she became nervous and her thoughts ran rampant. That night Charlotte couldn't sleep. She paced in conflict for so long she feared fraying the rugs beneath her. She looked over at George, who was sleeping soundly for the first time in the three weeks following the riots. The baby stirring in her belly reminded her of the continuing commitment she had made to her king. Wilkes was a dangerous enemy. His having access to this information, and the clever way in which he could use it threatened the Crown. She had to do something to mitigate its impact. Thus, the next day Charlotte sent for Christian Bach.

"I am afraid you must resign your position here at Buckingham. Send it to the king as your own decision. Tell him you want to write a symphony, or opera, anything. Just resign."

Christian was stunned at the abrupt nature of the request. "What has brought this on?"

"For the good of the monarchy, it is best we officially end our working association," Charlotte insisted. "I shall hire a new music master when you have quitted your position."

"Please tell me why. I have done nothing unseemly."

"I know. But I am not at liberty to reveal my reasons."

Christian looked into her eyes and could see she was conflicted. If only she could be truthful with him. He had complied with her every wish. He had sacrificed the physical aspect of their relationship for more than two years. He relegated himself to the background of her private life. Now she was asking him to absent himself completely from her. Why? Finally he acquiesced. "I will collect my music after the prince's lesson, and give the king my resignation in the morning."

Charlotte nodded and left the room. Outside the reception room she paused to steady herself gripping the amulet beneath her dress. Lady Lizzie was coming down the stairs and witnessed the queen's melancholy. "Are you all right, Your Majesty?" said the lady in her clipped Scottish brogue.

Charlotte nodded but did not answer directly, making her way up the stairs to her chambers. *Perhaps it is finished,* she thought. Perhaps when news of Christian's resignation spread, those partial to Wilkes would presume there is no validity to a romance. God knew she could not withstand a running scandal such as Wilkes' attacks on Augusta and Bute.

But as she entered her chambers, feeling better about the solution, she found herself haunted by its execution. She had hurt Christian.

She had hurt him badly.

The next morning, Johann Christian Bach was in the music room at Queen's House packing his music sheets into boxes. He had just finished a piano lesson with Prince George, and his head was pounding. Charlotte had been on his mind all night, and he kept searching for answers. He must have done something, said something, intimated something, however nuanced, to upset her. But he could think of nothing. His headache was mirrored on his face and he rubbed his temples a few moments. Then he heard:

"I'll do that."

Christian turned to find Charlotte in the doorway. He looked at her for a long, indecisive moment. Charlotte moved to him cautiously—placing her fingers on the pressure points of his throbbing head. The two said nothing as she began to massage his temples. Christian stared at her intensely. Charlotte knew what he was thinking for the same thoughts plagued her as well and she had to confess. "Sir Wilkes knows about our... friendship. He threatened to expose us in the newspapers as soon as he has irrefutable proof."

"So for the good of your reputation and the king's, I am to be dismissed?"

Charlotte stopped massaging her beloved. Her eyes cast to the floor in silent agreement.

"Have I ever failed you, Charlotte?" asked Christian, understanding why he had to go.

"Never. You have only been the most kind and loving...friend... whom I shall never forget. But the king is not always well and requires me."

"It's no secret he's mad."

"Then surely you know I cannot abandon his needs."

"Surely you cannot abandon the needs of those poor souls you've charged yourself to help free and protect." Christian then softened his tone. After all, he wasn't angry with Charlotte. He understood she had much on her mind. "I will resign as you ask, but I have a request."

"Anything."

"Think. Is it not mightier to sacrifice the suffering of a mad king, for whom you can do nothing, for the freedom of those less fortunate?"

Charlotte thought about this. He was right. He always was, yet she remained resolute. "I will see that you are compensated and I will arrange further employment for you after your resignation."

"No. When I finish the opera, I will accept Leopold Mozart's offer to tour with Wolfgang. I won't be back for a year. And when I do, I'll ask Cecilia for her hand in marriage."

Charlotte's heart dropped and Christian saw her disappointment. He instantly regretted his words, for he had only said them to hurt her as she had hurt him. Yet the words had been spoken. "I shall never forget you, and will always be grateful for your patronage." Christian finally turned and departed the music room and ultimately the palace, leaving Charlotte to remember—and quietly sob.

I refused all correspondence and visits from Christian. A year passed and Christian toured with Mozart. He wrote a series of new compositions and I stopped hearing from him. He had found himself and his art. And for that, I was grateful.

Forty One

George honored Christian's service by issuing a national proclamation the day he resigned. Christian found a way through
his pain and began a series of concerts with his longtime
friend Carl Frederich Abel called the 'Bach-Abel' concerts. The two
made a fortune and moved into a large house together in the fashionable
Soho district.

Twenty-two months later, Sir John Wilkes was released from
prison, more angry with George than ever. In issue after issue of the
North Briton, he sided with the Colonists and continued to condemn
George and the government's policy of 'No Representation' for the
Colonies. Though he served his duties as an MP for Middlesex in the
House of Commons, he also managed to get elected Lord Mayor of
London. Fortunately, nowhere in his newspaper was there ever any
mention of Christian and me—not even snide innuendo. I was pleased
about that.

But in 1774, Sir Henry Fox, who had been ill for a long while,
passed away in his sleep. The thorn in George's side died a deeply un-
popular man, having acquired a reputation as a 'public defaulter of
unaccounted millions,' and the most dishonest, unprincipled politician of
our time. He never received his much sought after Earldom.

Then, upon the king's return from a fox hunt, Sir William
Cavendish was awaiting him in the courtyard.

"Your Majesty, Major General Cornwallis has urgent business."

George quickly entered the palace and went into the Presence Room where Lord Charles Cornwallis bowed. "Your Majesty, 60 men calling themselves 'The Sons of Liberty' dressed up as Mohawk Indians, boarded the *Dartmouth*, then dumped 342 chests of tea, valued at more than £18,000, into Boston Harbor. The monetary loss is incalculable and they've amassed an army against us. I suggest we eliminate self-government in Massachusetts and close the port."

"Have you consulted General Gage?"

"I have, sir. He wants you to approve a full-scale deployment of troops at once."

George sighed, but agreed. "Then it shall be done. Close Boston harbor."

The day those Colonists masquerading as Indians dumped tea into the Atlantic, the king was duty-bound and honor-driven to act. All the rage the politically unrepresented colonists had toward England and King George finally erupted into one inspired moment.

Through it all, I had to be there for George. At 35, time and obligation had not been his friend. He was aging poorly, growing stout, and losing the lovely hair around his temples. The illness of the ancients encroached again. For weeks I had to cope with his erratic tantrums. He would fly into lunatic rages, flailing and screaming at the top of his lungs, 'Bloody malcontents! Close the harbor! Close the harbor!' Or he would lock himself in his room, scribbling orders to General Gage. Finally, on 9 August, 1776, the king was read the ultimate decree by Prime Minister Pitt.

"Your Majesty, the Colonists have officially elected to separate from England to form their own democracy," informed Pitt. "On 4 July their Continental Congress ratified this." He handed George a document. "It is a Declaration of Independency signed by all thirteen colonies."

The king read the document—and the words which inspired his wrath: "*...that these United Colonies are, and of right ought to be, free and independent states, that they are absolved from all allegiance to the British Crown, and that all political connection between them and the state of Great Britain is, and ought to be, totally dissolved...*"

George was incensed. "The Colonies are in rebellion, and if it's war they want, it is war they shall get!" He immediately dispatched more troops.

The Revolution raged for years. I spent my time with my family, which had now grown to twelve. I was 33 years old. Lady Hagedorn, Lady Schwellenberg, and Anne kept me occupied while George received reports on various battles won and lost by Britain.

Christian Bach, however, proved unrelenting in his pursuit of me.

✠

"Christian Bach is here and wishes to be received, Your Majesty."

Charlotte was in the nursery playing with Prince Adolphus and baby Princess Mary when a note was brought to her by Lady Hagedorn. Charlotte read it, shook her head, and handed the note back. "I will not see him. The queen is not receiving."

"He's quite insistent. He says if he is not received, he will seek audience with the king."

Now Charlotte was livid. "I will not allow a tribute exacted under duress in this way. You will tell Mister Bach the queen will seek an audience with the king herself—to have him banished from England, lest he forget to whom he is asking reception."

"Very well, Your Majesty." At that, Lady Hagedorn left.

How dare he, I thought. How dare he think he can show up and be seen simply because he felt he was able. This behavior went on for a year. Christian would seek an audience with me and I would refuse him. Then suddenly, the behavior inexplicably ceased.

A year later, Lady Lizzie was going through Charlotte's jewelry. She picked out a handsome diamond pendant and showed the queen. "These will do nicely for the theater. And won't Lady Dalrymple be jealous of you," said Lizzie, putting them on the queen.

"She's had her eyes on these diamonds since I wore them in May."

"High harlot," Lady Lizzie quipped. "She should be so lucky as to have diamonds like these. Thank God she's moved on from Prince George to Sir Charles Fox."

Lady Grace Dalrymple was one of the grandest courtesans, who chose her lovers from among royalty or the peerage. She had set her charms upon 18-year-old Prince George, and he, like most unsuspecting men of his ilk, lavished her with gifts of furs and jewelry, amassing an enormous debt. Now the Prince owed everyone in London.

"My son and his cultured whores," sighed Charlotte. "It'll be the death of me."

"Or him," chortled Charlotte's lady, and they both had a good laugh. Lady Lizzie handed Charlotte a hand mirror. "Now, have you heard the latest? It appears Minister d'Eon has given France our national secrets concerning combat tactics and strategies in America. The French can now anticipate our every move. Turns out he's been a spy. On top of that, the Stock Exchange has an ongoing bet that d'Eon is actually a woman who has been disguising herself as a man."

"How absurd," exclaimed Charlotte. "I knew him in Mecklenburg as a young girl. I see d'Eon every other week here. Slight, yes, a woman, no."

"Well, I say unless you lay with a man, you never know. And even then it's a puzzle."

Again, they had a good chuckle. Charlotte still liked Lady Lizzie. She always had the best gossip in London which she embellished with a dramatic aside. As she began to hook the back of the queen's dress, she continued. "Oh, I almost forgot. Mister Bach is about to be married," she said, the inflections of her Scottish accent more pronounced. "He and Cecilia Grassi were in a print shop in Soho Square where the invitations are being printed."

I can't remember the rest of Lady Lizzie's conversation, for I was too stunned. Yet my lady was correct. Christian and Cecilia Grassi were indeed married on the grounds of Newburgh Castle in Devonshire, England in a ceremony attended by several close friends and family. Suspiciously absent was George or myself. I was hurt, but had to overcome his nuptials, and it would be a full two years before I could think about

Christian and not become emotional. But little by little, I became stronger, for other issues prevailed.

In the midst of our conflict with the Colonists, General Cornwallis, whom I had met long ago at Sanssouci, had an idea. He could see that many American rebel leaders and soldiers were slave owners in the south. So, to hit them where it most hurt, he offered freedom to any slaves who could make their way to British occupied territory and fight for the Crown. Slaves abandoned their masters by the thousands, and many came to Britain. Lord Cornwallis had found a way to end the slaves' condition in America; and it was then I began to think about the words Christian spoke to me the day I forced him from my employ: '...Is it not mightier to sacrifice the suffering of a mad king, for whom you can do nothing, for the freedom of those less fortunate and used as beasts of burden?'

Thus, I decided to go back to Phillips Printing Shop and renew my commitment to the cessation of the slave trade...and ultimately slavery itself. But when I contacted Madame Lia de Beaumont to begin our subterfuge anew, unfortunately, she had plans of her own.

"Your Majesty, I must go back to France," Mme. Lia sighed. "Alas, my brother is embroiled in a legal matter and has been recalled to Versailles—to see the Dauphin. He has to answer some charges in court, and I must make a statement. I do not know when I'll return."

Charlotte's facade dropped uncontrollably. "What kind of trouble is Minister d'Eon in?"

"Have you not heard?"

Charlotte motioned for Lia to sit. "I heard some nonsense about a bet on the Stock Exchange as to his being feminine. It sounded absurd. London is teeming with feminine men."

"It's far more unsavory. My brother has been accused of... of actually *being* a woman."

Charlotte remained incredulous and stared at Madame Lia—her mind unable to absorb it. "There is one place which dictates whether one is male or female. It's the first place one looks when a child is born. Surely *you* know whether your brother is in fact your brother versus your sister. Did you not go before the Lord Justice and testify on his behalf?"

"I was not asked to. But that is what I must do in France as these charges affect my brother's post as ambassador. He left England last Thursday. I leave day after tomorrow."

Charlotte's head fell in sadness. She was already without Christian, now she would be without her best friend and confidant. Mme. Lia could see how much her news upset the queen.

"I could never leave without giving you this." She motioned for her footman to bring over a wooden crate and open it. Inside were a dozen bottles of wines. "I have another three cases waiting on my coach. Enough to last you."

"Oh Lia," said Charlotte wiping her eyes. "What shall I do without you?"

"What you've been doing, I suspect: tending your garden, playing with your children, nursing your husband through this fiasco of a war. In turn, when all the legal affairs are over, I shall send you more wine after I visit my mother in Tonnerre."

"Tonnerre?" Charlotte interrupted, her visage brightening. "You're going to Tonnerie?"

"Yes. That is where my mother and our vineyards are., in the burgundy region of Provence. In Tonnerre."

"How far is Provence from Mirepoix?"

"Three, perhaps four days south."

Charlotte was in a dilemma. Should she reveal to her friend her web of subterfuge? Could she trust Lia with so profound a secret as the reason for wanting to see François Antoine Gaston, Duke of Levis-Mirepoix? And if so, did she feel secure giving Lia any scrolls for the Duke?

Yet, even though these feelings of insecurity swarmed within, Charlotte took the leap. "I need an extreme favor from you, Madame Lia. One without your asking the reason for such."

Lia frowned, but understood. "Anything, Your Majesty. You only need ask."

"There is someone I need you to get something to. Duke François Antoine Gaston of Mirepoix. Tell him I need his help and he will understand why."

"Duke François?"

"But be careful," Charlotte implored. "You're giving him something most importance."

Mme. Lia saw in Charlotte's eyes this was a significant favor and she bowed. "Of course. I serve at your pleasure, Your Majesty, you know that."

"I shall see that you are rightfully compensated. But please, send any correspondence you have on this matter through my maid, Anne Josef. She will deliver the item for you to transport to Duke Francois tomorrow. That is all I can say on the matter at present."

Lia understood. "I shall do as you ask—and I shall miss you."

"And I, you. Please give my regards to Minister d'Eon."

At that, Charlotte and her friend hugged goodbye. Madame Lia de Beaumont left Queen's House as Charlotte wiped the faintest tear from her eye praying she was doing the right thing.

Forty Two

Charlotte had no idea she would not see Madame Lia for years. Nonetheless she gave the papyrus scroll to Anne who surreptitiously delivered it to Lia. Once again she would have to wait until it was given to Duke Francois. Wait until she would hear news.

On 22 September 1780, the queen gave birth to her 14th child. But Prince Alfred was sickly in every way—a helpless infant who suffered in pain most days. Charlotte always spiraled into tears when she looked upon him for after fourteen deliveries, she had finally given birth to a child blessed with Magragana's mark—the birthmark of the Merovingians. Yet she fretted. She knew her son would never live long enough to fulfill his destiny or birthright and it was a constant struggle for her.

The following year, on an unusually warm October day, Charlotte and George were enjoying a game of cricket near the pond at Queen's House with their children Frederick, William, Charlotte and Augusta when her eldest, Prince George, came out to give them news.

"Mother, father, I intend to marry Maria Fitzherbert next April. I am in love with her."

A vein the size of his thumb rose in the middle of the king's forehead portending disaster. "I forbid it," George growled. "I disapprove of Mrs. Fitzherbert and you know it. She is Catholic, she's not a royal, she's twice widowed, and at 26, far too old for you."

"I do not care what you think. I intend to marry her. I love her," Prince George insisted.

"Are you aware that through the 'Act of Settlement', no monarch can marry a Catholic, nor can a family member of the monarchy married to a Catholic ascend the throne of England? That means you will never be king. And if that does not convince you of your folly, I enacted the 'Marriage Act' so no Hanover under age 25 can marry without my consent. And I say no Maria Fitzherbert!" George hurled his cricket mallet to the ground.

But Prince George was primed with condemnation. "I will not be as you, father. I will marry the woman I love, not some woman 'assigned' to me," he snapped, then acknowledged Charlotte. "No offense to you, mother, but I will not allow my intended to go off and unhappily marry, have an affair, an illegitimate child, and live in sacrifice of her royal society. I don't know the woman, but thank God Lady Sarah has finally found true love with Captain Napier and married him. It will not take me twenty years to do so."

"What are you talking about?" the king blared.

The Prince of Wales narrowed his eyes smugly. "Your one-time lover just married a member of your 25th Regiment. At last she is finally happy—as I hope to one day be."

The prince walked off leaving the king in such a state it took twenty minutes to calm him.

Then the worse news arrived ten minutes later brought by a visibly shaken Lord Frederick North—the king's 7th Prime Minister in his reign thus far.

"Your Majesty, I must speak with you."

George, who was already upset, gave the rest of his offspring a look suggesting they leave. Dutifully they obeyed which left the king, the Prime Minister and Charlotte alone. When the queen started to go, George held her arm taut, indicating she stay.

"Sir," began Lord North in a grave voice, "17,000 men from Rochambeau and Washington's troops arrived at Yorktown and converged on Cornwallis' troops. Our soldiers were outnumbered two to one, stranded, blocked by French forces from the sea, and subjected to heavy fire for three weeks. They could not sustain and ran low on ammunition and food." He choked back emotion. "Cornwallis had to surrender. He handed over 7,087 men, 900 seamen, 30 transport ships, 154 cannons, and 15 galleys. Our troops are now American prisoners."

George's composure broke. There was a long, impenetrable silence before Lord North pulled a letter from his breastpocket and solumnly gave it to the king. "This is my resignation. I can no longer assist you in leading England at this time of so humbling a defeat. Let me not go to the grave with the guilt of being the ruin of my king and country."

Sadly, the king accepted North's resignation and watched the Prime Minister leave the palace grounds. Upon absorbing this crushing blow, George felt desperate and conquered.

Later that evening he drafted a letter of abdication, the correspondence of which was never delivered. I could not allow him to send it. 'Look at history, George,' I pleaded as he sat writing the letter. 'Every great man of wisdom and courage experiences defeat—some more than once. It is how great men learn—from their mistakes. Strong character lies not in falling off of the horse, but climbing upon it again.'

But George was despondent and took to his bed, remaining that way for months. During the next two years, I began to feel a bitterness consume me that I could not shake. My children were growing up, I learned my brother Adolph had died, my brother Charles was now Grand Duke of Mecklenburg, and my secret quest to have the reliquary scrolls translated had been thwarted by the absence of any response from either Mme. Lia or Duke Francois. It became difficult to assist George with his maladies when I could not take care of my own.

Then, on the last day of December 1781, Sir Albert Papendiek came to me with a letter.

"Your Majesty, this came for you from Bach."

"Send it back, Sir Albert," Charlotte instructed.

"But it is from *Madame* Bach."

Charlotte quickly took the letter and opened it. Her heart sank upon reading the emotional words: *"Your Majesty, my husband is dying and needs to see you. Please come."*

Charlotte had her coach immediately brought around and took Lady Schwellenberg with her to the Bachs' house in Soho. Madame Cecilia Grassi Bach met the queen at the front door of the sparsely furnished house in tears. Charlotte listened as Madame Bach told her the whole sordid story, and upon learning what had been Christian's life since their parting, the queen was racked with guilt. Christian's desire to have a larger career than his father Sebastian had eluded him.

Although he traveled extensively in France and Germany and had composed many operas and sonatas, his fame waned and his credit over-extended. In the last two years, to feel better about himself and recapture the acclaim he once enjoyed, he'd become a wastrel—buying carriages, bigger homes, jewelry—and amassing bills. As his debt rose his health declined, and he began drinking. Soon, he just gave up on life.

"Two men came on Monday. I begged them not to take everything in the house for the debts Christian had not honored," Cecilia lamented, "but they took everything anyway. The next day, other creditors came knocking. I pleaded with them to leave us some remote dignity. Alas, they would not. My husband lay ill from consumption. He could hear the commotion. He knew what was happening, but could do nothing. Not for his debt, nor for his health. He begged me for one last favor—to send for you."

Charlotte was shown into Christian's room while his wife served her lady tea in the main room. Seeing him after so long and in his condition startled the queen. Christian was weak and pale; a mere slip of his former self. His bountiful dark hair was now grey and thinning, and his striking green eyes in which Charlotte once saw his optimistic world now be-trayed that sanguinity with impending death. When those dying eyes could finally focus on Charlotte and realized she had come, he smiled and waved her forward. She sat on the chair beside him.

"Charlotte…I…," he tried to speak.

"Shhhhh," Charlotte quieted. "I'm here." Her heart was breaking as she touched his gaunt face, the bones of his cheeks prominent beneath her fingers. "I brought something. Something I still have and love." Charlotte pulled the silver ballerina music box from her bag and wound it up. The music of '2 Part Invention' played.

Christian squeezed Charlotte's hand. "I stood at my wedding…and before God and the world I declared my love for her. I felt all issues in my life had been resolved. I was clear about it—about all of it. Every-thing was perfect…except for what to do about my love for you.

Christian sat up slightly. "Charlotte…it shall never be finished," he managed, barely above a whisper, trying to quell the half-smoldering pas-sion which had driven him for so long. "Never."

Charlotte nodded, knowing full well the truth of it—that it would never be finished for her either, and her mind raced back to Mecklenburg, to that day at Mirow Palace when Emmanuel Bach introduced his talented, completely irresistible younger brother to her, and her world spun off on its own axis. She held Christian's hand until he fell asleep and instinct told her it was time to go. She said her goodbyes and whispered to him:

"Je vous verrai dans l'éternité, mon amour."

The next morning, New Year's Day 1782, Johann Christian Bach died. He was 47 years old. Though England mourned his passing, Charlotte knew the condition in which Christian's creditors left his widow. She wanted this wonderful man, this musical treasure of her time, to have a dignified and reverential funeral, so she paid for it from her privy purse through Sir Albert Papendiek, who was a pallbearer.

The following week Charlotte sent for Madame Cecilia Grassi Bach. She was brought before the queen at Kew Palace where Charlotte was mourning without the preying eyes of those at Queen's House who would not have understood. Cecilia, once a handsome woman, was now broken and the strain of her circumstance had aged her considerably. Upon motioning her forward she kissed Charlotte's hand reverently. "Your Majesty, thank you for seeing me."

"Please sit, Madame Bach. I understand the anxiety of your situation."

"I am at wit's end, Majesty. He has left nothing. Our debt exceeds £4000 and creditors have taken everything—our house, the furnishings, the paintings, our coach. Everything," she cried. "I loved him. And I know he loved you. I knew it the first time I came to Queen's House after my debut of *Orione*, and I knew it when you came the day before he died. But I do not know where else to turn." She fell to her knees crying in distress.

Charlotte extended her hand to her. "Madame Bach, you should not be in want simply because you loved he who could not help but love only the great music he gave the world. For Christian, music would always be his true lover, his true wife. In the end, we were all sacrificed for her. Now rise up, and go about your business. I shall personally see to it that you receive a pension and are provided for so you can live out your days in Italy, your homeland. As regards Christian's debts, I shall attend to as many as I can, but his funeral has already been settled."

Cecilia was disbelieving. "But I cannot repay such a kindness. What do you ask of me?"

At our next levee, a grateful Cecilia Grassi Bach sang for George and I. It was the aria from 'Artaserse'—the opera Christian wrote and dedicated to me. As I listened to the stirring voice which had so moved me and my former lover, I found myself caressing my amulet. There could not have been a more fitting gift than Christian's music, so beautifully presented.

Je t'adore, Christian. Au revoir.

Forty Three

Charlotte disparaged most of 1782. She mourned Christian's death for months. Thankfully George understood her sorrow and what their music master meant to them—and most particularly to Charlotte who was once again heavy with child.

This at least lifted the queen's spirits for she had suffered so many losses in a short span of time. On 20 August, her sickly child, Prince Alfred, her one hope for the continuance of the legacy that was Magragana's, her father's, and the ancients going back to King David, died in her arms. He was but two years old. Charlotte's grief was insurmountable, not only because of his death, but for the mission if the child she now carried did not possess the mark. This, and the human toll the Revolution took on the English forces, could have kept Charlotte in despair all that year.

But hope intervened. On a cool September morning, Anne came into the parlor at Queen's House and whispered to Charlotte as she was playing chess with Lady Lizzie. It had been four months since the queen had made a public appearance or desired to attend a salon. Anne's news forced her to go with the Ethiopian to Charlotte's private chambers. Once there Anne reached into her uniform pocket and gave Charlotte a letter. "This arrived for me a few moments ago. I did not want to give it to you in front of Lady Lizzie. The stamps are French."

Charlotte suddenly became nervous and quickly opened it. Though the handwriting was different from Duke Francois, as soon as she saw it, she groaned. "The words are in code."

"I'll decipher it, if you would like," Anne offered.

Charlotte nodded and for the rest of the afternoon, Anne translated the scroll. Finally Charlotte's maid handed the translation to the queen who read it:

Your Majesty,

I have located Duke Francois in Mirepoix and he has been busy translating your documents. I do not know when I shall return to England. The trial lasted far longer than expected and the Dauphin has asked for my assistance on other matters. But the reason for this letter is that I have found your heart's desire. When the translations are finished, Duke Francois will give it back to me so I can deliver it to you. But he seems both excited and troubled by the contents thus far and has asked that I be careful in spiriting them back to you as ministers of the Church in Rome could become quite interested in them. In any event, he has said it may take another month or so, but I cannot stay in Mirepoix. I must go to Bordeaux on business. But I shall write again as soon as I have that which you need in hand.

Yours faithfully,
Mme. Lia de Beaumont

"It sounds hopeful." said Anne.

"Also dangerous," replied Charlotte, her heart racing.

"What is dangerous?" they heard from behind them.

Charlotte turned quickly. It was George, who seemed to have appeared at the door without making a sound. "What is dangerous, Charlotte?" he repeated.

Charlotte could not answer. All this time she had kept this side of her world secretive. She had been afraid to share it with George, fearing he would dismiss both she and the information as insane. What could she tell him—that for ten years she had been chasing after a Duke who was her father's sole connection to the translation of the Magragana's scrolls? Or that her amulet was a part of a complex of nine which may reveal Templar treasure?

An unbearable silence engulfed the room. All that could be heard was the chiming of one of George's clocks which constantly kept the wrong time. Then, they heard:

"I think I have found my daughter," blurted Anne. "Her Majesty said she would try and help me buy her out of slavery…but that it may be dangerous."

"I'm sorry. Am I to understand that you, a scullery maid, have the ear and purse of the Queen of England?" balked George.

Charlotte remained silent, looking at Anne, praying that if the king did not accept her response as truth she would not unnecessarily suffer his wrath. But Anne held her head high, as though her words were the genuine reality. "Her Majesty merely suggested a loan."

George stared at Charlotte intensely, and she was convinced he did not believe Anne.

"More slaves purchased at the expense of your privy purse, my dear?"

Charlotte swallowed hard. Now she would be an accomplice to the deceit. She steadied herself. "Yes," she lied. "I know the pain one feels at the loss of a child. I won't add to it."

"And should you find her, do you intend to buy her as well?"

Suddenly, the queen was angry. Perhaps it was because Anne had been so helpful assisting her search for answers while George did nothing but harass and demean her.

"Leave," bellowed George to Anne. "Go!"

Anne gathered skirt and left while Charlotte glared at the king. "You treat her terribly. I am glad the Colonists revolted and won their independence. And if you continue your reluctance to do anything about slavery here in Britain, I swear I will declare to the world she who we are both descended from to be the very chattel you so staunchly refuse to free."

"You'll do no such thing. Do you know how difficult it is for one man to change centuries of ignorance? I have always held that freedom will come, just not in my lifetime."

"Why not in your lifetime?" Charlotte challenged. "Jefferson brilliantly stated in his Declaration why freedom and self-reliance is crucial to human happiness and survival. Is he more enlightened than you? More forward thinking? More sensitive to the subject than you?"

George's eyes narrowed, indicating he was incensed. "Do not quote Jefferson as a moral example. He holds over 200 Negroes in bondage. If ever there was a hypocrite it's that Jacobite with 'the gift of verbiage' from Virginia. Even *he* realizes the institution is too profitable to expunge from his personal economy."

"Damn you, George!" Charlotte angrily crashed her fist onto the marble tabletop of her desk, breaking a tea cup. A sliver of glass stabbed through her hand, drawing blood. Charlotte winced in pain, grabbing a napkin to stop the blood, and stormed to the door.

"Come here," George demanded. "You will not avoid me for days over this, as you do."

His command was in such a portentous tone Charlotte instantly stopped, her heart beating rapidly. George moved closer, slowly turning his wife toward him. He lifted her hand and unwrapped the napkin from around the cut. Tears from the pain and the ardency of their argument fell from Charlotte's eyes as George's voice dropped to a whisper. "Whether I like it or not, I have come to rely on your good judgment and counsel."

Charlotte said nothing as George dipped his handkerchief in the water pitcher and began to gently wipe the trickles of blood from her injured hand. His thoughts were engraved in the visible furrows on his forehead, but he appeared sincere. "I am sorry."

"If you truly are, do something about this cause."

The king was forced to issue a 'Proclamation of Cessation of Hostilities,' culminating with the Treaty of Paris. This officially ended the war. It was signed in February of 1783 one month after the birth of my fifteenth and last child, Princess Amelia. The new 'United States of America' appointed George Washington as 'President,' which they decided was more appropriate for a democracy than 'King,' and he, in turn, appointed John Adams, a signer of the Declaration of Independence, as Ambassador to England.

George was, of course, livid. 'How dare those bloody "Americans," as they are calling themselves, deign to position themselves in my court,' he fumed to me the evening before the new ambassador was to arrive at St. James. 'I shall ever have a bad opinion of any Englishman who would accept of being an accredited minister for that revolted state.'

But I countered, 'You were the last to consent to separation between Britain and America. Be the bigger man and accept that separation has been made and is inevitable. Meet the friendship of the United States as an independent power—and do it with humility and grace. Get on with it.'

George grunted and called me an eternal optimist—one who only saw the greenness of the grass when all about me saw a dung heap. I chuckled, for only I knew how tired and ancient I felt. I was 40 years old, had given birth to fifteen children and buried two—for my dear little Prince Octavius, who was but age four, also went to live with the Lord after a protracted illness. These disappointments had taken their toll, and I felt my life amounting to that very dung heap of which George so eloquently spoke.

The next day it was all the king could do to hold his anger as John Adams, the newly appointed American Ambassador to England, approached him. George was seated alone in the throne room. Just in the anti-room beyond, Charlotte, surrounded by a mass of bishops, state ministers, lords and courtiers, knew the king was seething. The queen excused herself and eased out of the room into a closed-off hallway which adjoined the throne room. It had a secret door which seamlessly blended into the wall, and she furtively looked through the tiny hole in the wallpaper to watch the proceedings.

The 50-year-old John Adams was ever the diplomat. After nervously making three reverences to "the presence," he approached the king, a man Adams considered "a tyrant unfit to be the ruler of a free people." He was gracious and soft spoken. George, however, maintained an aloof, detached demeanor, in an attempt to intimidate the already nervous ambassador.

Adams gave a passionate speech on how the two countries had an opportunity to put the war behind them and conduct themselves as allies.

Throughout the speech, George found himself touched by Adams' words. Little by little he softened his harsh disregard for the ambassador, and when Adams finally finished, Charlotte was shocked to witness George extended his hand and her own rose to her chest as she heard George remark, "I will be very frank with you. I was the last to consent to separation, but it having been made and inevitable, I would be the first to meet the friendship of the United States as an independent power."

Charlotte smiled to herself, for those were her exact words to George the evening before. Three days later, a drawing room was had in John and Abigail Adams' honor. They brought along their daughter, Nabby, and the palace was filled with MPs, aristocrats, peers and courtiers. Young Prince George spent most of his time drinking heavily and talking to Maria Fitzherbert. Just as the prince helped himself to another glass of brandy, the king balked.

"That's enough spirits. I shall not have you a drunken fool in front of my guests."

Charlotte witnessed the exchange and hurried over. "Gentlemen, this is a party. Behave."

Prince George, who was inebriated, countered with slurred indignity, "Leave me alone. Both of you!" and he marched off with Maria. The king turned in the opposite direction and walked away as well, leaving Charlotte in red-faced embarrassment.

Abigail Adams, cheerful and reverential, came over in an effort to quell the humiliation the queen was experiencing. "It appears we have much in common, Your Majesty," Mrs. Adams grinned, looking at their daughters, Nabby and young Charlotte, the princess royal, as they had punch and chatted like best friends. "Much in common indeed. We are both about the same age, our daughters appear to get on well, we have husbands in power," she looked the queen in the eye sincerely, "And, it appears, we have feisty first-born sons."

Charlotte smiled. "Sometimes I do not know how to handle him— or his father."

Mrs. Adams chuckled and attempted to sip her punch, but found her glass empty. Charlotte motioned for a servant, who came over. "A sherry, please. And you, Mrs. Adams?"

"More punch please," answered the ambassador's wife.

"She will have a sherry, too," Charlotte suggested instead, turning back to Mrs. Adams. "You and I shall be good friends, I suspect."

Soon Charlotte's attention was drawn to an enthusiastic young man standing just behind them, talking to William Pitt the Younger, the newly appointed Prime Minister, and Sir Charles Fox, the slovenly son of Lord Henry Fox. The young man was impassioned regarding the impropriety of the slave trade, and Charlotte's ears perked up. She listened as he announced his intent to draft a bill to submit to Parliament for the abolition of the slave trade. Sir Charles Fox thought it a good idea, and the young Prime Minister asked that he also submit any related documentation.

The idea that someone was as interested as she in ceasing the trade excited Charlotte, and she began to look around the room—until she found Lady Lizzie in conversation with, of all people, Sir John Wilkes. Eventually she excused herself from Mrs. Adams and signaled to Lady Hagedorn. "Fetch Lady Lizzie for me, please."

Lady Hagedorn went over to Lady Lizzie, who immediately complied and hurried to the queen. Charlotte pointed. "Who is the young man with the Prime Minister?"

Lady Lizzie looked. "It's William Wilberforce, an MP from Kingston-upon-Hull, elected to the House of Commons. Quite the rabble-rouser I understand. And darling looking."

"My word. A gentleman's appearance is all you seem interested in, Lady Lizzie. Which is why it's shocking to see you spend so much time with Sir Wilkes tonight, who is anything *but.*"

Lady Lizzie went blanch. "But I haven't, Your Majesty. Sir Wilkes was being obnoxious—trying to fondle me inappropriately." She curtsied and hurried away.

Charlotte looked around again, and upon finding Sir Allan Ramsey, furtively maneuvered through the crowd to him. She pulled him aside. "Sir Allan, invite that young Mister Wilberforce to one of your meetings," she whispered. "Apparently he is quite the advocate for abolition, I hear."

"He is indeed. He's spoken several dozen times at Phillips over the last five years. He will be the keynote speaker at our next meeting on Tuesday," said Sir Allan, who then lowered his voice. "'Tis a shame *you* are not able to hear him. He's something."

It had been years since Charlotte ventured onto the streets of London with Mme. Lia keeping with her pledge to help the anti-slavery cause—the same pledge she insisted upon George. Perhaps it was time she did so again, and she gave Sir Allan a knowing look.

The next morning, Charlotte, the king and their family were gathered at breakfast. Since Princes George, Frederick and William were of age, they had establishments at Frogmore House or Carlton House. But everyone was expected to be together at Queen's House for breakfast.

As they supped on eggs and toast, Charlotte eventually asked George what he thought of young Mister Wilberforce. George, aware of the MP's penchant for ending slavery, found him ill-advised. Prince William and Prince Augustus agreed. But Prince George was impressed with Wilberforce.

"I must say he is one of the wittiest men I have heard on the floor of the Commons," said the prince. "It is a pleasure to hear him speak, regardless of the subject."

"Well, I have a more pressing subject," insisted Princess Augusta, now a beautiful, dark-haired young woman. "I am in love with Dr. Ralph Thomas, and I wish to marry."

Charlotte, surprised by her daughter's assertiveness, was pleased that one of her daughters had found love. George however was rankled. "Out of the question," he balked. "Dr. Thomas is not royalty. He is not even a peer, and I have made no such arrangements for your betrothal."

"I am 16. The same age mother was betrothed to you," said Augusta irked at her father's tone. "Are we all to be spinsters? Shall we never find the affection we want for ourselves?"

"What do you mean by that?" George snipped acidly. "Why can you not be more like your older sister, Charlotte, who finds contentment in her solitude, and is grateful for the love she receives from her parents until the proper suitor is found for her."

"'Proper' suitor? My sister Charlotte is miserable. She will not tell you so for fear of your wrath. But she cries all the time. She tells me constantly how she longs for the affections of a man you deny her." Augusta turned to her eldest sister. "Tell him. Tell him how sad you always are."

Princess Charlotte was not thrilled to be placed on the spot and glared at her sister.

"The things I confessed, I did so in secret. They were not for public consumption."

"Then it's true?" asked the king.

Princess Charlotte looked down at her plate. She had not eaten much of her eggs or porridge. "You have denied every one of our requests for marriage, father. You have said no to Elizabeth, to Sophia, to me, and now Augusta. I am now 18 years old. Will there be no one suitable for any of us?"

"You see?" cried Augusta.

"Has the world gone topsy? Have you all gone mad?" exclaimed George.

"No. Only you!" cried Augusta, running from the room. "I refuse to remain a virgin forever."

In the midst of the chaos, Prince George stood in his sister's defense. "Augusta is correct. You are unyielding and obstinate upon this subject, father. It is the very reason I married Maria Fitzherbert secretly and consummated it over a month ago. I married for love. Not for position, bloodlines or political gain. *For love.* And if you cannot accept that, I am truly sorry."

Charlotte watched as vexation turned George's face crimson. He marched over to his son and slapped him. "I told you last year I forbade a marriage with that woman and have not given my permission. I shall have it annulled."

"No, George," Charlotte interceded. "Maria is our son's choice. Let him be happy."

"Happiness…is not a point of negotiation. He is the Prince of Wales, heir to the throne of England. He will do as he is told…as I had to."

Charlotte could only stare at George.

I was struck mute. My son was right. We were all puppets in a game of bloodlines and nobility. Obligation inevitably trumped love or happiness, which had no place in our world.

I then had to remember my own mission and place it at the forefront. I had to accept that since my last child, Princess Amelia, did not possess Magragana's mark—nor did any of my children, it was time to devote myself to my own interests without guilt or recrimination. It was time to pursue my own causes whether George liked it or not. Bloodlines be damned!

Forty Four

Spring, 1783

On the second Tuesday of May, Charlotte's plan was at the ready. She arose at six o'clock as usual. Because Lady Hagedorn had not been feeling well and it was Anne's day off, Lady Lizzie helped Lady Schwellenberg dress the queen. Charlotte came down to breakfast with her family, feigning a slight headache. She announced to Lady Schwellenberg that she wanted her to go to Strands Apothecary and have them mix a headache potion for her. At one-thirty she and Lady Schwellenberg went into the music room, where she told Lady Lizzie she did not wish to be disturbed and began to play the piano-forte.

Twenty minutes later, Lady Schwellenberg left the music room and got into her carriage by the side entrance of Queen's House to run the errand for the queen as Charlotte played her repertoire of compositions over and over. Outside the palace, at a predetermined location, the coach pulled over. Out of the shadows came Anne, who climbed aboard. No one in the palace ever suspected that the passenger was Queen Charlotte and not her lady in waiting who left Queen's House. Anne and the queen smiled and continued on their way to Phillips Printing shop.

Since the Revolution, London was a city in transition. In the seven years since Charlotte had ventured out in this way, the streets had a rousing, effervescent energy. Noise from new construction and the bustle of new shops and businesses was at times overpowering—vastly different from a decade earlier when food was at a premium and work slow if at all. The area known as the Strand was entirely given up to new shops and places of business. People felt heartened. North of Downing street, where the Prime Minister resided, were magnificent carriages carrying the well-heeled or members of the nobility. In the parks, couples strolled along taking in the views, or promenaded with parasols and high hats enjoying the sweet smell of flowers making their appearance for spring.

Yet, as Charlotte and Anne ventured further east, they were reminded why the queen desired to be more vigilant regarding the status of minorities. The contrast was stunning. Along the streets of the Spitalfields was wretched poverty and decrepit buildings. There was no improvement from two decades earlier when Charlotte and George stumbled onto the street in 1762.

Beggars, negro and white, were boundless, and women of all ages worked as prostitutes, some as young as 14. Anne turned to the queen in disheartened frustration. "This is how most of us live, Your Majesty. My daughter Mary would be 11 this year. I can only pray that I can find her before this life or worse befalls her." Charlotte patted her maid's hand gently and they continued until finally they reached George Lane—and Phillips Print Shop.

But today, as they entered the facility for the meeting, they were met with the distinct odor of urine. When they looked to their right, Negro workmen in the printing area were urinating on the disassembled presses and letters on the floor, then brushing, mopping and cleaning them off. Charlotte was befuddled and stared. Anne saw this and chuckled.

"For some reason, urine cleans the presses better than anything else," explained Anne, who subtly waved to one of the workmen. "Something is in it that dissolves the build up of oil and ink well."

"My word," Charlotte chortled. "How do you know this?"

Anne smiled and pointed to the workman she knew. "That man used to work for the Bethany's. He would always tell me about his second job working here. It would make me laugh—pissing for a living."

They both laughed, then Charlotte and Anne went into the back assembly room and looked around. Since Anne was new to the meeting, she appreciated being acknowledged by the others without regard to her color. Charlotte noticed there were at least thirty people there now, a dozen more today than years before. This included Sir John Wilkes, seated in front. The queen kept her head low, her veil down over her face, and sat in the back of the room, where she noticed a number of Quaker women. However, the hierarchy was still the same: women, whether white or black, were seated in back, and men in front, which again disturbed her.

On a nearby table Josiah Wedgwood, who'd had a leg amputated and was on crutches, had several pieces of blue and white pottery on display for sale to support the cause.

Then, Sir Allan Ramsey pounded his gavel and, as the meeting co-ordinator, called to order the Society for the Abolition of the Slave Trade. He asked the group for suggestions on how they could effectively organize a larger body of concerned citizens and raise money and aware-ness for their cause. An older woman raised her hand and introduced herself as Hannah More. She suggested that perhaps they get Mr. Phillips to donate his services to print flyers for placement in windows and trees. Another woman suggested they raise funds through bake sales, book sales, and the selling of cast-off clothing, then use those funds for adver-tising placement in newspapers.

Both women's suggestions were appreciated by the male majority, but they were asked to approach their husbands about the use of their homes for meetings, to get the word out. They requested the women help with cooking meals and baking products for the various sales, and Hannah and other women were offended by this. "I am not married, sir," snipped Hannah. "Can we women not be of service without the assistance of a man? Must we transpose the second-class condition of slaves to that of women?"

The other women applauded and Charlotte could see the tide was changing with more vocal female commentary. This pleased her. Finally, after a half an hour of informal conversation, Sir Allan Ramsey intro-duced the main speaker—William Wilberforce. Charlotte smiled upon seeing the young, energetic MP, who had several petitions which he passed out.

"I need your help to gather at least 3,000 signatures on these petitions attacking the slave trade for presentation to the Commons in the next three months," he implored. "I want the slave trade bill to pass this time. My first attempts in 1776 were futile because the war distracted everyone and nothing came of it. But now is the time. My colleague Thomas Clarkson is still collecting evidence against the trade and will be with us at our next meeting." He then motioned for some others to come forward from the back of the room. "Now, I could stand here and give you horrifying accounts which I've personally received from slaves who've suffered aboard slave ships, but I find it far more compelling when those who have survived the ordeal can expound on it themselves. So, I introduce to you three of the 'Sons of Africa' who have been traveling with me—Olaudah Equiano, Ottobah Cuguano and John B. Wainwright. These men, heroes all, have experienced the atrocities of the middle passage and slavery firsthand."

Three men of color came forward from the back of the room. The first to speak was an African, Olaudah Equiano, whose eloquence and heartfelt emotion about his challenging and horrid journey from the mother country to America in the bowels of a slave ship, was moving.

But it was the second speaker, a lighter-hued man whose story of his arduous, unexpected journey to London and freedom, struck an unanticipated, familiar chord within Charlotte. There was something about him. He had a lilting Jamaican patois, and his face—the smooth honey-colored skin and hazel eyes—had the comfort of an old friend. She knew him, but from where? Charlotte crept in for a closer look, then suddenly smiled in delightful realization.

He was so much older and depleted than I remembered. But his eyes—those unmistakable light brown eyes—were the shining eyes of the one whose friendship changed my life and the course of my goals so long ago. They were the eyes, the voice and indeed the presence of Jon Baptiste, my family's former slave—and my beloved half-brother.

Jon was now a "Son of Africa" and a 46-year-old abolitionist and activist who spoke with learned eloquence of his childhood in Germany and how wonderful the princess of his duchy was to him. He spoke of how he taught her to dance and this princess taught him to read in return. Then he recalled the brutal beating he received at the hands of her cousin for a rape he did not commit. He took off his shirt to further illustrate his tribulations revealing the permanent scars so visible and deep upon his back that Charlotte's tears could not be held back. Jon explained that he was taken away from the palace grounds and brought to the docks at Stadt where he was sold and placed on a slave ship bound for the West Indies. From Santo Domingo he was transferred to the slave ship *Brookes* with more than 500 other slaves.

"...We were chained two by two, right leg and left leg, right hand and left hand, packed tightly together in the cargo hold. We lived in our own sweat, vomit and feces. Once a month we were allowed on deck to be washed down with sea water. Most o' us were ill or dying. Two months later I was in the Colonies. The manacles had cut so deeply into my flesh I developed an infection and dysentery. On the auction block I was inspected and my teeth examined. Finally, I was sold to a plantation in Richmond, Virginia belonging to Mr. Gillis Wainwright, who kept his slaves in a terrible way—one shed for 200 of us. I ran away several times. Each time I was found by his hunting dogs. Then one day a new slave came. Her name was Lucy, and her face was like sunlight shining on my heart. We came to care for each other, and the next year we jumped the broom. She became my wife. My master gave us his last name 'Wainwright' like all his slaves..."

Jon's story of rebellion and refusal to adhere to servitude moved Charlotte. She learned Jon and Lucy had a son and that during the war they escaped attempting to reach British-occupied territory.

"...The best course of action for the slaves in America was the Revolutionary War. For many of us, British commanders issued proclamations of freedom in exchange for joining British ranks. My salvation came from General Cornwallis, who vowed to grant us our freedom. Lucy, my son and I had to get to his forces. We ran as fast as we could. I had Lucy's hand and she held our baby. But my master let loose his dogs and slave hunters on us. Lucy fell and twisted her ankle. She stayed with the baby and screamed at me, 'Run, Jon. Run. Get to freedom." I started running again, but Lucy and my son..."

Jon paused, too overcome to continue. Anne wiped her eyes, for his story was too emotional for her. Finally, Jon forced himself to finish. "My wife and son...were caught and mauled by the dogs. Both died. Lucy was having my second child."

Anne wept openly for the story made her long even more for her missing daughter; and Charlotte's hand went to her chest—to the amulet that was never far from her heart—trying not to cry. Jon recounted how he reached British territory and fought for the redcoats after a promise of freedom from Cornwallis. In 1779, he was allowed to board a British ship bound for London. "And this is where I've been for the last five years. Free here in England where we all are when we reach British soil."

Charlotte emitted a sigh of relief thanking God her half-brother and friend survived and emerged stronger. Eager to go to Jon and say something after his tale she stood. But Sir John Wilkes was monopolizing his time. So she wrote a note and gave it to Anne.

"Give this to him. Tell him it's from an old friend, but do not indicate me."

Anne did her queen's bidding and approached Jon, placing the note in his hand. "It's from an old friend."

Jon smiled at Anne. He liked her face. He then read the note, and become flustered. He looked for the woman who had given it to him, but Anne had exited the building with Charlotte, and Jon's audience was waiting on his time.

Upon returning to the palace, the queen wept. Finally, she told Anne that *she* was the princess to whom Jon was referring—that it was her family who sold Jon into slavery. "But why did he protect me? Why did he not say that he was the Queen of England's former slave?"

"Perhaps he doesn't know you are queen."

"Perhaps." Still Charlotte was forlorn. Jon had been through a horrible ordeal—one for which she felt in some way responsible. How could she ever make it right?

The carriage stopped at the side gate of the palace and "Lady Schwellenberg" and Anne the maid entered by the service entrance. No one said a thing, for at Queen's House it was business as usual. Even when Charlotte and Lady Schwellenberg exchanged clothes, life went on as before with no one the wiser.

Forty Five

"Lady Hagedorn has been complaining of stomach pain for the last two days," said Anne as she and the queen were in the garden gathering the first rose blooms of spring.

"She has also been crabby for months," added Charlotte. "I am going to have Doctor Hunter give her a full examination. The cold she suffered last winter lasted well over two months."

"Your Majesty, you have a visitor," they heard Lord Montagu announce from behind them. Charlotte stood as he approached her. "It's a Mister John Wainwright."

The queen frowned. "I do not know a John Wainwright."

"He said if Her Majesty did not know him as such, you may remember him as 'Sir Jon'?"

Charlotte's face lit up gleefully. "Oh my, yes. Yes, send him in." She stood smoothing out her skirt, and handed the flowers to her maid. "Anne, it's Jon Baptiste, whom you met at Phillips Print shop. He's come at last. Please get us some tea and bring it here to the garden."

Anne curtsied and left excitedly as Montagu went to admit Jon. Charlotte's heart was beating in anxious anticipation, and when the Jamaican was finally announced to her in the garden her face beamed at the sight of him.

Jon had dressed formally for her, even wearing a gentleman's periwig. He instantly fell to his knees.

"I never thought I would ever see you again, Your Majesty."

"Nor I, you, Sir Jon," Charlotte responded.

Jon grinned, remembering their long ago game, and their reunion was heartfelt. "I knew you had become Queen of England. My master said so many cities were named in your honor in Virginia where I was sold...Charlotte County, Charlottesville, Mecklenburg County. I only wished the people there could know you as I did, and I prayed you were happy. Have you been?"

Charlotte looked at him, at his still beautiful albeit aging face and kind eyes, and at his lanky body, which was a bit thicker but elegant in his clothing. She wondered how he could have survived with any sanity after enduring his ordeal of the middle passage, enslavement, escape, and still be curious as to her happiness.

"Yes. I would say I am happy," she answered brightly. "I'm told I tend to look at the greenest of the grass when others around me see a dung heap."

They both chuckled. "The king is good to me, and I have my children and causes I care about."

"So I see." Jon smiled knowingly.

"I have been secretly working with the abolition society without them knowing I'm the queen. The king knows nothing of it either. I dress up as my lady in waiting, sneak out of here, travel in a non-ceremonious coach, and listen to every sad and horrid detail of slavery and the trade wishing I could do more."

"It is my mission to see both end. I do it in memory of my wife and son."

Charlotte felt for him. "Your story saddened me. I am so sorry about Lucy and your son."

"You would have liked her spirit. I think your determination regarding this cause is admirable. I'm proud of you—especially knowing what you've been through in your own life."

Charlotte became reflective, and told Jon about the day Wilhelm nearly molested her, and how she felt when she could not reach him in time to prevent him being beaten or sold. She also told him about his mother, Sister Lena. "She took her own life, Jon. Right after she learned you were sold. She and I had a talk, she read her cards, then a few hours later she was found hanging from the rafters with her apron strings tied around her neck. I was devastated."

Jon's head fell in despair, and tears formed despite his fight to control himself. Charlotte motioned for Jon to walk with her through the gardens to the pond, where the water was so still it looked like a smooth sheet of glass. She asked God how to unburden her heart with other information she had to tell him. Finally, she sat on the stone bench on the water's edge and indicated he sit with her.

"Jon, there is so much I must tell you…things I've known for quite some time which will no doubt shock you." She turned from him. How could she say it? It had been such a surprise to her own sense of self all those years ago, she knew this news would leave Jon just as staggered. But Jon took Charlotte's hand and squeezed it a moment before respectfully withdrawing it.

"Just say it, Your Majesty. Can it be worse than telling me of my mother's death?"

Charlotte acquired her full resolve. "Your father was not Joe Herford, the blacksmith. Your father …was *my* father. You and I are siblings."

Astonishment possessed Jon as he shook his head. "My mother and your father?"

"Lena explained their relationship to me before she died. He did not ravage or defile her. They loved each other—and he loved you. But my mother was cruel and vindictive to her." Charlotte stared at the ripples of light glistening on the water. "Just as you know that she was unbearable to me her own flesh-and-blood daughter."

There was a long pause as the truth of the situation sunk in for Jon. "It all makes sense now. Your father was always kind to me and mama and I never saw him go out of his way with any of the other servants like with us." Jon stood and stared at the pond himself embarrassed to look at Charlotte. He became resigned and fiddled with his fingers. "Mama always said I was descended from kings. But it was grandma who insisted I was Joe Herford's boy." Soon, the revelation answered other questions. "I never understood where my hair texture or eye color came from. Or my skin color."

Charlotte began to fiddle with her amulet. "There is more, Jon. Much more." She stood and moved to him. "I am descended from a Moor—an African woman named Magragana ben Bekar. Her family was killed by Portuguese King Alfonso who abducted her and kept her as his concubine. They had a son named Martim who was banished from Portugal. Subsequent generations of Martim's progeny became powerful and far reaching. They ended up in the Netherlands, Portugal and Germany where my family and I were descendants. I was the darkest of them. It's why I always wore face chalk."

Jon was taken aback as Charlotte continued.

"It turns out the king is Magragana's descendant too—as are you. There is far more you need to know but we will leave it here for today." She could see the incredulity and bewilderment reflected on Jon's face. "I am just so happy you survived, Jon. Despite it all, you've become a strong, intelligent, committed man whom I respect and am pleased to have as my half-brother. I'm just sorry the story was born out of your mother's death." Her fingers clutched her amulet. "And my own defilement by Wilhelm."

The two were quiet. Jon remembered that horrible day and his vow to avenge Charlotte's debasement, and the brutality and sale into slavery he suffered. "I have had but one desire that I never shared with anyone, not even my wife," said Jon as he turned to Charlotte, his eyes smoldering. "The only dream I have is for the day I can wrap my fingers around Wilhelm's throat and squeeze the life out of him. I could die a happy man."

"We must work to get past these feelings," Charlotte cautioned her half-brother. "They eat at you and make you bitter."

Jon looked back at Queen's House, Charlotte's domain, and a wistful smile emerged. "Do you know my fondest memories other than being with my wife? They are always of my time with you at Mirow, teaching you to dance the Betty Blue, then seeing your face at Sanssouci when you were ready to try it with Herr Bach. Did you ever hear from him?"

Charlotte nodded wistfully. "Yes. He was music master here—before he died." Then she heard Anne announce, "I've brought tea, Your Majesty."

Turning, Charlotte motioned for Anne to pour their cups, and then introduced them.

"Jon, this is someone very special to me here at Queen's House. Anne Josef from Ethiopia. I met her at Sanssouci that night. Anne, this is Jon Baptiste, my friend."

Jon smiled at Anne, taking in her presence with curious intensity. He took her hand and kissed it. "You were also at Phillips Print Shop. How could I forget such beauty."

Anne blushed, something Charlotte had never seen, and it suddenly occurred to the queen that all the pain of the past could potentially be relegated to yesterday without compromising their tomorrow. And that tomorrow, though informed by their past, could actually be whatever they chose for themselves.

After lunch Charlotte invited Jon to visit she and Anne at Kew Palace where George seldom visited so they could all enjoy each other's company undisturbed.

Jon allowed himself another look at Charlotte's maid, his eyes flashing a private message of admiration. He accepted the invitation and came to call every two weeks like clockwork.

Forty Six

George awoke feeling a sense of foreboding. He had been having his usual headaches, and had slept in his own suite at Queen's House. But this morning he wanted some air and went to the leaded glass window to open it. *How beautiful the foliage of Charlotte's gardens looks today*, he thought. The colors were so rich and vibrant, and he sat in the window thinking. He was 48 years old, and as sovereign felt like a failure. As much as he would not speak about it, the loss of the colonies still caused despair and he felt he had ushered in the end of British greatness.

The king's stomach began churning. But just as he was about to call for Lord Parly to get his bitters, he saw something out the window. It was the elegant black lacquered carriage belonging to Madame Lia de Beaumont at the south entrance of Queen's House. "The undue influence has returned," he mumbled. And a horrible abdominal pain hurled him back to bed.

"Madame Lia is back?"

Charlotte was ecstatic upon hearing from Lord Montagu that her friend was waiting to be received in the Reception Hall. After eight years in France, Lia had finally returned to England. The queen hurried from her chambers and told Lady Schwellenberg that Mme. Lia was waiting. Her Lady made sure the queen looked presentable, then opened the door to the Reception Hall where Madame Lia anxiously waited with a heavy velvet bag at her feet.

When Charlotte entered the room the two women hugged each other for dear life. Lia dropped into a deep curtsey. "Oh, Your Majesty, how I have missed you."

"And I you, Madame Lia." The queen took a moment to have a good look at Lia. Though Lia had grown older in the intervening years she was still a handsome woman, and today she was splendidly dressed in a light-blue silk ensemble. "Look at your dress. It's spectacular."

"Yes, the French do have a way with a needle and thread," Lia chortled. "This is called a *Petit-maitresse en grand robe a corps ouvert*. It's the latest rage at Versailles. All the fashionable ladies at the court of Marie Antoinette wear them. I daresay the Duchess of Devonshire won't have this, and she is the best-dressed woman in London." Lia pulled a large, wrapped bundle from her bag. "So I had one made especially for you so for once you can outdo her."

Charlotte laughed and unwrapped the bundle. Inside was a coral dress of similar design as Lia's. Charlotte gasped, looking in the mantle's mirror. "It's fabulous. How can I thank you?"

"Easily. We shall have some of my wine versus that dreadful earl grey you serve here," Lia chuckled, pulling two bottles of burgundy from her bag. "Only the finest, darling."

As Mme. Lia poured two glasses, Charlotte became serious. "I want to know everything. You were gone so long. I wish to know about your brother's case, and your travels," then her voice dropped, "Especially your trip to Mirepoix."

Mme. Lia took a deep breath, her expression morphing into dour contemplation. "I was hoping we would have had a few more moments of pleasantry before embarking on this."

Charlotte sat back on the divan and gave Mme. Lia a few moments to gather herself. "First, you should know that I am now in Britain for good," stated Lia. "My allegiance to France has soured, and my brother will not be able…to return as you knew him."

"Really? Why?" inquired the queen.

"Suffice to say, Chevalier d'Eon cannot return to England on orders from King Louis."

Lia was quiet for a moment. So was Charlotte. Both knew what now needed to be addressed directly and it was Madame Lia who began after a sigh.

"I was glad to be of service to you, Your Majesty, for so many reasons."

"I hope I have not involved you in this private matter unfairly, Lia. And I certainly pray it has not undermined your safety."

"My concern…is for your own safety, my dear," replied Lia who looked at the queen with a measure of disquiet. "The documents and the amulet you own are…dangerous."

"Is that what the Duke said?" queried the queen.

Lia looked away and found her eyes perusing the floor. She could not face Charlotte. "When I appeared at Duke Francois' door, I became nervous at my mission. I gave him a specific handshake. The handshake indicated my membership in a secret organization which protects its own and any secrets in our possession. It was also designed to put the duke at ease regarding whatever it was I was giving him from you." Mme. Lia then sighed. "I was soon to discover what you gave me, was of world-wide interest and importance."

Charlotte remained silent for a moment then walked to Lia and extended her hand. Lia, in confusion, extended her own in response. Charlotte shook Lia's hand using the lion's paw handshake her father had taught her. "Is that the handshake, Madame?"

Lia stared at the queen. "How do you know such a thing?"

"The question is, how do you?"

Mme. Lia's mind raced. She poured herself another glass of wine to steady her nerves while Charlotte waited patiently, wondering what could possibly create such wavering in her friend. Finally, Madame Lia looked up at the queen.

"I am a Freemason. In 1759 I was initiated into the Lodge of Immortality. Soon after, I became a Fellow craft member. We would meet to discuss matters requiring discretion and honor. Things I cannot divulge now. That handshake is a symbol of Masonic membership."

"I know that. I am a member of the Daughters of David, a secret sister Order which is a subset to the Knights Templar of old."

Mme. Lia frowned. "I suspected you were a Daughter when I saw your amulet that day at St. James. What I did not know was if you knew its significance."

"I do not. Not entirely."

"All of the crowned heads of Europe are related in some way. Families intermarry to keep successions strong, countries associated and aligned politically, and royal bloodlines pure." Lia sipped her wine. "I am of noble birth as well. My maternal descent connects me to the Bourbons of France, from whom King Louis is descended. My paternal descent, however, can be traced back to Robert de Crayon—the second Grand Master of the Knights Templar. As such, it has been my family's task to hide certain knowledge or artifacts from the world."

A staring match occurred between Charlotte and Mme. Lia, as the queen was now coming into a realization. "But there are no women freemasons. Certainly none in the Lodge of Immortality."

Madame Lia looked at Charlotte for a long time, wishing she could bypass this moment. Finally, she had to confess. "I was a member of 'The Secret'—Louis XV's clandestine order of operatives who infiltrated various royal societies and delivered sensitive information to France."

Charlotte was stunned. "So *you* were the spy? I thought it was your brother, Minister d'Eon. Lia, surely you know that such an undertaking is a treasonous act against England."

Mme. Lia then stood never breaking her look to Charlotte. "Do you trust me, as a keeper of your secrets—which I now know?" she asked intensely.

"Of course," Charlotte answered. "You are as close to me as my ladies from Germany."

"Well, it's time I trusted you...with *mine*." Mme. Lia took off her gloves. "It is a curious thing, the sense of entitlement men possess. They have every advantage, every opportunity to succeed because they are instructed from birth to keep women in their place. " Lia began to undress causing Charlotte's eyebrows to raise. "Yet I find that, in most cases, all it takes for a man to yield to change are the gifts God gave to women..." Lia took off her doublets. "You see, women have their allure, their sexuality, their coquettishness..."

Charlotte was uncomfortable as Mme. Lia continued to take off clothing, but said nothing. "As suspected by women all over the world, men are dictated to by their penises. Only the enlightened ones are motivated by their hearts and minds," Lia mused as she unhooked her dress bodice. Charlotte's hand clutched her amulet as Lia stood there in her whalebone hoop skirt, and under-pantaloons. "Men are members of an exclusive club whose credo is to provide for defenseless women, whom they assume cannot fend or think for themselves, nor get on in the world because they lack intellect, cunning, or skill..." She unhooked the hoop skirt and it dropped to the floor. "...So, if you endeavor to effectuate change, and you encounter a group of men who require the company of other men in order to get things done, function with decency, or get your point across..." Lia then pulled off her wig and dropped her under-pantaloons. She was now naked from the waist down. "...I find it more productive to *be* a man."

Charlotte looked at Mme. Lia's flat male chest, then her eyes traveled downward until she saw *it*, and her mouth dropped in stunned amazement and shock.

"It" was Lia's exposed penis. In a deep male voice, her true voice, Lia smiled. "Allow me to re-introduce myself, Your Majesty. I am Chevalier Charles Genevieve Louise Auguste Andre Timothee d'Eon de Beaumont—former French plenipotentiary Minister to Great Britain, and friend to your family, at your service."

The air left the queen's lungs, and seconds later she had fainted to the floor.

✠

When Charlotte awoke on the settee D'Eon had redressed himself as "Mme. Lia." The queen was still in disbelief as she stared at her friend. "All this time, how could you deceive me when you knew how much I liked you as my friend? What do I do now? What do I even call you? Lia? D'Eon?"

Not knowing where to start, d'Eon sat beside her. "For whatever reason, my mother dressed me as a girl when I was young, and I suppose I just became comfortable in women's clothing and identified as one. Years later, as an adult in the French Dragoons, Louis XV wanted to reconcile with Russia and sent two emissaries to discuss the matter with Empress Elisabeth. But the mission failed because her court was closely guarded and consisted primarily of women. Male emissaries were banned. So, in order to infiltrate her court to discuss the issue, Louis had to send a woman. But no woman was capable of handling such a mission. Since I was slight of build, I put on a dress and rouged my lips and cheeks. I pretended to be my sister 'Lia' and easily fooled Louis. He gave me the assignment—and I was successful. Empress Elizabeth and I became close friends. She divulged her secrets—and I gave them all to the

Dauphin. The French monarchy had a victory. I was then inducted into a secret network of spies called *Le Secret du Roi*. We worked for King Louis personally. From then on, it was suggested that my services to *Le Secret* would be better served if I continued spying as a woman—as Lia."

Charlotte sat transfixed as d'Eon continued, not certain if she was infuriated by his betrayal, or awed by his cunning audacity. "So that is what you did with me—befriend me so you could turn our secrets over to the Dauphin?"

"In 1762, I was retained to spy on the Court of St. James. I used my position as Minister to England to collect information for a potential invasion. But I began to provide false information; nothing which would harm England…and most especially you. I did so because I liked you. You and I shared the same ideas, the same desire for bettering British citizens, for freeing Negroes, and ending the slave trade. I liked your spirit and vulnerability. Then I saw your amulet—and knew you and I shared a greater purpose. That meant I had to protect you. Your Majesty, I have known and kept secret your ethnicity ever since that dinner in Mecklenburg. So, no. I did not betray you."

He went on to explain that their friendship brought him great joy as 'Madame Lia' and that he loved their adventures together in London. "Make no mistake. I am no buggerer. I enjoy the affections of women too much. It is just that speculation as to my gender began causing concern here in London, and created a lawsuit in France. It also threatened my pension from the French government. So I had to return to testify in the French court. One of my lovers stood firm, testifying that I was indeed a woman," he chuckled. "What else could he say? He would never admit he'd slept with a man. In the end, they all keep my secret. But now, since I am no longer French minister, Louis XVI, the new king, has forced me to maintain the role of a woman permanently or not receive my pension. So I am now in exile here in London as 'Lia d'Eon.'"

I could not believe the events of that day. The woman whom I trusted with my secrets and my heart—was in fact a man. And so clearly male. Why had I not seen it? She did have a masculine demeanor now that I knew the truth. Lia was never a beautiful woman, but I myself had been deemed an unattractive woman, so I tended to look past these elements to find the beautiful core of a human being. How amazing that what you see, or fail to, is due to that which your mind dictates. Now that Lia had revealed herself to be a man—a man in a dress was sitting before me. Did it change my opinion of her as a person? Or him? What a confusing, fearsome thing to behold. I did not wish to discriminate as so many others had done. Was not d'Eon, someone who struggled with his identity, to be pitied? Understood? Was it any different from my husband, the king, who needed the same pity.

"Does the king know about your pension or exile here?"

D'Eon shook his head. "No, but to satisfy the bets I will accept to being a woman. In fact, my friend Chevalier St. George wants to duel with me dressed as such in an exhibition here in London. We'll make a fortune."

"Duel?" Charlotte was incredulous.

D'Eon chuckled. "I am the best swordsman in Europe—dress or no dress."

Charlotte didn't know what to make of it, but d'Eon became emotional. "Please allow our friendship to continue despite my secret. I adore you, Your Majesty. I'd be lost without our relationship and would be content to paint your portrait on the canvas of my gratitude for the rest of my life. Please do not abandon me."

Charlotte reached out her hands to touch his smooth face. "Do not worry. I will not abandon you." She now stood, wobbly at first, but soon finding her bearings. "However, I suggest you find the strength to declare Lia and d'Eon to be one and the same."

"Yes, but *which* one of the same?" Lia whispered humorously.

Charlotte chuckled, then became serious. "Now. What about my scrolls and my amulet?"

Madame Lia raised the dress she wore to reveal the underskirt.

"Not this again," moaned Charlotte. But Lia continued to turn up the underside of the underskirt until she reached four carefully sewn deep pockets. Each held one wooden container which she retrieved for the queen. Then in another pocket, she retrieved a roll of carefully folded pages and gave those to Charlotte as well.

"This is everything you asked for: your original scrolls and their translations. They were in Hebrew, Coptic and Aramaic—which was in such an ancient form of the language it was difficult to decipher. Some of the words or pages are missing. But you must read it."

Charlotte looked at her friend, then gave her a kiss. Mme. Lia took this to mean it was time she left. Respectfully, she bowed to her queen and turned to leave.

"Lia?" said Charlotte with a warm smile, "Thank you."

Lia nodded and then left. Charlotte bolted the door behind her, then used the back stairs and went to her chambers where, with rapt fascination, she began reading the translations.

Forty Seven

The Diary of Magragana ben Bekar

On a sweltering June morning in 1249, my honey-colored baby labored to push its way through the labyrinth of my womb. Even at this vulnerable, most susceptible moment its destiny was already charted, for this was no ordinary child, and it was no ordinary birth. I painfully struggled in my confinement, for my child was upside down within my birth canal. Clarissa del Soto, the old Portuguese midwife and, some said, mystic, was muttering to herself as she reached inside of me to turn the baby around and help birth it.

'Esta es un chico,' Clarissa said when she finally laid the slippery child on my breast next to the gold amulet hanging from my neck. I smiled, for the first thing I noticed was the unusual raised birthmark on the baby's body which was bright red in color on his left shoulder. Clarissa nodded, 'Marca del destino.'

I touched it. Yes. It is a 'mark of destiny,' I thought, then touched the almost identical birthmark on my own body. "Perhaps he is the one." I prayed my son was the destined one, for even though he was a bastard, he was a bastard with royal blood coursing his veins. He was the son of the fifth King of Portugal, Afonso III, whose ancestor, Afonso the Great, killed or expelled huge numbers of Moors during the original Christian reconquest of Portugal one hundred years earlier. The proud Moors, from the north shore of Africa, were primarily Muslim. After Portugal was reclaimed from our reign we were forced to choose between two faiths if we were to remain in the country. Those who accepted Christianity were called Moriscos. Those faithful to the Islamic faith were called Mudejares. I was a Mudejares and the king was intent to rid Portugal of my sect. Afonso had marched through city after city, killing Moors including my father King Madrem and my brothers, Myoda and Ennis. He then took me as his rite of conquest and had me baptized with the Christian name, Magdalena Gil.

But I was too proud and would never accept this new moniker, and chose to remain faithful to my Muslim faith and name. I had been born Magragana ben Bekar, and that is who I shall remain.

Upon learning that I was to bear his child, King Afonso commandeered me to the hilltop home of his uncle Hertos where I remained under arrest for the duration of my confinement. I was never allowed to return to the palace.

Every day Clarissa brought my son to be nursed, then took the baby away. I had to accept that he was being raised Christian as evidenced by the Christian name he had been given: Martim Afonso Chicorro. My child was being reared without knowledge of my existence, or access to his rightful religion and heritage.

Then one day Clarissa turned to me as she was about to leave, and with vision-ary sincerity exclaimed: "One day the stars will converge to bring you and this child together. On that day, it will unite you and the fruits of David." Clarissa touched the amulet hanging from my neck, then left. That day I stopped crying, and started to write. I removed my amulet and looked at its raised markings, wishing I could ac-quaint my son with its meaning, as well as his religion. Then I thought about the amulet's journey, which my father had recounted so many times.

During the first Crusade, after the fall of Jerusalem to the Saracens, the amulet was smuggled out of the bowels of King Solomon's Temple along with other treasure and artifacts by the nine original Knights Templar. The Templars had excavated under Temple Mount below which were the ruins of Solomon's first Temple, and in addition to confiscating coins, gemstones and gold treasures, they also took sacred relics, charts, and scrolls containing forbidden knowledge and Gnostic teachings dating back to the time of the Essenes. Under the guise of safeguarding pilgrims in and out of Jeru-salem, the Templars secretly transported and housed the Solomon treasure in secret locations along with other scrolls and sacred relics from the crucifixion. They also pro-tected descendants of the persecuted bloodline of King David.

Then, to commemorate the founding of the Order, nine amulets were designed af-ter the original Solomon amulet. The original, designed by Solomon himself in 892 BC, was created to house small amounts of myrrh used for medicinal purposes and, it is said, his famous ring used to possess and control the demons and spirits who helped build the first Temple. On the top he placed the Solomon sigil—the five point star with the name of God on it, and along the sides he had the five words that can invoke

the demon Asmodeus into service, for good for Solomon had dominion over them given to him by God. Before King Solomon died, he placed the amulet with his impressive treasure in the bowels of the great temple. Each amulet designed for the Templars was handed down to a succeeding Grand

Master or Seneschal or their family from the original nine. My amulet was passed on to the second Grand Master, Robert de Craon, upon the death of Hughes de Payens. Then, the amulet mysteriously went missing. Years later, it emerged just as mysteriously around the neck of Prince Hazub—the last Prince of the Davidic dynasty who was also descended from a 5ᵗʰ century Frankish king named Merovech. King Merovech was noted as the first ruler of the Merovingian bloodline. He and his offspring could be identified by a red, raised birthmark which became the insignia of the Grail Guardians. Prince Hazub is said to have hidden a sacred treasure inside the amulet—two thorns from the rush bush of thorns driven into the head of Jesus Christ and removed by Joseph of Arimathea after His death. It is said Joseph kept many thorns from the Crown of Thorns as keepsakes of Christ—until the persecution of the Jews drove him from Jerusalem. Joseph was also an ancestor of Prince Hazub who thus received both the thorns and the amulet from separate inheritances. After placing the thorns into the amulet, Hazub, who was versed in ancient languages, deciphered the five word invocation but added that these words should never be spoken aloud. He then created a way to open and close the amulet so only future generations of Merovingians knew how. A drawing of the procedure accompanies these scrolls.

Thereafter, the amulet was handed down to the first-born male of each succeeding generation who bore a striking birthmark until it reached Yahya Ha Nasi, known as "El Negro," Lord of Aldeia dos Negros in Portugal. Yahya was my fourth great-grandfather, who passed it down to Yahia Ben Yahi III, who passed it down to Bakr Ben Yahia I, who passed it down to Yahia Ben Bekr, who passed it down to Bekr Ben Yahia II, who passed it down to Aloandro Ben Bekar—my father—also known as King Madrem. So we became a mosaic of Mudejares, Morisco, and Judaic. My father would have passed the amulet to my brother Ennis, but knowing he and his sons would be dead at the hands of King Afonso, he put the amulet around my neck and commanded me to 'run.' As expected, my father and brothers were beheaded by Afonso, who caught me as I ran. The rest is my current life. I have asked Allah to allow me to be the portal through which his words flow that I might have vengeance, and so my son would come to know his birthright.

Many years have passed, but I write and pray. I tear the lining from the velvet drapes hanging in my room and hide my writing and these scrolls in the folds between them, less Afonso's uncle came to spy. I have watched my son, who is called Prince Martim, grow tall and proud. He has been well educated and speaks several languages. I witnessed him standing with Afonso and Queen Matilda, the barren woman who has raised him, as the city rejoiced in the annual harvest. I saw Martim at 18 triumphantly march into the city having continued Afonso's conquest to expand Portuguese Christian domination into Spain.

Then my prayers were answered. In 1270, King Afonso III of Portugal and King Alfonso X of Spain made a deal to avoid war. If Afonso married the Spanish king's illegitimate daughter Beatriz, Spain would relinquish all rights to the Algarve when a male heir was born of the union. King Afonso agreed. The moment the marriage was announced, Afonso's still alive wife and Queen, Matilda, died of heartbreak. Upon Matilda's death, Beatriz became Queen and Prince Dinis, the son she had with Afonso, became legitimate heir to the throne. King Afonso publicly bestowed all his possessions to Prince Dinis and not to my son Prince Martim, who was forcibly removed from the palace and banished from Portugal.

When word reached me of Martim's expulsion, I had to find him. With Clarissa's help I gathered my most prized possessions, my writing and the amulet, and escaped from a window Clarissa left open. Two days later, I found my son on the road out of the city and hurled myself in front of his carriage with my arms outstretched to prostrate myself before him.

Martim emerged from his coach mixed with curiosity and disdain for me. In front of him was his enemy—a Moor woman. Yet I stood and reached out to touch his cheek and inexplicably, Martim did not recoil from me. I told him who I was and that I had asked Allah to allow me to find him so he could take comfort in the great destiny which lay before him. Martim did not understand me and questioned that 'destiny.' I told him he was the son of greatness and a great people. But he had been denied knowledge of it by his father—that he had come to believe his mother was Queen Matilda but she had not bore him. Martim perused my face, affronted and with a mind to strike me. I prayed Martim had inherited my compassion rather than his father's impenitence. In a small voice, choking back tears, I told him I was his mother, that it was I who bore him. At that I fell to my knees before him, which left Martim stupefied. I saw the tiny dark hairs rising on his golden arms as they stood against the sweat from the hot sun. Finally, he backed off to his carriage then, surprisingly, returned to me. He drew his sword, pointed it at my throat. He asked what proof I had. I spoke softly, for the tip of his sword was a whisper from killing me. I explained that he possessed a raised, red birthmark on his left shoulder.

After a moment Martim lowered his sword. He unhooked his tunic to reveal the raised red birthmark. Through my tears I pulled my dress top to the side, revealing my own birthmark. In the long, incredulous silence which followed, I reached into my bag and gave him the wooden containers with these writings. I told him they were proof of my claims and our family legacy. Martim opened a container and uncurled my writings to read it. Soon, he sat on the grass and I watched him turn the color of milk as the contents overwhelmed him.

"Do you have the Solomon amulet?" he asked.

"Yes," I nodded, then gave it to him. "We must protect it."

"According to your writings, this amulet is made of zahab mufaz gold—the God-ordained gold of King Solomon. The symbols on it are the 'Magen David'—the Solomon Seals—the same symbols on the ring given to King Solomon by God which gave him power over demons."

"Yes. It allowed Solomon to command them during the building of the first Temple. It is said that when Solomon wasn't wearing the ring, he hid it inside a talisman fashioned from the same special gold commanded by God that his father, King David, use for the Temple. He then placed the holy name of God on the talisman, as well as the sigil of God. You know it as the Star of David. They say the talisman is also imbued with power if you know the proper incantations."

Martim opened the amulet according to the diagram and found himself awed by the two thorns inside. He then swore to protect what he had with his life. He also swore to kill his father and Prince Dinis. It was the only way to not only take his revenge, but to correct injustices done to the Moors; injustices of which he had been a part. I warned him against such a deed. I told him to have his revenge in a way so as to profit us with power. "Plant your seed with Moors, so we may grow strong and prosper in our rightful greatness and place in the world..."

✠

Charlotte sat transfixed as thoughts bombarded her. The amulet she had been given charge of all these years had possessed the infamous magic ring of King Solomon and now contained precious thorns driven into the head of Jesus before the crucifixion. Could it be true? Was it possible? And what about the five word invocation? Was it possible to summon and command demons just by speaking the words? What were those words?

Charlotte trembled with nervousness and went to the reliquary and retrieved her father's diary. She matched what he had documented with what was written on the translations, which went many generations back. Her father's charts going forward showed that King Afonso III's legitimate son became King Dinis of Portugal. But Afonso's bastard son with Magragana—Martim Afonso Chicorro, married Ines Lourenco de Sousa, a mixed Moor from the House of de Sousa. They left Portugal, but Martim maintained his family's tradition. He passed the scrolls and amulet to his son Martim Afonso Chicorro II, who also inherited the birthmark, and who, upon becoming a Templar at age 19, was responsible for the amulet reemerging in Templar hands. In turn, his son Vasco Martim de Sousa III begat Alfonso de Sousa Chicorro, whose daughter Mencia gave birth to Margarita de Castro y Sousa. Margarita married Count Jean II de Neufchatel, a descendant of Geoffroi de Charny—the Templar knight who owned the Holy Shroud. From there came Charlotte's father and mother's family genealogy down to Charlotte herself. This explained the reliquary and amulet being passed down to the queen herself.

Charlotte began pacing the room, thinking about what to do. She looked at her amulet differently now. She saw the foreign words. She saw the strange sigil. Now she wanted to open the amulet to see the thorns. But how did it open? Every twist and turn yielded no movement and there was no scroll in her possession which offered instructions as Magragana indicated.

Soon, there came a tap at the door. Charlotte quickly gathered the translations and containers and hurried them under her bed. "Yes?"

Lady Lizzie entered the chamber with a dress. "Good morning, Your Majesty. I thought you might want to wear this for breakfast," she said with her lilting Scottish brogue.

"Breakfast?" wondered Charlotte aloud.

"Yes. It's six-thirty." Lady Lizzie looked around. "Have you been up all night?"

Charlotte threw open the drapes. Indeed the sun was out. "Good Lord." She turned to Lizzie. "Send Anne in."

"But Your Majesty, *I* am responsible for your wardrobe and dressing you," Lizzie lamented. "There is protocol…"

"…Which, I remind you, is to carry out your queen's demands," Charlotte snapped.

Lady Lizzie hurried off, leaving Charlotte rueful, yet unapologetic.

When finally Anne appeared, Charlotte gave her an order trying to hide her concern. "Find Madame Lia and bring her here immediately."

Forty Eight

By mid-afternoon, Lia Charles d'Eon de Beaumont was standing before Charlotte in the music room. The king had been in constant abdominal pain and doctors were regularly attending him. He was cautioned against moving about and thus consigned to his apartments. This freed Charlotte's use of the palace, and she invited Lia into the room farthest from the king's ears.

After a sip of wine her maid poured, Charlotte turned to Anne. "Go get the item."

Anne curtsied and left. But when she reached Charlotte's chambers, she was surprised to see Lady Lizzie leaving them. Anne hid behind a corner observing as Lizzie quickly moved down the hall and up to the third floor. She then entered Charlotte's chambers as directed.

In the interim, Charlotte and Lia d'Eon were still unsure how to proceed in the uncharted waters of d'Eon's "female revelation" the day before. Charlotte perused her former "girl" friend.

"It will take me a moment to absorb all that I have read, coupled with what I have seen and now know about you. But I do thank you for your assistance in my highly private matter."

D'Eon nodded in gratitude. "I was worried you changed your mind and I'd be arrested."

"Never. But I do have another favor." Charlotte removed the amulet from her neck and gave it to d'Eon. "I assume you read the translations, or were told of their content."

"Some," nodded Lia.

"Do you know how to open the amulet?"

At first Mme Lia was tentative, but soon after held out her hand for the amulet. She beheld it as it gleamed in her fingers and she squeezed it. Her eyes closed praying for absolution. This was the amulet of Solomon in her hand and she tried to open it. Yet it wouldn't budge.

"Apparently I cannot," she confessed. "I wish to God I could."

Anne then knocked and entered with a purple velvet sheath. Charlotte placed the amulet back around her neck as her maid gave the sheath to her then left. Charlotte motioned d'Eon closer and pulled out the contents of the sheath—her father's 14th century Templar sword. Charlotte caressed the shaft of it. "This sword once belonged to the Templar knight from whom I am descended. It was passed down to my father and then to my brother, who gave it to me when I left Mecklenburg." She pointed the razor-sharp tip at d'Eon's chest. "If you are indeed a swordsman as you say you are, surely you must know how to use one."

"Of course."

"Teach me to use this one. I will need to know how to protect myself."

Mme. Lia gasped at the request, yet was challenged. "But you have guards, a husband. Everything you need for protection. What if something happened…"

"Something has already happened," Charlotte stated flatly. "I know I possess information and an object of significant interest to those who would do me harm. Now teach your queen how to parry—as men do. For I shall want to go away from Queen's House sometime and not have the king or my guards know. For those times I want to know how to protect myself."

Lia d'Eon bowed. "Very well. Then let us begin our lessons starting Monday." Then he left Queen's House. In the stark silence of the room, Charlotte thought. The past could not be changed—only her perception of it. The future was what she needed to manage. Though the amulet and the scrolls were part of her past, their translations renewed a purpose in Charlotte—and she knew what she had to do.

Thus, every Monday and Wednesday for the next month Charlotte, dressed in male fencing attire, learned the rudiments of sword fighting from Lia d'Eon while George was either hunting, in meetings or in bed.

Lia, having given Charlotte's suggestion some thought, and knowing she was forced to be female or risk losing her pension from France, asked Charlotte to continue to call her "Lia." Charlotte, who valued their friendship, agreed, and kept Lia's secret.

"Your low quarte is not protected," warned Lia during a lesson. "And keep your wrist pronated like this." Lia showed the queen the move. "Your sword arm should be higher here so it doesn't veer to the right during the moulinet leaving the left side of your head open. All your opponent has to do is hammer a horizontal quarte into your left temple to kill you."

Two weeks later, having dispensed with her father's Templar sword for the more appropriate saber sword, Charlotte quickly adapted, enjoying the competition and a newfound confidence. She kept her arm up, anticipating Lia's left quarte jabs. The metallic sound of their swords crashing against each other created a remarkable feeling in Charlotte who loved when they parried, fenced, or dueled. Eventually, the queen became so skilled that Mme. Lia told her she "handled her saber well." Having this skill at her command gave Charlotte a sense of self-assurance and the cocksure smugness of a man. Finally, Lia felt Charlotte was ready.

"Your Majesty, I have an excellent idea for your next meeting at Phillips Printing Shop."

⊱✠⊰

The following month, Lia d'Eon arrived at Queen's House carrying a valise. She and Charlotte met in the queen's chambers, where Lia instructed Lady Schwellenberg and Lady Hagedorn to undress the queen and bind down her breasts with a length of muslin.

"I told you I had an idea for your next meeting at Phillips, Your Majesty. Now you'll know what it is to be taken seriously by men." Lia asked her ladies to help Charlotte into a pair of maroon pantaloons, a jacket and a powdered gentleman's wig she had brought in the valise. Afterward, she scrubbed off Charlotte's makeup and tucked the queen's hair under the wig.

Soon, the hard work began. Lia had to teach the queen how to act masculine, to speak deeply, and walk with the pride and character of a man. Lady Hagedorn, Lady Schwellenberg and Anne looked on and found it humorous. Charlotte did too, for if her ladies or Sir Albert knew that her teacher was in fact a man, it would cease to be.

Lady Schwellenberg, jeweled, wigged and dressed as "the queen," accompanied the others to the music room, passing Lady Lizzie, who was also none the wiser. She played cards with Sir Albert, Anne and Lady Hagedorn, who was feeling poorly. Meanwhile, Lia insisted Charlotte choose a male name for herself, as this is how she would be presented at Phillips. The queen nodded, knowing exactly who she would become, then she and Lia left the palace.

Within the hour they arrived at the anti-slavery meeting at Phillips Printing Shop as Madame Lia d'Eon de Beaumont and "Sir Charles Frederick." Charlotte as Sir Charles sat down in the front row, with Sir Allan Ramsey on one side and Sir John Wilkes two seats over on the other. Neither recognized the newcomer. Once again, the women were seated in the back. But today Mme. Lia would not stand for it. She boldly sat in the second row, challenging anyone who insisted she sit with the other women.

Soon, Hannah More and other women slowly moved to the front. Charlotte smiled at d'Eon. It had begun. Change was in the air and the agents of freedom at Phillips Printing Shop were forced to accept every precious step.

Thomas Clarkson began the meeting with an update on the signatures he and William Wilberforce had collected for the petition for Parliament. "Through our collective efforts, we have 1500 anti-slavery and anti-slave trade petitions with which to lobby Parliament signed by over a million people in Britain."

There was applause. "We have also sold several hundred pieces of Josiah Wedgwood's pottery, which has brought in enough money to print campaign flyers." He pointed to a table where several books lay on top. "I am also offering copies of my book *A Summary View of the Slave Trade and Consequences of Its Abolition* and pray you all buy it, read it, and pass it on."

"Sir Charles" purchased a book and, as the meeting went on, offered up ideas. One such idea was that they initiate a boycott against sugar or tobacco harvested in the West Indies on the backs of slaves, and transported by slave ships. "If we can organize such a boycott effectively, I believe we could get as many as 200,000 people to refuse to buy those products. That would clearly send a message of strength," he insisted.

The group agreed, including Clarkson and Wilberforce, and all went about formulating a method by which to initiate this.

> *My opinions were being valued. And whether that value was due in part to the visual perception that I was a man or because they were valid, solid ideas did not matter. A difference was being made and I was part of it. I loved being a part of something important, something meaningful, something larger than Drawing Rooms at St. James, or Wilkes' condemnation of the king. The feeling was deeply satisfying and powerful—one I wished women could experience as part of their natural birthright. But then, that was a cause I had to place in second position.*

On the return trip to Queen's House, Lia asked Charlotte how she felt in the guise of a man, if it had given her some sense of perspective. Charlotte mused at the scenario. Here was Lia d'Eon, a man, dressed as an undervalued woman, and the Queen of England, a woman, dressed as an aristocratic man. It was sublime, and she had to admit it was one of the most powerful feelings she had ever experienced and could not wait to chronicle it in her journal.

But as they reached the side entrance of the palace, Sir Albert ran out in a panic. "Thank God you're here. Your chamberlain has been searching for you everywhere. When he entered the music room and saw Lady Schwellenberg in your clothing he became unhinged. She gave him an excuse that you gave her the clothing as a gift, but we know he did not believe her."

"What's happened, Sir Albert?"

"It's Lady Hagedorn."

Charlotte ran up the stairs pulling off the wig and man's jacket. After a stop in her chambers to drop off the book, and put on an over-robe, she ran to Lady Hagedorn's quarters.

Haggy was in bed sweating from fever. She'd had a stroke. Lady Schwellenberg, still in the queen's clothing, was there as well as a doctor tending the 45-year-old Lady-in-Waiting.

The queen held Lady Hagedorn's hand. "How bad is she?"

"I'm afraid the stroke has affected the left side of her body," said Stockmar. "It's been coming on for some time—the dizziness, fevers, general malaise. All we can do now is wait."

Lady Hagedorn's right hand motioned slightly for Charlotte to bend in closer. The queen did as instructed. In a slurred whisper Lady Hagedorn implored: "If I survive the next two days, I want to go back to Mecklenburg. I wish to die in my home country."

Charlotte promised her lady she would accommodate her. A month later, boxes, luggage and trunks were carried out of the palace by pages and placed into a carriage. Lady Hagedorn was carried out by Sir Albert Papendiek and placed inside the coach, along with a nurse. They were followed by Charlotte, Sir Albert's daughter Charlotte Papendiek, age 19, and Lady Schwellenberg, who was in tears. Everyone hugged Lady Hagedorn. But when it came to the queen, her lady was overcome with emotion and held Charlotte tightly with her good right arm.

"I have loved every moment taking care of you," Lady Hagedorn slurred with difficulty.

Charlotte cautioned her lady not to talk for she, too, was distraught and had no words without tears. The nurse closed the door and drew the velvet drapes inside the coach, then tapped at the roof.

Charlotte's tears flowed into Lady Schwellenberg's chest, for neither knew how to say goodbye to their trusted friend, companion and partner in crime, Lady Juliana Hagedorn.

Forty Nine

For weeks after Lady Hagedorn's departure, Charlotte was depressed. Though she had solved part of the mystery of her amulet and the reliquary scrolls, and had become instrumental in the abolitionist plans taking place at Phillips Print Shop, losing Haggy, her beloved cohort weighed heavily.

Anne, however, found a satisfying reason to keep her own spirits above the fray. She found great delight in her short visits with Jon Baptiste. They took place at Kew Palace every other week. After Charlotte and Jon would have tea, he would walk with Anne in the formal gardens. She would point out all of the flowers the queen was cultivating, and Jon was impressed by her knowledge of their scientific names, as well as her ability to speak several languages. Little by little Anne taught Jon a phrase and he remarked on how much she was like Charlotte in humor and temperament. It wasn't long before Anne found him to be the most agreeable man she had ever known, and she began to melt at the sight of him.

Equally, Jon's heart was not immune to the charms of Charlotte's maid, and after a short while he began to visit the queen as much to spend time with Anne as to see Charlotte. One afternoon, as Lady Schwellenberg was dressing Charlotte for lunch at Kew Palace, the queen glanced out of the window and saw a wondrous sight. There in her garden, amongst the azaleas and delphiniums, were Anne and Jon, exchanging a moment of affection. She motioned to Lady Schwellenberg to come take a look. Both women watched wistfully through the glass like two voyeurs as Jon took Anne into his arms and kissed her. Anne's arms encircled his strong body as she leaned into his passionate embrace. Perhaps now Jon would find some small happiness again despite all that went before, thought Charlotte, and for a brief moment her mind trailed back to her time with Christian all those years ago. Perhaps for Jon and Anne a new future was possible. One Charlotte vowed to help them attain.

Later that evening, as Charlotte was at her desk reading Thomas Clarkson's book, Anne entered to turn down the bed. She took note of the book and a curious smile betrayed her otherwise serious countenance as Charlotte looked up. "You seem in want of unburdening yourself, Miss Josef."

"Perhaps, ma'am."

"Then, unburden," insisted the queen, putting the book on the desk top. "Let me guess. You are in love with Jon Baptiste."

After a moment, Anne finally nodded. "He is unlike any man I have ever known—not that I have known many men. Most have been brutes that merely used me for folly." She smiled to herself. "But Jon is so tender, such a loving, respectful, humorous man." She stopped a moment before continuing. "Your Majesty, I carry his child."

Charlotte's hands first went to her mouth, and then reached out to touch her maid's belly. "Shall you marry? Oh, do marry him. Make this child legitimate."

"We intend to," smiled Anne, who took a moment to think about how to approach the queen with her other news. Charlotte saw that Anne's expression had tightened. "What is it?"

Anne bit her lip slightly. "You once asked me to be your eyes and ears here. Well, I have seen things I need to present to you."

"Such as?"

Anne began fiddling with her own amulet concealed beneath her dress. "It's Lady Lizzie. You cannot trust her. I have seen her lurking where it's inappropriate for some time."

But before Anne could finish or Charlotte react, George barged in, holding the pair of maroon men's pantaloons Charlotte used for her escapes into London. He motioned for Anne to leave, which she did, then he hurled the pantaloons at Charlotte.

"As these do not belong to me, nor Prince George, why were they in your chambers?"

Charlotte quickly lied. "I don't know. Perhaps one of my ladies was entertaining."

"In Her Majesty's boudoir?" Suddenly George became distracted by the book on Charlotte's desk. He picked it up, and read the title and author's name. "Thomas Clarkson? The abolitionist? What are you doing with this?"

Charlotte said nothing. Suddenly there was an anxious knock, followed by Anne's hurried re-entry. She curtsied to the king. "I'm sorry, Your Majesty. I forgot my book."

George glared at the maid. "How dare you bring such reading material into this palace. How is it you even own such a book?"

"Do not threaten her, George," warned Charlotte. "She can read whatever she likes."

"Here, freedom of what is written and read has limits."

"Yes, and those limits and freedoms are conditioned by you and Parliament." Charlotte jibed, taking the book from George and giving it to Anne, with whom she exchanged a knowing look. Anne left. George angrily waved the pantaloons. "You can dismiss and relegate abolitionist literature to your maid, who I suspect cannot even read, but I know your opinions on the slave subject. It's one you pound into my head daily. Remember, I also found out about Bach, and I will find out about this man, whoever he is, too," he snapped, tossing the pantaloons to the floor. "I make a point of knowing what goes on in all of my homes!" He left rubbing his temples.

I became worried. What else did George know? And what would he do about it? Then there was the business of Anne's revelation about Lady Lizzie. Was she the one giving George information? I had to not only be sure, but more careful than ever. Who knew what insane notions George could take up in his condition.

The next morning, Anne waited until George left the palace to approach Charlotte. She returned Clarkson's book to the queen who thanked her for the rescue from George the previous night and the information she conveyed to her. Anne curtsied and hurried away just as Lady Lizzie came up to Charlotte and handed the queen her mail. She reminded Charlotte she was to sit for Sir Thomas Gainsborough for a family portrait later that afternoon.

Charlotte took the letters and absently fished through them—until one froze her in place. She looked at the handwriting, opened it, read it, then began to physically shake. Turning to Lady Lizzie, she became shrill. "Lady Lizzie, where did this letter come from?"

Lizzie shrugged. "It was amongst the others delivered by post."

"And it was not opened for inspection? How can that be?"

"I am sorry, Your Majesty. I was not paying much attention."

"You will do so henceforth, Madame. All manner of illegal imports can be slipped to His Majesty or I if not disposed of first. That is why we have inspectors!" she yelled. "Now find Anne and bring her to me at once!"

Lady Lizzie bowed and hurried out as Charlotte held her stomach, then re-read the letter.

As she went through each and every word of the horrendous, loathsome bile it contained, her stomach churned as much as the king's had the evening before. Her world should have been coming together. Instead, it was falling apart because of one letter. She had to find a chair in which to sit and think. *Of course he would write to her*, she thought. He knew she had what he wanted, and she was surprised he had not contacted her sooner.

Moments later, Anne ran up to Charlotte who ushered her maid into the nearby library. "Tell Jon. I need to see him at Kew Palace tomorrow afternoon. It's important."

"Yes, ma'am." Anne rushed off.

☩

Charlotte's arms were tightly folded across her chest as she listened to the music from Christian's music box. The letter was in her hand and she was pacing. Finally, at two o'clock, Jon was admitted to the Drawing Room at Kew Palace and he rushed over to her.

"Your Majesty, I came as soon as I got your message."

Charlotte handed him the letter. As Jon read it Charlotte paced.

"Dear Cousin Charlotte.

Forgive my not writing since you became the queen of such a wealthy and powerful country as England, but I have been concerned with more pressing, selfish needs—my own survival. Your brother Grand Duke Adolph unceremoniously excised me from the royal stipend as punishment for what he determined was an assault by me on your person. As a result, my wife Helena left me at the behest of Lord Gregory, and I have been struggling for years. I now find myself financially insolvent and Grand Duke Charles will not help.

Now, I look to you for assistance. I will be frank. I require a home in Germany or perhaps England, 20,000 talers, and a steady pension to allow me to live comfortably. In return, I shall not publicly discuss, sell, or reveal matters of most embarrassment to you as queen, and you can continue to remain silent on the same. I await your speedy response in the form of a bank draft sent to the address below. In the meantime I hope all is well with you and most especially the king, whom I am anxious to meet.

Yours faithfully, Wilhelm."

Jon was disbelieving. "After all he's done to you, your cousin is demanding money?"

"And I'm afraid he has at least two scrolls from father's reliquary."

"What will you do?"

Charlotte took the letter and hurled it into the fireplace. "That!"

"Wilhelm is dangerous. Perhaps you should negotiate with him."

"No. Such action begets a repeat action. Blackmail never ends."

The queen wandered to the window and gazed out at a wren as it flew from the ledge. "How I long for our days in Mecklenburg when all I cared about was dancing."

Jon's heart was breaking for her while trying to contain his own anger. He went to the mantle and wound up Christian's ballerina music box. Both listened to the music for a while.

"We are too old now, with too many responsibilities for pretending, Your Majesty."

Charlotte nodded. But deep in her heart she lingered on two small words that embodied big sentiment: "If only."

Fifty

On 11 July 1788, Sir Albert was brushing back my hair to place it under a wig in preparation for our Tuesday levee. Suddenly, Swelly ran into the room and announced that Anne had just given birth. Though I was queen and should not have expressed so much emotion as I did over an 'underling servant,' I nonetheless rushed from the room and quite strikingly went below stairs to the servant's quarters where I found my maid in bed holding the most beautiful pecan-colored baby girl. I sent for Jon and within two hours he was with her. The two had been married a month earlier and I was approving, for I wanted legitimacy for their child. When Jon saw his daughter he burst into tears. I had never seen such a display of emotion from him ever before. Then he pulled aside the blanket to hold her aloft in the air and I saw the baby's birthmark. I held my heart. This baby, my niece, this little brown angel, was Merovingian, thus a Daughter of David. She was the destiny which blood could not deny. Yet Wilhelm's letter continued to haunt me.

Two months later, Charlotte was writing in her diary as Lady Schwellenberg did her makeup, using a fresh jar of Sir Allan Ramsey's natural-looking chalk paint. Lady Lizzie and Lady Charlotte Papendiek, the queen's new Mistress of the Bedchamber, who replaced Lady Hagedorn, helped her with the pannier and doublets of her gown. All of her helpers were frustrated, because Charlotte was determined to finish writing and sometimes they had to wait until she completed a line or phrase. Writing in her diary allowed Charlotte to think about a good many things, and that afternoon she found herself concerned about Anne. Charlotte was worried because she had not seen her since sending Anne to Phillip's Printing Shoppe three days earlier. Nor had she seen Anne and Jon's baby.

Finally, Charlotte finished her entry and put her diary away to allow her ladies to dress her. Lizzie watched as the queen put the diary in the drawer of the secretary, locked it, then left the key on top as she became distracted by something—stains on the lace of her gown.

"Why was this not cleaned properly?" queried Charlotte.

"I apologize for the stains, Your Majesty," answered Lady Papendiek. "But when I called for Anne to re-clean it, I was told she no longer worked at Queen's House. She was sold."

"Sold? On whose authority?" demanded Charlotte.

No one answered quickly and Charlotte was outdone. "Get out. All of you!" she snapped. Sir Albert, Lady Papendiek, Lady Schwellenberg and Lady Lizzie all started out. Charlotte angrily gathered up her skirts and marched out of her chambers, pushing Lady Lizzie out of her way. Lady Lizzie thus became the last to leave and, upon noticing everyone else had gone, furtively stayed behind. She saw Charlotte's key on top of the desk. All manner of thoughts ran through her mind, and the lady in waiting found herself tempted. She knew Charlotte, and she knew an altercation would ensue between her and the king that would last at least twenty minutes. She had seen it happen before. More importantly, she knew Charlotte's diary was in the desk. How many years had she seen the queen writing in it? What secrets were in those pages?

She had to know, but she had to be careful. Lady Lizzie crept to the desk and picked up the key. Her hands were trembling and she shuddered at the idea of the wrong she was doing. Yet, she furtively unlocked the drawer and eased out the red leather diary—the keeper of Charlotte's clandestine life—and began to read it. Soon she found what she was looking for and was shocked. She learned of Charlotte's love for Bach, the guilt she felt over their trysts, the molestation and hatred of her cousin Wilhelm...and her sacred genealogy. A cunning smile emerged on Lizzie's face. The queen's life was a shocking narrative—a secret, scandalous saga that could earn her a pretty pence. She knew time was of the essence and she could not read it all. But what she had read was enough.

She replaced the diary, locked the drawer, placed the key back on top of the desk, and snuck out undetected.

Meanwhile, it had only taken a minute for Charlotte to reach George's chambers, and she burst in angrily while he was being dressed by his Lords of the Bedchamber.

"She was my friend, and you sold her! It was *my* book, George, mine! She lied to you about it to protect me."

George dismissed his Lords and turned to Charlotte. "What are you talking about?"

"I am talking about Anne, my maid. You sold her."

"I most certainly did not. My chamberlain gave me a note that said the woman had been sold. I assumed you came to your senses."

Charlotte was incredulous. "*Came to my senses?* You bastard! Anne had been bought and sold like meat—her body used like a breeding ground, and I saved her from all that." Charlotte's fist punched against the wall and her voice became shrill. "Now you expect me to understand when the one human being I personally saved from such a life, *you* sold back into it! I shall never forgive you!"

But during Charlotte's tiraid, George began to experience cold sweats and tremors. His left side throbbed, and suddenly a stabbing pain shot up through his head, forcing him to sit down. Suddenly, George collapsed and twitched from pains darting from his side to his back, making his breathing difficult. His feet were swollen and the whites of his eyes quickly turned yellow.

Charlotte ran to the door and called out: "Get Dr. Baker, now!"

Later, when Dr. Baker finally arrived, he thoroughly examined the king. After an hour he told Charlotte that George had another spasmodic attack worse than all of the others. By this time, most of the royal children had come to the king's bedside. Prince George, however, stayed away. His father's illness too well indicated what he could one day succumb to.

George suddenly regained consciousness, and began to speak so fast and so long no one could get a word in. By the next morning the king had been talking nonstop for twelve hours, interrupting his patter with nonsensical injections of "What, What?" or "Hey. Hey!" Belligerent with anyone who tried to get him back into bed, he developed a habit of running naked in the halls. Prince George finally came to see his father one day and asked if there was anything he needed. The king became so enraged, he grabbed his son by the throat, hurled him to a wall, and tried to choke him. "You ask me what I need now, hey, hey—after embarrassing the monarchy with that woman you married?"

Prince George could not breathe and it took several pages to pull them apart. Charlotte ran from the room crying, and Princess Augusta followed her.

George was blooded again. When the pages removed his toilet water Dr. Baker checked it and again the king's urine was bright purple. He tried to administer James Powder, a powerful medicine, to George, but the king refused it. The two struggled. Finally, George pulled Dr. Baker's wig from his head and flung it out the window. Baker left the palace in an agitated state, sans wig, and went straight away to see the queen at Queen's House.

"The king is under an alienation of the mind. Bleeding him has not resolved his rapid pulse or violent temperament, and he is not responding to Senna. I recommend you utilize the services of Dr. Francis Willis. He is the foremost authority on mental illness."

Charlotte slumped onto a chair. "A 'mad' doctor?"

Outside the door, Lady Lizzie heard all, reacted, then instantly left the palace.

The following Saturday, Dr. Francis Willis arrived at St. James. The 71-year-old physician, who had once been a minister, was considered a tough, taciturn man. Willis examined the king who asked what kind of doctor he was. Willis said he treated conditions of the mind.

"So you, too, think me mad, what, what?" ranted George. Willis said nothing and instead gave the king some medicine, which George refused, screaming, "Answer me fool!"

Willis assured the king that was why he was there and not as the minister he once was. The king questioned why Willis left the church to join the medical profession.

"Our Savior went about healing the sick," answered Willis.

"Yes, but I never heard he got £700 pounds for doing so," George retorted.

After the examination, Willis told Charlotte that George should be confined to one of their smaller residences such as Kew Palace. "I need to try a few unconventional treatments on the king, and the family should not visit except as appointed."

Charlotte acquiesced to this request and George was moved to Kew where soon he became violent. Willis blooded him and treated him with leeches. The king started to have eye problems and had trouble seeing. In a state of anxiety, he attempted to jump out of a palace window when, thankfully, Dr. Willis was just entering the room and stopped him. Thereafter, George was restrained in a straitjacket and given Laudanum to keep him sedated.

Prince George, still annoyed by his father's attack on him, his marriage, and the king's refusal to pay his mounting debt, summoned Sir Charles Fox, Sir John Wilkes and other Whig colleagues. He discussed who would receive what office or pension if he was named regent. He boasted of the power and influence they'll have. Charlotte overheard the conversation and angrily entered the room.

"Do not be so hasty as to presume the crown before the jewel is handed to you."

But the Prince of Wales dismissed her. "Mother, this is a private conversation."

When Prime Minister Pitt and Dr. Willis were shown into the king's room. Prince George wanted to determine if a regent should be named immediately. Willis would not commit, but Pitt pressed, "Is the king of reasonable ability to rule?"

Finally, Dr. Willis responded. "There is more reason to assume insanity than death."

"Gentlemen, you have your answer," said Prince George confidently.

Prime Minister Pitt still had concerns. "Regencies are rare in British history. There is no precedent for this situation. It is clearer when there is death or a child involved, but an incapacitation such as this is unique. On whose authority does the regency rest? Parliament?"

After two months, it seemed as though George's delirium had abated enough so that the king was allowed to visit his family accompanied by Dr. Willis. But twenty minutes into the visit, George saw Lady Elizabeth Pembroke in the hall, ran up to her, and lasciviously felt her breasts. Lady Elizabeth, a beautiful 60-year-old, tried to run, but George followed her, howling like a dog. He caught the terrified woman and felt her derriere. "*This* is a firm, appealing English ass, hey hey!" Charlotte stood aghast as George was subdued and placed back in a straitjacket, his eyes turning the color of black currant jelly. She wondered about the fate of England.

> One afternoon Prime Minister Pitt came to see the king with Prince George and me. We walked on the grounds. Dr. Willis stayed close. Mister Pitt tried to discuss the pending slave trade bill. George told him he was feeling better and assured all he would be able to resume his duties. Two minutes later he ran up to an oak tree, grabbed a branch and shook it, referring to the tree as the King of Prussia. He talked to it for ten minutes. Mister Pitt clearly saw George was anything but well, and I could not contain my grief.
>
> My son, Prince George, gave Pitt a look and was resolved. "Even you have to concur a regent must be determined."
>
> All of this, and the fact my dear Anne was still missing after all this time and Jon was beside himself with grief, weighed heavily on me and I was besotted with anguish.

Fifty One

By September 1788, there was no improvement in the king's condition. It had been a sad summer for Charlotte and her family. On the 13th, Prince Augustus went to the University of Göttingen in Germany along with his brothers Prince Adolphus and Prince Ernest. Queen's House was a tomb without them. With George squired away at Kew Palace, and Anne nowhere to be founde, the queen was more dependent upon family and friends for her happiness than ever before. Yet she could not share all of her concerns. As she sat in the window of her chambers sipping tea and absently watching the snow cover her garden, she found she was dizzied by the turn her life had taken. It was then her chamberlain knocked at the door. When she allowed him to enter, he bowed reverently.

"Your Majesty, your brother Grand Duke Charles is here from Mecklenburg. I put him in the Receiving Room," announced Montague.

"Charles? Here?"

This news instantly pulled Charlotte from the doldrums and she was thrilled. Her brother was at last in London. She excitedly ran down the stairs as fast as her 45-year-old legs could carry her from her chambers to the Receiving Room. Happily out of breath, she threw open the doors and dashed inside.

"Charles, oh Charles, how wonderful you're here."

"M-most w-wonderful, indeed."

The queen instantly halted upon hearing the familiar stutter, then her face contorted in horror. The man before her, grinning from ear to ear, was *not* her beloved brother Charles...

...but her demented, 53-year-old cousin Wilhelm James Albertina.

Anger, fear, and incomprehension overtook Charlotte, and her breathing ceased as she slowly backed up. But Wilhelm rushed over to her, grinning fiendishly.

"N-not d-delighted to see me, d-dear cousin? It's b-been such a long time w-without so much as a hello or r-returned letter," he mused in his frightening stammer.

An unwelcome tension stretched tighter between them, and Charlotte could say nothing.

"I had to c-come in p-person as obviously my letters were m-met with silent derision. So allow me to update you. An emissary of Sir John Wilkes arrived in M-mecklenburg a year ago, seeking information on you. Information S-sir Wilkes is most willing to p-pay for—and as you are no doubt aware, I need funds. So, after exchanging several letters I t-told him I would be willing to p-part with all I knew and have in my p-possession on condition I be allowed to come to London for a p-personal meeting. Sir Wilkes agreed and p-paid for my passage. I've been here for a while investigating my needs. Now, Wilkes and I are scheduled to meet this Thursday to finalize things.

Suddenly, it occurred to me that my d-dear cousin is, after all, Queen of England. Consort of the k-king. So, as I have yet to meet Sir Wilkes in p-person, surely Her Majesty w-would not want this most embarrassing and damning information in the h-hands of a Member of Parliament w-with a newspaper p-printing so much against the king. It would be r-remiss of me not to offer you the s-same consideration for, let us say, *double* w-what Wilkes will pay me."

Charlotte was livid. "Blackmail? Nothing you have could possibly affect me," she lied.

Wilhelm chuckled. He had risked all to come to the palace in person for just this reaction, so he could finally have his comeuppance. His once lust for his cousin had now degenerated into a hatred for her success and continued censure of him. In his mind, he had the upper hand now. He was in control and, as always, Charlotte would have to deal with him on his terms.

"Come, come n-now cousin. Don't m-make it so sullied and dramatic. After all, you h-have always underestimated and ignored me." Wilhelm reached into his bag and pulled out a scroll identical to the ones she'd had transcribed. Charlotte reacted, but did not outwardly express it. "For years I hid my aunt's amulet," Wilhelm continued. "She had asked me to get rid of it. But I never did. I kept it—until that day she made me give it to you."

Charlotte began to breathe harder. Her heart pumping so fast she thought a heart attack was eminent.

"I know you're wondering how I got this," he said indicating the scroll. "In fact, I have two. The two scrolls she gave me to destroy. When the Grand Duke was alive, I once saw him go inside the secret b-bottom of his chest. I never told anyone—not even your mother. T-then two years after your f-father died, while Aunt Elizabeth was at Neustrelitz, I went into her r-room to her h-hiding place for the c-chest and I opened it." Wilhelm informed Charlotte that he stole some old gold coins from the chest. But not knowing what the scrolls were, he hid them in the woods abutting Mirow palace. "Your f-father barely left enough m-money for the b-basic needs of our family," Wilhelm chided. "Short of an auction, there was nothing of value except what was in t-that chest."

Charlotte learned that Wilhelm eventually sent a tracing of one scroll to be translated by Father Gretchen the priest in Berlin who had baptized him. Eight months later, Father Gretchen sent Wilhelm a letter urgently insisting they meet at the old chapel in Neustrelitz. That it was a matter of great importance. When they convened, Father Gretchen offered him 1,000 talers for the scroll and told him that the people he represented would pay more for any others. Wilhelm asked the priest what information did the scroll contain, and was told it was an ancient, forbidden codex written by King Solomon containing mystic teachings the church had deemed sacrilegious to the faithful, but would pay handsomely for. But when Wilhelm asked the priest who his contact was, Father Gretchen declined to answer. So, after some consideration, Wilhelm sold him one scroll and informed him he had access to five more.

"I told the p-priest to have his people p-prepare to negotiate a high p-price. But when I returned from Neustrelitz, your m-mother had hidden the chest s-somewhere else. I did not see it again until the day she gave it to you—the day she died. I contacted Father Gretchen again last summer only to discover he died three years ago. But fortunately his protégée, Father Savio is interested in the scrolls on b-behalf of the Church. And I n-need money." His eyes narrowed in sinister determination. "S-so you see, *you* have what I n-need, and queen or n-not, I expect my due f-for you h-have no idea w-what you have."

But Charlotte *did* know what she possessed. It had occupied her every waking moment since she landed in England. "You underestimate me if you think I haven't investigated my own property."

"Good. T-then you know that y-your amulet contains a relic," Wilhelm reached into his pocket and moments later pulled out an item which he dangled before her. "Just like this one."

It was Anne Josef's amulet—the sight of which alarmed and stopped Charlotte's heart.

"Where did you get that?" the queen demanded. "It belongs to my friend."

"*Belonged* to your f-friend," informed Wilhelm. "The African w-woman f-from around whose n-neck I relieved this w-weeks ago, is w-well on her way to her rightful destiny. And having it, d-dear cousin, adds to m-my advantage," he stammered.

"You bastard. Where did you find her?"

"I was informed t-that she was your p-personal maid and I f-followed her one day after she left here. As I rather f-forcefully asked her questions about you, her amulet f-fell from her p-pocket and I recognized it as similar to y-yours if not in fact yours. W-when she would not t-tell me how she acquired it, I s-snatched it. T-then I made sure she was t-taken to Bristol where she w-was sold."

The queen was teary. She realized George was truthful when he said he didn't sell Anne.

"I know that these amulets are of g-great importance to the Church. They were only handed d-down to d-descendants of Merovingian blood w-who have a distinctive b-birthmark. You—h-have such a mark. So did Jon. I s-saw it when I beat him. unless A r-raised, red birthmark on his s-shoulder just like yours. Imagine. How could s-such a thing happen unless your p-precious father f-fornicated with that Jamaican whore."

"You know nothing. You have nothing. No proof whatsoever," declared the queen.

"I have the p-pages I t-tore from your father's d-diary admitting your father's lust for Sister Lena."

The queen's eyes grew and a knot formed in her stomach.

"*You* have the torn pages?"

"And much m-more. I still h-have your love letters from Christian for I never burned them. And I have p-proof that you were molested b-by a Schwartzer who was s-sold to keep him from h-hurting you again because I have the receipt and r-reason for the sale." Wilhelm crept in closer to her, "My, won't Sir Wilkes' *North Briton* newspaper be thrilled by the reportage t-that not only is the woman w-who sits upon the throne of England black, b-but was ravished by one who, as it turns out, is also her half brother. Naturally, this w-would have nullified her v-virginity at the r-royal wedding. Incest, m-my dear, was the undoing of Anne Boleyn. And oh h-how they will revel in the knowledge that the queen w-was the lover of Christian Bach, a man who conveniently b-became music master of the p-palace. F-fornicating under the king's nose, were we?"

Charlotte slapped Wilhelm's face. "You will not threaten me or the king. I'll see you arrested or dead first!"

"Oh, let's n-not bandy idle t-treats about so casually," Wilhelm sneered. "I also have a chart your f-father drew tracing your lineage b-back to not only a Moor, but reveals George is also descended from that same Moor. Imagine. I can t-tell Wilkes my t-truth, give him my proof, and woe to you, Madame. A-after he c-contrives, t-twists, and manipu-lates it in the p-press, you and the king will be so maligned, revolution will be as eminent h-here as it is in France. And if you a-arrest me, I have g-given instructions to have my documents d-delivered to Wilkes imme-diately."

Wilhelm put his hat on his head. "Fifty thousand talers, a home, and a stipend. That is w-what I demand for my silence, m-my proof..." he then held up Anne's amulet, "...and this." He smiled fiendishly. "I am at t-the Hotel Villers, room 3 under the n-name Sir Charles Frederick. I'll await your d-decision by Wednesday at six p.m., or my v-valuable inter-ests go to S-sir Wilkes first t-thing T-thursday morning." Wilhelm walked away.

Charlotte's hands were clenched so tightly she had driven her fin-gernails into her palms.

✠

The next afternoon, the queen was sitting in her rose garden with Lady Schwellenberg, where she had been all day. She was clutching her father's Templar sword and had barely slept. She had prayed all night and all that day, yet was still as upset as the day before. She couldn't eat, her nerves were frayed beyond understanding, and she had forced herself to refuse strong drink. Wilhelm had to be stopped.

But she needed an enforcer—an ally and confidant who could take care of things quickly and quietly. So she sent a note through Swelly to the only person she felt could assist her. But as it was now three in the afternoon, where was he? And why did she think he was the answer?

Twenty minutes later he finally sprinted up to her with a concerned expression on his face. He was wearing a gentleman's wig and dressed in his best white pantaloons, shirt and tunic. He bowed the moment he approached Charlotte. "I came as soon as I got your note, Your Majesty. I dressed and did all the things you asked according to your instructions."

"Thank you for coming, Sir Jon. I am at wits end and desperately need your help."

"I'm at your service, you know that."

Charlotte smiled at him—at the kind eyes that had always brought her peace. "Do you remember when we were young and played our pretend game of 'Lady Charlotte and Sir Jon'?"

"Of course. I never felt more valued than in those times."

"Well, I no longer find the game to my liking," said Charlotte.

Jon frowned in confusion, trying to understand what his half-sister was trying to say as she continued. "Once upon a time, if a squire wanted to become a knight, he had to train and acquire special skills, sometimes sacrificing years toward his apprenticeship. In those days, the procedure began with the squire praying in vigil, then he would be bathed with special oils, and in the morning, he would dress in a white shirt, pantaloons and an overjacket. He would come before his king or queen who drew a sword and touched first one, then the other of his shoulders declaring: "Be thou now a knight."

Charlotte drew her father's elaborately bejeweled sword from its holder and faced Jon. "Eventually, the process evolved and the squire was made to vow that he would obey the guidelines of chivalry and never flee from battle. On the eve of his knighting, the squire would take a cleansing bath, fast, make his confessions, and pray to God to ready himself for his new life. He would dress all in white—the symbol for purity—and vow to follow a code of chivalry, which promotes honesty and respect for God and their sovereign."

Jon now understood. "All these things you asked of me in your letter."

"Yes," nodded Charlotte, "for you have always protected and done right by me."

Jon could not believe it as Charlotte placed her hand on his shoulder. "Kneel."

Jon instantly fell to his knees, his eyes brimming with tears as Charlotte placed her father's Templar sword upon his right shoulder. "So, my dear Jon, it's high time you actually became a knight in the service of your queen, your king and the Empire." She tapped his right, his left and then his right shoulder again. "I dub thee Sir Jon Louis Charles Baptiste, Knight of the Queen's Realm, and a gentleman. Be thou now a knight, and arise Sir Jon."

Jon heard applause as Lady Schwellenberg, there to witness the event, beamed in congratulations for him. As he stood, his legs wobbled in disbelief. His tears flowed freely as Charlotte touched his face. "It is no longer pretend. Your queen needs your help, Sir Jon."

"Anything. Anything, Your Majesty."

Charlotte did not know how to begin. "It's Wilhelm," she finally admitted. "He came here to Queen's House yesterday under a deception as my brother Charles. It is how he gained entrance into the palace. But his blackmail is far more formidable than we suspected."

Somehow Jon knew and waited for Charlotte to confirm the depravity. "He has several items in his possession which could prove embarrassing to both George and I should they fall into the hands of Sir John Wilkes and his newspaper—or in fact, anyone. Now he is asking for 50,000 talers, a home and a lifetime pension in exchange for them."

Jon looked at Charlotte askance, "Fifty thousand? His letter only demanded 20,000, was bad enough. How embarrassing are these items?"

"He has my letters of affection from Christian, which he stole from my possession in Mecklenburg," admitted Charlotte, finally sitting on a stone bench. "He knows about Magragana, and he has a chart my father drew tracing our lineage back to her; a chart which, by accident, reveals George is also descended from her as well as King David." Charlotte turned away, her voice dropping to a frustrated whisper "You are on the chart too, as my father's illegitimate son. Father drew a duplicate in his diary he left me. I have the actual chart. But several pages had been torn from his diary. Wilhelm stole those long ago."

After an impenetrably long pause, Jon forced Charlotte's eyes to meet his. "Why would a chart traced back to King David be a bad thing for the king...or the world?"

Charlotte knew she had to reveal it, for it was Jon's lineage as well. "The scrolls he has were taken from the Temple of King Solomon, and they reveal secrets about the whereabouts of Templar treasures—including pieces of the Holy Shroud, relics from the Crucifixion. He also has the receipt for your sale in Germany and the reason. It said that you ravaged me...which we know is not true, but would nullify my perceived virginity for a royal wedding. He could conceivably ruin me—again."

Jon needed to assess the situation, and he stared into space. "He must be stopped."

But Charlotte felt Jon needed to know it all. "Jon, there is more. I bear a mark upon my body which ties me to historical artifacts, relics, documents and a specific royal bloodline. That bloodline, the Merovingians, have taken vows to protect these secrets. None of my children received this mark, and George does not possess one. And all those who did that I personally knew are dead or presumed dead." Charlotte took a moment to scan Jon's face. "You bear such a mark, I understand. It looks like this."

The queen pulled her dress top over and revealed her raised, red mark to him. Jon was at first stunned, then he pulled over his white tunic to reveal his own red mark. "Then we share a secret—with my daughter as well."

Charlotte sighed for she knew she had to tell him the rest. "Jon, Wilhelm got to Anne, and I fear something bad has happened to her. He said he had her sold to Bristol and stole her amulet." Charlotte removed her amulet from its hiding place and showed him. "He showed it to me. It is the one which looked like this. Anne would have killed rather than ever willingly remove it from her body."

"I know. I asked her about it. I used to see a similar one at Mirow your father wore."

"This—is that amulet, and it contains two thorns from the Crown of Thorns worn by Jesus. That is why Wilhelm stole Anne's. There is something of value or importance inside of hers."

Jon's eyes scalded with the fire of decision. "If your cousin hurt Anne, I will kill him."

"We need a plan. Whatever is to be done must be executed by Thursday. That is the deadline Wilhelm gave me before he goes to Sir John Wilkes."

Jon asked Charlotte if she had any public plans. The queen answered that she was scheduled to see Mr. Mozart's newest opera at King's Theatre the next day, Tuesday. The muscles in Jon's jaw soon relaxed a bit. "Tell me how to contact Madame Lia d'Eon, and go on with your schedule. Do exactly what I ask you. D'Eon and I will take care of the rest." He paused a moment. "But I have one favor to ask. It has been on my heart for a while."

"Anything."

"My daughter is all I have left in the world, other than you. If anything should ever happen to me, promise me you'll find a way to see after her. Let her know who she is. Let her know who I was. Be good to her, as you've always been to me."

Charlotte nodded. "I will, Sir Jon. I promise."

At that, Sir Jon Charles Louis Baptiste, half-brother to the Queen of England, left the gardens.

Fifty Two

Sir John Wilkes was in the Grand Hotel making love on a dreadfully rainy day. Upon fully sating himself, he poured a glass of brandy and looked back at his conquest lying naked beside him. He smiled wickedly. "What I love most about this arrangement are the bonus benefits I derive from it," he chided, as he caressed her bottom. "They do so 'lift' my most ardent support."

Lady Lizzie turned over and set about putting on her clothing. "Then I am happy to engender that support, sir," she mused in her soft Scottish brogue, "as my own tend toward the neglected." She put on her stockings and garters and tied up her bodice, feeling at odds with herself.

"Ooh. Do I detect a note of irony in your voice, my dear?" said Wilkes, tossing back his brandy.

"The queen is at wit's end now that a specialist is treating the king. Why can you not leave her alone? Nothing ironic in that, sir."

Wilkes became annoyed. "I pay you to get me definitive, credible proof of any infractions committed by the king or queen which I can print in my newspaper, so I will not be sent to the Tower again. But for the last three years all you've done is *tell* me information I cannot have corroborated in writing. Now, I already know the king is mad. Get me the proof—a doctor's note. Or get me the queen's actual diary, proof of any affairs or forged signatures on bills. Tangible evidence I can print—and leave my objectives to me. Remember, all I need do is tell His Majesty that the queen's Mistress of the Bedchamber...is a traitor."

Lady Lizzie sat on the bed in misery as Wilkes finished dressing and left the hotel room.

⊦┼⊣

Later that evening at a pub, Wilkes met with members of the Whig Opposition: Sir Charles James Fox; Richard Sheridan, an MP and play-wright; and the Dukes of Devonshire and Portland. Wilkes told the group over fish and ale that the king was indeed insane. "I have it on good authority that the foremost specialist in diseases of the mind is treating him as we speak."

"Then we must demand a committee be formed to investigate the need for a regent now that the king is ill. We should make sure the Prince of Wales has no impediment to his appointment, as we can control him as regent," said Fox.

"I agree," said Sheridan. "He is a Whig, he is against everything his Tory father stands for, and no matter what a cuckold he may be, his poli-cies and opinions on war and foreign affairs are in keeping with our own."

Wilkes sat back, grinning confidently. "And I shall print all that fits our agenda in earnest, including a list of possible ministers to his coun-cil." He stood and held out his glass. "Gentlemen, to the Whig Party!"

The men stood and held up their glasses as well. "Here, here!"

Within two days, all Britain knew the king was mad. Every newspaper reported every detail and weighed in on the consequences of a regent appointment. As George could make no personal appearances, the regency crisis supplanted all others as the chief topic of conversation. All bills and policies requiring the king's signature were put on hold— including the bill to end the slave trade, which Mr. Wilberforce had so earnestly put forth.

That Monday, I was having breakfast with my family, when a page handed Prince George a letter. "It's from Prime Minister Pitt," pro-claimed my son. But as he read it, his elation turned to ire, and he threw the letter to the floor and left. I picked it up and read it. It stated that The House of Commons had come to a decision. By a majority vote, it was declared that Prince George would become regent, but would be sub-

ject to four restrictions which severely limited his powers. He was, in ef-
fect, king, but with no absolute control, and he could do nothing about it.

But my concerns were more worrisome. I had but 48 hours before I
needed to locate 50,000 talers in blackmail money and explain its need to
Parliament, or allow Wilhelm to go to Wilkes with his information and
sensational stories.

✠

Sir Jon and Mme. Lia d'Eon entered the Receiving Room at Queen's
House insisting on an audience with the queen. With them was a young
man with dirty blond hair who was not very well dressed and in seemingly poor health. Jon appeared as though he was trying to control his
emotions as his eyes were beet red. Charlotte quickly received them,
dismissing Lady Papendiek and Fanny Burney, a writer and the new Mistress of the Bedchamber being trained by Lady Schwellenberg.

"We have information on Anne," said Mme. Lia.

"Where is she?" asked the queen clasping her hands with a sense of
foreboding.

"Dead," Jon blurted out, his voice throttled with despair.

Charlotte's eyes clouded with grief then Mme. Lia indicated the
young blond man who was with them. "This is Mister Jonas McBride. I
promised him a hot meal and a warm bed for rest if he shared with you
the fate of dear Anne."

The queen motioned the man to her. "What do you know of Anne
Josef?"

The man bowed to the queen, then looked at Mme. Lia, who nodded for him to respond.

"I was a crewman aboard the slave ship *Recovery*. I joined when it left
Bristol on its way to Senegambia on the West Coast of Africa. John
Kimber was its captain. We had fifty-two Negroes aboard. Anne was
one. When it left Senegambia it was carrying 406 tightly packed African
men, women and children. All were being sold into slavery. Our destination was the West Indies. Three weeks into the journey, there were only
300 slaves left. In order to amuse himself and the crew Captain Kimber
demanded some of the women dance naked on the deck of the ship. He
picked out Anne. But when she refused he…he began to beat her with
his whip."

Charlotte trembled as he went on. It took all her strength not to col-
lapse.

"Anne refused to cry out. Instead she kept chanting something like:
'God will deliver me,' over and over. She would not stop chanting, even
when the Captain insisted, so he..." The man stopped. This was hard
on him and his face went wet with tears. Charlotte's hand went to her
hidden amulet to steady herself as the man wiped his eyes. He looked
over at Jon, whose eyes watered as well. "He...he tied a rope around
Anne's ankle and made two crewmen hoist her up. I was one of them.
The Captain left her suspended upside down hanging by the ankle over a
pulley. The dress she wore came over her head, revealing her nakedness
anyway...and he had her beaten until...she died. Then he threw her
overboard. I vowed when I was able I would never do work such as that
again."

Tears spilled from Charlotte's eyes and she stumbled onto the settee. The very thing Anne feared in that nightmare so long ago had come
to pass. "Take Mister McBride to the kitchen. Make sure he gets a hot
meal and a bath," Charlotte asked Lia who nodded.

After Mme. Lia and McBride left. Charlotte turned to Jon who was
weeping uncontrollably.

"I want you to take care of Wilhelm, do you understand? I do not
care how it is done. Finish him."

"If it's the last thing I do," Jon vowed.

Fifty Three

The next afternoon at King's Theater the audience applause was just dying down for Queen Charlotte, meticulously dressed and coiffed by Sir Albert, as she acknowledged all from her royal box. Her children were seated around her including the Princess Royal, Princesses Augusta and Elizabeth, and Princes George, William, Ernest, Edward and Augustus. *Don Giovanni*, the latest opera from Wolfgang Mozart, was having its British premiere, and Mozart, now 22 and the toast of the world, was seated on the other side of Charlotte.

The queen had much on her mind as the curtain rose. She knew the public needed to see how she was holding up under the stress of the king's illness. But she was depressed by so many issues now. Anne was dead—a woman who meant so much to her—*a human life unceremoniously tossed into the sea.*

As she watched the performance she thought about George who, just that morning, had been purged twice in three hours by Dr. Willis, causing the king great pain. Then Charlotte thought about her role in how Wilhelm and her enemies had to be eliminated and what was expected of her as dictated by Jon. That morning when Charlotte had arrived back at Queen's House from her ordeal with George's illness, she found Lady Schwellenberg standing at the top of the stairs. She gave Charlotte a look which Charlotte understood was their sign. The two entered the queen's chambers where Charlotte removed her amulet and handed it to Swelly folding her fingers around her lady's. "Be careful."

"I understand my assignment, my girl," said Lady Schwellenberg, who left the room, went down the hall, and knocked on Lady Lizzie's door. When Lizzie answered, Swelly went into a diatribe about stomach pains from which the queen was suffering and asked Lady Lizzie to get Lord Montagu. During the request, Swelly helped Lizzie put on her blue over-robe, stealthily slipping the amulet into the pocket. Then, as Lady Lizzie's red velvet shoes hurriedly clacked down the stairs, Swelly went back to Charlotte's room nodding affirmatively to the queen.

A few minutes later, Lord Montagu was shown into Charlotte's room by Lady Lizzie.

"Your Majesty, you need my help?" asked her Lord Chamberlain.

Charlotte indicated Lady Lizzie. "Yes. Fetch the palace guards and arrest this woman."

Lady Lizzie was shocked. "Why? What have I done?"

"You stole a valuable family heirloom," Charlotte responded, then turned to Montagu. "Search her."

Montagu searched Lady Lizzie's pockets and instantly found the amulet which he returned to the queen. He called for the palace guards as Lady Lizzie protested cried and cursed.

The palace guards arrived and took Lizzie away.

Now Charlotte was sitting at King's Theatre, trying to control her anxiety. She knew the rest of the plan was being executed as she watched the second-act duet. She glanced over at Mozart enjoying his new opera and began to worry about Jon and Lia.

✠

Wilhelm was in Room 3 of the Hotel Villers, re-reading the note which had been delivered to him the day before: "Sir, at the behest of HRM, I will be expecting you in Room 5 of the Hotel Villers tomorrow, Wednesday, at three o'clock, with your request from same. Please have your exchange participation available in its entirety. Mme. de Beaumont."

He went to the bed where underneath he had hidden the valise that held his future, his salvation. Wilhelm had manipulated the situation perfectly, he thought. His cousin was forced to acquiesce to his demands. It was far more important for her than for Wilkes. After all, *she* had to keep the truth hidden. *She* had the birthmark which obliged her to harbor ancient and esoteric relics. *She* was the queen consort tainted with African blood no one knew about.

Within the valise were the scrolls, Christian's letters, charts, torn pages from his uncle's diary—and Anne's amulet. He had everything he needed in front of him, and upon looking at the clock, he grinned. It was almost two. Soon he would be rich. And rich was enough.

Forty-five minutes later Jon, wearing a servant's wig and white gloves, and d'Eon, dressed as a man, were in a buggy which pulled in front of the hotel. Jon got out and "assisted" d'Eon by carrying his bag and walked behind him as they entered the hotel. D'Eon checked in as "Sir Charles Frederick" and asked for his key to Room 5. Jon kept his head down, playing the dutiful servant. Upon entering the room d'Eon quickly changed into his "Madame Lia" clothes and he and Jon waited.

At precisely three o'clock, Wilhelm knocked at the door, carrying his valise. Mme. Lia answered sizing him up. "I have brought what you requested of Her Majesty. Now I wish to see what she has requested of you, sir."

But Wilhelm insisted on seeing the money first. Mme. Lia pointed to Jon who, keeping his head down, opened the bag to show Wilhelm the money. Because Jon was a Negro, Wilhelm never paid any attention to him. He was too interested in the money and when he saw it in Lia's bag, he smiled at her. He then opened his valise and showed it to Lia who went through it all—torn pages, a scroll, letters tied with red ribbon, a bill of sale for Jon, etc. She smiled at Wilhelm, then gave Jon a subtle look. Wilhelm reached into Lia's bag and pulled out a fistful of pounds and grinned.

Suddenly his grin faded and his body jerked. Jon's gloved hands were tight around his neck as he was throttled to the floor gasping and kicking grotesquely. While Jon held Wilhelm down, d'Eon pulled off Wilhelm's clothes, shoes and wig, leaving him naked, then changed into them. Now dressed as Wilhelm he grabbed Wilhelm's valise which contained Charlotte's sensitive documents and the bag of money he and Jon had brought. Next he rifled through Wilhelm's clothing to make sure he had Wilhelm's identification papers, money, and the hotel key. "Do not forget to put Sir Charles' identification papers in his suit pocket when you are done. I am going next door to get his luggage."

Jon nodded. "I'll meet you at the appointed place."

D'Eon, dressed as Wilhelm Albertina, put on a hat and left. But revenge overtook Jon. As he looked at his former tormentor, his fingers
choking the life out of him, Jon thought about his justification for mur-
der. He thought about Charlotte whom Wilhelm had violated and nearly
raped. He thought about his own beating, the scars of which were still so
clearly evident on his back. Then he thought about his two wives: Lucy,
who died along with his son because she wanted freedom from the slavery Wilhelm had consigned Jon to; and Anne, who bore his daughter and
was killed as a result of Wilhelm's greed.

He thought about his mother Sister Lena, who took her own life
when his own was sold into enslavement by Wilhelm. *Yes*, thought Jon,
he has to die. But before he broke Wilhelm's neck, he taunted him.

"Do you remember me, you bastard? Look into the eyes of the last
man you will ever see on this earth!"

Wilhelm gulped for air, and when he could focus he finally recognized Jon. "You!"

Somehow Jon managed to draw a knife from his pocket. His look to
Wilhelm was resolute as he began reciting, *"Holy Mary, Mother of God, pray
for us sinners..."* and showed no regret as he thrust the knife deep into
Wilhelm's chest, *"...now and at the hour of our death."*

He thrust it into Wilhelm eight times.

D'Eon, disguised as Wilhelm, came down with the suitcase to the
front desk. "I am checking out of Room 3. The name is Sir Wilhelm Albertina." He paid the bill in cash and left the hotel while the real Wilhelm
slumped to the floor. He was dead.

Jon was breathing hard, his heart thumping loudly. He looked at his
white gloves stained with the blood of his revenge. He had to move
quickly. *Stick to the plan*, he told himself as he pulled off the bloody gloves
and put identification papers into the pocket of the suit he and Lia
brought to leave behind.

Suddenly there was frantic knocking at the door. A man on the
other side called out, "What's going on in there? Hello? Is everything all
right in there? We heard noises."

Jon panicked. What to do? Nervously, he looked around, then saw
the window. He had no choice. He had to climb out of it. Soon, two
men kicked down the door and found Wilhelm's body. One went to the
window and saw Jon climbing down the gable. The other ran for help. In

the lobby the man ran up to the front desk yelling, "A man's been stabbed! The killer is getting away! It's that Negro! Shoot him. Shoot him!"

A hotel guard quickly grabbed his musket and ran outside with the man. They saw Jon running away. The hotel guard yelled "Stop!" But when Jon did not, he aimed his weapon…

…and shot!

Jon felt the red-hot bullet pierce into his back and pass through his chest. His body instantly dropped with a thud and he rolled over onto himself twice before landing face down in the dirt. Excruciating pain exploded through every part of him and he could feel the warm ooze of his own blood as it spread out in an even crimson circle around him. As his chest rose for the last time, he thought about Charlotte. *"Dear God, my daughter. Please let her take care of my daughter,"* he prayed. Then his eyes closed and a strange smile incongruously crept to his face.

A melee ignited in the street as people fled or screamed. The hotel guard ran to Jon, turning over his body. Jon was dead. Around the corner waiting in the buggy, Lia d'Eon, still in disguise, had seen the entire event yet could do nothing. Sadly he was forced to ride away, wondering how he would tell the queen that her beloved half-brother was no more.

At King's Theatre, Charlotte jumped suddenly sensing something was wrong. Prince Frederick frowned leaning in to her.

"Mother, are you all right?"

"No. I'm not well, Frederick. I should go. The rest of you stay."

"I'll have them get your coach and guard," assured her second son.

When Charlotte got into her carriage she unloosened her over-jacket. Her stomach was fitfully churning and she could not shake her feelings of dread. When the carriage turned down Manchester Street, Charlotte was overwhelmed by a single thought. She tapped the roof of the coach for it to stop. When it did and her coachman leaned down the queen stuck her head from the window. "I must make a stop."

Lady Lizzie was crying in the Tower of London. Her cell was a dreadful place with just a wooden bed and no window. The only food she'd had all day was a bowl of broth. Soon, there was a commotion as

Queen Charlotte, accompanied by a guard, approached her cell. Lizzie was overcome with emotion and told the queen she did not steal the amulet, that she had been deceived. Charlotte stared at her lady, then asked why Lizzie revealed vital secrets to George's enemies. "The king's chamberlain said it was *you* who gave him the note saying Anne Josef had been sold. Will you lie and say you are not in league with Wilkes?"

But Lady Lizzie just cried, which made the queen more furious. "Confess, or suffer the consequences. I will remind you, your misdeeds are treasonous, and I will insist on death."

Lizzie fell to the floor and wept hysterically. "Please, no. Please."

Charlotte let her lady steep in her unfortunate predicament a while. "I do not understand, Lizzie. I only showed you kindness all these years. I trusted you, I liked you, yet you betrayed me. It is an unconscionable deceit for which any other queen would métier with the appropriate punishment. But I have a suggestion. Reveal who you have been working with and what you have done, in writing, and I shall allow your arrest to be expunged. You may leave here in the morning. If this is not to your liking, perhaps you will prefer the gallows. It is your choice?"

Lady Lizzie looked up, wiped her eyes, and nodded. Charlotte motioned to her guard. He gave her a pen, inkpot and paper for Lizzie who, feeling she did not deserve this option from her beloved queen, tried to find the words. "I never meant to hurt you, Your Majesty," she repented, in her soft Scottish lilt. "I was working for Sir John Wilkes and the Opposition because he said he loved me and wanted to marry me. I also liked the money. But when I was in too deeply, he threatened to go to the king. I have no family, few friends, and the position I enjoyed at the palace became frustrating. I had been fortunate to get it, yet you preferred that…that Negro woman, Anne, to me. You had her function in my stead which made me feel inadequate. Sir Wilkes made me feel special. Every time I gave him information, he made me feel valuable."

Lizzie admitted to all of her actions over the last several years in writing, and when she was finished, Charlotte read the confession, and left without further word. Lizzie realized at that moment her life was over, and she looked at the pen, inkpot and paper…

…and wept again.

Fifty Four

Charlotte's bloodcurdling wails reverberated throughout the palace like a desperate, wounded animal. Madame Lia had been waiting for her with Wilhelm's valise when she arrived from Tower prison and gave her the staggering news of Jon's death. The queen sank onto the settee, inconsolable in bereavement. "He cannot be dead," she cried in disbelief over and over. "First Anne, now my Jon."

When the queen was sufficiently subdued with medicine from Doctor Baker, Lia and Lady Schwellenberg were finally allowed into her chambers.

"Your Majesty, Jon gave his life for you, for the greater good, and the satisfaction of his own revenge," said Lia holding the queen's hand. "We must take comfort in the fact he died in fulfillment of his goals—and ours."

"All of our goals?"

"Yes, ma'am. Your cousin is dead. He can harm you no more, thanks to Sir Jon, and as a result I have with me everything you hoped to acquire in this valise." Lia handed the small bag to the queen, which she opened. Amongst all the items she sought to forever keep from public scrutiny she found Anne's amulet and squeezed her fingers around it. Charlotte wiped her eyes and took a moment to consider all that had happened. Two people she loved dead in a matter of days; Anne and now Jon. Such sad lives they had. Even after enduring the ordeal of enslavement, both found a modicum of happiness; Jon with Lucy and later Anne with Jon. Yet neither could totally escape the condition of unhappiness as if it were an ordained circumstance of birth. Jon and Anne deserved so much more. Charlotte looked away, thinking about them, then stared at Anne's amulet. She had to reassure herself that neither she nor Jon had died in vain.

"Where did they take Jon's body?"

✠

The next morning a carriage pulled in front of London's city morgue. The queen, dressed simply and without royal ceremony, entered with Mme. Lia, clad in women's garb. Charlotte placed a kerchief over her nose as the unsavory odor of death was distinct and unbearable, and the melodic sound of running water punctuated the silence. A chill ran through her as she saw several bodies stretched on grey slabs behind a glass partition. Pressing her face against the glass, she looked at the corpses. Some were covered with sheets, some not. Some retained their natural look in the rigidity of death; others appeared like masses of bloody, rotting meat.

One of the bodies belonged to a Negro man.

Soon Charlotte heard the water pump turn off and Mr. Whittaker, the morgue director, a stodgy, cheerless man, came from a back room. "May I help you?" he asked, peering over his spectacles.

"I am looking for my Negro servant," Charlotte lied. "He may have been shot."

Whittaker nodded and walked her to the Negro, whose arm was visible under the sheet. When he pulled back the sheet to reveal who it was, Charlotte held the kerchief tightly to her nose not just for the smell, but for the tears she valiantly tried to suppress.

It was indeed her beloved Jon. She could see the scars visible on his chest from Wilhelm's beating years ago and the manacle scars on his wrists from his ordeal on the slave ship. Most importantly, she saw his red birthmark and a gaping hole from the musket shot.

"Is this your servant?" asked Mr. Whittaker, seeing she was upset.

As hard as she tried Charlotte could not control her emotions, yet she shook her head, no.

"Well, it's a good thing," said Whittaker pointing to another corpse. "He stabbed that one to death. At least eight times." He went to the other body and pulled back the sheet, revealing Wilhelm's mangled body.

"Sir Charles Frederick. According to the hotel, he checked in three days ago, but no one's come to inquire about him."

Charlotte could not speak. She saw the stab wounds in Wilhelm's chest which caused her to turn away. Wilhelm was dead. He could harm her no more. It was then she noticed something else which further alarmed her. She slowly eased toward another sheet-covered corpse behind which hung a familiar blue over-robe and red velvet shoes against the bare plaster of the wall. Charlotte's heart fluttered and she yanked back the sheet herself, gasping at the sight.

Lady Lizzie's body lay there with the ink pen still jammed into her jugular and dried blood visibly staining her neck and torso. Charlotte cried out and covered her mouth.

"That one just came in. Suicide at the Tower," Whittaker offered. "Do you know her?"

Charlotte turned away asking what would happen to the bodies if no one claimed them. Whittaker explained that he would keep them there three more days. But if no one claimed them he would have them dumped in Potter's Field outside of London. Charlotte nodded, then told the morgue director her servant was not there. She thanked him and ran out in tears with Mme. Lia who helped Charlotte into their carriage. As the queen picked up her father's Templar sword from the carriage floor, she became tearful. "The poor man never had any happiness until Anne."

"I will take care of Sir Jon's body. He deserves better than Potter's Field," sighed Lia.

"They will never allow a Negro at Westminster. Where can he be buried?"

"I will take of it, Your Majesty. It will be respectful and dignified."

Charlotte thought a moment. "Take care of them *all* when this is over."

Mme. Lia nodded. "I shall. Now let us finish this. I need a drink."

The two headed to the Hotel Villers to complete their mission.

✠

At noon that day, Sir John Wilkes strode into the lobby of the Hotel Villers carrying a small bag. He went to Room 3 and arrogantly knocked on the door. From within, Mme. Lia, opened it and smiled. Wilkes looked at her, then grinned seductively. He took her hand and kissed it. "I remember you, lovely creature. But you never contacted me after my stay at King's Bench."

"No. Fortunately I found employment elsewhere," swiped Lia.

"Bonny for you," Wilkes retorted. "Now where is Sir Wilhelm Albertina?"

Suddenly, Charlotte stood from behind the chair in which she was sitting wearing her father's Templar sword and sheath. "He has returned to Mecklenburg after some sensible coaxing," she answered.

It took Wilkes a moment to realize that the person in front of him was actually the queen. "Your Majesty?"

"Now, Sir Wilkes, I have some sensible coaxing for you," Charlotte continued. "You will stop your spying, your unlawful manipulations and blackmail. All of it is treasonous and actionable by death. And trust me I will have no reluctance in having you prosecuted."

But Wilkes was belligerent and defiant. "You have no proof of any infractions, ma'am."

Charlotte drew her sword and pointed the tip at his jugular. "Au contraire, sir."

Madame Lia took the small bag from Wilkes' hand and opened it. Upon seeing its contents, she nodded to the queen.

"We now have the blackmail money you brought," retorted Charlotte, "and a witness to it in Madame Lia here. Most importantly, Lady Elizabeth Wells confessed to aiding you in your crimes and begged for immunity from prosecution."

Mme. Lia pulled out a piece of paper and handed it to Wilkes as Charlotte continued. "She gave me that written confession last night in the Tower of London where she was incarcerated. It contains dates, times and places of financial transactions between the two of you going back over seven years. For it, I have provided her with a safe hiding place until such time as the king decides to bring charges of treason against you. Then she will testify against you."

Wilkes became visibly nervous as he read the paper Lia had handed him. He tore it to shreds.

Charlotte was incredulous. "Surely you do not think me so inept a female as to come here with the original? I had it copied word for word last night." She shook her head in disgust. "Sir Wilkes, I have long ad-mired your tenacity where personal freedoms were concerned, most es-pecially freedom of the press, freedom of speech and the cessation of slavery. In those honorable pursuits you actually had me as an ally, de-spite the king. But it is your methods which repulse and offend me. Do it again, sir—and I swear on this, my father's sword, I will see you hanged." Charlotte retracted her sword.

Mme. Lia winked at Wilkes. "And if that isn't enough, I'll make it publicly known that you are my lover. Everyone at Phillips Printing Shop and King's Prison has seen you flirt with me."

Wilkes frowned. Lia took Wilkes' hand and placed it on her crotch. Wilkes felt a penis and jumped in mortification.

Charlotte smiled, "I assume we have an understanding?"

The queen and Lia d'Eon left the room, leaving Wilkes completely unraveled.

> *I never saw Sir John Wilkes again. He did not return to court as a courtier and was defeated in his bid for reelection by a narrow margin in the Commons. Curiously, he retired from politics and lived without incident with his daughter Polly until his death.*
>
> *Mme. Lia and I left the Hotel Villers still reeling from the experience. We talked in the carriage and decided it was important to find Jon and Anne's daughter in fulfillment of my promise.*
>
> *Three days later, dirt was tossed onto an elegant mahogany coffin as Jon's body was respectfully laid to rest in a small cemetery next to a church in London's east end. As a minister spoke a few words of comfort and re-cited passages from the bible, Chevalier d'Eon, still dressed as Madame Lia, and members of The Society for the Abolition of the Slave Trade, stood in attendance and respect as Jon was buried. His gravestone read 'Sir Jon Louis Charles Baptiste 1742–1788.' No one questioned his heredi-tary title as a Knight.*
>
> *The day after that, a headstone bearing the engraving 'Lady Elizabeth Wells, 1745-1788' was placed atop the grave of Lady Lizzie in another small cemetery in Sussex. Once again, Mme. Lia was there to make sure all was carried out to my satisfaction.*
>
> *At the same time, on the outskirts of London, in Potter's Field, the body of my cousin Wilhelm James Albertina, wrapped mummy-style in a*

white sheet, was unceremoniously dumped, along with several other unidentified similarly wrapped bodies, into a mass grave. Several baskets of lime were hurled over the corpses by grave workers, followed by dirt piled on top of that. There was no pomp, no spoken religious words, no dignity—and no absolution.

The next day, I had Mme. Lia urgently send for the Duke of Levis-Mirepoix by coded letter.

Fifty Five

The face underscored enormous infirmities. It was accentuated with deeply grooved lines, an unkempt beard, and the fingernails on his weathered, blue-veined hands were far longer than male protocol suggested.

The Duke of Levis-Mirepoix was now an old, thin man who held up his weight with a cane. He was gingerly escorted into Filbert House by Mme. Lia. When he was presented to the queen he was overcome with emotion and struggled to his knees in prayer. Charlotte hurried over to take his hands for it had been twenty-eight years since she had seen him at Sanssouci and his appearance unsettled her.

"Your Grace. How wonderful to see you again," she said, offering him to the settee nearby.

Duke Francois Antoine Gaston nodded in kind and slowly sat. "You as well, Majesty."

"He's a bit hard of hearing," informed Mme. Lia. "But he's quite fond of strong drink."

Charlotte smiled then motioned to Mrs. Delacourt, the caretaker, who poured a brandy and brought it to the Duke. The queen stared at him, her expression resolute. "You do know why you're here?"

✠

Duke Francois had understood completely. It is why he chose to finally journey so far in his condition. The queen had him secretly ensconced at Filbert House, a residence Charlotte used for complete privacy. He would stay there until he had translated Charlotte's amulet and the final scroll which had been in Wilhelm's possession. He would be well paid. The Duke worked as fast as his 76 year old body would allow while Charlotte fretted and worried back at Queen's House.

Finally, on a gloomy autumn afternoon a month later, the queen received a note in code that said: *"The information you want is at hand."* As she had learned how to decode a Caesar cipher herself, Charlotte contacted Lia d'Eon and both hurried to Filbert House.

"Well?" the queen urged Duke Francois the moment she stepped foot into the residence.

Duke Francois did not answer right away and Charlotte's palms became sweaty.

"Your Majesty, there are some truths better left undisclosed as their consequences could be too much to bear."

"You will speak plainly, Sir. I want to know what I have."

The duke sighed. "On one of the Magragana scrolls is a gnostic tractate, a codex of grimoires ascribed to King Solomon. It contains evidence contradictory to Christian theology—teachings Rome would rather the world not know."

"What kinds of teachings?"

"Things such as the invocation of underworld spirits, detailed diagrams and conjuring charts, sigils and seals giving power over demons. I told your father so when I translated part of this same scroll for him decades ago."

Charlotte recalled her father's diary. "Then it's true. Solomon could command and control spirits."

"And you can too—if you use these incantations."

"My God."

"The scroll also reveals the forbidden words on your amulet and how to open it."

Charlotte held out her hand. Duke Francois hobbled to the table and slowly came back with the fresh paper upon which he had written the translations. He crossed himself, then gave them to Charlotte who sat on the settee and began reading. Duke Francois went to a chair and prayed aloud while Charlotte tried to control the dry lump growing in her throat as she read.

Half an hour later, Charlotte was shaking as sweat poured from every pore. Her hand went to her heart to steady her nerves. "You cannot be serious," she stammered. "Seals of evil spirits? Beelzebub, Asmodeus, blood sacrifices, geniis, devils? This is a work of black magic, sir. It's blasphemous."

"I would agree with you. That is why I caution you not to recite the words aloud and certainly not in the order presented."

Charlotte folded the papers and paced back and forth a moment. She looked over at Mme. Lia who was as shocked as she.

"Open my amulet," Charlotte insisted to Duke Francois.

The duke drew in a nervous breath as the queen removed the amulet from her neck and gave it to him. There was a silent, emotion-filled moment exchanged between them before the aging duke began a unique process of twists and turns to open the ancient piece. As Charlotte carefully watched he pushed up from the bottom and depressed the top. He twisted it twice and pulled the middle portion down and depressed the top which came off easily. A moment later, out of this talisman the queen had worn for twenty-seven years, the same one worn by her father and his father before that, dropped an old dried piece of linen cloth, which Duke Francois unwrapped and removed two thorns with stained dark tips.

He looked at Charlotte with resignation. "Ego ago per is verum. Vos praecipio mihi," he said in Latin then handed them all to the queen. "You possess one of the oldest relics in Christendom, next to the Shroud, nails and the Holy Cross itself. Those thorns have Christ's divine blood on their tips, and it is said *His* blood could heal the sick."

Charlotte could not calm down as she looked at the cloth and thorns in her hand. She had solved the mystery of her father's quest. The amulet was a magic sigil of protection that contained relics from the passion of Solomon's descendant. Both thorns were two inches long although one was longer and thicker. She wondered when was the last time they had seen the light? Was it the day Prince Martim was shown them on the road by his mother Magragana? Or had another family member utilized the secret opening technique to unveil their presence?

"Remember. You cannot *un*-know a thing once you know it," cautioned the duke.

Charlotte looked at her amulet, at the five words and symbols she now knew evoked either the name of God or a demon. She thought about the pain Jesus suffered when the very thorns in her hand were driven onto his head. She felt their tips which were still sharp. Her fingers squeezed around them feeling humbled. Then the queen gathered her composure from an unknown source and placed the thorns into the amulet which she placed back around her throat.

Suddenly, it struck her. "Is it possible?" and she motioned to Mme. Lia. "I must go to Kew!"

Within the hour, the queen had arrived at Kew Palace and could hear George's howls throughout the residence. Servants, guards and chamberlains came and went as though the freakish screaming was a daily event to be ignored. Charlotte was aggravated by the nonchalance and summoned Dr. Willis, who told her she shouldn't be there for George was having a bad day. He was burning with fever and foam constantly ran from his mouth. None of Willis' methods were working, and he needed more medical help. Even Prime Minister Pitt's physician, Dr. Lowe, felt the king was at death's door—and the newspapers concurred.

Charlotte and Willis went into George's room and the queen was shocked by what she saw. Her husband was again buckled into a straitjacket and his mouth was gagged with cloth. His eyes were bloodshot, he had soiled himself, and the putrid smell of urine filled the room.

"Get His Majesty cleaned up and take that infernal gag off of him," she chastised Willis.

Willis nodded and sent for two personal pages. It took half an hour for them to restrain and clean George. Finally, it grew silent, and after an acknowledgement to her, the pages, who were disheveled and exhausted, carried soiled sheets, clothing and George's chamber pot from the room. Charlotte squeezed her amulet to calm herself, then asked Dr. Willis to leave as well.

"But Your Majesty, it is not safe."

"I will be fine, sir. I am protected by a higher authority," she said, with her own meaning.

Dr. Willis obliged and finally left the room. Charlotte waited until he was gone to approach the king. George was still restrained, but was in clean clothes and lying on clean sheets.

I reached out my hand until I felt his forehead. It was hot and damp and his eyes were red, watery and glazed. George began to whimper in agitation and finally, he looked at me and pleaded: 'Kill me.'

I took off my amulet and prayed. 'Please Lord, help me,' I beseeched aloud. Then, remembering how Duke Francois had opened it, I pushed the bottom of the amulet up and twisted the top, which disengaged the locking mechanism. After another few twists, the inner compartment clicked open and I turned the amulet upside down. Out of it dropped the two thorns in the old linen cloth. I held the longest one and took a deep breath. What on earth was I expecting? How could I ever think dried blood over 1,700 years old would still be present, much less retain some purported divinity? And what made me think I could invoke it or the amulet's power?

Still, I gathered my resolve and opened George's bed shirt, exposing his left shoulder. I closed my eyes and dared say the words aloud. Those words: 'Tra gram ma ton te.' Then I stabbed his shoulder with the thorn. George cried out and when I opened my eyes I saw the blood ooze from the wound.

The king soon fell back onto the pillow and was quiet.

Fifty Six

Charlotte was in the music room at Queen's House playing the harpsichord. It had been two days since she had learned the contents of the last scroll and pricked George with the thorn. As she played, she prayed for God not to be angry with her but guide and protect her.

Suddenly she heard a voice behind her: "Look who I have found."

She turned to find Madame Lia d'Eon holding a baby. Charlotte pulled back the blanket covering the infant's face and smiled. It was a beautiful Negro baby; the daughter of Jon and Anne Baptiste. She seemed to gravitate to the queen holding out her arms with a grin as wide as the Thames. Charlotte looked at the birthmark on the child's shoulder and smiled. "She will not suffer the consequences of her gender or ethnicity. This one will have every advantage. I'll see to it."

"Your Majesty, why do you seek more for this child than your own children?" asked Mme. Lia.

"It's simple really," Charlotte replied. "My children are royalty. They already have every advantage. They will be fine no matter what. But not one of my living children carries the mark. And I must pass the knowledge to a blood relation who carries the birthmark." Charlotte asked to hold the baby and they sat on the settee. "How did you find her?"

"I went to Jon's flat. But there was no answer," started Lia. "Just as I was about to leave, I heard a baby crying in the flat below and just had a feeling. I knocked at the door and a Negro woman named Mrs. Bailey answered. I asked about Jon and she said she was watching his daughter. She had been watching Lotte-Anne all this time for she was the child's babysitter."

"Lotte Anne?"

"That is her nickname," Lia smiled. "Her full name is Charlotte Anne Lena Baptiste."

Charlotte was touched. The last time she spoke to Jon about his daughter, he and Anne were deciding between "Anne" or "Lena." But this moniker felt appropriate and royal.

Lia further explained that even though Mrs. Bailey loved the baby, she was fraught with worry and knew something was wrong. Jon had never been gone so long and would never have abandoned his child. He was so happy to have her even though he had suffered through the tragedy of his wife's loss.

"I told Mrs. Bailey I was Jon's benefactress and that I would provide for the baby now. Mrs. Bailey gave her to me with some reluctance, but she said if I ever needed help not to hesitate to contact her. So I gave her a few quid for her generosity then I left."

"Lotte Anne is blessed," replied Charlotte. "But now I must find a place for her to be raised and schooled; somewhere safe and not necessarily connected to me or the king."

"What about Filbert House?"

Charlotte smiled, happily kissing the baby. "Of course. The caretakers can keep an eye on her until a governess can be hired."

"I have an idea for a governess as well," Lia smiled.

Two hours later a carriage arrived at Filbert House. Out of it emerged Mme. Lia and the baby now carried by Mrs. Bailey. When they entered the residence Mrs. Delacourt, the caretaker, showed them into the parlor then prepared tea. Mrs. Bailey looked around in awe. "Is this where we will be living?" she asked Mme. Lia.

"Yes. The rest of your things will be brought over in a few days."

Mrs. Bailey looked at the baby. "You are the luckiest child."

Mme. Lia saw how wonderful Mrs. Bailey was with the infant and knew Charlotte had made the right decision in hiring her to look after Lotte-Anne. Lia left Filbert House satisfied that Charlotte's promise to herself had been fulfilled. Jon's daughter would be well cared for.

Meanwhile, Charlotte was being changed for dinner when Princess Augusta knocked on her chamber door and entered. "Mother, come quickly. It's a miracle, an absolute miracle."

Charlotte followed Augusta down to the reception room where to her surprise King George was presented to her by Dr. Willis. Also there were most of their children along with Lady Schwellenberg and Lady Papendiek. George came over to Charlotte and smiled.

"As quickly as it had appeared, George's illness disappeared."

"I have no explanation for it," exclaimed Dr. Willis. "He seemed to improve overnight."

George kissed Charlotte's forehead and apologized for any embarrassment he may have caused her during his malady. "I was trapped inside my own head until a warm sensation flooded over me the moment you left. All at once I felt renewed and needed to see you. To hold you."

Charlotte fell into his arms and cried.

George returned to me intact and more affectionate than ever before. Whatever took him mentally was gone and the miracle, however interpreted, left him grateful for all he had including us and our life together. I thanked God that day, praying in earnest as George slept peacefully. Was it the thorns? Was it the words? Divine intervention? Coincidence? I shall never know with certainty. Only what I suspect.

✠

Over the next several months Charlotte's purpose was clear and she put it into action. She wanted an end to slavery, the slave trade, and most of all, she wanted retribution for Anne Josef.

To that end, she contacted her friend and painter Sir Allan Ramsey to get a message to William Wilberforce, who was still trying to get his anti-slave trade bill through Parliament. She recounted all the details of Anne's ordeal onboard the slave ship *Recovery* and wanted to know what recourse there was in bringing its captain to justice. Cartoon depictions of Anne hanging naked from a pulley on the deck began to circulate in London and people were outraged.

Revolution had begun in France. By 1789, the French king and queen had been beheaded and England was in another financial slump. People did not want to engage in another war and they were no longer tolerant of issues such as the continuation of slavery. Charlotte felt change in the air.

Wilberforce agreed to be an advocate in the case of Anne's slave death on the *Recovery*. In a speech before the House of Commons, he accused Captain Kimber of having caused the death of a slave girl by inflicting injuries on her because she had refused to dance naked on the deck of his ship. As a result of Wilberforce's speech, Kimber was arrested and tried before the High Court of Admiralty. Even though he was ultimately acquitted, Charlotte felt some vindication for Anne. When she visited Anne's baby daughter Lotte-Anne at Filbert House, she gave the girl a doll and told her it was from her parents in heaven, who were at peace.

Months later, Charlotte learned Duke Francois died in his sleep upon his return to Mirepoix. She also learned that John Stuart, the Earl of Bute passed away from complications following a fall on his property. George mourned him even though they had not spoken in years.

But it was the death of Sir John Wilkes which gave Charlotte the most solace. He had been a great activist for social change and America utilized many of his ideas in the formation of their government. America's citizenry enjoyed the rights of freedom of speech, freedom of the press, freedom of assembly and freedom of religion as guaranteed by their constitution. But for Charlotte, Sir John Wilkes would always represent the man responsible for some of the worst, most emotionally challenging times in her life.

And yet, his passing had not the resonance of the death which took place four months later. Charlotte was in her chambers writing in her journal. Strands of graying auburn hair haphazardly fell onto her face as she looked over at the clock. It was quarter past four in the afternoon and she felt as ancient as Methuselah. She was more than aware of the physical toll having fifteen children in twenty years had taken on her 53-year-old body as each movement gave way to aches of muscle and spirit.

Suddenly Lady Papendiek tearfully ran in emotionally distraught.

"Your Majesty, it's Swelly."

Charlotte's lady was dying. Her breathing slow and labored. The stomach tumor had come up quickly and overtaken her in just a few months. Charlotte rushed in and sat at her side holding her hand and praying. Her tears began to flow like the Thames into the North Sea.

"Swelly, I cannot let you go. Who will care for me? With whom shall I have adventures?"

Lady Schwellenberg opened her eyes, sensing Charlotte's fear and grief, and held up a finger which Charlotte clutched desperately.

"No crying, my girl. I'm going to a much better place."

"No, no…"

"Charlotte, you are strong. Your strength has always amazed and prided me, child. Be who you are. You don't need me."

"But I do. Please, Swelly. Don't leave me," Charlotte cried. "You are like a sister to me."

"And I have loved you like a sister. Oh, the adventures we have had, you and I. Make me proud. Let Lady Papendiek and Mrs. Burney show you they can be your confidants in my stead. Let me go, my…girl… Let me go."

Lady Johanna Schwellenberg's chest fell for the last time.

Charlotte was inconsolable and refused all food and drink. She refused all company and gifts of condolences. She would not see George or any of her other ladies in waiting for weeks. She stopped entertaining and grew cold and sullen.

Her friend Mme. Lia d'Eon found a lover and spent more time in the country making jam and canning apricots. Charlotte heard that Lia and Nadejda were even seen holding hands—two old women strolling along the Thames together.

So Charlotte's daughter Augusta took it upon herself to send a note and invited Mme. Lia to take tea at Queen's House to cheer her mother up. Lia came and brought apricot jam, wine and Charlotte's favorite—snuff. As they enjoyed all of Lia's treats in Charlotte's chambers, Lia chastised the queen with her typically robust attitude.

"My dear, you must get out more. Queen's House has become the most boring royal establishment in Europe. You and the king have not had a levee in months and people are talking."

"Let them talk."

Lia rifled through the queen's perfumes looking for something to dab on her neck then frowned in exasperation. "Darling, English perfumes are far too spicy and masculine. Don't you have something French? Something more floral, or fruity?"

"There is quite enough fruit in this room—at the moment," Charlotte chuckled.

Mme. Lia turned in mock condemnation, placing one hand on her pearls. "My, my. Cruel and bitchy today, aren't we? Well, never you mind. I have just the thing to sooth that savage, ever so unattractive beast residing in you."

"Not your fabulous port from Tonnerre?"

"The very one. We simply cannot have a grousing session without formal libation."

Charlotte smiled realizing how much she enjoyed Lia's company. "Oh, how I have missed you, Lia. What would I do without you?"

"Be ignorant of the absolute best gossip. Now, have you heard? Mr. Wilberforce may have enough signatures to go before the Commons."

Charlotte's face brightened as Lia poured a glass of wine. "I think it's time you got back into the cause, darling. He presents his bill next Tuesday. Should not we be there in support?"

Charlotte grinned. This was all she needed. The next Tuesday she returned to her old tricks. Dressed in plain, undistinguished clothing, she and Lia went up to the gallery of the House of Commons where regular citizens could watch the proceedings. William Wilberforce stood before the MPs and gave an impassioned address as he presented his bill for the cessation of the slave trade—for the sixth time.

> *My devotion to what Thomas Jefferson called the 'inalienable rights' of man had not altered, and I kept my attention on the ongoing evil. Mr. Wilberforce, who had brought forth a bill every year since George's madness, had accumulated enough signatures and petitions to once again present it to Parliament. But this time the mood had changed. Wilberforce's passion could be felt throughout the Commons, and many of the MPs and others could be seen nodding in agreement. Thomas Clarkson and Granville Sharp were sitting in the gallery listening with me. I was excited because this time I felt the tide was turning. As each member of the Commons voted yea or nay, Wilberforce was nervous but expectant. Clarkson smiled at every yea. Finally, the vote was tallied and announced. "The House of Commons votes 114 to 15 in favor of abolition!" There came a resounding cheer from the chambers. Now the bill had to go before the House of Lords.*

On the day of the vote in the Lords Queen Charlotte Sophia was squeezing her amulet waiting for news. Sir Allan Ramsey promised to tell her as soon as he knew anything. The queen waited and paced. With her was the king, Lady Papendiek, Mme. Lia d'Eon, and Princess Augusta. Charlotte's own sons Prince William and Prince Augustus were absent as they were dead set against the bill's passage. Three hours later, a gleeful Sir Allan Ramsey was admitted into Queen's House. He announced for all to hear: "The House of Lords voted 41 to 20 in favor of the abolition of the Slave Trade!"

I was thrilled. The slave trade was no more. And by ending it, England began the process by which the slave trade ultimately ended in most countries in Europe. I thought about Jon, Anne and their daughter Lotte-Anne. I thought about all the disaffected Negroes, bought, sold, and placed onto ships. People who would never see home again but would know their children would not suffer the same atrocities. Best of all, I saw George smile when he looked into my jubilant face, for he knew the right thing had been done, and he was finally on the correct side of the issue.

With deep pride I watched as the bill was signed into law abolishing the Slave Trade on 7 March 1807, and as I stood with the wind of change swirling about me, I felt a haunting presence. I looked up and there in the distance I could faintly see the diaphanous figures of my beloved Jon, Anne, Christian, and my father, Grand Duke Charles Louis Frederick. They were all smiling proudly.

Then I saw someone else with them; a dark-skinned woman—a Moor of uncommon beauty with long ropy hair. I could only surmise it was Magragana, my ancestor, who smiled as broadly as the others and nodded to me. Had I gone mad myself that day? I shall never know. But I felt satisfied.

Fifty Seven

October, 1818

Charlotte Sophia stayed largely out of public view for the next seven years. She and George were devoted to each other and their lives were quiet and loving. The queen had also been lucky. When Buckingham caught fire later in 1807, Charlotte was escorted from the building in haste. But when she got outside and saw that the king was safe, she realized that Christian's music box, Magragana's scrolls, her father's diaries, and most especially her own diaries—50 years of the events in her life—were still inside her beloved chest in her private apartment. They could not go up in smoke. She *had* to retrieve them.

Though staffers and her ladies tried pulling her away, Charlotte ran back inside the raging inferno. Prince William ran after her, but once inside he could not find his mother through the smoke. He called out to no avail, then, overcome with smoke, ran back out. Everyone feared the queen was lost. George began to weep aloud.

After several agonizing minutes, Queen Charlotte emerged from the palace dragging the reliquary behind her wrapped in a sheet. Her dress was burning and she collapsed on the lawn. Prince Augustus ran up and carried the queen, whose legs had been badly burned, while Prince William carried the reliquary.

For four days worried doctors treated her and waited. On the fifth day Charlotte's eyes opened and she saw she was still alive. When she learned her memories were safe, that Queen's House could be repaired, and nothing was lost entirely, she knew her prayers had been answered. Anything else could be dealt with.

Charlotte was now 72 years old, and her once kinky auburn hair was white and sparse. She no longer bothered with white makeup to hide her ethnicity. Her burned left leg never healed properly and always caused some discomfort. Yet she told Lady Papendiek, who had now become indispensable to her, that it was worth the sting of her burns to save her legacy.

Lady Papendiek confessed that Lady Schwellenberg had instructed her to be of singular, secret service to the queen. "And I vowed on my sainted father's grave to protect you and guard your secrets as mine."

Charlotte nodded knowing that to be true. "Then I need a favor. A promise you cannot carry out until I have gone to my Lord. It will be the last promise from you in service to your queen."

Lady Papendiek understood and swore. Once the queen revealed the duty she asked her lady to leave and allow her to get some writing done. Lady Papendiek obeyed.

Charlotte opened her aged red leather diary, cracking, worn, and imbued with wisdom and began to write:

I am old now, and the rigors of my age prevent me from writing as frequently as I would like. But I feel I have honored my family with a life well lived, on my own terms, and faithfully chronicled within these pages. Having outlived all of my siblings—even my youngest brother George—I have endured many losses in my time, many hurts and regrets. Some have shaded my well-being. Others have been insurmountable.

One such loss was my dear friend Madame Lia d'Eon de Beaumont. I stood at d'Eon's funeral, looking down at her casket, and I had to smile despite my grief. Lia lived her life her way—or rather his way. She was 81 and still fabulously dressed as 'Madame Lia.' Her wife had instructed the undertaker to dress her as such, for she had long ago accepted d'Eon's peculiarness. At the time of her death, all of London thought that Chevalier Charles Genevieve-Louise Auguste Andre Thimothee d'Eon was a woman who had once dressed as a man. But it was at his autopsy that certainty was established. George made the doctor tell him exactly whether d'Eon was a male or female.

Shortly thereafter my poor George went permanently mad, never to recognize me or his children again. They say it was brought on by the revelation that d'Eon—was indeed a man.

My son Prince George is now regent with all the pomp and power attended it. He rules with an iron fist and a cold, calculating heart. I pray for England—and now for you.

It is your time now, and you must find a cause worth living and dying for. To make choices for the betterment of the oppressed of which there are many. Realize that freedom for some is only as meaningful as the freedom we allow for all, and that the privileged must do more, as their needs are less. Do something greater than yourself, for it is the only way to be at peace.

Charlotte closed her diary and placed it into the wooden reliquary next to her. The entire history of her life was in that chest; all the bits and pieces of her journey—including the Testament of Solomon. She thought about her father and then her gaze turned to the amulet hanging proudly on her still magnificent cleavage. She held it in her hands and smiled, knowing its power—and its secret.

I think about the day I pricked George with the thorn still stained with the living blood of Jesus, and I think about his miraculous healing in Christ's name. I ponder the fate of my amulet and its marvel within. Even with all I now know, I believe. And I pray for peace.

CS

Soon, almost as though summoned, *She* appeared to Charlotte in a vision.

Magragana ben Bekar. Her ropy hair gently settled upon her shoulders. She held out her arms to Charlotte and smiled.

The Moor smiled in return and held out her own arms welcoming like a cool breeze on a summer day.

"Indeed," Magragana whispered to Charlotte. *"Have some peace."*

Epilogue

LEGACY

Filbert House
London, England - 1818

"History is no more than recorded experience – generally the experience of its winners – and it is common sense to learn from the experience of yesterday. Indeed, it is that very experience which holds the moral, cultural, political and social keys of tomorrow..."

Sir Laurence Gardner

Fifty Eight

Bells were tolling on the first day of December, 1818 as Queen Charlotte Sophia was privately lying in state at Kew Palace. England was in mourning. Lady Papendiek stood at the casket looking down at her mistress whose face appeared so peaceful. She wished the king could be present to pay his last respects but he could not be there. George was locked away muttering to himself forever confined to the dementia of his mind. He never knew Charlotte was dead.

As she stood there forcing back tears, Lady Papendiek took solace in knowing she had honored the two promises made to her queen. She knew that just beneath the folds of Charlotte's silver funereal gown, to be buried for eternity, she had placed the queen's requests: the love letters from Christian Bach and the Solomon incantations.

✠

Just after three o'clock on the same afternoon the Queen Charlotte's special carved wooden reliquary arrived at Filbert House delivered by courier. Its recipient, Charlotte Anne Lena Baptiste was in mourning for the beloved queen, her hazel eyes swollen from grief. She instructed the courier to place the chest on a nearby table. Afterward he handed her an envelope for which she had to sign, and he left.

Charlotte-Anne opened the envelope. Inside was a note attached to the fully executed deed to Filbert House. The property was now hers. The note said: *"A solicitor will send a stipend every month for your care and the upkeep on the house. The queen wanted you to know she loved you, your father and your mother. Because you possess the mark you must read everything in the reliquary, for it explains who you are."*

Charlotte-Anne was stupefied. Also confused. The house she had lived in for thirty years was now hers. But why would the queen give it to her? She went to the carved chest and opened it. Inside she found two old red leather diaries, one brown leather diary, four parchment scrolls in wood containers, a white Masonic apron, a silver music box, and a velvet pouch out of which fell two similar gold amulets and a letter which stated:

Dearest Lotte-Anne,

My time is short and there is much to confess. Your father and I were half-brother and sister, and I loved him as deeply and as purely as I love my children.

Why should you be shocked? Why should you disbelieve? It is not as though the origin of my being is unique in the annals of history. Stories of miscegenation, conflict and defilement—or even affection—between master and slave, conqueror and conquered, have been with us before the Bible chronicled Abraham, Hagar and Sarah.

That said, the story I must tell you, and the resultant secrets and unpalatable truths which emerge, do not begin with me. Nor, if I have studied history correctly, will the disputation inherent in my being end with my demise—especially once the secret of my amulet and me are revealed to you. I find I must concern myself with legacy—and legacy can be such an abstract and ethereal thing, so open to misrepresentation. I began these diaries to correct the record for, in the end, as Napoleon has stated, 'History is but a lie agreed upon.'

We all have our confidences we conveniently sweep under the rug of acceptability. And oh, the price we pay for perception as we stand in the face of judgment and tell the occasional, little, white lie. The problem is, this lie is neither little...

...nor white.

I am Charlotte Sophia Albertina Frederick Hanover, Queen of England. And though history is but that 'agreed upon' lie, this is mine...

...and now yours.

As Charlotte-Anne held one of the amulets it began to feel warm in her fingers and she suddenly felt a haunting presence.

When she looked up she saw *Her.*

Queen Charlotte's niece then smiled. For without knowing the reason, somehow she understood.

Author's Notes and Acknowledgements

Although *Charlotte Sophia: Myth, Madness and the Moor* incorporates the real life story of Queen Charlotte Sophia of Great Britain, it is none the less a work of fiction and a product of my imagination. However, there are actual places, facts, events, people, and artifacts in this book which required research and verification. I am indebted to my researcher Denise Y. Gillman whose mammoth contribution of time and energy cannot be calculated; and to Austin Foxxe, my editor, who helped me shape the work.

Grateful acknowledgement is also made to the following "angels" without whose help this book would not have been possible: historian and genealogist Mario de Valdes y Cocom, who first discovered and completed the original research on the genealogy of Queen Charlotte's Moorish roots, and shared my love for the story's ethnic components; my manager Todd Harris who constantly encouraged; Dave Ingland who never disappoints; my dear friends George Alexander, Stanley Bennett Clay, Frank Fletcher, Tracy Grant, Deborah Gregory, Sharon Johnson, Mondella S. Jones, Wendy Kram, Joanne (JM) Morris, Marion Ramsey, Cheryl Terry, Erik Aston Washington, and Sherri Williams who read various drafts and gave great notes.

Most importantly, several source references and documents were used in conjunction with this novel that were essential. They are not responsible for any interpretations, omissions, misrepresentations or errors I may have made, but acknowledgement must be paid to the following authors and their works: *Queen Charlotte*, by Olwen Hedley; *Memoirs of Her Late Majesty, Charlotte, Queen of Great Britain and Ireland (London, 1819)*; *King George III*, by Christopher Hibbert; *John Christian Bach*, by Heinz Gartner; *King George III*, by John Brooke; *Monsieur d'Eon Is A Woman: A Tale of Political Intrigue and Sexual Masquerade*, by Gary Kates; *Royal Spy: The Strange Case of the Chevalier d'Eon*, by Edna Nixon; *The Maiden of Tonnerre, The*

Vicissitudes of the Chevalier and the Chevaliere d'Eon, by Roland Champagne, Nina Ekstein, and Gary Kates; *John Wilkes*, by Arthur H. Cash; *The Shroud of Turin*, by Ian Wilson; *The Templar Revelation*, by Lynn Pickett and Clive Prince; *The Templar Papers: Ancient Mysteries, Secret Societies, and the Holy Grail*, by Oddvar Olsen; *Bloodline of the Holy Grail*, by Laurence Gardner; *The Sign and the Seal*, by Graham Hancock; and *The Essene Odyssey*, by Hugh Schonfield.

You can also chart Queen Charlotte's descent from Magragana ben Bekar the Moor, the Knights Templar, and King David by going to: http://fabpedigree.com/s029/f648648.htm.

I would also like to thank Leo Garcia, Artistic Director of Highways Performance Space in Santa Monica, California for allowing my play *"Charlotte Sophia"* based on this novel, to initially be presented; and for the artistic contributions of my talented cast. That play, now entitled *"Buckingham"* had its East Coast premiere at The Southampton Cultural Center thanks to Executive Director Kirsten C. Lonnie; and is enjoying performances across the country.

Finally, I am and will always be grateful to God for allowing me to live through the process of writing this book after a health crises in 2009. I extend my deepest and most heartfelt appreciation to my various physicians whose talent and medical skill saved me to write another day with a smile.

Peace & Blessings

Tina Andrews
New York City

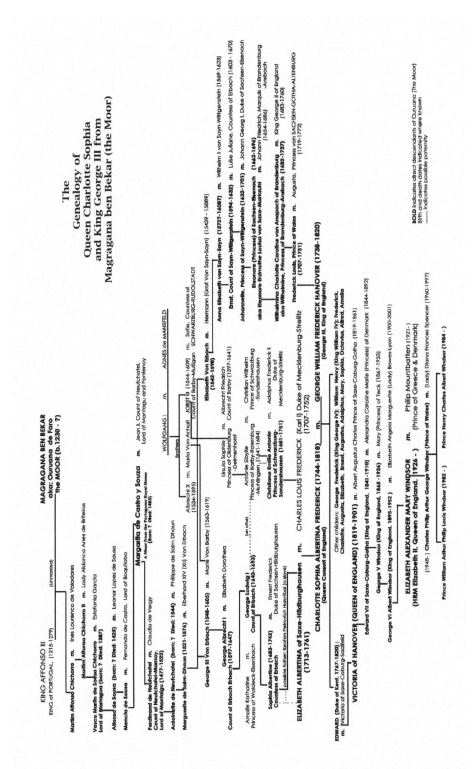

About The Author

TINA ANDREWS won the Writers Guild of America award, an NAACP Image award, and the MIB Prism award for her mega-hit CBS miniseries, "Sally Hemings An American Scandal." She also won an NAACP Image award, and the Memphis Black Writers Conference award for her bestselling nonfiction book, "Sally Hemings An American Scandal: The Struggle To Tell The Controversial True Story. "

She wrote the plays "The Mistress of Monticello," "Buckingham" and "Frankie" as well as the screenplays for the Warner Bros. film "Why Do Fools Fall In Love," the CBS miniseries "Jacqueline Bouvier Kennedy Onassis," and the Showtime animated series "Sistas 'n the City."

Miss Andrews lives in New York City.